WILDFLOWER HILL

Kimberley Freeman

A TOUCHSTONE BOOK
Published by Simon & Schuster
New York London Toronto Sydney

Touchstone
A Division of Simon & Schuster, Inc.
1230 Avenue of the Americas
New York, NY 10020

This book is a work of fiction. Names, characters, places, and incidents either are products of the author's imagination or are used fictitiously. Any resemblance to actual events or locales or persons, living or dead, is entirely coincidental.

Originally published in Australia in 2010 by Hachette Australia Pty. Ltd.

Published by arrangement with Hachette Australia Pty. Ltd.

First Touchstone trade paperback edition July 2011

TOUCHSTONE and colophon are registered trademarks of Simon & Schuster, Inc.

For information about special discounts for bulk purchases, please contact Simon & Schuster Special Sales at 1-866-506-1949 or business@simonandschuster.com.

The Simon & Schuster Speakers Bureau can bring authors to your live event. For more information or to book an event contact the Simon & Schuster Speakers Bureau at 1-866-248-3049 or visit our website at www.simonspeakers.com.

Designed by Renata Di Biase

Manufactured in the United States of America

10   9   8   7   6

Library of Congress Cataloging-in-Publication Data is available.

ISBN 978-1-4516-2349-9
ISBN 978-1-4516-2351-2 (ebook)

for Janine, who is precious

PROLOGUE

Sydney, 1989

The girl danced.

Right leg, pas de chat. Right leg, petit jeté.

"Emma, your grandmother asked you a question."

"Hm?" *Left leg, pas de chat. Left leg, petit jeté.* On and on across the parquetry floor, from one sunbeam to the next. She loved Grandma's house, especially the music room, where the sun patterned through the gauzy curtains, and there was enough space to dance and dance.

"Emma, I said—".

"Leave her be, dear," Grandma replied in her quiet, musical voice. "I'm enjoying watching her dance."

Right leg, pas de chat . . .

"If she practiced her manners as regularly as she practiced her dancing, she wouldn't have been booted out of two schools already."

Right leg, petit jeté . . .

Grandma chuckled. "She's only eleven. Plenty of time to learn manners when she's older. And you do insist on putting her in those uppity schools."

Left leg, pas de chat . . . "No, no, no!" Emma stamped her foot. *Deep breath. Start again. Left leg, pas de chat. Left leg, petit jeté* . . . She became aware of the silence in the room and glanced up, expecting to find herself alone. But Grandma was still there, on a deep couch beside the grand piano, watching her. Emma shook herself, pulled her spine very upright, and gazed back. Above Grandma's head hung a large painting of a gum tree at sunset: Grandma's favorite painting. Emma didn't really understand how anyone could be so interested in a tree, but she liked it because Grandma liked it.

"I thought you'd gone," Emma said at last.

"No, I've been watching you. Your mother left ten minutes ago. I think she's with Granddad in the garden." Grandma smiled. "You certainly love your dancing, don't you?"

Emma could only nod. She hadn't learned a word yet to describe how she felt about dancing. It wasn't love, it was something much bigger and much weightier.

Grandma patted the couch next to her. "Sit for a wee minute. Even a prima ballerina needs to rest."

Emma had to admit that her calves were aching, but she didn't mind. She longed for aching muscles and bleeding toes. They told her she was getting better. Still, Grandma had been very kind to watch all this time, so she crossed the room and sat. Somewhere deep in the house, music played: an old big-band song that Grandpa liked. Emma preferred Grandma to Grandpa infinitely. Grandpa went on and on, especially about his garden. Emma knew her grandma and grandpa were important people with a lot of money, though she cared very little about what it was they did or had done. Grandma was fun and Grandpa was a bore, and that was that.

"Tell me about your dancing," Grandma said, taking Emma's slight hand in her soft fingers. "You're going to be a ballerina?"

Emma nodded. "Mum says hardly anyone is a ballerina, and I should do something else just in case. But then there wouldn't be enough time to dance."

"Well, I've known your mother all her life." Here Grandma smiled, crinkling the corners of her blue eyes. "And she's not always right."

Emma laughed, feeling deliciously naughty.

"You must work hard, though," Grandma said.

Emma grew serious, lifting her chin. "I already do."

"Yes, yes, by all accounts you work so hard on your dancing that you haven't time for anything else. Including making friends." A look crossed Grandma's forehead, one that Emma couldn't decipher. Was it worry? Or something else? They sat in silence a few moments. Outside, the autumn sun slanted on rattling branches. But inside it was very still and warm.

"You know," Grandma said, shifting in her seat and squeezing Emma's hand before dropping it, "I'd like to make you a promise."

"What is it?"

"It's a little incentive."

Emma waited, unsure what the word meant.

"If you do become a ballerina, I will give you a present. A very precious one."

Emma didn't want to seem rude, but she couldn't fake excitement. She smiled sweetly and said, "Thank you," as her mother would want her to.

This made Grandma burst into laughter. "Oh, dearie, that doesn't thrill you at all, does it?"

Emma shook her head. "You see, Grandma, if I become a ballerina, then I will already have everything I want."

Grandma nodded. "A dream come true."

"Yes."

"Nevertheless, I will keep my promise," Grandma said. "Because you'll need something for after. Ballerinas can't dance forever."

But Emma was already off again. Thinking of making her dream come true had lit up all her nerves and muscles with desperate energy: she had to move. *Pas de chat. Petit jeté.*

"Emma," Grandma said softly, "do try to remember that success isn't everything." She sounded sad, so Emma didn't look around.

She just kept dancing.

ONE

Beattie: Glasgow, 1929

Beattie Blaxland had dreams. Big dreams.

Not the confused patchwork dreams that invade sleep. No, these were the dreams with which she comforted herself before sleep, in her trundle bed rolled out on the floor of her parents' finger-chilling tenement flat. Vivid, yearning dreams. A life of fashion and fabrics; and fortune, of course. A life where the dismal truth about her dismal family would fade and shrink and disappear. One thing she had never dreamed was that she would find herself pregnant to her married lover just before her nineteenth birthday.

All through February, she obsessively counted the weeks and counted them again, bending her mind backward, trying to make sense of the dates. Her stomach flipped at the smell of food, her breasts grew tender, and by the first of March, Beattie had finally come to understand that a child—Henry MacConnell's child—was growing inside her.

That night she arrived at the club as though nothing were wrong. Laughed at Teddy Wilder's jokes, leaned in to the warm pressure of Henry's hand in the small of her back, all the while fighting the urge to retch from the smell of cigar smoke. Her first sip of the gin cocktail was harsh and sour on her tongue. Still, she kept smiling. She was well used to navigating that gulf between how she felt and how she behaved.

Teddy clapped his hands firmly twice, and the smoke rose and moved with the men and their brandy snifters to the round card table that dominated the room. Teddy and his brother, Billy, ran this not quite legal gambling room above their father's perfectly legal restaurant on Dalhousie Lane. It was at the restaurant that Beattie had first met them. She'd been working as a waitress; that's what her parents still believed she did. Teddy and Billy introduced her to Henry, and soon after, they'd introduced her to the club, too: to the darkly glittering underbelly of Glasgow, where nobody cared who she was so long as she looked pretty. She worked half the night serving drinks and half the night keeping Teddy's girl, Cora, company.

Cora patted the chaise to invite Beattie to sit down. The other women gathered near the fireplace; Cora, her short curls flattened over her ears with a pink satin headband, was the acknowledged queen of the room. Though none of the others liked the idea, they were careful enough not to stand too close for fear of unfair comparisons. Beattie probably would have done the same if Cora hadn't decided that they should be bosom friends.

Cora grabbed Beattie's hand in her own and squeezed it: her usual greeting. Beattie was both in sacred awe of Cora and excruciatingly jealous of her heavily made-up dark eyes and her platinum hair, her easy charm and her endless budget for tasseled dresses in muslin or crepe de chine. Beattie tried, she really tried, to keep up. She bought her own fabric and sewed her own clothes, and nobody could tell they weren't designed and made in Paris. She wore her dark hair fashionably short but felt that her open face and large blue eyes ruined any chance of her seeming mysterious and alluring. Of course, Cora was born to her confident glamour; Beattie would always struggle for it.

Cora blew a long stream of cigarette smoke into the air and then said, "So, how far along are you?"

Beattie's heart spiked, and she looked at Cora sharply. Her friend looked straight ahead, her red lips closed around the end of her cigarette holder. For a moment Beattie even believed that she'd imagined the question: surely her shameful secret couldn't make its way from the dark inside to the brightly lit club.

But then Cora turned, fine curved eyebrows raised above her sloe eyes, and smiled. "Beattie, you're practically green from the smoke, and you've not touched your wine. Last week I thought you might be sick, but this week . . . I'm right, aren't I?"

"Henry doesn't know." The words tripped out, desperate.

Cora softened, patting her hand. "Nor a chance of me saying a word. I promise. Catch your breath, dearie. You look terrified."

Beattie did as Cora said, forcing her limbs to relax into the languid softness expected of her. She accepted a cigarette from Cora, even though it made her stomach clench. She couldn't have another soul noticing or asking questions. Billy Wilder, for example, with his florid cheeks and cruel laugh: oh, he would find it great sport. She knew, though, that she couldn't hide it forever.

"You didn't answer my question. How far along?" Cora said in a tone so casual she may as well have asked Beattie what she'd eaten on her lunch break that day.

"I've not had a period in seven or eight weeks," Beattie mumbled. She felt unbearably vulnerable, as though her skin had been peeled off. She didn't want to speak of it or think of it another moment. She was not ready to be a mother: the thought made her heart cold.

"Still early, then." Cora pulled her powder compact from her bag and flipped it open. Loud laughter rose from the card table. "Still a chance it won't stick."

For a breath or two, the oppressive dread lifted. "Is that right? I know nothing. I know I'm a fool, but I . . ." She'd believed Henry's promise that if he withdrew from her body at precisely the right moment, this could never happen. He'd refused to take any other measures. "French letters are for the French," he'd said. "I know what I'm doing." He was thirty, he'd fought in a war; Beattie trusted him.

"Listen, now," Cora said, her voice dropping low. "There're things you can do, dearie. Have a hot bath every day, take cod liver oil, run about and wear yourself out." She snapped her compact shut, her voice returning to its usual casual tone. "It's early days. My cousin's friend was three months along when the bairn just bled away. She caught the wee thing in her hands, no bigger than a mouse. She was devastated, though. Longed for a baby. Married, of course."

Married. Beattie wasn't married, though Henry was. To Molly—the Irish wolfhound, as he liked to call her. Henry assured Beattie it was a loveless marriage made between two people who thought they knew each other well but had slowly become strangers. Nonetheless, Molly was still his wife. And Beattie was not.

She puffed her way inelegantly through half of the cigarette, then excused herself to start work. As she brought round the drinks tray, she considered Henry's square jaw and his red-gold hair, longing to touch him but careful not to break his concentration. She dared not tell him yet about the child: if Cora was right and there was a chance Beattie could miscarry, then why create problems? Nothing may come of it. It might all be over tomorrow or next week. All over. A few long, hot baths; certainly, it was hard to spend too long in the shared bathroom on their floor of the tenement block, but if she went down early enough in the morning . . .

Henry glanced up from his cards and saw her looking. He gave her a nod: that was Henry, no grand gestures, no foolish winking or waving. Just his steady gray eyes on hers. She had to look away. He returned his attention to his cards as she returned her tray to the little bar in the corner of the room and lined up the bottles of gin and brandy along the mirrored shelves. She loved Henry's pale eyes; strangely pale. She could understand him through them when he didn't speak, and he spoke rarely. Once, right at the start of their relationship, she'd been watching him play poker and noticed how stark the contrast was of his pupils against his irises. In fact, she could read his hand in his eyes: if he picked up a good card, his pupils would grow, while a bad card made them shrink. Almost imperceptibly, noticeable only by the woman who gazed at those eyes endlessly.

This led her to watch the other men at the table and try to predict their hands. Not always easy, especially with Billy Wilder, whose eyes were practically black. But in instances of high stakes, when the men were trying hardest to keep their faces neutral, she could nearly always tell if they were bluffing. Henry thought it a load of rot. She'd tried to show him what she meant, but he'd tipped her off his lap and sent her away from the card table. He'd lost the game for not following her advice and had been in a devil of a mood for days. So now she stayed away. It wasn't so important.

Cora signaled for her to return; she had gossip to share. "Can you believe what Daisy O'Hara is wearing?"

Beattie switched her attention to Daisy, who wore a sequined tube of beaded net over a silk slip, a silk flower at her neck, and a pair of high Louis heels. The shimmering dress was cut too tight for her wide hips: modern fashion was so unforgiving of hips. It wasn't Daisy's fault. A good dressmaker could drape those fabrics so she looked divine, tall, a goddess.

"Lordy," Cora said, "she looks like a cow."

"It's the dress."

Cora rolled her eyes. But tonight Beattie hadn't the heart for Cora's razor-sharp analysis of every other woman's failings. She listened disconsolately for a while, then returned to the bar.

The evening wore on—clinking glass and men's laughter, loud jazz music on the gramophone and the ever present smoke—and she began to feel bone-weary and to long for bed. She could hardly say that, though. Teddy Wilder liked to call her "break-of-dawn Beattie"; many was the time she'd turned up for work at Camille's dress shop after only an hour or two of sleep. Tonight Beattie felt removed from the noise and merriment. In her own little bubble of miserable anxiety.

At length, Henry rose from the table and scraped up an untidy pile of five-pound notes. He'd had a good evening, and unlike the others, he knew when to stop. Half-joking recriminations followed him across the room. He stopped in front of the bar, seemingly oblivious to what his friends were saying. Without smiling, he stretched out his hand for Beattie. Henry exuded a taciturn authority that nobody resisted. Beattie loved him for it; other men seemed such noisy fools by contrast. And just one glance at his hand, at his strong wrist and his clean square fingernails, reminded her why she was in this predicament in the first place. Her skin grew warm just looking at him.

He pulled her close against his side with his hand down low on her hip, and she knew what he wanted. The little back room waited, with its soft daybed among the stacks of empty crates and barrels. As always, she shivered as she moved out of the warmth of the firelit club, and Henry laughed softly at her, his breath hot in her ear, assuming her shivers were of desire. But in that instant, Beattie felt the full weight of her lack of wisdom, and it crushed her desire to dust.

If he sensed her reluctance, he gave no indication. The last sliver of light disappeared as he closed the door and gathered her in his arms.

The rough warmth of his clothes, the sound of his breath,

the beat of his heart. She fell against him, all her bones softening for love of him. Away from the eyes of his friends, he was so tender.

"My dear," he said against her hair. "You know I love you."

"I love you, too." She wanted to say it over and over, in bigger, brighter words.

He laid her gently on the daybed and started pushing up the hem of her skirt. She stiffened; he pressed himself against her more firmly, and she saw how foolish it was to resist. It was already too late. Why shut the gate after the horse had bolted, as her father would say.

Her father. Another wave of shame and guilt.

"Beattie?" Henry said, his voice soft, although his hands were now locked like iron around her knees.

"Yes, yes," she whispered. "Of course."

Beattie's skin was pink from the heat of the bath as she dressed in the dank bathroom. A week had passed, and the hot baths were giving her nothing but odd stares from Mrs. Peters, their neighbor. She returned to the flat to find her father at the kitchen table, already at work on his typewriter. A sheen of anxious perspiration lay across his nose, despite the chill air. She couldn't remember the last time she'd seen Pa relaxed. With every passing day, he drew himself tighter and smaller, like a spider drawing its legs in to die. Laundry hung from the pulley that ran parallel to the kitchen ceiling. Ma was still asleep behind the curtain that divided the living area from the sleeping area.

"An early start?" Beattie asked.

He glanced up and smiled a little. "I might say the same for you," he said in his crisp English accent. Ma's Scots accent was thicker than Glasgow fog, and Beattie's lay somewhere between the two. "You were late home from the restaurant, and here you are up and ready to work again."

Beattie worked at Camille's boutique on Sauchiehall Street. Or at least she had for the last three weeks. Prior to that, she'd worked in the dress section at the Poly, a department store where the customers were far less demanding but the clothes were far less beautiful. All the latest fashions from the continent came in to Camille's, and the wealthiest women in Glasgow shopped there: the wives and daughters of the shipping magnates and railway investors. Beattie regularly witnessed them spend fifty pounds or more on a gown without blinking, while she was taking home four shillings a week.

"You won't need to work two jobs much longer," he said, ducking his head and adjusting his spectacles. "I'm sure to be finished soon."

"I don't mind." Guilt pinched her. Pa would be appalled if he knew she was working at the club, relying on the tips of men who found her pretty, or on Henry to slip her a few pounds if he'd had a good night's winnings. Pa thought she was a respectable lass with her virginity intact.

He returned to his work. *Tap, tap, tap . . .* Seeing him, anxiety so apparent on his brow, made Beattie's chest hurt. It had all been so different just a year ago. Pa had been a professor of natural philosophy at Beckham College in London. They'd not been well off, but they'd been happy enough, living in a

tidy flat at the college with sun in its windows in the afternoon. Life in London had been exciting to Beattie after growing up in the little border town of Berwick-upon-Tweed, with
their tiny cold garden that Ma tended so carefully. But Pa had
been an outspoken atheist—even though Ma had strong Scottish Protestant objections—and the new dean, a Catholic, had
quickly developed a dislike for him. Within two months he'd
lost his job and the flat with it.

Just as she was about to step through the curtain to roll
away her bed and find her shoes, Pa said, "Do take care of
yourself, Beattie, my dear."

She paused. Her father never showed real affection, and
this little morsel—*my dear*—grabbed her by the heart. She
returned to the table, sitting opposite him to watch while he
typed. She'd inherited his dark hair and blue eyes but not,
small mercies, his distinctive nose and lipless mouth. He
seemed to her in that moment as he had always seemed: a
stranger right beside her, somebody she knew well but didn't
know at all. Lack of money had driven them from London
to Glasgow, where Beattie's maternal grandmother delighted
in taking judicious pity on them. Nobody had yet offered
Pa another teaching job, but he refused to look for any other
kind. He clung to the idea that his intellect would triumph.
So he worked on his book, certain that when it was finished,
a publisher would buy it and a university—somewhere in the
world—would have him. Granny thought this was rot. If Ma
agreed, she didn't let on.

Pa became aware of her gaze and glanced up, puzzled.
"Beattie?"

"Do you love me, Pa?" Where had those words come from? She'd not intended to say them.

"Well . . . I . . ." Flustered, he pulled off his spectacles and rubbed the lenses vigorously on his shirt. "Yes, Beattie."

"Whatever I do? Will you always?" Her heart sped, driven by a primitive fear that he could read her thoughts.

"As a father should."

She stood, thought about touching his wrist softly, then changed her mind. "I'm not tired," she lied. "I'm just fine."

He didn't look up. "Good girl. I must keep working. This book isn't going to write itself."

The sound of the typewriter followed her to the bedroom, where she found her shoes and buckled them on. Ma snored softly, and it cheered Beattie a little to see her face looking so peaceful. She hadn't seen Ma looking anything but tired and anxious for a long time. Pinned to the wall was the pattern for a dress Beattie had been working on. The brown paper sagged against the tacks that held it up: she hadn't had the heart for it since she'd discovered she was pregnant. Why make a dress that wouldn't fit for much longer?

Beattie sat on the edge of the bed and pressed her forearm across her belly. What mysteries unfolded in there? What strange new life was moving and growing? The thought made her dizzy with fear. She drew her eyebrows down tightly, willing her womb to expel its contents. But nothing happened, nothing ever happened.

TWO

Weeks passed, and the stubborn thing clung to her insides. She imagined cramps where there was nothing but twitches of fear. In the meantime, her girdles grew tighter and—because she'd always been slight, almost bony—the first swell of her stomach became visible. She gave thanks for the figure-skimming shift dresses she wore, for her wrap coat, for Henry's preference to make love in the dark, and for her ability to let seams out invisibly. And soon, surely, the bleeding would start, just as she'd imagined it a hundred times, a thousand times. The nightmare would be over, and life could go on as it was supposed to.

She found it increasingly difficult to get out of bed, and one chilly April morning, she hung on to sleep in the gray dark until her mother gently woke her.

"Beattie. Beattie, dear. You'll be late for work."

Beattie squeezed open her eyes.

"I'm sorry," Ma said. "But I'd hate for you to get your boss offside. These aren't easy times. You canna lose your job."

"Thanks, Ma," she said, pushing off the covers and rubbing her eyes.

Ma stood, coughing loudly. The coughing seemed to go on forever, then finally, she had it under control. Meanwhile, Beattie dressed quickly.

"That cough sounds bad," she said.

"Och, I'll be fine."

"It's been a week. Perhaps you should go to see a doctor."

Ma turned to her with sad eyes. Her eyelids drooped at the outer corners, as if this were where she wore the weight of all her worries. "We canna afford a doctor, child, nor a day off. I'll be well in a day or two."

Beattie watched as she went through to the living area, then ran a comb through her hair and put on her makeup in a dim little mirror propped up on a pile of suitcases. Did Pa not see what Ma was going through? Did he not think once that if he just got himself an honest job . . . Of course he didn't see it. Ma had married him for his brilliant mind, and now she was shackled to it.

Camille's boutique, where Beattie worked four days a week, was owned by Antonia Hanway, sister of the famed James Hanway who ran a dress-cutting business on Bath Lane. Beattie's secret hope was that she would make a good impression on Antonia and one day turn this goodwill into a position with James: as a seamstress, a dress cutter, perhaps even a designer. She kept a few folded sketches in her handbag, just in case he ever came by the boutique. He never did.

She was still yawning when she arrived at work, which drew a stern glance from Antonia. Antonia was a difficult woman, though Beattie didn't think it was her intention to be so. Clients had to make appointments before coming to shop, and then Beattie and the other assistants had to wait on them as though they were royalty. Sometimes, in fact, they *were* royalty, and Beattie presumed the constant anxiety was what made Antonia so insufferable to work for. Beattie didn't mind, because she loved the shop. Racks of dresses waited in straight lines across the checkboard floor, the basement fitting rooms were lit by glittering chandeliers, and a yellow canary in a wrought-iron cage fluttered his wings as he watched the street through the bay window. His name was Rex. Lorna, one of the other assistants, had told her that he was the fourth yellow canary named Rex that Antonia had sat in the window. "One dies, and she brings in another the next day," Lorna said. "Doesn't like her clients to have to think about death, even though it will happen to them all. Uppity cows."

Beattie learned to love some of the clients who came into Camille's, but others she hated with passion, none more so than Lady Miriam Minchin, a razor-thin woman in her forties who was as tight with her kind words for others as she was easy with her money for herself. It happened that Beattie was serving her that morning when she felt the first shaft of pain, hard in her left side.

At first she thought she could ignore it. She fetched gown after gown from the racks and hurried them downstairs to the fitting room. Her heart picked up its rhythm, hope filtering into it: it was really happening. The hot baths, the cod liver oil, the endless wishing had finally worked. But at the same time, she was terrified. What if it were painful? Messy? How was she to deal with it discreetly at work?

"I like the blue on you," Antonia was saying to Lady Miriam as Beattie tried to appear calm. "What do you think, Beattie?"

"The cut is beautiful," Beattie said. "And the color is so flattering against your skin—" A spasm of pain shooting deep into her groin made her gasp involuntarily and clutch at her belly.

"What is it, Beattie?" Antonia asked sharply.

"I have . . . a pain . . ." This wasn't how it was meant to be! She was meant to bleed quietly and quickly at home, with the bathroom close by. Nobody was ever to know.

A moment passed when nothing happened, when the only movement was Lady Miriam's eyes as they skipped from Beattie's face to her belly, then back to her face. Beattie shrank. Lady Miriam knew.

"I have to go home," Beattie managed, turning away, running for the stairs.

"Wait, lassie!" Antonia said, clearly panicking about the impression Beattie was making on Lady Miriam.

"Let her go," Lady Miriam said.

She escaped. Up the stairs and out of the boutique into the drizzly street.

An instant later, the pain disappeared. She caught her breath.

Home: she had to get home. She was three blocks away before she realized she'd left her coat at the shop. Goose bumps prickled along her arms. The damp gray street unfolded beneath her feet; her breath was louder than the clatter of traffic.

Then another pain. Hard and sharp; it bent her in two. She forced air into her lungs, knowing she couldn't go home like this. Pa would see her, and besides, she needed a doctor.

She found a dry place under a shop awning and tried to clear her mind sufficiently to think. She had no money for a doctor: Ma had spoken of it only that morning. But she was consumed by selfish panic. Then she remembered the time at the club when Henry and Billy Wilder had been too drunk to wear each other's jokes any longer, and they'd come to blows. Billy broke a glass on Henry's head, and the bleeding wouldn't stop. Henry—a handkerchief pressed against the wound—had made a midnight visit to Dr. Mackenzie on West George Lane, along with a freshly contrite Billy. Dr. Mackenzie had delivered Henry into the world thirty years before and been his family physician ever since. Perhaps if she asked for his help, threw herself on his mercy, told him the child she was losing was Henry's . . .

But the shame, the trouble, she would bring to Henry.

The pain was too intense; she needed help. She turned and headed back toward West George Lane. The clouds overhead darkened, and the drizzle deepened to rain. Hard, cold rain that sluiced into the gutters and jumped after the wheels of motorcars speeding past. She stayed close to the buildings so she wouldn't get splashed, but by the time she arrived, her shoes were sodden. Then she stood in those sodden shoes, unable to push the door to Dr. Mackenzie's surgery open. There were no awnings to shelter under, and the rain fell on her as though she were no more important than one of the rubbish-filled crates that sat outside the door across the narrow lane.

In that moment, she believed that she wasn't.

Tears welled in her eyes, and for the first time since she'd realized she was pregnant, Beattie allowed herself to cry about it. To cry for the loss of her innocence, her pride, what tatters of self-respect remained after her family's demotion in life. But also to cry for the child, who did not ask to be conceived and would never have a chance to breathe the damp air of Glasgow, feel its mother's touch, nor see its father's storm-gray eyes smile. She wept into her hands as the rain thundered down on her, and then, like magic, the torrent suddenly stopped.

"Are you well, lassie?"

She looked up. All around, the rain still bucketed down, but a tall, broad-shouldered gentleman with a huge black umbrella stood next to her, sheltering her.

Beattie palmed away her tears, gathering herself. "Thank you, you're so kind. I . . . I should just go home."

"You need to see the doctor?" He indicated the door to the surgery.

She glanced from it to the gentleman and shook her head. "I've not enough money."

"Och, it will be fine. Come in. I canna leave you out on the street in the rain in such distress." He shook out a set of keys and opened the door to usher her forward, and she realized that the gentleman *was* Dr. Mackenzie. He placed his umbrella in a stand near the door and asked her to wait in the empty front room, dripping on the wooden floor, while he unbuttoned his coat. The front desk was unattended. From behind it, he fetched her a scratchy white towel.

"I usually don't work on a Thursday afternoon," he said. "You're lucky you found me."

She toweled her hair. The room smelled strongly of lemon polish and ointment.

"Come through," he said, and led her to an examination room with a narrow bed under a white light hanging on a chain. He sat at his desk, but she didn't feel comfortable enough to do anything but stand in front of him, like a naughty schoolgirl.

"Go on, then, lassie, what's your trouble?"

"I'm pregnant and . . ." Her cheeks flushed hot despite her shivering body. "I think I'm losing the baby. I've got a terrible pain . . ."

He didn't frown or give her any indication of disapproval. Instead, he stood and helped her up onto the bed. "Let me see, then," he said, smoothing her damp dress over her belly and running his hands firmly over it. She watched his face, half a breath held in her lungs. The pores on his nose were large, and his gray whiskers grew up high on his cheeks.

"Do you mind?" he said, "I'll have to lift your dress out of the way."

She nodded, closing her eyes. Then his cool hands were on her bare skin, rolling down the top of her girdle, pressing, feeling. Assuredly reaching lower, to places that only Henry had ever touched. But it felt different this time. Not hot and wild. Cold and clinical.

"You're not bleeding at all. Has there been any blood?"

"No," she managed.

"How old are you?"

"Twenty-one," she lied.

"The pain, is it similar to the cramps one has during one's monthly courses?"

Beattie squirmed with embarrassment to be talking about such things with a man. "No, it's much lower down, on the left side. In fact . . ." In her shame and fear, she hadn't noticed. "I think it's going away."

He fumbled with her clothes, and she realized she was dressed again. She opened her eyes and sat up. Dr. Mackenzie was back in his seat, but she remained on the bed.

"It's quite common at this stage of pregnancy to have the kind of pain you're describing. It's your body getting ready for birth. The ligaments in your womb are stretching. You're young, so it hurts a little worse for you. You've probably only just stopped growing."

Birth? She hadn't even contemplated it. Her head swam.

"So you needn't be worried. The baby is perfectly well and safe."

The inescapability of her situation was like a stone dropped on her stomach. "No!" she said before she could stop herself. Tears brimmed again, but she held them back.

Dr. Mackenzie's eyebrows shot up. "Oh, I see."

"Thank you," she said, pretending everything was fine, climbing down from the bed. "I shan't take up another moment of your time . . ." But the sobs were bubbling out of her then, and he sat her firmly in a chair next to his desk and handed her his handkerchief.

"You're not married, are you?"

"No," she said.

"Does the father know?"

She thought about Henry, about how Dr. Mackenzie had known him as a wee lad. "Not yet."

"You need to tell him." His voice grew soft. "You've a babe in there, lassie. He or she has been in there about three months. The chance of you miscarrying now is very small. Do you understand what I'm saying to you? There's no way out now. You need to tell him."

She pushed her toes hard into her shoes. "He's married," she managed.

He pressed his lips together, creating two deep lines that disappeared into his beard. "I see."

"Should I still tell him?"

"Lassie, I don't see that you've got any other option."

Outside, the clouds had lifted and the rain had thinned. Beattie returned to Camille's, ready to apologize to Antonia, to make excuses, to hang on to her job somehow. This wasn't a time to be out of work. Everyone was talking about "the slump"; even the big shipping companies were wary about putting people on. Beattie knew she would have to beg. So she rang the doorbell and moved to the bay window to peer in. Antonia emerged from the downstairs fitting rooms. When she saw Beattie, her face took on a scowl.

Antonia opened the door a crack. "What is it?"

"I wanted to say sorry, I—"

"You look like a drowned cat. I don't want the likes of you in my store, Beattie Blaxland. I've a reputation to uphold."

"I'll go home and change and come straight back," Beattie said, aware that she sounded hopeless, frantic.

"Change? You can change your clothes, but you canna change what you are. Lady Miriam pointed out to me what's been right under my nose. You're with child. Not even married. And there are rumors that you run with Henry MacConnell. Is the bairn his, then? He has a wife, you know."

"Please, Antonia," Beattie begged, desperate. "I can't manage without my wage. My family is—"

"You should have thought of all that before you brought your trouble through my doors. A dozen girls a day beg me for a job, and every one of them *not* pregnant. I'm not hard up for people to choose from. Why would I choose to keep you?"

"Please . . . please!"

"Lady Miriam has specifically said she won't be back unless you're gone. I have to think of my business."

Beattie swallowed hard. She must have looked utterly desolate, because for a moment Antonia softened.

"I'm sorry, child." Her voice was quiet, and she wouldn't meet Beattie's eyes. "But you're not to set foot back in my store." Then she pushed the door closed.

THREE

B *reathe in, breathe out.*

Beattie stood on the street below the club. Tonight she was going to tell Henry. Her breath made a faint fog in front of her. Her stomach itched with anxiety. She tried to understand why she was afraid of him. He loved her, or so he said. He would stand by her. He wouldn't be angry . . . would he? She had taken extra time with her makeup, making her eyes dark and soft, her lips red and peaked. If she were pretty enough, he would be kind to her. Take pity on her.

And yet how did she get to this place where she longed for pity? She had always been proud of her big dreams, her loud laugh, her brash casualness. Standing on the street, with the smell of roasting meat and cigarette smoke wafting from the restaurant, she realized horribly that those things were all a show, a childish pretension. After all, it was easier for her to talk about her big plans than do anything about them. It was easy to match Cora's barbed wit and brazen confidence with a gallon of drink in her. But all she was, really, was the awkwardly thin and poor daughter of a maddeningly weak mother and a foolishly idealistic father. Beattie knew this with such force that she almost turned and ran.

But she didn't. Because it wasn't just herself she had to take care of now. The child, whose first soft bumps against the wall of her belly she had felt that morning, needed a father.

The first stair was the hardest. Then she smelled the familiar cigar smoke, heard the familiar laughter—much louder than usual tonight—and rose toward it. Her heart was too big for her chest. She would tell Henry, she would have it out in the open. And then, however the pieces fell, they would fall.

She hadn't counted on a party.

The club was bursting at the seams. Streamers hung from one side to the other, dangling dangerously close to the fireplace. The card table was gone, and in its place was a long dining table bearing an orgy of food. She blinked rapidly, searching the room for Henry. She didn't want to have to speak to anyone else. Her lips were ready to say only one thing: "Henry, I'm pregnant." But Henry was nowhere in sight.

"Come in, come in, Beattie!" This was Teddy Wilder, in his checked trousers and Fair Isle pullover. His cheeks were red and shining. "It's a goodbye party. We'll need you at the bar straightaway."

"Goodbye?" Her heart jumped. Henry was leaving. Running away with the Irish wolfhound. "Who's going?"

"Nobody you like, don't worry," Teddy said, snorting with laughter. "My brother, Billy. He's skipping town. Off on a ship to Australia day after tomorrow."

Then Cora was there, taking Beattie's hand in her cool white one, dragging her toward the bar, shouting over the loud jazz music on the gramophone. "Did you hear? Billy's going!" Cora could barely keep the excitement out of her voice. She despised Billy. Most people did. He was unpredictable, rude, vain. He was rumored to run with a street gang, to smoke opium, to misuse prostitutes. Beattie was never sure how many of the stories were true.

Teddy raced off, shouting and laughing at another friend, while Beattie clung to Cora. "Where's Henry? I need to speak to him."

"Not here yet. Cigarette?"

Beattie shook her head, but Cora lit up, her chin lifted so her elegant white throat was on show. "So, Billy's being investigated over diddling the figures at Proudmoore's."

Beattie refocused, bringing her attention back to Cora, to the present. Henry wasn't here. All her courage started to flee; she hoped she could regather it when he arrived. "Diddling the . . . ?"

"Aye, falsifying the account books. He's running off before the police catch him up. His pa got him a job with a friend in Tasmania. Bottom of the world. Where he belongs." She glanced around, making sure nobody was listening. "He did it, sure as anything, Beattie. He told Teddy so. Skimmed two hundred pounds for himself."

"Henry's not involved?" Billy worked in accounts as Henry's supervisor at a shipping firm.

Cora shook her head emphatically. "No, Henry's not got it

in him. But Billy, he's a bad seed. I'll be glad to see the back of him."

Beattie forced a smile. "Teddy will miss him. He'll be lonely."

"Teddy will be fine," Cora purred, lifting her eyebrows suggestively. "I'll keep him very close company."

Beattie couldn't look at her. Why was it she, not Cora, who had fallen pregnant? The injustice of it burned, and suddenly, she needed to get away from Cora, with her perfect flat bust and stomach. She turned, began to hurry away, her head down, pushing people out of the way. Cora called after her imperiously, not used to Beattie cutting her out, but she ignored Cora's voice, all of the other voices, the laughter, the pressing mob.

Then he caught her. "Beattie?"

"Henry!" Her voice was half relief, half fear.

"What's wrong? You're quite pale."

"I'm . . ." She pulled herself together. "I have to speak with you. Now."

"You're speaking with me."

"I mean about something important." She looked around wildly. "Somewhere private."

He drew his eyebrows down, an expression so familiar to her. She loved his serious face, his intelligent eyes. She loved them so much it hurt her. She tried to hope. He would know what to do. He would help her.

"Well, then," he said, and grasped her wrist gently. They approached the back room, and Henry pushed the door in only to find another couple, half dressed, on the daybed. With a muttered curse, he closed the door again. "Outside," he said, not letting her go.

Now he led her through the crowd and down the stairs. His firm fingers were reassuring, and Beattie started to feel a strange peaceful acceptance, almost as though she were in a dream. The night air was cold in contrast, and she hadn't brought her coat. She could smell approaching rain, the strong odor of bus fumes from up on Douglas Street.

"What's this all about, then?" Henry asked. He gazed down on her with his steady gray eyes, and she savored the moment. She was madly in love with him; love would solve everything. Then a chill breeze sprang up and reminded her she had bare arms and a belly full of baby.

"Henry, I'm pregnant."

He froze. A statue. Even in the dark, she could see his pupils shrink. For the first time since she'd met him, he looked uncertain. A second passed, another, and another, and her dreamy sureness washed away. He didn't move nor say a word. She felt the sting of approaching tears, then the warm relief of them forming and flowing over.

"Oh, Beattie," he said at last, so softly and so tenderly that it terrified her.

"I'm sorry," she said. "I'm so sorry." As though it were solely her fault, as though there were something bad and faulty about her that had caused her to fall pregnant. As though he had nothing to do with it at all.

"No, no. I'm sorry," he said. "I can't . . . ." He dropped his

head, pinching the bridge of his nose. Then gathered himself
again and met her eyes. "My darling, I am married to somebody else. You know that."

Her veins grew cold. "But . . . what about me?"

"Molly is my wife. It's not that easy to—"

"Oh, God. Oh, God." Beattie reeled away from him, all her
instincts urging her to run.

But he caught her, pulled her close, covered her tear-stained
face with kisses. "I love you, I love you. But here's the truth.
Molly will never grant me a divorce."

"What shall I do?" Beattie sobbed. "I've already lost my
job. I can't even look after myself, let alone a babe."

"I'll help if I can," Henry said. "Please be calm, and keep
your voice quiet, my dear. Please be calm. You must tell me:
does anybody else know?"

"Cora," she confessed.

"Has she told Teddy?"

Beattie shook her head.

Henry drew a deep breath. "Here's what will happen. We
will go upstairs and fetch your coat, and we will tell everyone
that you're unwell and heading home. Then you must stay
away from the club a little while."

"But—"

"I just need some time. To organize things," he said. "You
do trust me, don't you?"

A vast emptiness opened up inside her. She *didn't* trust
him. Of course she didn't. It was the reason she had taken so
long to tell him, after all. Agony to realize it.

"Will you do as I say?" he asked.

What choice did she have? She nodded but couldn't find her voice to say yes.

Two weeks passed, and still no word from Henry. Each day, she fell further and further into the well of hopelessness. Every morning, she dressed and left the flat, so that Ma and Pa wouldn't know she no longer had a job. Of course they would find out, when Ma went through her handbag looking for money and found none. Daily, she walked until her feet were swollen and invariably found herself at Glasgow Green. Everywhere new life was unfolding. The tight green shoots on the bitch and lime trees; the wildflowers bursting into color along the banks of the Clyde; the proud geese with their trains of clumsy-footed chicks. Inside her, too. Her child gently twitched against her belly, which grew manifestly and inescapably rounder.

But as well as new life, she saw other things on her walks through Glasgow, images that haunted her. Ragged women without homes, dirty children begging for coins or food, a grubby collection of old blankets in a back alley, waiting for its owner to come home to sleep in it. Her imagination, once given over to dreaming about dresses and successes, trod those back alleys without her permission. She saw herself and her child, she saw winter's cold grasp approaching like a shadow. She saw a bleak, hungry future.

She returned home each day at dusk. Pa still on his typewriter, Ma easing her shoes off her tired feet after a day at the laundry where she worked and saying nothing to Pa with her lips, although her eyes silently begged him to find real work. Beattie withdrew and they didn't notice.

Cora didn't call on her, either, to see how she was. She was surprised by how sad that made her. Had Beattie's friendship been so peripheral to Cora? Cora had not once, since the day Beattie had confessed she was pregnant, asked her how she was or if she, Cora, could help. It was as though she had forgotten Beattie's predicament. Just as quickly, now, it seemed she had forgotten Beattie, too.

Beattie waited. She waited for Henry. She waited for her parents to notice she had no job. She waited for her belly to grow large enough that her dresses no longer hid it. She waited for the consequences to come.

And then, one morning, they did.

Beattie was in the bathroom, stepping out of the bath with its chipped enamel and rusty taps. Her mother walked in.

It was deliberate, of course. The suspicions must have been prickling her, and she knew Beattie was in there. The bolt on the bathroom door hadn't worked for months, but all the residents who used the bathroom had grown used to leaving their slippers just outside the door, a signal that the room was in use.

Beattie gasped, reaching for a towel. Naked, there was no hiding her swollen belly. Ma kicked the door closed behind her, strode over, and snatched the towel away. Then she grasped Beattie's hands in hers roughly and spread them apart.

"Ma . . ."

Her eyes traveled Beattie's body from throat to thighs, then she dropped her daughter's hands and finally looked at her face.

"Ma, I'm sorry," Beattie said, but she saw no pity in her mother's eyes. Just panic.

"You have to go."

"No! Ma, don't throw me out."

"Your father must never know. The shame. The *shame*." Ma's hands flapped like trapped birds. "Get dressed. Go."

Beattie gathered her towel against her, heart thudding in her throat. "I've nowhere to go."

"I dinna care!" Ma's voice was growing hysterical. "Your father will die for shame. He'll never get another decent job if it's known his daughter is a . . . a . . ." Ma couldn't find the words, descended into noisy coughing.

"But I—"

Beattie's protests were cut short by a sharp slap to her face. She stared up at her mother, who was wild-eyed.

"Ma?" Tears in her eyes. She flailed to catch Ma's hands, but she pulled them away sharply.

"No," Ma said. "Leave me be. Things are hard enough."

A small shred of memory came back to her then. Ma brushing her hair before school one morning, snow outside the window, Ma's warm hands, Ma's quavering voice singing an old Scottish folk song. The memory contrasted so sharply with this moment that Beattie's stomach lurched as though she might throw up. "You can't do this," she gasped. "I'm your daughter."

"No," she said grimly. "You're not. We have no daughter."

* * *

On the street, the air was thick and oily. Beattie was dressed, had the purse her mother had flung at her in the stairwell, but was otherwise empty-handed as she hurried away from the tenement block. A few streets away, she stopped. Her pulse fluttered as she paused, unsure which way to turn. To Henry's office, to plead with him? To Granny's house in Tannochside, with its sodden back garden that grew more moss than grass? Or to the warmest, driest alley she could find to prepare herself for her final ruin? For long, horrible minutes she stood, and it was as though she could feel the world turning, feel her own tenuous perch on it.

There was only one person she could think of who might know what to do. Cora.

Beattie had never been to Cora's house, though she knew where it was. Henry had pointed it out to her one night when walking her home. A honey-colored sandstone townhouse on Woodlands Terrace. Cora's father was a shipping magnate, with a country estate as well. Beattie tried not to think about what it would be like to have two houses instead of one tiny, cramped flat. To have a father who provided for her.

Beattie was panting by the time she arrived, and she stopped at the bottom of the wide stairs to catch her breath. She hadn't even realized she'd been running. The morning sun had broken through clouds and was evaporating last night's rain from the road. In the park, the birds were in full chorus. Beattie waited for her heart to still, palmed her tear-stained face, then walked up and rang the bell.

The heavy door creaked open. An imperious face under a frilly white cap peered out at her.

"Yes, lassie?" the old woman said.

"Can I see Cora?"

The woman—Beattie assumed she was a housekeeper—arched an eyebrow. "Who are you?"

"My name's Beattie. I'm her friend. Please. I just need to talk to her for a few minutes."

"Wait here," the housekeeper said, then closed the door.

Time passed. It felt like hours but was probably ten minutes. Traffic noise in the distance: the day starting as normal for everyone else. Beattie started to think she had been forgotten. Then the door opened again, and Cora stood there.

"Lordy, Beattie Blaxland. It's only nine in the morning."

"I'm sorry. I hope I didn't wake you. Only I didn't know where else to go."

"It's no matter. You look dreadful. Have you eaten? I can make you tea."

"I . . ." Beattie took a deep, shuddering breath so that she wouldn't cry. "I would love tea."

"Come in, then. Mind the wee step here. You're not wearing an ounce of makeup. You look like death. Do you want me to find some lipstick for you?" Cora's voice rattled on as she led Beattie up a wide hallway and into a parquetry sitting room with windows that went all the way to the floor. "Here, sit down. I'll fetch you tea, and then you can tell me what this is all about."

Beattie waited in the quiet, sunny room, clasping and unclasping her hands anxiously. She felt as though she were sitting outside herself, watching from a distance. For surely none of this could be real. She felt so young, looking at her thin pale wrists. A child's wrists. Cora returned, carrying a tea tray, smoking a cigarette. She set it down and poured Beattie a cup. Strong, black.

Beattie took a sip, scalded her tongue.

"What's this about? I thought you'd had enough of me," Cora said with a pretty pout. "The way you cut me out at the party. You didn't ever come back to the club."

"Henry told me not to."

"He did? Why?"

"Because of the baby."

"The . . ." Her eyes drifted down to Beattie's midsection and widened to saucers. "Lordy, Beattie, you're not still pregnant! I thought you'd got rid of the bairn. You didn't mention it again."

Beattie could do nothing but shake her head, her lips pressed tight against sobs.

"What's happened, then? Has he come to see you? Is he going to look after you?"

"He said he would, but I've not heard from him. His wife . . ."

"Haggard old cow who can't have children herself, that one. She should let him go." Cora put a protective arm around her shoulders. "How can I help?"

"Ma's kicked me out. I don't know where to go. Should I go to Henry? Only I don't want to make life hard for him . . ."

"And why not? He's made it hard enough for you." Cora butted out her half-finished cigarette with her free hand. "No, don't go to Henry. He'll not treat you right."

"Henry's not so bad. He's a good man, he's—"

Cora shushed her with a raised white hand. "There are two types of women in the world, Beattie, those who do things and those who have things done to them. Try to be the first type." She sat back and looked Beattie squarely in the eye. "I know of a place in northern England. A friend of my auntie runs it. Girls like you go there, they have their babies, then leave them there for adoption. You could be back in Glasgow by Christmas, as if this never happened. I can organize it all for you."

Beattie's mind spun. Here was Cora, offering her everything she'd wanted: shelter, comfort, an end to the responsibility of mothering. But Beattie had changed. Slowly but certainly, as the weeks had progressed and her fate had become inevitable, she had come to feel an unexpected affection for the child inside her. Soft as a silk rope, it tied her to the baby. They belonged together, didn't they?

Cora's eyebrows drew together. "You've got no silly ideas about keeping the wee thing, I hope?"

She was desperate. It was either do what Cora suggested or face her ruin. She forced a bright tone. "Of course not," she said quickly. "I never wanted it anyway."

FOUR

Through the rimy window of her shared room at Morecombe House, Beattie could see the rooftops that blocked the view of the sea beyond. Once a week on a Tuesday afternoon, the fourteen girls who resided here were taken down to the beach—late, so few people would be offended by the number of unlawful pregnant bellies—where they collected shells in their handbags and stood up to their ankles in the stinging seawater and took enough deep breaths of fresh air to last them until the next time they were allowed out.

Beattie would have inched up the window, only it had been nailed shut. A seagull on the roof opposite ruffled its feathers against the afternoon breeze that tore off the sea every day at dusk. She dropped her hand to her belly. Inside, her child wriggled and kicked.

Not her child anymore. The matron had informed her that a family had already been found for the baby, a good Christian couple from Durham who had two adopted daughters and were hoping this time for a son. The matron had told her this sternly, almost as though warning her not to disappoint them with a girl. Beattie tried not to think about whether the baby was a boy or a girl: those thoughts made it seem too real, too close. If she had to give up the child, it didn't do to imagine it in any detail.

What she wouldn't give now for her mother's comfort. For her father's wisdom. Here she was, about to birth a child, and yet she still felt as if she were a child. Young and frightened and longing for comfort. But there was no comfort here at Morecombe House. Just a daily diet of instruction about how ashamed she should be, always served stone-cold.

Beattie turned from the window and found a book to read. The matron allowed only the Bible and classics in the rooms. Beattie had no desire to read the first and was largely bored by the second, but she had managed to find a Charles Dickens novel that held her attention. She lay down on her bed and tried to read.

The room was small and would be cold when autumn came—when her baby came. No rugs to warm the floor, no wallpaper or paintings to break up the cool stone walls, between which she listlessly wandered from morning chores to lunch, from craft time to supper. Her bed was made neatly, but Delia's was a mess of sheets and blankets. Delia had been her roommate for the three weeks since she'd arrived. Last night at midnight, Delia had been ushered out, groaning and crying, to deliver her baby. Then, half-awake, half-asleep, Beattie had dreamed strange dreams of blood and death and crying children. Her nerves were frayed. She couldn't focus on the lines in front of her.

The door thumped open, and Beattie looked up to see Delia in a floral dress so faded that the daisies were gray.

"Delia? You're back?" she said, sitting up.

Delia smiled, but it was brittle. A smile stretched over a dark fissure. "All finished."

Beattie glanced at Delia's stomach, which had been round and ripe. Now it bulged softly against the dress. "You've—"

"It's done," she said grimly. "I'll be out in a week."

"The baby?"

"Didn't see it. They held a . . . a blanket up . . . in front of my face . . ." Delia's smile faltered, fell. "I don't even know if it was a girl or a boy." She sat gingerly on her bed and lay down.

Beattie's heart pinched. "Did you hear it?" She slid across to sit with Delia, smooth her hair off her face.

"Such a little noise," Delia said. "Like a cat." The smile was back. "So now it's over, and I'll be off home next week and can get on with life. Thank God." She brushed Beattie's hands away and pulled up the covers.

"Did it hurt?"

"Like hell." She yawned. "I'm tired, Beattie. Can you leave me be, so I can sleep?"

Beattie rose and returned to the window, leaned her forehead against the cool glass. She wasn't due for months, but already the dread crept up on her. Delia's baby was gone. That wriggling bundle of life that had been attached to her was now in somebody else's care, and her womb was empty. The thought made Beattie cry, and she let the tears run silently down her face and drip off her chin, knowing all the while that the tears weren't really for Delia. They were for herself.

* * *

The sea churned gray, and thick foam lay in waving lines across the beach as the girls picked their way down the path. Beattie glanced up at the leaden sky, holding her hat on firmly against the wind. It was sure to rain, which would mean their weekly outing would be cut short and they would be sent back early to Morecombe House. Perhaps they would get extra Bible studies for their sins.

"Get some good fresh air, girls," the matron called as they fanned out across the beach. The ones closest to giving birth sat, exhausted and fearful, watching the gray waves. The ones who were barely showing ran down to the water's edge to dip their toes. The ones in between, like Beattie, wandered up the shoreline looking for shells or pieces of colored glass washed smooth by the sea. Beattie, determined to make the most of her time outside, walked briskly up the damp sand. The sea air and the thump of her heart washed out the cobwebs that had gathered in her mind while she was stuck inside the cabbage-scented linoleum halls.

Up on the verge in the distance, she saw a figure. She paid it no attention until she saw it lift a hand, almost as if waving to her. Tentatively waving. She slowed. Peered. It was a man in a gray suit, his face obscured by his hat. Definitely waving.

She looked behind her. The other girls were twenty yards away from her, and none of them were looking at the man. She turned back, and her heart started dancing: it recognized him before her eyes did.

Henry.

Beattie froze with shock. She couldn't just run up to him; the matron would see. But nor could she ignore him.

At the precise moment, the clouds above her parted and rain began to fall. The matron's voice was loud against the wind. "Come back, girls. We'll return immediately."

Return? How could she? Henry was there, just a hundred yards down the beach, standing in the rain.

"Somebody get Beattie! For the love of God, Beattie, we're all *waiting* for you!"

A hand closed around her arm. One of the new girls; Beattie had forgotten her name. "Come on," she said in a thick Geordie accent, "we'll catch our deaths out here in the rain." Beattie shook her hand off, turned back to look at Henry.

He was gone.

"Come *on*," the girl said.

Beattie could see ahead that the girls were hurrying away from the beach, that the matron was waving her meaty arms in fury. She glanced back: there was no figure.

What if it had never been Henry? Just an imagining thrown up by her desperate heart?

Wiping away angry tears, Beattie stomped down the beach toward the others, caught up just as they were crossing the road. Parked behind the pavilion was a black Austin precisely the same as Teddy Wilder's.

Beattie shook herself. Many men drove black Austins. But still, it was enough to make her hope. The rain had intensified, the matron had her head down under her black umbrella. Nobody was looking at her. Not right at this moment . . .

Beattie peeled off from the group and dashed for the beach. Nobody called after her. She ran as fast as her body would allow with its recently acquired clumsiness and slowed when she realized she was standing on the sand alone.

Gray sea, gray sky, completely alone. No Henry. He wasn't coming. He was never coming.

And then a heartbeat later, it all changed. She heard him call her name.

"Beattie!"

She turned. He stood at the verge, beckoning her. She hurried up the sand, threw herself so hard into him that she was afraid she might knock him over. But he was as strong and steady as a rock.

"I thought you'd never come."

"I lost you! Your parents knew nothing. Cora finally confessed to me. I'll never forgive her for keeping it secret."

The rain soaked them, but they held on to each other tightly. Finally, he stood back. "You'll be seen. Quick. Come with me, I have Teddy's car."

Her eyes darted around. She *would* be seen. The matron would send somebody back to find her. Henry swept his arm around her, hurried her up toward the car.

Inside, she dripped into the seat while the rain pounded on the roof. Henry didn't start the car. Rather, he turned to her and fixed on her with his gray gaze. Her pulse was hot and thunderous. She dared not speak.

"Run away with me," he said. Was she imagining it, or did his breath smell like gin?

"What do you mean?" But it was already too late. He'd said the words she longed to hear, had not even dared to imagine.

"I've telegraphed Billy, in Australia. He's going to find me a job."

A wave of dizziness.

"We can be together."

"Your wife . . ." she said, struggling for air.

"I don't love her. I love you. I love our child. She'll never find us. I've organized a berth for us on a cargo liner leaving from London in eight days. I've forty pounds in my pocket. Will you go with me? Now? To London?"

Outside the squally rain eased. Beattie gazed at him, thoughts flitting across her mind: of letting Cora down after she had done so much to help, of moving so far from her home, of never seeing her parents again . . . But none of these thoughts settled because, in the deepest well of her spirit, she wanted to go with Henry. And that desire overrode everything.

"Yes," she said. "Let's go."

Evening closed in on the windows of the little hotel room in Bayswater. Beattie watched the street for Henry; he was late. And every moment he was late, she wondered if she was doing the right thing. It was not right, surely, for her to lose faith in him the moment he was out of her sight.

In the next room, through the thin walls, she could hear someone whistling "Bye Bye Blackbird." The cheerful tune was at odds with the chill of the room, the approaching dark, the pressing sense of caution in her heart.

Tomorrow they were off on a cargo ship that had enough space for two passengers and not even a steward to tend to them. Henry would have to do some cleaning to pay for their passage. They were to travel via India and would not be in Hobart for eight weeks.

Eight weeks at sea. In the moments when she wasn't tired and overwhelmed with doubt, it seemed an adventure. But now it was hugely, horribly daunting.

The promises Henry had made her! Eternal love. Raising their son together (he was sure it was a boy, a little Henry). A new life in a new world. They would pose as husband and wife. She would cease to call herself Beattie Blaxland and would henceforth be known as Mrs. Henry MacConnell. She would bear babies; he would work hard and bring home money. They would have a little place of their own and grow old together.

But there were too many false notes in this symphony of his imagining. He would be working with Billy Wilder. His wife may track them down. And he hadn't found himself able to make love to her pregnant body.

"It's nothing," he'd muttered, gently turning away her advances. "You look different, that's all. Not my Beattie. When you've had the child, it will be the same again."

Had Henry not come for her, she would still be in Morecombe House, waiting like all the other girls to give birth and give away the child. She curled her hand around her belly. Why could she not escape this terrifying ambivalence? One moment she wanted Henry, the baby, the new life. The next moment she did not. She simply wanted this to have never happened.

But it *had* happened.

There he was, striding casually along the street. He'd been finalizing the arrangements for their journey and picking up a bag full of roomy dresses for her from a friend of Teddy's in Paddington. Beattie had nothing but what she had fled the beach in, and it wouldn't fit for much longer.

He glanced up at the window, saw her watching for him, and lifted his hand in a greeting. No smile. That wasn't Henry's way.

She simply couldn't doubt herself, not now. She had made her decision, or rather, her heart had made it for her.

Tomorrow the journey would begin. Tomorrow there was no looking back.

FIVE

Emma: London, 2009

I was running late, but I supposed by now that Josh was used to it. The rehearsal had ended right on time; I'd dressed and grabbed my handbag from my locker. I'd started out with such good intentions from the Shaftesbury Avenue studio—don't stop to look at anything, don't stop to buy anything—but up on Euston Road, I'd been recognized.

"Excuse me! Excuse me!" A toffee voice behind me, growing closer.

I stopped and turned.

A middle-aged woman and her awkward preteen daughter were hurrying up to me.

"Hello," I said.

"You're Emma Blaxland-Hunter, aren't you?" the woman asked, smoothing her shirt as though preparing for esteemed company.

"I am. I'm very pleased to meet you."

The woman glanced at her daughter, then back to me. "This is my daughter, Glenys. She loves to dance. Do you have any advice for her? She wants to be just like you."

"Mum!" Glenys exclaimed, as mortified by a simple thing as only a twelve-year-old can be.

This was the point where I should have smiled politely and backed away, offered my apologies but claimed to be terribly busy, and so on. But I couldn't. Gran always said to share the good times and they would last forever. London had been the city of my dreams as a child. To live and work here, exceling in my field, was an honor, and to be welcomed with such enthusiasm by its residents was something I never grew tired of. I wasn't naturally good with people, especially children, but it was only twenty minutes out of my life. So, while the traffic roared past and the long summer afternoon wore on, I talked to Glenys, gave her some tips, danced with her on the footpath as puzzled commuters hurried by on their way to King's Cross or St. Pancras. Glenys shed her awkwardness quickly, became shiny-eyed with excitement. Finally, I autographed the back of an old envelope for her and encouraged her to keep dancing.

"Thank you so much," Glenys said, pressing the envelope against her chest.

The mother nodded appreciatively. "It was such a pleasure to meet you. I've long been a fan of your grandmother's brand, you know. There must be something in the blood with the women in your family. Such creativity, such drive."

I bit my tongue so I wouldn't say "You haven't met my mother," and turned to be on my way. Late now. Quite late.

Even so, I arrived at the restaurant before Josh. Our reserved table waited, and I sat at it, feeling daunted by the sharp edges of the folded linen napkins and the posh quiet.

Josh was born into privilege; for me it had come only lately, and I still felt like an impostor sometimes, waiting for the tap on the shoulder, the polite "You shouldn't be here."

Ten minutes passed. He still hadn't arrived. This was unusual. I'd been living with him in our roomy rented apartment in Chelsea for six months, and he lived his life like clockwork. The alarm went off—he got up! Not like me, hitting the snooze button over and over, clinging to the last thin shard of sleep until I heard him putting on his shoes near the front door and guilt finally prompted me to rise. If he said he'd be home at six, then at six he'd be home: no later, no earlier. If anything beyond his control held him up—and there was little beyond his control—he'd call and . . .

My phone! Did I even have it switched on?

I rummaged in my bag. I hated the damned thing, but Josh had insisted on it. I barely knew how any of its functions worked, and 90 percent of the time, I forgot I owned it. Dozens of calls were usually piled up on my voice mail every week. Sometimes I just ignored the tiresome task of listening to them all; it was time taken away from more important things.

My hand closed around it . . . Four missed calls. I was thumbing through the functions, trying to remember how to retrieve my voice mail, when I heard the door to the restaurant open, briefly letting in a blast of traffic noise. I looked up, knew it would be him.

He smiled. Oh, that smile. It had been the start of everything. A smile that hinted at the man beneath the polished surface, at primal urges and passions balanced against immaculate manners. I'd never been much good at men until Josh. I'd had boyfriends, of course, but I had a record of picking the ones with big dreams and no way of making them come true: would-be artists and aspiring rock journalists. Josh was ambitious and razor-sharp, with a job in a stockbroking firm and a family of terribly old money. The love that had bloomed under my ribs for him was fierce.

But there was something different about his smile tonight—some wariness, something held back—and I found myself on my guard.

"I'm sorry I'm late," he said, sitting down and gesturing to the waiter.

"It's fine. Now I know how it feels," I joked.

He didn't laugh, didn't even seem to have heard me. He beckoned the waiter over; we ordered wine but said we'd take a few more minutes to decide on meals. He laced his fingers together and looked at them for a moment.

"Good day?" I asked.

He looked up. "My mother called."

"Oh?" His family had moved to Spain a year ago; I'd never met them. "Everything okay?"

"Yes. Yes." He glanced around again. He was nervous about something, that was for sure. "They're all coming up to Paris for a week. End of October. My mum, my dad, my sister. They want us to meet them there."

"Great, I . . ." My mind was spinning through my diary. Damn, where was Adelaide, my PA, when I needed her? What was I doing in October? Would *Giselle* be over? But here was Josh, asking me to meet his family. A sign—a clear sign—that he was thinking of more permanent arrangements. A week in Paris with him would be lovely. We'd never been away together. I'd always been too busy. Then it occurred to me: casting for the Christmas season. I couldn't miss it.

"Would we have to go for the whole week?"

Irritation crossed his brow. "Most people have holidays, Emma. It isn't unthinkable."

"It's complicated. I'm on contract. I'll need to make sure I have another contract lined up for when it's finished. In this business—"

"You can't have a break. Yes, I know, you've told me this before. But you *need* a break, and I *need* to introduce you to my family."

"Need to? Why?"

"Because they're my family."

"You haven't met mine."

"They're in Australia. And I can guarantee that if they were just across the Channel for only a week, I'd make the effort to come and meet them."

"Look, Josh, don't be upset. I'll check with Adelaide; she has my diary. If you can give me the dates, I—"

To my surprise, Josh stood up, fists clenched by his sides. People at the neighboring tables glanced up sharply; he realized he was creating a scene and sat down again. Leaned forward and, obviously keeping his anger in check, said, "This cannot go on."

By now I was growing annoyed. He was overreacting. "I think it's reasonable that I should be able to look at my diary before committing to anything."

"Before committing to *me*?"

I shook my head. "What are you asking me?" I felt as though we were playing a game and I didn't know the rules. It was so unlike Josh to be unreasonable that I suspected darker motivations. It was almost as if he wanted to find fault with me. "Where has all this come from?"

"Do you know what I want from life, Emma?" he demanded.

"Of course. You want . . . to do well at work and . . ." I trailed off. Did I *really* not know what he wanted from life?

"Marriage?" he said. "A family?"

"You've never spoken of it."

He exhaled sadly. "I have. You just haven't listened." He looked me squarely in the eyes and said, "Do you want those things, too?"

"Maybe. One day."

"You're nearly thirty-two."

"Plenty of time." What was that constricted feeling in my chest? "Lots of dancing to do first."

Josh ran his fingers through his hair, took a deep breath, then said, "I'm sorry. This relationship isn't working. I want to end it."

A bolt of electricity slapped my chest, and the world became sharp-edged. A vacuum, a long silence. I was afraid to speak, in case I said the wrong thing. *Not working?* From my perspective, it had been working just fine. And so that was the word I said. "Fine."

He cocked his head, a brief moment of anger crossing his brow. He thought I didn't care. But I did. I had just been shocked into silence. People always misunderstood me. I just didn't know how to say the right things.

Josh, regathering his efficient self, ruled out a long, messy goodbye. He picked up his keys and phone and stood. "I'll head off. I'll book a room at the Berkeley tonight, and I'll nip into the apartment to collect my things tomorrow while you're at the studio." He reached for my hair, but I flinched away. "I'm sorry, Em," he said softly, in the intimate voice I had grown to love. "I really am. But you're not the girl for me."

I wanted to shout. To upend the table. To kick him so hard in the groin that his face turned blue. But I did none of these things. I was too visible: I was Emma Blaxland-Hunter, prima ballerina with the London Ballet. Granddaughter of the Blaxland Wool empire. I carried the family's reputation on my slight shoulders.

He left. I waited five minutes and left, too, ignoring the curious stares in my wake.

I refused to believe that Josh wasn't coming back. Certainly, the following day he'd moved out his clothes and toiletries and CDs while I was at rehearsal, but he hadn't taken any of the potted plants on the terrace that he'd so lovingly tended. I was confident he'd return, so I didn't call him. I wanted him to call me. He owed me an apology. A big one.

The summer days dragged on. I longed for the dark of winter. But instead the days lingered, a bright light shone on my uncertain heart. The heat just added to my misery. At least back in Sydney the houses were designed to cope with hot weather, to let the air flow through. Here, every building seemed designed to trap the stuffy warmth.

So, because the emptiness and the heat were all that waited for me at home, I stayed at the rehearsal studio later and later. The perfect way to forget about Josh, about how I was waiting for him to come back, was to throw myself into my work. Rehearsals for a September production of *Giselle* were in full swing, and from the moment I arrived at the studio till the moment I left, I barely thought about him. But the sadness hung, waiting for me as I dressed in my street clothes and brushed my long hair out of its tight knot. The emptiness. No Josh to meet for dinner. No Josh to come home to.

I spent every evening of those first two weeks walking from one end of the city to another. Sometimes the traffic got too much, and I escaped into parks; sometimes I idly stared in shopwindows. On the second Friday night, I caught sight of a Blaxland Wool display in Selfridges & Co. and went in to look closer. Blaxland Wool specialized in classy women's wear. This year it was forties-inspired suits with short, short skirts in bright colors. I doubted Grandma would have liked them, and the thought gave me a pang. *Grandma.* If she'd still been alive, she would have been the first person I'd call. "Gran, I think he's left me. I don't think he's coming back." And Grandma's voice would have soothed me down the line. *Shh, Emma, you will be all right. I know you, and I know you will be fine.* Grandma had more faith in me than I had in myself.

I fingered the cuff of one of the suits, getting my panic under control. Josh would come back. *Stay positive.*

"May I help you?"

I turned, found myself looking up at a tall, coltish young woman with miles-long French nails. "No, no, I'm fine," I said.

"Hey," the young woman said, "you're Emma Blaxland-Hunter."

"Yes, I suppose I am." The jokes that Josh and I had made about our surnames. His was a double-barrel, too: Joshua Hamer-Lyndon. Modern parents and their need to keep maternal surnames, Josh had complained. Our children, he declared, would be Bill and Ben Hamer-Lyndon-Blaxland-Hunter, and pity the poor generation that came after them.

I'd never taken him seriously. Children hadn't been in my plan—not until the distant future, at any rate—so I'd assumed they weren't in his, either.

"Do you mind if I get my boss over here? She'd be ever so thrilled to meet you."

And that night I simply couldn't do it. I would look like a stuck-up cow, I knew. It would be shop-floor gossip for weeks: "Emma Blaxland-Hunter came in to look at our display, wouldn't even talk to us."

"I'm sorry," I said. "I have to be somewhere . . ." I backed away, nearly knocking over a mannequin with legs identical to the shop assistant's. "I'm very sorry."

I escaped, hurried down to the crowded street. My stomach grumbled lowly. I ducked into the Bond Street underground and made my way home.

Every time I opened the door, my heart held its breath, hoping Josh would be back. But no, the flat was dark and empty. I hung my keys on the hook and switched on a lamp. The message light was blinking on the phone. Surely it would be Josh this time. This silly game had gone on for too long. I dialed the message bank. No Josh; Adelaide, my part-time personal assistant.

"Call me. Important. Really important. Not work-related but important nonetheless. I want you to hear it from me."

I frowned, hung up the phone. I didn't want to call her. She sounded rattled. As though she had bad news.

I set about opening every window in the apartment; a grudging breeze, warm and laden with the smell of petrol fumes, leaked in. I poured a glass of wine. I looked in the pantry for food. There was none. When had I last shopped? I glanced at the phone. *Really important.* I didn't want to know; I was afraid of what I'd hear.

Finally, I marched up to the phone, lifted the receiver, and dialed.

Adelaide had it on the first ring. "Emma?"

"How did you know?" My heart thudded softly in my throat.

"Caller ID. Are you sitting down?"

I perched on the arm of the couch. "I am now."

"I saw Josh this evening."

"Josh? My Josh? Is he . . . ?" *Coming back?* But I knew from the tone of her voice that he wasn't coming back; that this would not be happy news.

"He was with someone else, Emma. I'm so sorry."

My stomach sank. I hung on tight to the edge of the couch with my free hand. "You mean . . . ?"

"A woman, yes. Not just any woman. Sarah. His assistant."

I barely remembered her and was surprised that Adelaide did. But they had probably organized appointments together. Josh and I were both very busy people.

Somehow I managed to keep my voice even. "Thank you for letting me know."

"I'm so sorry. I wish I had good news for you."

"No, no. I'm glad you told me." Was I? Or was that the kind of empty platitude anyone said when her heart had been torn out and crushed to pulp on the ground? "I'll see you at the studio."

I hung up, slid down into the couch with my eyes closed. Josh and his assistant. What a horrid cliché. He'd moved quickly: less than two weeks since we . . .

But wait. *Sarah.* I was remembering now. She had a hard face, not pretty at all. Her name had popped up many times in our conversations, not that I'd paid much attention. And now it seemed that I'd been overlooking some very important facts. Josh's late nights at the office, at least one business trip a month, the endless attachment to his BlackBerry, furiously two-thumbing messages every minute of the day and night. Had he been having an affair all along? Was his ultimatum a way of finally deciding between me and her?

I felt myself crumbling from within, turning to sand. I didn't want to be alone, but I had so few friends. Two away, abroad with the ballet. One old friend from Australia who now lived in . . . where was it again? And for the first time in a very long time, I wanted my mum. I wanted her very badly.

I scooped up the phone again and dialed before I could

think better of it. At the other end, thousands of miles away, the phone rang. And rang. I realized that I would be terribly disappointed if it rang out. That, despite the fact that my mother would nag me to come home, I still needed desperately to hear her voice.

Just when I was about to give up, the line went live.

"Hello?" Out of breath.

"Mum?" I said, my voice already breaking.

"Oh, Em, what's up? You sound—"

"Josh has left me." Big sobs bubbled out of me, the first I had allowed myself since Josh had abandoned me at the restaurant. "He's run off with his assistant."

"Darling, I'm so sorry," Mum said, and while I cried, she kept up a comforting string of sounds and words. For the first time in years, I actually wished I were home in Sydney, just so I could put my cheek against her cool throat and be comforted like a child. Mum and I had a tense relationship, a clash of personalities that we hadn't been able to resolve. But she was still my mum, the person who had smoothed Band-Aids over my cut knees and driven me to every ballet class.

Finally, I got my tears under control. "God, Mum, one minute I think I'm living the perfect life, and the next, it all falls apart."

"You could come home," my mother ventured.

The familiar sting of irritation. "No."

"Just for a visit. You haven't been back since before your grandma died."

"I can't. I'm in rehearsal for a production."

"After that."

"There will be another production."

A sigh on the line. "Emma, you're nearly thirty-two. You can't dance forever."

But I could: that was the thing. My body still felt fine. If not forever, I hoped to get at least another ten years out of my work. Maybe more. I'd seen footage of Maya Plisetskaya *en pointe* at sixty-three. Since childhood, I'd wanted to do nothing but dance; I couldn't even think of stopping. I didn't know how to stop.

"Mum," I said, "I promise you I'll come home when I stop dancing. But for now it's still my life." In fact, it was all I had left.

I must have heard the expression "broken heart" hundreds of times in my life. But now I understood with every muscle and nerve in my body what it actually meant. My heart, the vital organ that pumped blood through my body, and love and longing through my veins, never stopped hurting. I would wake up with the pain, then go to sleep with it again at night. I cried into my hands over the bathroom basin getting ready for work. I couldn't think straight. I didn't know myself.

The only way I knew to shut out the awful feelings was to move. After rehearsals every night, I stayed on, dancing and dancing and dancing. Adelaide gave up on me at six every evening and wisely went home to her family in Clapham. I cherished the gleaming empty room, its high white lights and its long mirrors. I had all the space in the world to express my anger and my pain. The more my feet ached, the closer I knew I was to getting over him. I danced like a mad person; I danced as though it were the only thing keeping me alive. And in some ways, it was.

Thomas, the janitor, rattled around the hallways. I heard the vacuum cleaner, the water running in the bathrooms. One evening he came and cleaned the mirrors from one side of the room to the other, studiously not watching me as I tortured my body. By the second Friday afternoon, Adelaide couldn't hold her tongue anymore.

"You've been doing this for two weeks. You *know* it's bad for you."

"Practicing is never bad for you."

"You can push your body too far. If Brian found out—"

"Don't you dare tell Brian!" Brian Lidke was the artistic director. The last time he'd cast me, he'd pointedly asked me how old I was. "I need to do this, Adelaide. I spent far too much time with Josh, missed rehearsals, lost form."

"You've never missed a single rehearsal, Em. I manage your diary. I should know."

"I could have attended the extra ones."

She snorted a cynical laugh. "For God's sake—for your *own* sake—go home."

Home. To the empty flat that I couldn't afford much longer. "One more hour."

Adelaide hitched her bag onto her shoulder and huffed away. I pushed down my guilt and headed for the barre. Calves aching. *Up.*

I worked particularly furiously that night. Didn't notice at first that I couldn't hear Thomas's vacuum cleaner. When I was done, working through some cooldown exercises, I slowly started to realize that I truly had the theater all to myself. I went to the door and peered into the hallway. Usually, the wooden panels and wide stairs were lit by soft downlights. But it was pitch-black. Either Thomas hadn't come, or he had taken off early and forgotten me. I was probably locked in.

A war took place inside me: whether to laugh or to cry. I did neither. I needed to get to my locker for day clothes, so I left the door of the studio open in hope that some of the reflected light would follow me to the changing rooms. I'd never be able to get the key into the locker in the dark, so I decided instead to head downstairs and see if I could open the door from the inside. If not, I guessed I'd be curling up to sleep on the floor for the night and I wouldn't need to get changed. The idea somehow suited my miserable, lonely mood. I thought about my mobile phone in my locker but knew it would be uncharged. I hadn't laid eyes on it in a week.

I walked down the hallway. The light ran out near the stairs, but I found the railing with my right hand and slowly felt my way down to the next step. And the next. And the next.

But the one after that wasn't there. At least I couldn't find it with my toes, and something strange happened in the dark. My muscles, tired from a week of punishing practice, were off duty and simply couldn't compensate for the sudden change in terrain. I had a moment to remember that the stairwell curved to the left just at this point, but it was too late for my falling body.

It all happened horribly quickly, though later, I would

remember it as taking forever while I watched outside myself. I skidded down the stairs and landed on the rough carpet like a doll that had been dropped by a careless toddler.

No immediate pain. Not so bad, then. Though why was my heart pounding so urgently, as though it knew something my brain did not? I tried to stand.

And my right knee buckled beneath me, almost as though there were no knee there at all. The pain came from everywhere at once, making me cry out. And the joint began to fill, just like a balloon filled with water.

What have I done? What have I done? This couldn't be happening. My blood pounded in my ears, nausea filled my stomach. I collapsed to the ground, clutching my knee, calling out for help in the dark, empty theater.

SIX

From one specialist to the next, day after aching day, and each wore an unbearable expression of serious consideration and sympathy. I had heard the story a hundred times by the end of the first week, a thousand by the end of the second. The angle of the fall had torn my ligaments. Not just ice-pack-and-rest torn. Torn-to-shreds torn. The pain was mediated only by heavy painkillers. The specialists were already muttering darkly about a "mixed" prognosis. One orthopedic surgeon opened up my knee and then closed it again only to refer me to another orthopedic surgeon. This time the operation went ahead, but the outcome was "not as we'd hoped."

It took a full three weeks—because of the painkillers and the shock and the stupid euphemisms the surgeons used—before I realized they were telling me that my knee was beyond repair. I would be able to walk, though as I got older and weaker, the pain might increase to the point where it would be better to give me an artificial joint. As for dancing . . . well, that was not going to be possible.

The bottom fell out of my world.

* * *

The very worst had happened, and I was constantly surprised that life kept going. That, in fact, I had to accommodate this very-worst into my life as it continued on without pause. As the traffic kept moving outside my window. As the season of *Giselle* went ahead with another, younger dancer in the lead. My heart didn't stop, my body didn't forget to draw breath. In my apartment, with all the curtains drawn against the summery brightness, I continued to live.

I longed to dance. I longed for it so intensely that it caused my chest to hurt, sometimes even more than my knee hurt. I wasn't ready to stop dancing; but then would I ever have been ready to stop dancing? In truth, I couldn't deny the increasing caution with which I'd been offered roles, the microscopic stiffness in my hips at the beginning of rehearsals, the bunions on my feet and ulcers between my toes caused by years of wearing unforgiving shoes. Last year's production of *Swan Lake,* with its infinite *pas de bourrés,* had filled my legs with cramps. I'd had to ice my feet to get my shoes on. In reality, perhaps I'd had only two or three more years left of dancing professionally. Some dancers did go on forever, I knew that. I might not have been one of them. But if I stopped, I had nothing left. Nothing.

At night, when sleep took its time coming, I refused to dwell on these things. Instead, I imagined myself dancing. So far, I could only hobble, but I hoped to be able to walk by the end of the month. And then . . . well, why should I believe the doctors? If I could walk, I could run, if I could run,

I could jump, if I could jump, I could dance. It might take a year, or two, or . . .

And then I would clutch my pillow in the dark, afraid of the emptiness that lay in wait for me.

By mid-September, I was packing boxes and preparing myself to say goodbye to the rooftop terrace. Managing the rent by myself would be tough under ordinary circumstances, but in the wasteland between my last paycheck and my insurance payout, it was impossible.

Adelaide, bless her, came by to help. I suspected that she felt bad about the accident. If she had made me go home that evening, I wouldn't have stayed until after dark and fallen. But I didn't blame Adelaide, or the janitor, or anyone else. I understood entirely what was happening: I had been heaped with bad luck, the blackest kind, and I waited—tensed like a cat—for the next bad thing to happen.

For surely it would. I had lost my lover, my career, my home. Next it would be something worse. I worried obsessively about cancer, car accidents, abduction, terrorism, the warming of the planet, the possibility of a new ice age, the extinction of the species. I never stopped worrying. It gave me something to do in those long hours between when the sleeping tablets wore off and when it was safe to take them again.

"Where are all your books?" Adelaide was asking. She had organized me a serviced one-room unit at Holborn, where

I would stay until I could find a more permanent place. Ground floor. No stairs.

"I don't have any books," I confessed, wrapping another dancing trophy in tissue paper. "I read them, then give them to Oxfam. They take up so much room."

Adelaide feigned horror. "Once you've read a book, you and it belong to each other for life. Did you not know that?"

"Even the pulpy ones?"

"Even the pulpy ones." Adelaide looked around. "In fact, you really don't have much . . . stuff. I came prepared for hard work and lots of dusting. If the furniture isn't even yours, there's really only your clothes and—"

"I know," I said. "It's all dancing awards. Josh used to say the same thing. He once bought me a photo frame and put a picture of us in it. I knocked it over and cracked the glass, put it in my bedside drawer. It's in there somewhere." There. I'd managed to talk about dancing and Josh without crying. No, wait, I was crying.

Adelaide gave me a squeeze around the shoulders. "You'll be fine."

"I won't be."

"Of course you will."

I indicated the box of awards, their attractively designed angles carefully softened by the tissue paper. That was my life in there. Wrapped up and ready to be sealed away. "I feel as though I've lost my anchor. I've lost my boyfriend. Now I'm losing my apartment . . ."

"Do you have to move? Really? Could you wait a little longer?"

"I'm going to run out of money soon."

"I don't get in, Em. Your millionaire grandma died a few years ago. She didn't leave you anything?"

"No. Nothing. And I didn't want or expect anything, so I don't mind." When Grandma died, she left nothing to her family. From my earliest childhood, I had understood that my grandparents were very important people: Grandma for her business, Grandad for his work in parliament. But they had never flaunted their wealth nor forgotten their responsibilities to the community. Grandma's company was now in the hands of the shareholders, and the personal fortune went to sixty different Australian charities. It was one of the reasons I had been reluctant to return to Australia. My mother and my uncle had become so bitter, even though they were both company shareholders and were quite wealthy enough. There had been legal investigations and long, stupid arguments. Nothing ruined a family like a rich relative's death. "Besides, I can't manage the stairs here at the moment. It's best if I just get away."

That's when the doorbell rang.

"I'll get it," Adelaide said. "Don't get up."

I anticipated the moving van arriving an hour too soon. What I didn't expect to hear was my mother's voice at the bottom of the stairs, explaining who she was to Adelaide.

My heart jumped, and I tried to get up too quickly. Hurt my knee. Sat back down. Then my mother was there, striding toward me gracefully, her back erect, her dark hair shining and straight and caught in a long ponytail at the nape of her neck. I had always known the sting of having a beautiful mother. When I was a teenager and my mother was still modeling professionally, I would pin photos of her to my bedroom mirror, then sit among them with sick wonder at the difference between our complexions, our eyes, our mouths. Then I'd tear down the photos and put them away, practice for an hour as though exorcising a demon. All that mattered to a ballet dancer was that she was firm and fit and light enough to be picked up. Which I mightn't have been if I'd grown as tall as Louise Blaxland-Hunter.

"My darling," Mum said, leaning down to enclose me in a hug. "You look pale and tired."

"Thanks," I muttered.

Mum knelt and I envied her the ease of movements in her joints. Despair tumbled over me like a wave. "Let me look at you," she said.

I glanced at Adelaide, who nodded and quietly left the room.

"Was this your idea or Dad's?" I asked my mother.

"Both of ours," Mum said. "But I organized it. I'm offended . . ." A little-girl pout, a flutter of eyelashes, entirely inappropriate on any other fifty-eight-year-old woman but somehow still appealing on my mother. "The first thing I wanted to do was come to you. My baby. But I kept thinking you'd come home on your own." She stood, smoothed her skirt. "But you didn't. So I've come to take you home with me."

"I'm not coming home."

"Why not?"

I opened my mouth to reply, but her question caught me

off guard. Why not, indeed? I'd been lying in bed being miserable for weeks. I didn't eat properly, I took too many painkillers; I'd seen myself in the mirror, and the light had gone out of my eyes. There was nothing here for me in London now. Would it be so bad to go home, to be with my family?

My mother sensed me wavering and moved in for the kill. "We have some of the best specialists in the world in Sydney," she said, puffing up with national pride. "They will take such good care of you and your knee." Then the words that sealed it. "Your father knows a physiotherapist who helped one of the Sydney Swans rehabilitate his knee. She's quite famous, and I believe he's gone back to the game now."

My heart caught on a hook. Was she saying this physiotherapist could help me to dance again? Because if I could dance, I had a future. If I couldn't, I was this wreck of a human being.

Mum held her breath.

"All right," I said, "I'll come."

It took me six full minutes—fingers locked like iron around the banister, sweat beading on my brow, knee twinging—but I finally made it up the narrow stairs to the rooftop terrace.

It was unseasonably cold, with squally rain clouds blowing in from the northeast, as though they'd gathered up the gray sea on the way. I made my way over the timber decking to the railing, past the scruffy pots of marigolds and impatiens, leaned against it, and took deep breaths.

This was the view—over the Thames toward Battersea Park—that Josh and I had fallen in love with. Melancholy slid its arms around me. I remembered the day we'd moved in. I'd been in rehearsals for a regional tour of *Daphnis and Chloe,* Josh had just gotten a promotion. We'd left the packing and putting away to come up here with Chinese takeaway and a bottle of Veuve Clicquot. As the sky darkened and the lights all over London flickered into life, Josh had brought up an armful of blankets and we'd made love under the sky. All his kisses tasted like champagne and soy sauce. I froze and laughed at the same time. We were sure everything would go our way from that moment on.

Perhaps, for Josh, it had gone his way. I didn't know. I realized I knew too little about him. I never asked about his work because it bored me, even though he always wanted to know about mine, what I was thinking and feeling about it. Had I been that self-obsessed? It seemed so. Perhaps there was always an assistant waiting in the wings for the partners of women like me.

Mum would be here to get me within an hour. The flights had been booked before she even left Australia. Business class, so I could have my leg stretched out for the entire trip if necessary. Still, I dreaded it. Such a long way. It would take the last of my sleeping pills and painkillers to get through it, and I had deliberately refused to renew my prescriptions. From the moment I touched down in Australia, I was determined to regain my fitness. My dignity. Perhaps even my ability to dance.

How I wished Mum would stop banging on about "other careers." Especially teaching dancing. Teaching! I could barely relate to adults, what would I do with children? Break them, probably. Choreography: no. It would only make me jealous to see other people moving, fluid, alive, their hearts thundering, while I stood on the sidelines and watched.

I sighed and sagged against the railing. "Goodbye, goodbye," I said to the London sky and the river and the cars and the people and the dream, and all of my insides were in a tangle of grief. "I'm going home."

SEVEN

To her credit, Mum waited a week—long enough for me to recover from jet lag and withdraw from the painkillers—before she revealed her ulterior motive. Perhaps she would have waited longer, but Uncle Mike dropped by unexpectedly and, just as unexpectedly, said what he shouldn't have.

It was spring in Sydney, and the air was alive with the scent of the jasmine that Mum grew in the deep back garden. I had started physiotherapy with my father's acquaintance and, at her recommendation, was resolutely walking up and down the entrance hall, avoiding the overly friendly wet nose of Tiger, the German shepherd pup Dad had given Mum for Christmas. Without the painkillers, I was more able to feel the joint, know it. The physiotherapist hadn't given me any false hope. My injury, she said, was a one-in-a-million piece of bad luck for anyone, let alone a dancer. But she had given me good advice: just concentrate on today. To think of all the tomorrows ahead would overwhelm me, immobilize me. Walk for now. Rebuild the leg muscles. Live in the present, in case thoughts of the past or future flattened me.

Dad was at work in the hardware store he owned. Mum and Dad had never married; that's how I had ended up with my mother's double-barreled surname. Periodically, they made noises about a "celebration of their love," a thought that both embarrassed me and filled me with soppy happiness.

Up and down the hallway.

The knock at the door.

"Uncle Mike!" I tentatively offered him a hug, silently begging him not to perform one of his Uncle Mike moves like sweeping me up and shaking me around. He was a giant bear of a man, known for bomb-diving swimming pools and complicated prank handshakes.

"Em! So good to see you. You look beautiful. The Australian sun is doing you some good, then."

I didn't tell him that I wouldn't cross the road without a hat and sunscreen. I was very attached to my ivory skin. Instead, I said, "It's nice to be home."

"How long you staying?" He closed the door behind him and walked toward the kitchen, not waiting for an answer. "Has Hibbins been on to you yet? What's the story?"

I didn't know what he meant, but it wasn't unusual for Uncle Mike to go off on a tangent that nobody could understand except him. I followed him slowly, catching up just as he was pulling a beer out of the fridge and setting it down with a clunk on the marble countertop.

"Want one?" he said.

"Mum!" I called, aware that she'd want to know Uncle

Mike was here. Whether she wanted to see him was another thing. "Visitor."

Uncle Mike twisted the top off the beer and leaned his back against the opposite bench. "So, what did you get?"

"Get?"

"Hibbins. Your Nana Beattie's solicitor."

"Nana Beattie. I haven't called her that since I was eight." I shook my head. "I haven't a clue what you're talking about."

"Jeez, you sound like a Pom. We're going to have to knock that accent out of you."

I heard footsteps on the carpeted stairs. Mum was coming to save me. She emerged into the kitchen looking more poised and glamorous than anyone had a right to while ironing. When she saw Uncle Mike, her whole body tensed.

That's when I started to suspect she hadn't told me everything.

"Mike," she said.

"Louise," he responded.

"I asked you to give Emma some space."

"Space? I'm her uncle. I wanted to come and see how she was."

"Don't lie. I know why you're here."

"Someone's got to tell her. You obviously haven't."

"You selfish fool. My daughter has just suffered through two operations and has been told she'll never dance again. Those other things can wait."

Uncle Mike snorted a laugh. "Don't pretend you're protecting her, Louise. You want to know as much as I do."

I watched the exchange with growing apprehension. "Can somebody explain what's going on?" I asked with a dry throat.

Mum turned to me and forced a smile. "It's all right, we can talk about it later."

"I don't see why we should have to wait till later," Uncle Mike said. "We've already been waiting for years."

I shrugged. "I'm curious now. I want to know."

Mum glanced at Uncle Mike. Her nostrils flared slightly, a sign that she was pulling her emotions under control. "We'll take tea in the garden. These things should be done properly."

Of course I had figured out this was something to do with Grandma's estate. Mum and Uncle Mike had never quite recovered from the shock of being left nothing. Had she left me something, then? It was no secret that she doted on me. I'd always had a special bond with her. Sometimes I'd even wondered if my mother was jealous of my relationship with Grandma; they'd been so prickly with each other. I was intrigued but not excited by the idea of an inheritance. The only thing I wanted was to dance again. And maybe to have Josh back, but the Josh who didn't cheat on me. Material things had never been particularly important to me.

It was late afternoon. In the distance, a lawn mower growled, and the scent of freshly cut grass was heavy in the air. As the sun moved down in the sky, the blue velvet foretaste of evening set in, and my knee began to pulse with dull pain. I waited for Mum and Uncle Mike, whom I suspected were arguing as Mum filled the teapot and arranged the cups on the tray. That would explain why the tea was taking so long. I leaned back in my chair and stretched out my injured leg. A flock of birds, distant black shapes, shot past overhead. For some reason, the late part of the day always brought on a miserable, hopeless feeling. I missed London, I missed Josh, I missed the rehearsal studio. The painkillers and sleeping pills had been an easy addiction to break, but those other things—those things that had underpinned my happiness for so many years—were impossible to withdraw from. The sadness built up inside me, and I had no way to express it. I had always expressed myself through moving my body. My entire adult life, if not before, I had chaneled my most intense feelings into my muscles and sinews, then danced them out. All I had now were tears, and I was nauseatingly bored with them.

I glanced up to see Mum and Uncle Mike approaching. Did I imagine the avaricious gleam in their eyes? They were mad. No amount of money could buy me back my happiness; my insurance payout had already proved that to me.

With a practiced politeness that was stretched tight over their tension, they settled at the wrought-iron table, one on either side of me. Mum poured tea for her and me; Uncle Mike stuck with beer. There was small talk. I watched it all as if from a distance. Then I finally said, "How much?"

Mum and Uncle Mike exchanged glances.

"What I don't understand is why you couldn't tell me until now," I said.

"We don't know how much," Mum blurted. "That's the thing. Mr. Hibbins has said—"

"We couldn't tell you because your Nana Beattie put a stupid condition on the will."

"She was adamant, love, that you be back in Australia before you received anything. Or even heard about the inheritance." Mum stirred her tea vigorously. "It was intended as a gift on your . . . retirement."

Memories drifted back to me. Sitting with Grandma in the music room of her big house at Point Piper. I must have been about eleven. She had promised me a present for "after." *Ballerinas can't dance forever.* All the nerves in my body lit up with indignation.

"I'm not retiring," I said forcefully. "I don't want anything from Grandma. It'll be something small, anyway. She gave her money to charity, and you two just have to get over it. I'm not going to be an heiress. I'm going to get better, and I'm going back to London to keep dancing."

A vacuum of silence followed my tirade. Uncle Mike stopped with his beer can halfway to his lips. If I'd been physically capable of it, I would have stormed off. I had to settle for carefully drawing myself out of my chair and hobbling away.

"Come back, Em," Mum said.

"Let her cool off, Louise," Uncle Mike said.

"We really should talk about this," Mum called.

But I didn't turn around, I didn't look back. If I had, they would have seen my tears.

I locked myself in my room. As though I were fourteen again. I didn't come down when I heard Dad's car in the driveway, nor when I could smell frying garlic, nor when Mum knocked and called through, "Are you going to eat?"

My silence sent her away.

Evening deepened toward night, and I sat on my bed with

the window ajar, listening to the crickets chirping, listening to the gentle breeze in the leaves of the giant camphor laurel trees that lined the creek running parallel to the street, listening to the distant sounds of cars on the highway. Darker and cooler. I didn't turn on a light. It was as though I were paralyzed, as though I couldn't think and move at the same time. But I wasn't thinking, really. I was trying *not* to think.

I heard my parents watching television. I heard Dad come up the stairs, the creak of the pipes in the bathroom as he showered. I heard Mum lock the front door and turn out the lights. I heard them go to bed, soft voices in the dark. Talking about me, I supposed. About how I had lost touch with reality, how I didn't want inheritances but still believed I could dance.

Midnight, and still I was a statue. Finally, I rose. The half-moon outside gave me enough light to find my suitcase under the window. I hadn't unpacked yet. Denial. In the side, in a satin-covered box, I found my shoes. New Russian pointe shoes, worn in just enough to be comfortable and flexible but not yet starting to break down. Perfect shoes. Next to them was the tiara I had worn for *Swan Lake* in Yugoslavia the year before. It had been designed especially for me by a Czech jewelry designer, and even though the jewels weren't real, it was exquisite. I slid it onto my head and eased myself onto the floor, hitching my skirt up to my hips to lace the shoes on. The movements were reassuringly familiar: I hadn't worn them since the accident. Then I struggled to my feet. I had danced through pain before.

I stretched each foot gently, then . . . up.

For a microscopic space of time—perhaps a billionth of a second—it felt normal. My muscles did what they were supposed to do, replayed their memories faithfully. But the searing pain was quick to blot out my glimmer of hope. I cried out, crumpled to the ground. And allowed myself to sob. For my pain. For my disappointment. For the loss of the thing most important to me. My head had known it all along, but now my heart did, too. By the time I rehabilitated my knee—if that were even possible—I would be too old to cast. Too risky. And because semi-professional work or small roles were so vastly beneath me—there, I admitted it—that meant my career was definitely over.

A gentle knock at the door.

"Go away," I called.

But it was Dad. He let himself in. "Em? Did you fall? Are you all right?" He turned the light on; it was hideously bright. He took a glance at me, at the tiara on my head, the pointe shoes on my feet, and rushed over to pick me up. I cried into his chest, my face awash. He sat me carefully on my bed. For a large man—a real bloke's bloke—he had always been infinitely gentle.

"Are you hurt?" he said. "Should I call a doctor?"

"I didn't fall," I replied in a bubbling, hiccuping voice. "I'm crying because . . . I've realized . . ." I couldn't finish.

He pushed my hair off my hot face. "I'm so sorry, my sweetheart," he said. "I would do anything to make it better. But I can't."

Of course he couldn't. Nobody could. I carefully pulled

off the tiara and handed it to him. "Throw it away," I said. "I never want to see it again."

By the following Monday, I found myself in the offices of Mr. Hibbins, who had been our family's solicitor for as far back as I could remember. I'd never heard anyone call him anything other than Mr. Hibbins, though I'm sure he had a given name just like the rest of us. But there was something old-fashioned about him, with his carefully pressed shirts and slightly too-wide ties. It would have been wrong to address him any other way.

Of course my mother was there. Much to her delight, I'd refused to allow Uncle Mike to come. Mum fidgeted, a clear sign that she was nervous. I wasn't nervous. I didn't anticipate money, while Mum clearly did. Grandma would know better than to leave me money. I expected, perhaps, an item of treasured jewelry, or a book that had some meaning to her. I expected a token, something with a lesson in it for me: probably a lesson I didn't care to learn just now.

Mr. Hibbins opened the folder on his oak desk with all due ceremony. Clocks ticked, paintings watched, dust accumulated on bookshelves. He already knew what was in the folder and was playing the part like a host on a reality television game. "The winner is . . ."

Mum twisted her elegant hands together.

"Emma, your grandmother gave me very clear instructions. She has left you something of great sentimental value, but there are conditions attached. One of those conditions has been that you return to Australia." He smiled. "Welcome back."

I couldn't meet his eye. He knew nothing about my injury, my loss. My misery must have been brutally evident. His smile faded and retreated.

"In any case," he continued gruffly, "the object in question also has some monetary value, though you can't actually sell it for six months after it is transferred to you."

"What is it?" Mum asked, unable to hold still any longer.

Mr. Hibbins didn't even glance at her. The fallout from Grandma's inheritance had put him at odds with Mum and Uncle Mike. "It's a house, Emma."

"A house? But you sold off the Point Piper place," Mum said, leaping from her seat. "I remember. The money went to some bloody animal refuge."

Mr. Hibbins cleared his throat, shuffled his papers back into the folder, waited for Mum to sit down again. A house. Grandma had left me a house. That was a good thing, surely. I shouldn't feel this sense of being burdened.

"As I said, the house had enormous significance for Beattie." He pushed the folder across the desk to me. "It's in Tasmania."

"That old place?" Mum said. "I thought she sold it years ago. Is that all? Are you sure?"

"Thank you," I said to Mr. Hibbins, tucking the folder underneath my arm. "But I don't know what I'll do with it. Is it in salable condition? I mean, I don't have to go there, do I?"

Mr. Hibbins's voice softened. "Your grandmother was very keen that you go, but she knew she couldn't make you. As

I said earlier, you can sell it in six months but not before. I think she was rather hoping you'd spend some time there."

"In Tasmania?"

"Yes. It's very pretty. You'd like it."

I knew about Grandma's sheep farm. One of my earliest memories was sleeping over at Grandma's place and waking with a fright in the middle of the night. I'd run out to where she sat, up late, reading in the music room. She'd put my head in her lap and told me to look at the gum tree painting that she loved so much. That was her favorite view from the homestead, she'd told me, and it always made her feel calm and happy to look at it. I'd watched the painting carefully for a long time while she stroked my hair, until I'd drifted back to sleep.

I was curious to see the place. Stepping down from London to Sydney was one thing. But to head down to an island full of farms at the bottom of the world . . .

"Just sell it," Mum was advising me, sotto voce. "You can't go down there in your condition. You need me to look after you. You might get a nice sum for it."

I thought about Mum and Uncle Mike, both of them telling me what to do, anxiously trying to control the last small piece of Grandma's estate. And I thought about Grandma, about what she might be trying to tell me by leaving me this house—I knew how much it meant to her—and I decided I would rather listen to Grandma than to Mum.

"I'll go," I said.

Mum was blessedly silent with astonishment. Mr. Hibbins smiled, and this time I found that I could smile back.

"I'm so pleased, Emma," he said. "Beattie would have been pleased, too. Perhaps you can breathe some life into the old place."

"I'll go and have a look, that's all," I said, hands in front of me, palms out. "I'm not going to stay for any length of time."

He seemed to be about to say something, then stopped. Adjusted his tie. "There was no estate sale, so the house is still rather . . . full. Somebody will need to sort through the things."

"What things? Books? Knick-knacks?"

"Actually, all the furniture is still there. Under dustcovers, I imagine. Boxes and boxes of . . . I don't know. She sent a lot of her things there for storage. You might find it a big job sorting them."

"Do you want me to come with you?" Mum said.

"No," I replied, probably too quickly. I gave her an affectionate rub on the arm. "No, I'll be fine. In fact, I'm rather looking forward to it."

EIGHT

Beattie: Hobart, 1933

Beattie was hanging out washing on the thin line that
ran between the eaves of the house and the side fence
when she heard the postman's whistle from the street.
That sound, so innocent, had lately filled her with dread as
their debts mounted up and increasingly frustrated creditors
reminded them just how much they owed.

She finished hanging up Henry's shirts with wooden pegs,
wiped her hands on her apron—her knuckles were red and
split from a morning of scrubbing and wringing clothes over
the steaming copper—and headed to the letter box with trepidation.

It was a fine March morning, briskly cool, yet the sky
seemed wide and sunny. Doris Penny from next door beat a
rug on her front patio, and the rhythmic thump echoed between the houses on the narrow street and sent clouds of dust
up in the air to catch the sun. Beattie retrieved a single envelope from the letter box, flipped it over, and didn't see the name
of anyone they owed money to. Her relief was short-lived.
Because the name was far worse than the name of a creditor.

"Hello!" Doris called in a hopeful voice.

Beattie tucked the letter in the pocket of her apron, kept her head down, and returned to the house. Henry had been very clear that she wasn't to make friends, she wasn't to speak for too long to anyone, unless their secret was found out. Doris had been energetic in her attempts to build a relationship, but Beattie only ever offered her hurried apologies, a hand raised in a gesture that could have been a greeting or a warning to stay away. Nor was Beattie allowed to contact anyone from home—though she had sent two letters to Cora via Billy. Cora had not replied. Beattie missed home, she missed her friends, she missed her parents. She longed to be able to unburden her heart to someone, but Henry had forbidden it.

The door clunked shut behind her, and she moved through to the little kitchen to sit at the table and pull out the letter. She read the sender's name again. *Molly MacConnell.* Henry's wife. His *real* wife, not his make-believe wife, as Beattie had been for over three years. Her fingers were desperate to open it, but she dared not. Henry's temper was unpredictable, grew more unpredictable as their financial difficulties deepened. And their financial difficulties deepened the more Henry drank to forget how deep they were, the more he gambled to try to dig them out of their hole.

Beattie carefully propped the letter on the mantel. She would have to wait for Henry to come home, read it, tell her what it meant. For surely they had been discovered now: if Molly had gone to the trouble of finding him, then maybe she wanted him back. Beattie experienced a tiny thrill of guilt; the idea of Henry being somebody else's problem brought momentary relief, a weight lifted off her chest. But she still loved Henry. And they were bound together now by a sticky web of complications.

Down the hallway, the sound of a door opening. Then a sleepy-faced child peered out.

"Mama?"

Beattie rose, collected Lucy in her arms, and kissed her warm cheek. "Did you have a nice sleep, darling?"

Lucy nodded, rubbing her eyes with her soft fists. "I want lunch."

Beattie desposited Lucy at the kitchen table and set about making her a very thin sandwich with the food they had remaining. She cut it into four small pieces and put it in front of Lucy, who turned up her nose and said, "I don't like it."

"You haven't tried it. It's cheese and pickles."

Lucy shook her head, but her cheeks dimpled.

"It's Daddy's favorite," Beattie said, as she said every day at lunchtime.

Lucy theatrically rubbed her tummy and made a slurping sound, then started in on the sandwich. To say that the girl was attached strongly to her father was to understate the case by a thousand miles. Lucy and Henry were cut from the same cloth. They even shared the red hair and the gray eyes. Only when Lucy smiled could Beattie see any resemblance to herself. From the moment she'd been born, Henry had doted on her. She'd been a cranky child, impossible for Beattie to settle. And yet every evening when Henry returned from work, all he had to do was pick her up and talk to her softly and she would finally stop crying, nestle into his shoulder, and sleep.

Beattie had been far too shocked and exhausted by parenthood to be made jealous.

Now that Lucy was three, the daddy-daughter love was so deeply cemented that it sometimes felt as though Beattie were a long way outside them, her voice heard less clearly, her face seen less distinctly. She was the one who spent all day with Lucy, who made peg dolls with her and lay down to sing her to sleep for her nap. But that physical proximity could not compete with the emotional proximity Henry and Lucy shared. So on the days when life with Henry was hardest—when he came home too late and too drunk, when he bullied Beattie over the smile she exchanged with the baker, when he smashed the kitchen table with his fists in anger and her heart grew hot knowing it was her body he would rather hit—she could not allow herself to dream of taking Lucy and leaving him. The child would not be moved.

As Lucy ate, Beattie's eyes were drawn again and again to the envelope. Perhaps it was good news. Perhaps Molly had met somebody new and finally wanted to divorce Henry. Perhaps she had spent months tracking him down to set him free. But Beattie couldn't shake the feeling of dread.

Lucy pushed her empty plate away from her. "Can we play in the garden?"

"No, darling, we have to go to the shops. We have no food for Daddy's dinner." And no money to buy food, but she hoped the general store would allow her just one more tick on the books.

Lucy climbed down from the chair and ran to fetch her shoes. Beattie glanced one last time at the letter, then told herself to put it out of her mind until Henry came home. Praying he would come home early for once.

Beattie walked down the hill toward the shops, Lucy running several feet ahead of her to pick up rocks or pet a stray cat. From up here, Beattie could see across the masts in the harbor all the way to the clock tower on the post office. Seeing the ships never failed to give her a sense of dread. She and Henry had spent two months aboard a stinking cargo liner to get here. The first ten days were a blur of roiling seasickness, and all those that followed were a claustrophobic nightmare inside their grimy cabin, waiting and waiting for the world to turn underneath her so she might finally come to rest. But reaching land brought her no joy. For this was not home but a strange wide-skied country where some people still used horses and carts. The homesickness was almost too much for her to bear, and some days she wondered if it was only the prospect of another long journey that stopped her from turning around and going back. She swore she'd never set foot on a boat again.

Henry had started work quickly, and their days fell into a routine. They were renting a little house from Billy Wilder on a street of brick cottages behind hawthorne hedges. Lucy had arrived in the very early hours one weekend, quickly and painfully. There hadn't been time for the midwife to attend, and Henry had been the one to take the squirming baby from Beattie's body and wrap it in a soft blanket until help came. With misty eyes, he'd told her they had a little girl, a daughter, and they had sat close by each other in sacred awe, holding the child—little Lucy with her fierce eyes and tuft of red hair—until dawn. Such happiness had beaten in her heart. But that happiness had been fleeting.

The general store was run by two elderly women whom Beattie had always found difficult to tell apart. Jean and Lesley. Not sweet old ladies, either. Rather the stern, self-righteous variety. They were close but not sisters, and Beattie suspected that they might be much more than friends. Henry, when she'd suggested this, lost his temper at her for thinking scandalous thoughts. It had made her sad: did she have to second-guess before sharing her thoughts with him? How could they be close if he judged her so fiercely?

But then had they ever been close? Fervent dalliances at the club aside, the first time they'd spent concentrated time together was on the ship to Hobart. And they'd found they had little to say to each other.

Jean and Lesley were running a thriving business but always complaining about money. For this reason, they left the lights in the shop off during the day, so that the windowless back corner was always in semi-darkness. This was the corner they had chosen to put the toys, high up on oak shelves, tantalizingly out of reach. It was Lucy's favorite corner. She stared up longingly at the Madame Alexander dolls. The fat baby in the red pajamas was her favorite, and Beattie was certain that only fear of the sharp voices of Jean and Lesley stopped her from climbing the shelves to get it. Beattie left her to gaze and took the basket around the shop, collecting only the essentials but still alarmed at how quickly the basket was filling up.

Then, fearfully, she approached the glass counter, which was lined with jars of sweets and rotating racks of postcards.

Jean—or was it Lesley . . . no, Jean was the one with the steel-gray hair—smiled at her tightly. "Good morning, Mrs. MacConnell."

"Good morning. I . . . wonder if my husband could come down and pay for these later?"

Jean's smile didn't falter, though her eyes grew cold. "I believe we are still waiting for your husband to pay for groceries from last Thursday."

"Yes, I know. He will come down and pay for them all this week." Friday, payday. Not that there was ever much left. Eight months after Lucy's birth, Billy Wilder had formed his own company and employed Henry. Within weeks, he'd told Henry he couldn't afford to keep him on—so many men were losing their jobs—unless he took a much lower salary. And from that salary every week, before a penny had made its way into Henry's pocket, Billy deducted rent and gambling debts. What they had left over was sometimes less than the dreaded welfare: she'd be better off with a food relief card. "We have to eat," she said softly.

Jean sighed. "Some folk are so ill-starred that they make soup from grass, Mrs. MacConnell. But as your husband actually has a job, I'll give you another chance." She turned and opened one of the drawers behind her to pull out a well-thumbed notebook. She slapped it on the counter and opened it. "I'll extend your credit until the end of the month. On March thirty-first, if your debt isn't cleared, you won't be able to shop here again. Do you understand?"

Beattie merely nodded. As Jean rang up her bill, then pinned the receipt in the notebook, she carefully hid her squirming, hot-faced shame. Today it was a little easier to bear, because there was something even more worrisome on her mind. A letter waiting at home for Henry, and she didn't know what it signified.

Beattie hoped Henry would come home early and put her out of her misery. She went about tidying the house and preparing dinner. She thought about steaming the letter open but stopped herself. It wasn't worth Henry losing his temper. Finally, she bundled Lucy up and took her out into the garden. As the long shadows crept across the patchy grass, Lucy ran about with her arms outstretched, demanded endless games of ring-a-rosy, buried her peg-doll family alive, then dug them up again. Henry's usual arrival time came and went, and as the sun set and Lucy started moaning about being hungry, Beattie realized he had decided to stay out, probably to drink with Billy.

She took Lucy inside and fixed her dinner—bread and dripping and some leftover pea soup—but had no appetite herself. The evening was taken up with chores: bathing Lucy, cleaning up, making up bedtime stories. Lucy cried a little that her daddy wasn't home, but Beattie reassured her that the sooner she went to sleep, the sooner it would be morning and she would see him then.

Beattie sat up with her sewing kit and worked. She made all of her own and Lucy's clothes, often looking out for castoffs that could be unpicked and resewn. Her childish dreams of being a designer now seemed laughable, but she did still love drawing ideas for dresses, and many of the local women had commented on Lucy's beautiful clothes. Beattie always kept her head down, nodding politely, though not engaging in conversation. But she had suggested to Henry that she could start a little business making children's clothes to sell.

Henry had scoffed at the idea. "Nobody has any money, and children grow so quickly, they'd be fools to spend it on new clothes. Just keep to yourself."

As Beattie sewed, she was aware of the night deepening. She had no appetite, but she ate a little bit of dinner and left the rest for Henry when he came home. Her eyes returned again and again to the letter, and as the wind off the water intensified and it grew cold enough to light the fire, her dread grew exponentially. Molly. The Irish wolfhound. A woman she had never met and yet was inextricably connected to. Beattie had stolen Molly's husband. There, she'd allowed herself to think it. And what happened to women who stole husbands? Beattie suspected she was already finding out.

It was ten o'clock before Beattie gave up. Even if Henry came home now, he wouldn't be sober enough to talk to. She changed into her nightdress and climbed into bed. Gusts of wind periodically shook the windows, and she slept fitfully, half-dreams and anxious imaginings punctuating her rest.

In the very early hours of the morning, when the world seemed farthest from the sun, she heard voices.

She sat up, sleep falling away from her in an instant. It was Henry. Had he seen the letter yet? She rose and cracked open the door. Across the hall in the sitting room, the lamps were blazing, the fire roaring. They were talking some nonsense about a rich client, making lewd jokes and laughing uproariously. She heard the clink of glasses. They were drinking. She hoped that Billy had bought the alcohol, because Henry had no money for it.

Beattie returned to bed, leaving the door ajar so she could listen. Their conversation drifted in and out of her hearing. Then there was a burst of loud laughter and, briefly afterward, the sound of Lucy's bedroom door opening. They had woken her up.

As Beattie pulled on her dressing gown, she heard Lucy's sleepy voice in the hallway. "Daddy?"

"My wee lass!" Henry effused drunkenly. "Come here, dearie. Come and say hello to Uncle Billy."

Beattie's skin crawled at the idea of "Uncle Billy" anywhere near her daughter and hurried out to intercept Lucy in the doorway to the sitting room. "Come on, love. Back to bed."

Henry glared at her. "I haven't seen her all day. Give me a chance to say hello, woman."

Beattie bit her tongue so she didn't tell him it was his fault he hadn't seen her all day because he'd been out drinking. Probably gambling.

Lucy threw herself in Henry's arms, and he gathered her up and cuddled her savagely.

"Och, she's the image of you, Henry," Billy said.

"Until she smiles. Then she's all Beattie."

Billy glanced at Beattie, his eyes drawn to her nightdress.

She drew together her robe tightly at her neck. He smiled cruelly—in truth, she'd seen no other kind of smile from him—and held out an empty whiskey glass. "Drink?"

"It's one in the morning."

"It will help you sleep."

Beattie didn't answer. Her gaze skimmed the mantel. The letter was still unopened.

Henry put Lucy down and said, "Will you sing a wee song for Uncle Billy? The one about the birdies that you made up?" He turned to Billy. "She's a clever lass, Billy, you wouldn't credit it."

Beattie intervened. "She really should be sleeping, Henry."

"I want to stay up with Daddy."

Henry conceded. "Your mother's right. I'm just so happy to see you, my chick." He stroked her hair gently. "Go on, off to bed with you. You can sing for me in the morning."

Beattie took Lucy back to bed and tucked her in. By this stage, the child was wide-eyed and restless, and Beattie doubted she would sleep.

"Just close your eyes," Beattie said. "Off to dreamland. I'll meet you there under the big chestnut tree. We'll have a picnic."

Lucy smiled. "Can we have cake?"

"Yes, cake with jam in the middle."

The little girl mimed eating a giant slice, then turned over and screwed her eyes shut. Beattie left her, closing the door quietly, then paused in the threshold of the sitting room. Henry was more subdued now, but Billy was screeching with laughter over some wild joke. She waited for him to quiet, then smiled politely. "Have you news of your brother, Billy? Did Cora have the baby yet?"

"Yes, yes, Teddy's a proud father. A wee boy they named Frank. They've moved to Edinburgh, bought a house with a garden. Domestic bliss."

Beattie found it hard to fight her jealousy. "Give them my best, won't you?" She turned her eyes to Henry. "And Henry, there's a letter up there for you." She nodded toward the mantel. "Might be important. I'm off to bed."

She turned, heart thudding, and returned to her room. Closed the door all but a crack and peered out. A long quiet. He was reading it.

"What's wrong, MacConnell? Bad news?"

"It's nothing," Henry said quickly. She saw him cross the room to the fire. He was going to burn the letter. "Just some nonsense. Another drink?"

Beattie got into bed and closed her eyes. He burned it. That meant he didn't want it. That meant everything was all right. Didn't it? Sleep eluded her. Within half an hour, Billy had clattered out the front door and Henry was sliding into bed next to her, quiet, trying not to wake her.

She turned to him. "Henry, the letter—"

"Don't ask."

"But what did she want? What—"

"*I said don't ask!*" he shouted, and it was so loud in the dark quiet that her whole body twitched in shock.

She opened her mouth to speak, to ask for reassurance, but

didn't want him to shout again. He'd burned it. He wanted to forget it. That would have to be enough.

Sometimes, Henry thought, it was better to take care of things himself. It didn't matter how many times he'd told Beattie that she must go down to the general store and negotiate with them; she insisted she couldn't, that the two hard-faced women who ran the store would not extend their credit another penny. Henry didn't believe that for a second. Beattie was a mite lazy and a mite too worried about what other people thought. So he'd put on his hat and marched down there, Lucy clinging firmly to his hand, to make Jean and Lesley see sense. He couldn't pay, not just yet, though he anticipated a windfall soon. His luck was bound to change at the card table. Frankly, it couldn't get any worse.

"Daddy, you're walking too fast."

Henry slowed, giving her soft hand a squeeze. "Sorry, my dearie."

"Mummy lets me collect rocks."

"We haven't time today." But the sting of being unfairly compared to Beattie undermined him. "Och, I'm being a grouch. Go on, Lucy. Find your pretty rocks."

Her warm fingers left his, and she dashed off to the edge of the road. He watched her with a grin, aware as he always was that the child made him into an idiot. Every time he looked at her, even thought about her, his heart turned to warm water. The night she was born—a collection of hellish images of blood and bodily contortion that he could not forget when he looked at Beattie—it was as though Lucy had emerged directly into his hands, as though she were telling him, "I'm yours, never let me go."

They arrived at the bottom of the hill. The store was late-afternoon quiet. The larger woman, Lesley, was bringing in the news banners while Jean counted out the cash register inside. Lucy ran off to the back corner to look at the dolls, and Henry approached the counter.

Jean looked up, unsmiling. "Mr. MacConnell? I do hope you've come to pay your bill."

Henry wasn't one for smiling or charming people. He spoke plainly and with dignity. "I am unable to pay at this point. I want to extend our credit until April thirty, when I expect to pay it in full." There. Not so hard to say, so why did Beattie balk at it?

"No."

Henry winced. "I'm sorry?"

"No. I'm not in the business of extending credit to bad debtors. Many people are in financial difficulties, Mr. Mac-Connell. *Genuinely.* But yours is the only family who asks for more than we can give you."

The rage began to build within him. What did she mean "genuinely"? Had Beattie told them about his gambling debts? Could she not keep her mouth shut? The silly, young fool! His hands balled into fists, and he wanted to smash the cabinet they rested on, to hear the satisfying shatter of its glass.

"I can see you don't like what I'm saying to you," Jean said, "but nothing you can do can change my opinion. Unless you give me some of the money I am owed."

Henry gathered himself. He nodded once, then wordlessly turned on his heel. He marched up to the back corner where Lucy was gazing with huge, round eyes at a collection of little dolls up out of her reach.

"Daddy," she said, "the baby."

He looked and saw a tiny baby doll, smaller than his hand, dressed in red. Lucy looked at him with pleading eyes. He cursed himself. If he hadn't lost so much to Billy—damn Billy, damn him for everything!—he'd be able to buy this little toy for his child. But instead . . .

Henry checked behind him. Jean was counting her money, Lesley was still outside, the back corner was dark.

In one swift moment, the doll was in his pocket. He herded Lucy out quickly, shushing her excited laughter. He swept her up in his arms and hurried down the hill to the empty marketplace, where they sat together and she made a game out of checking every one of his pockets until she found the doll.

Then she threw her little arms around his neck and shrieked with happiness.

As Lucy played with her dolly, as the plane tree leaves scattered about them, as the boats slowly bobbed on their moorings in the harbor, Henry's anger subsided until he felt quite normal again. And a little embarrassed. Stealing toys for his daughter. Is that what he had been reduced to? Once he had known what to do with himself, with life. But then Beattie had come along, with her wide blue eyes and her soft white skin . . . For a long time, she had seemed to be his greatest love. Now, though, she was his greatest regret.

Especially now that Molly had found him. Especially now that Molly had written to tell him her father in Ireland had finally died and left her a small fortune. She still wanted him back, despite everything. That was the kind of person Molly was. She was good: a heart handmade by angels.

He shook himself. That was not his life anymore. This was. He watched Lucy a little longer, smiling again. The child brought him such happiness, and every choice he'd made that had brought him here—to this moment of togetherness—was worth it. He would endure without Molly's money, without Beattie's adoration. For the love of his daughter, he could endure anything.

NINE

Even though Henry had expressly forbidden it, Beattie found herself knocking quietly on her neighbor's front door. To say she was desperate was true on so many levels, but she was most desperate for money. Her one pair of shoes, brought with her from Glasgow, the ones she had used to run away from Morcombe House, were finally beyond repair.

Not that she was going to ask Doris for money. The thought mortified her. But she knew the elderly woman lived alone, and perhaps she had odd jobs that Beattie could help her with and be paid for when Henry was out and wouldn't know.

Beattie crouched down and straightened the hem of Lucy's dress. It would have to come down again. The child was growing so fast.

"What are we doing here, Mummy?"

"I have to speak very quickly to the lady who lives here. Her name is Doris." She stopped short of saying "Daddy mustn't know" because that was a sure way to get Lucy to say something. No secrets could be kept from Daddy. She would rely instead on the fact that Lucy was young and easily distractible. An afternoon playing with the peg dolls in the boat made out of a soapbox would make her forget.

The door opened, and Doris was standing there, looking down at her curiously. "Mrs. MacConnell?"

"Beattie," Beattie said, standing and extending her hand.

Doris took it briefly, smiling. "How nice of you to drop by. Can I make you tea?"

"I . . ." Beattie hesitated. Then decided she could not form half a friendship with this woman. "Of course. Thank you, I would like that very much."

She ushered Lucy in ahead of her and sat her down in the sitting room with the little baby doll that Henry had bought her—Beattie had held her tongue: there were so many things they needed more than dolls—where she played happily while Doris made tea and Beattie eyed the room. It was immaculate. Clearly, this woman needed no help with household chores. Every gleaming surface was adorned with little glass statues, china candleholders, silver boxes. Over the mantel hung a heavy, decorated crucifix. A watercolor painting of Jesus—blue-eyed and fair-haired—sat on the mantel just like a photo of a favorite relative.

"I must say," Doris said, pouring the tea, "I never thought I'd find you in my sitting room."

"I'm very sorry," Beattie said. "My husband and I have rather kept to ourselves." Not entirely true. Henry was well known in the bars. His indiscretion was no doubt how Molly had tracked him down.

"You don't need to explain anything to me," Doris said, sitting next to Beattie on the high-backed sofa. "I'm just glad you came. I've been very lonely since my husband died." She blinked rapidly, then forced a smile. "I do hope you'll come again."

"Well, that is one of the reasons I wanted to speak to you. I'm rather hoping to find some work: cleaning, perhaps? Or cooking? I'm very good at sewing, if you need anything repaired."

Doris shook her head. "Oh, no. I like to do all those things myself. It keeps me fit. And I don't really have the money to hire anybody. Since Tom died, I do have to be careful with what I've got."

Lucy was circling the room slowly, admiring the knick-knacks gleaming on every surface. Beattie tried to hide her disappointment.

"It's a shame you don't live a little farther north. My cousin Margaret in Lewinford is a seamstress, and she always has more work than she can manage. She often employs young women like yourself."

"Lewinford? How far away is it?"

"Fifty miles, dear. Too far to travel. Especially with a young one." Doris's eyes settled on Lucy, and she smiled. "She's a pretty thing, isn't she? That lovely red hair."

"She looks like her father. He was always a handsome fellow." As Beattie said this, she wondered where her desire for Henry had gone. Those days, when one look from his pale eyes could set her heart thundering, were so far behind her.

Beattie drank her tea as quickly as she could, keen to get

home now that Doris couldn't help her. If Henry found out, there would be trouble. But Doris had settled into a long tale of her husband, how they'd met, the thirty-five good years they'd spent together, their six children who were living in various places all over Australia. Finally, she'd stopped to offer to make another pot of tea.

"No, I mustn't," Beattie said. "I've rather a lot to do at home."

"You must come by again tomorrow. Or the next day. It has been so lovely to have company."

Beattie squirmed. "Thank you for inviting me. I'm sure I'll come again soon."

Doris saw them to the door, crouching in front of Lucy to say goodbye. Beattie watched curiously as Doris put her arms around Lucy's body, then rummaged in her smock. Just as Beattie was about to protest, Doris produced a small glass statue of a mouse. "I don't think this is yours, little one," she said kindly, and stood.

Beattie's face burned with shame. "Lucy! You stole that! How could you?"

Lucy looked confused. "I liked it."

"I'm so sorry, I—"

"Think nothing of it. I saw her hide it under her dress and thought I'd give her a chance to put it back." Doris turned kind eyes on Lucy. "You mustn't take other people's things. Jesus is watching you always."

"Who's Jesus?"

Beattie turned Lucy around. "We must go . . ."

"If you ever need somebody to mind the child, just drop her by. I'd be delighted to have her."

Beattie marched Lucy home, wishing she'd done exactly as Henry said and not tried to make contact with the outside world.

They made it through winter by burning rubbish in their fireplace, by brewing their tea increasingly weak, by begging Billy to give them a month off paying rent even though it left them further in debt. Billy was always cheerfully willing to extend their credit, and Beattie didn't know if it was because he could not imagine how desperate their situation was or if he was pleased to get the extra interest on the loans. For all other purposes, he was Henry's best friend. Some weeks, the only food she could afford was porridge oats, bread, milk, and honey. She noticed her dresses growing looser around the waist, though she made sure Lucy always had plenty to eat. Because Henry was employed, they could not qualify for government assistance. But his money was gone before he got it, and he couldn't, or wouldn't, see the approaching disaster.

Others had it so much worse: she had come home with Lucy from a walk one day to see the family across the road—a thin, gray-faced woman, a pair of crying babies, and a man with a stricken face—sitting on their dirty mattress on the side of the road. Evicted. The man had looked at her and called it out in a cracked voice, "Please? Have you anything to give us? My children haven't eaten today, and we've nowhere to sleep." Beattie had kept her head down. If she'd had anything to give them, she would have. But by then she hadn't held a coin in her hand for four days.

"We have nothing," he called after her. "Less than nothing."

Beattie ushered Lucy inside and shut the door, her heart thudding.

"What were those people doing there?" Lucy asked. "What will they do if it rains?"

But Beattie wouldn't answer, distracted her with a game, and tried to forget what she had seen and heard. By the next morning, they were gone.

The winter cold mercifully lifted, and Beattie resisted as long as she could telling Henry that he simply must stop drinking and gambling, because his patience grew thinner and thinner with her until he would snarl at her for the least reason. But as Lucy's fourth birthday approached and Beattie feared there would be no money for a present, or even for sugar and eggs for a cake, she couldn't hold her tongue any longer.

It was a rainy night, and the sound of it sheeting off the roof made her anxious. The ceiling in Lucy's room leaked, and the steady drip-drip into the bucket sometimes kept her awake for hours. Beattie wanted to be sure Lucy was asleep before she spoke to Henry. She feared an argument. Beattie worked distractedly on a skirt she was rehemming for Lucy, while Henry read. Ordinarily, they would sit there for hours without speaking, conversation long since lost between them.

Beattie rose and peeked into Lucy's room. The child's breathing was deep and even. She closed the door and returned to the sitting room, stood in front of Henry.

At length, he looked up. "What is it?"

"You love your daughter?" She hadn't meant for it to sound so much like a challenge, but huge, buried feelings of resentment were firing into life.

"Of course."

"Is she not worth new shoes? Is she not worth a full tummy? Meat more than once a fortnight?"

Henry's eyes narrowed, his pupils shrinking to pinpoints. He pulled himself to his feet, and her heart turned to water. "What are you suggesting?" he said.

"You are lucky. You earn a living. And yet you throw it all away on gin and card games. We are *poor*, Henry."

"Everyone is poor." He sniffed, looking away.

Beattie took a deep breath. "If you loved your daughter, you would stop drinking and gambling."

His reaction was alarmingly swift and stinging: a flat palm across her face.

"Know your place, woman," he hissed. Then he turned and stalked off while helpless tears gathered in her eyes. She couldn't find her voice to call him back. He had frightened it away.

When the second letter arrived, she wasn't in a mood to ignore it.

This time she recognized the handwriting without having to read Molly's name on the back. Her chest grew hot.

Beattie set Lucy up at the kitchen table with an old wooden jigsaw puzzle and put the kettle on the stove. She hesitated before paying a penny for the gas to boil it, then decided that it was worth it. Once the kettle was boiling, she checked that Lucy wasn't watching and held the envelope carefully in the cloud of steam, her fingernail gently working its way under the back flap, all the while feeling her pulse flutter in her throat. If Henry found out . . .

The flap gave, and Beattie quickly switched off the gas. With shaking fingers, she unfolded the letter and read it.

Dear Henry, I cannot tell you how pleased I was to receive your letter . . .

Caught between disbelief and fury, Beattie put the letter down for a moment. He had written to Molly? He had forbidden Beattie from contacting even her own parents but had thought it acceptable to write to his wife? Her breathing had become shallow, her lungs seemed to shake.

"What's wrong, Mummy?" Lucy was looking at her, watching with those steady gray eyes.

Beattie forced a quick smile. "Nothing, darling. Have you finished the puzzle?"

"The kitten's head is missing."

"Oh, dear." Beattie forced herself to stop shaking, took Lucy's hand, and pulled her gently out of the chair. "Why don't you go into my room and find one of my dresses to play in?"

"Yes! Can I wear your bead necklace?"

"Just this once."

Lucy skipped off, and Beattie returned her attention to the letter, swallowing hard before unfolding it once more.

I have never stopped wondering about you, if you are
well and happy. You are still my husband and always
will be, no matter what foolish decisions you have made.
I must admit that it has given me terrible pain to hear
that you have a child, as you know it was one of my
fiercest desires to bear children. But I was not blessed. If
you could send a photograph of the child, it would give
me great joy and relief.

The tigress inside Beattie snarled. This woman wanted a photograph of Lucy? What on earth for? She hadn't a claim on the child and never would have. Beattie would kill somebody first.

Then wonder began to dawn on her. What was wrong with Molly? How could she be so nice? Henry had abandoned her, set up a life on the other side of the world, taken another woman as his wife. Where was the rage? Where was the venomous hatred? Was it hidden or really not there?

The next two paragraphs were about Glasgow, the weather, the traffic, her elderly aunt. Then the final paragraph cut Beattie to her heart.

I deduce from the tone of your letter that you aren't
opposed to the idea of me having a role in your life
again. Perhaps I am foolish (not a young, pretty fool
like Beattie, I'm afraid, as my thirty-third birthday
approaches), but when I agreed to marry you, I saw
it as a lifetime commitment. Nothing has changed. If

you want me to send you money for a passage back to
Glasgow, I gladly will.

Your wife, Molly.

How dare she? How dare she tempt Henry away with . . .

She realized Molly was only doing what Beattie had already done. Beattie had tempted Henry away. She'd known he was married; she'd listened to all his stories about Molly and how dull she was, how she never wanted to make love, how unfashionably she dressed. And she'd not given Molly a moment's consideration.

She wanted to tear the letter to shreds. Instead, she carefully slid it back into the envelope, pressed the flap down until it held, and put the letter on the mantelpiece. Would Henry leave her? Surely not. He wouldn't leave Lucy. She comforted herself with that thought for a while, joining Lucy in the bedroom for a raucous game of dress-up. Lucy, swimming in one of Beattie's dresses, had pulled on a hat and turned into a demanding customer. Beattie was cast as Jean, the general store was open for business. They played and laughed, then Beattie caught a glimpse of Lucy in the mirror. Her shining red hair, so like Henry's, turned her mind to the bond between father and daughter. Realization hit her, and her blood ran cold.

Henry might think he could take Lucy with him.

At once, every nerve in her body began to sing in panic. If Henry got it in his head to bundle her daughter off to Glasgow with him, what could she do?

She hurried out of the room, leaving Lucy protesting loudly. She seized the letter from the mantelpiece and set it alight in the fireplace. Watched it curl and blacken. Molly's words, her invitation, were ash now.

"What are you doing, Mummy?"

Beattie turned to see Lucy, still dressed up, at the threshold.

"Never mind." Beattie rose and came to crouch in front of Lucy, putting her hands around the girl's little shoulders. "You are so precious, my love," she said.

Lucy, always prickly with Beattie, shrugged her off. "Come on. I need to buy honey and pork."

Beattie followed Lucy into the bedroom, her heart thudding, but certain she had done the right thing.

There were only two ways that Henry could alleviate his guilt over Lucy's fourth birthday. Either borrow money off Billy for a present and a cake, or drink sufficiently that the feeling simply went away. His stomach clenched at the thought of it—as it did every day—and yet the foretaste of the searing liquid across his tongue made his heart stop fluttering for a moment.

He decided to do both.

The little desk he worked at was under the window of the office, on the second floor, so he could see down to the darkly gleaming Derwent River. But he rarely looked up to admire it. Billy kept him very busy, always silently holding over his head the amount of money he had borrowed, the amount of goodwill he had already presumed upon. Henry felt the weight of that debt, leaden on his heart.

Still, he rose and went to Billy's office. The door was always open. Billy worked hard, no matter what anyone said about him, and was a good employer. Too good.

Henry knocked. Billy looked up and beckoned him in. "How can I help?"

Henry spoke plainly. "It's Lucy's birthday today, and I don't get paid until Friday."

"You want an advance on your wage?"

"Aye." Henry eyed the brandy decanter on the corner of Billy's desk.

Billy nodded. "Go on. Pour me one, too."

Henry did as he was told.

"They are generous serves for this time of day." Billy laughed, holding up his glass.

Henry gulped the brandy. Closed his eyes for a moment as the warmth spread through his chest.

"How much do you need?" Billy asked.

"Five shillings?"

Billy reached into his pocket and pulled out the coins, lining them up on the table. "Here you are, then."

Henry scooped them up. "Just take the money out of—"

"Actually, Henry, I'd best not take them out of this week's pay, for you'll have none left at all."

Henry looked up, licked his lips. A silence ensued, stretched out for long moments.

Billy reached for the brandy and poured him another. "I feel responsible for you, man. You were always a good winner back in Glasgow. Knew when to stop. I don't know what happened, but the bad luck started when you chose that young lass over your wife. Molly kept you straight. With Beattie, you're blowing all over the place."

The coins were growing warm in his palm. He couldn't give them back, not now. It was his girl's birthday. He'd been promising her a present for weeks. How could he bear to see her face disappointed this evening? He'd sooner go blind.

"Just take the money, Henry," Billy said.

"Take it out of my next win at the table."

Billy smiled bitterly. "You don't win often enough for that to be a safe promise, man. Never mind. Just take it. Consider it a birthday bonus."

Henry thanked Billy profusely, hating himself for sounding so grateful. So unmanly.

After work, he walked into town. He couldn't go to the general store for a present, as he owed them money and they would want to be paid that first. His head cleared as he walked. What a depressing place the center of town had become, with grim, desperate people gathered to beg for jobs or money or just to be near other grim, desperate people in the hopes of not feeling so bad. Henry was proud that he was properly employed. Beattie complained constantly but had no idea how much better off they were than these low people whose hollow eyes followed him as he walked past. In and out of shops he went, spending his earnings. He bought a doll with china legs and rooted hair, and a sticky cake, stopped for a quick drink with the money left over, then returned home. The gate scraped on the flagstones as he opened it, and Lucy was at the door a moment later, in the little cotton frock her mother had made for her out of one of Henry's old shirts. That was the best Beattie could do for a birthday present.

"Daddy, Daddy!" she shouted, grasping his leg and hugging it savagely. "Did you bring me my present?"

"Inside, dearie. Give me a chance to catch my breath."

Beattie was inside at the gas stove, stirring a thin soup. She barely looked up. She was angry at him. She was always angry at him.

"Well, now," Henry said, taking Lucy on his lap. "Have you been a good lass?"

"Yes."

"I shall ask your mother. Has she been a good lass today, Mother?"

Beattie raised a smile, touched the child's hair. "The best."

Henry indicated the bundles on the table. "Which one first?"

Lucy pointed at the square box, her little fingers dancing with excitement. Henry unwrapped it and lifted the lid. Lucy squealed. "Cake! Mummy, cake!"

Beattie glanced over and her eyes widened. "How much did that cost?"

Henry didn't answer. He put the other bundle into Lucy's hands, watched with joy as she unpicked the string, pulled aside the brown paper, and found the doll inside. Rather than squealing, she went completely silent.

"Do you like it, my love?"

Lucy touched the doll's silky hair reverently. "I will love her forever," she said.

"Henry—" Beattie began anxiously.

Henry shushed her with an irritable wave of his hand. "You wanted the child to have a cake and presents. Don't be complaining now."

"But—"

Henry pushed his chair back quickly. He couldn't bear to be in the same room as Beattie's anxious disapproval. "Call us when dinner is ready."

"Can we have cake for dinner?" Lucy asked.

"No," Beattie said quickly, as though she imagined he might say yes. "Dinner first, then cake."

Henry pulled the little girl by her free hand. Her other arm was wrapped possessively around the doll's middle. In the sitting room, she immersed herself in play. Henry sat in his chair and watched her. She chatted to the doll, long monologues punctuated by spaces for the doll to reply.

"What are you going to call her?" he asked.

"What's your name again? When you're not Daddy?"

"Henry."

"I'll call her Henry."

"Henry's a boy's name. How about Henrietta?"

"Oh, yes. I like that. Do you like it, Henrietta?" Another silence. "Good, it's decided, then."

Lucy carefully tucked Henrietta into bed on the threadbare sofa, then put her finger against her lips. "Shh, now, Daddy. She has to sleep."

"I'll be quiet," he whispered.

She clambered into his lap, wrapping her arms around his neck. Her face was close to his, her breath smelled milky and sweet. "I love you, Daddy."

"I love you, too, my dear."

"I love Mummy, too."

He was silent.

"But I love you better," she continued.

Henry tried not to smile. "Your mother's a good woman."

"Sometimes she is sad."

"Is she?"

"Yesterday she was sad. A letter came and she got so sad, and so sad, and so sad. She didn't cry, but I could tell. And then she played dress-up for a while, but then she went back and burned the letter in the fireplace. Even though winter is gone."

Henry felt himself tense. She'd burned a letter? Why? What letter? What was she trying to hide from him? But then he remembered the drunken missive he'd sent off to Molly weeks ago. Had she replied?

"Daddy?" Lucy was looking at him with her clear gray eyes. Did she realize what a claim she had on his heart?

"My dearie," he said, kissing her cheeks tenderly. "Don't you worry about Mummy. When you've gone to bed tonight, I'll speak to her and see if I can cheer her up."

Beattie emerged from Lucy's bedroom. The child had been so excited by the cake and the doll—Henrietta was firmly tucked in the crook of her arm in bed—that Beattie had to sing a dozen songs until she calmed enough to sleep. While Beattie was relieved that Lucy's birthday had been such a happy one, the pressure of worry was building up again. How had Henry afforded the treats? And how long did they have until he had to pay it all back?

She was wary of him. She feared he would hit her again. But she needed to know where the money had come from and how much they now owed. She closed Lucy's door and crossed to the sitting room. Henry was not in his chair. He was leaning on the mantelpiece, his head resting on his forearms. Staring into the unlit fire.

She waited for him to notice she was there. Long moments. Then he looked up. "What letter did you burn?"

The question was unexpected, terrifying. Adrenaline spiked her heart. Her eyes went to the fireplace. How did he know?

"Lucy told me," he said, reading her expression. "At least you're not denying it. Perhaps you're not clever enough to lie." His words were acid. He pushed himself upright and moved close to her. Her feet were rooted to the floor. He was so close that she could smell his slightly sour sweat, the brandy on his breath. His face was florid, his ginger stubble catching the light of the lamp. Had she ever found him desirable? What had happened to those feelings of mad love? She held still, tensed against the blow she felt sure would come.

"Who was the letter from?" he asked, a low whisper, full of menace.

Was she clever enough to lie this time? No. Because if Molly wrote again, asking why he hadn't replied, she'd be caught out. "Molly," she said, as clearly as she could.

His eyes narrowed. "Did you read it first?"

"Yes."

"What did she say?"

Beattie pressed her lips together and shook her head. She was aware that his hands had balled into fists. Her breath quickened, every muscle and nerve in her body braced.

This time he roared. "What did she say?" Spittle flew from his lips, past her ear.

Beattie took a step back, her hands up in front of her face. "Don't hit me!" she sobbed.

Henry's eyes rounded. Was it surprise? Beattie couldn't read his expression. Then she watched as he forcefully got his body under control, relaxed his hands, stepped away from her. He wanted to hit her: that much was clear. But he seemed to have made the decision not to. For some reason, she found this more terrifying than an actual blow.

His voice was icy. "You won't tell me what was in the letter?"

She shook her head again.

Henry stalked away.

"Where are you going?"

He didn't answer. He seized his hat and coat at the door and slammed out of the house.

Beattie barely slept. Tensed against Henry's return, she fell into a state of half-dreaming, startling herself to full wakefulness throughout the night, hot panic under her heart. Every time she woke, she checked the bed next to her. Empty. She listened for sounds of him in the house. None. He hadn't come home. She pulled the thin blankets over her and tried to sleep again. But her mind turned and turned.

He would write to Molly again, of course he would. Perhaps he would telegraph her this time. And as soon as he found out what she offered, he would want to go to Glasgow, and he would want to take Lucy. No matter how she thought about it, this was the conclusion she reached. What reason was there for him to stay here? He clearly didn't love her anymore. He had no money. He hated his job. His life must be utter misery. If somebody offered for her to return to Glasgow, to look after her financially, she would be desperately eager. Perhaps she was paranoid and not thinking straight, but it seemed too great a risk not to believe he would go. And then what would become of her?

An idea started to form in Beattie's mind, one that she was reluctant to admit. Henry wasn't here. He was probably sleeping on Billy's couch, then he would be at work all day. It would be hours before he returned. There was plenty of time to get away.

Because as much as he said he loved his daughter, he was cruel to her, too. He spent their money before he'd earned it, he let Lucy go without essentials every day, then bought her ridiculous presents. And how long before she irritated him enough that he hit her, just as he had hit Beattie? With the drink in him, he couldn't control himself. Self-righteous indignation puffed her up. Why, the best thing she could do for the girl was to separate her from her father. Even if she adored him beyond all reason.

Beattie knew this was going to be almost impossible. But only *almost*. She remembered Cora's advice to her, all those years ago when she was leaving Glasgow: *There are two types of*

*women in the world, Beattie, those who do things and those who
have things done to them.* Had she listened? No. Cora had tried
to warn her about Henry, but she had been determined to be
the wrong type of woman: she had been determined to have
things done to her.

Now she waited for dawn, drifting in and out of confused
dreams. Waited for it to be daylight so she could go next door
and ask Doris about her cousin the seamstress, about the possibility of a new life, somewhere Henry wouldn't find her.

Over breakfast, Lucy was cranky and demanding, wanting cake rather than thin porridge. Beattie gave it to her, too
tired and distracted to care. Lucy missed her father, almost as
though she had intuited that he hadn't been in the house all
night and felt cut adrift by his absence. This was going to be
difficult.

Just as Beattie was clearing the table, she heard the rhythmic thump-thump of Doris beating her rugs on her front
verandah. Clattering the cutlery in the sink, she wiped her
hands on her apron and hurried to the door to throw it open.

"Doris?" There. She had set it in motion.

Doris looked up, curious. They'd had no contact since the
day Lucy had tried to steal from Doris. "Yes, dear?"

Beattie cleared her throat, tried to keep her voice even.
"Would you . . . please come by for a cup of tea?"

Doris smiled. "I'd love to. I've a few chores to—"

"Now, please," Beattie said. "I'm sorry. It can't wait."

The older woman nodded once, draped her rug over the
wooden railing, and came up the front path. Beattie's heart
was thudding as she let Doris in, and she willed it to slow

down. This was only the first step. She had to get through much more today.

"Come through to the kitchen," Beattie said. "I'm afraid it's still untidy from breakfast." She lifted Lucy out of her chair and urged her to play with Henrietta in her room. When they were alone, Beattie dropped a penny in the gas meter and put the kettle on the stove.

"Is everything all right, my dear?" Doris said, still standing warily.

"Please, sit down," Beattie said. "I'm afraid I'm not thinking straight this morning."

Doris sat at the table, looking around. Beattie tried to see the kitchen from Doris's perspective. The dingy walls, the up-turned fruit crates for spare chairs, the bareness. Doris's own kitchen had been painted green, and every countertop had held china containers: for sugar, flour, spices, rice, even biscuits. She wondered if Doris had realized how poor they were.

Beattie went through the motions of making tea, as though watching herself from outside. Then she sat with Doris and tried a weak smile. "Could you help me? I'm in trouble."

"I've no money to give you," Doris said quickly.

Beattie shook her head. "I don't want money. I want to know about your cousin the seamstress."

"Margaret?" Doris's face grew soft. "She's a long way away."

"I want to be a long way away."

"I see. Does your husband know this?"

Beattie swallowed hard, then forced herself to say the words she never thought she'd say to anyone else. "He drinks and he gambles. He has a violent temper. He's forbidden me to make friends or even contact my own parents. I'm afraid he'll hurt me and my child."

Doris nodded, setting her chin. "Then I'll help you get away. Margaret will take you in, and she'll give you work for your board."

"Will she? And my girl, too?"

"Margaret's a good Christian woman, and I know she has nobody working for her at the moment. She could use an extra pair of hands but hasn't much money to spare. She will treat you with kindness."

For some reason, the word "kindness" set Beattie off into tears. She had long ago become used to unkindness.

"There," Doris said, patting her hand. "There, child. You are making the right decision. When he sees that you've gone and taken the girl with you, he will see the error of his ways and he will come to the Lord's light. Then you can be reunited."

Beattie said nothing. She didn't want Henry back, ever. "You won't tell him where I am?"

"On my honor. I wouldn't help a violent drunkard." She rubbed Beattie's arm. "Go on, get your things packed. I'll give you threepence for the coach fare."

Within an hour, Beattie was ready for the walk into town to the coach stop. She had a pathetically meager collection of things in a cardboard box: the suitcases that had come from Scotland with them had long ago been sold. She threw in a photograph of the three of them—Henry, Lucy, herself—but wondered if it mightn't be better if Lucy forgot about her father. Beattie had no memories of her own life at four; perhaps it was kinder not to remind her of Henry. Lucy, with her new doll under her arm, asked repeatedly where they were going, what they were doing. Beattie hushed her, saying it was an adventure, that she would explain everything when they got off the coach at the other end.

Doris waited by the door, her eyes applying steady pressure. *You are doing the right thing.* Beattie tried to make her limbs feel like steel rather than flesh. She took Lucy firmly by the hand and, without a backward glance, closed the door of the cottage behind her.

TEN

The rattling motor coach rolled along beside the black water and up through small towns and farmland. It was a different green to Scotland: duller, lighter. But the sun was brighter, and Beattie allowed herself to be cheered a little. Doris had written instructions for her on a piece of paper. They had to get off the coach at New Norfolk and get on another that would take them farther northwest. Finally, at a tiny town called Bligh, they had to wait for the antiquated horse-drawn coach to Lewinford.

She made the first coach change without problems, but by lunchtime, the traveling had made Lucy throw up all over her clothes. Beattie cleaned her up roughly with a clean shirt out of the box, but the smell lingered, and Beattie started to feel queasy herself.

They arrived at Bligh, found the location for the coach to pick them up, and sat to wait. Beattie had brought sandwiches with dripping and honey, and she and Lucy shared them on the side of the road.

Beattie was glad to have come to a rest, even for a short

while. Her lack of sleep the night before had imbued all the events of the day with a nightmarish, not-quite-real color. In her mind, over and over, she repeated the phrase "I have left Henry, I have left Henry," but it still didn't feel true.

For what uncertainty had she chosen? Despite Doris's reassurances, she didn't really know whether Margaret would take her in. Or even if Margaret was home. What if she'd decided to go visiting? Or on holiday?

"Mummy?" Lucy's voice cut through her worry.

"Yes, darling?"

Lucy leaned in to her side. "Where's Daddy?"

"He's at work.".

"He wasn't at breakfast today."

"No. Daddy's . . . We aren't going to see Daddy for a little while."

Lucy looked up at her. The sun made her red hair gleam. "Why not?" Already tears were threatening.

Beattie turned the question over in her head. How to explain the situation to a four-year-old? "Daddy is sick," she said. "It's a kind of sickness that is bad for us to be around."

"But I love Daddy." She offered up her Henrietta doll as if to prove it.

"And Daddy loves you. But he can't look after us just now, so we have to go away and look after ourselves."

Lucy began to cry in earnest. "He will miss us."

Beattie crouched down to hug the little girl. "He'll miss you. I know that."

Eventually, Lucy grew tired of crying and sat down on the grass. Beattie paced, watching the road for the coach.

According to Doris's instructions, it should have been here an hour ago. She looked at the note again and again. Yes, she was in the right location, under the town sign, heading northwest, a hundred yards from the pub. She thought of going in to ask about the coach but was afraid that the coach would come the moment she stepped away from the designated location. The day grew too warm, sticky. She made sure Lucy was sitting in the shade. In the distance, she could hear a creek running over rocks and longed to find it and have a drink of water. But she didn't. She waited and waited until she was sure another hour had passed and the coach was surely not coming. Her stomach turned to water. Now what would she do?

"Come on, Lucy," she said, rousing the girl from where she sat, miserable, in the grass. "I need to go into that pub and ask about the coach."

Lucy dragged herself to her feet and took Beattie's hand. They walked together—Beattie casting her glance over her shoulder again and again—into the cool pub. Five or six men sat at the bar, and they all looked around curiously to see a woman and a child. It smelled as though beer had soaked the floorboards.

"No ladies allowed, love," the bartender said, but kindly.

"I just need to know . . . The coach to Lewinford?"

"Ah, that'd be old Frank. Miserable bastard. Won't run it on stormy days; reckons the thunder spooks the horses."

"Stormy?" She thought about the weather outside, hot and clear.

"We have a room round the back if you need to stay here the night."

"No, I . . ." She had no money. Just a penny for the coach. But the coach wasn't coming. "Is it far to walk?"

He squinted as he calculated. "Hm. Maybe three hours. The little one might slow you down. Can I offer you a drink of water?"

Beattie took the water gratefully, making sure Lucy had plenty, too. She listened as he gave her instructions to get to Lewinford, and resigned to their lot, they began to walk.

Half an hour up the road, she noticed the first dark clouds gathering on the horizon. Half an hour after that, with Lucy already whining that she couldn't walk another step, she heard the first rumble of thunder.

Her heart by now had experienced so much today—fear, hope, uncertainty—that it nearly collapsed under this new dread. Here they were, walking along a dirt road in the middle of nowhere, and it was going to storm. She stopped for a moment, and Lucy sat gratefully on the verge of the road. Sweat trickled under her blouse.

Shelter. That had to be the priority. It was unsafe to shelter under trees in a storm, so she had to find a house, or a shed, or *something* with a roof. Anything. She turned in a slow circle. Off to the east were miles of dense scrub, but to the west were wide fields fenced off by low barbed wire or tall poplar trees, starlings flitting between their branches. Farms. Farms meant houses.

"Mummy? I'm tired."

"I know, darling." Beattie eyed the sky. The storm front was moving fast, but still there was no rain or wind. "We're going to go up into that field and see if we can find somewhere to rest."

Lucy nodded, pulling herself to her feet.

"Good girl," said Beattie, and led her to the fence. "You'll have to lie on your tummy and wriggle under. Careful, now." Beattie gingerly held the wire up as high as she could, watching as Lucy slithered under it so that none of the spikes caught her clothes or hair. "Just like a snake. That's it."

Beattie pushed the box under after Lucy but knew she would never fit under it herself. Instead, she tried to separate the two middle strands to go between. On the way through, she caught her dress and calf on a barb. It stung.

"Mummy, you're bleeding."

She pressed her skirt against the wound, which stopped bleeding quickly. "It's nothing. Come on. There's a storm coming." As she said these words, the wind started to pick up.

They trudged up a hill, and from up here, Beattie could see miles and miles of farmland. Green hills, softly curved, punctuated with large flat rocks. Solitary eucalyptus here and there, alive or dead and white, homes for crows. But no homestead. In fact, no cows or sheep, either. She started to suspect that the farm was either much bigger than she imagined or wasn't in operation at all. But she could see a small white structure in the distance. A shed. The rumbles of thunder were coming closer, and a cool darkness was closing over the land.

She swept Lucy up in her arms and hurried down the hill and across the field as the first spits of rain came. *Please, don't let us get wet as well.* As she approached, she could see the shed was missing half its roof, that it had no door. Her heart sank farther.

Bright lightning forked the sky. The shed would have to do.

They reached it just as the rain started in earnest. The floorboards were stained and warped, but by sitting in the far back corner, they could stay dry. Beattie took Lucy on her lap and forced her muscles to relax. Lucy still smelled faintly of vomit. The storm moved overhead, its damp winds whipping the sweat on their bodies to ice. Lightning and thunder one on top of the other, then a torrent of rain in their wake. Lucy began to cry softly, calling for Henry. So Beattie cried with her. She cried for Henry, too, for the man he had seemed to be but wasn't. She cried for her loneliness, her isolation from her family and the life she'd once known. And she cried for her daughter, who was pure beauty and deserved every good thing in life but had ended up with poverty and uncertainty, shivering in a storm far from home.

The rain didn't ease. An hour or more it fell, until the floor of the shed was awash and they had to stand up, the water filling their shoes, to avoid getting wet. Lucy clung to Beattie's skirt, while Beattie considered what to do next. They couldn't stay here all night; it was too wet. And Lewinford was still hours away by foot. If they didn't want to still be outside walking in the dark, they would have to leave now.

But how was she to tell her small, exhausted child that she had to walk in the rain? And so she stood, frozen, waiting for a sign. But there were no signs, there was only this awful reality, this heavy moment.

"Lucy," she said, "I'm sorry, my darling, but we will have to go back to the road and keep walking."

"Why?"

"Because when things seem very bad, strong people keep going."

Lucy stood back resolutely, putting her hand up for her mother's. "All right, Mummy."

Beattie took her hand, and they walked out into the rain.

Mile after mile they walked, and the rain eased but didn't stop. The cardboard box under her arm grew sodden and sagged against her. Lucy soldiered on, one sturdy foot in front of the other, and Beattie felt the first glimmers of hope. They would get to Lewinford—surely they must be within a few miles by now—and Margaret would take them in and they would have a new life, a simple life, without fear. Gradually, the rain turned to drizzle, then she became aware that it had stopped altogether. Low on the horizon, a beam of sunlight struggled through the clouds.

They rounded a bend, surely only half an hour from their destination. And Beattie saw it.

The road was cut. The causeway over the creek was flooded. The creek itself was engorged and running with brown water. Beattie stopped, and Lucy stopped behind her.

Her mind was blank. She couldn't make it focus. What were they to do? They couldn't go back and around: she didn't know the way, and Lucy was exhausted. They couldn't just wait for the water to go down. It might rain further, making them even wetter than they were. Besides, the temperature was dropping as night approached, and they would catch their deaths if they didn't get somewhere warm and dry soon. All she wanted to do was cry. To sit down, put her head on her knees, and sob.

"Wait here," she said to Lucy, placing the box on the ground.

She approached the causeway and noticed that branches and debris had gathered at the edge. That meant the water wasn't too deep after all. Very carefully, she set one foot on the causeway. The water raced around her ankles. Another step. No deeper. Slowly, slowly, she walked forward, measuring out the whole crossing. The water was fast but not deep. If she carried Lucy across, she could—

At that moment she turned and saw that Lucy hadn't waited for her, was struggling through calf-deep water toward her.

"No, Lucy!" She began to slosh back, slowed down by muddy shoes and racing water.

Then the debris at the edge of the causeway began to move. At first it just slipped sideways, but then, with a surge, it came free and was carried across, knocking Lucy's feet from under her. Lucy pitched over and was washed off the causeway. She caught a low branch ten feet up the creek.

Beattie screamed. "Lucy! Lucy!" Her throat was raw. She ran back over the causeway and onto the bank of the creek, throwing herself out flat and flailing for Lucy's arm.

The little girl howled, "Daddy! Daddy!"

"Take my hand, darling!"

Lucy reached for her—inches too far away.

"I want Daddy!"

Beattie inched out farther, aware that were she to tumble into the swollen current, they would both be lost. "Please try again, darling."

Lucy extended her arm again but this time lost her grip on the branch. Beattie felt the brush of her fingers, then she was gone, under the water.

"NO!"

And then a splash out of nowhere. A man, on the other side of the creek, throwing himself into the water. Beattie had no idea who he was or where he had come from but saw a smooth, bare back the color of milky coffee disappear into the water. A moment later, he was up again, Lucy clutched in his arms.

"Lucy!" Beattie cried.

"Mummy," she moaned fearfully, struggling from the stranger's arms.

At least she was breathing. "Hold on to him! Hold on tight!"

The man pulled himself out of the water and laid Lucy carefully on the scrubby bank. He stood and flashed Beattie a smile. "I'll come across and get you."

Tears pricked her eyes. "Thank you. Thank you so much."

She ran back for her box, by which time the man was on her side of the causeway. With a firm hand on her upper arm, he accompanied her across the water. She ran to Lucy, who pressed herself into her mother's arms with grateful desperation. The child sobbed, and Beattie held her, rocked her, listening to her own heartbeat grow quiet and calm.

Finally, she turned her attention back to the man. He had pulled his shirt back on but hadn't yet buttoned it.

"How can I ever thank you enough?" she said.

He shrugged. "What else was I going to do, missus? Watch the little girl drown?"

She smiled at him, extending her hand. "My name's Beattie. This is Lucy."

He took her hand and squeezed it once, then dropped it. His skin was very warm.

Lucy looked up, her eyelashes still holding drops of water. "What's your name?"

"Charlie," he said.

"You saved her life," Beattie said.

"I was watching you from about a hundred feet off," he said. "Tried to run down and warn you. Saw the little one following you."

Beattie squeezed Lucy hard. "I should have known she wouldn't listen to me." She considered Charlie in the late-afternoon light. He had dark, curly hair; his eyes were almost black. She slowly realized he must be Aboriginal; she had never seen one of his kind before. She couldn't tell how old he was: perhaps a few years younger than her. He had a boyish look about him, with his unruly curls and his long lashes and clean-shaven chin. Then she realized she was staring and glanced away.

"Where you heading?" he said, casually buttoning his shirt.

"Lewinford. We've walked all the way from Bligh. The coach didn't come."

"He never runs it on stormy days." Charlie squashed his

hat back on his head. "I just come from Lewinford," he said warily. "You got friends there?"

"Yes. No. We're going to see Margaret Day. Her cousin said she might take us in."

"Yeah, Mrs. Day will take you in. Don't you worry."

"Is she . . . nice?"

Charlie shrugged. "Not to me." Then he laughed. "But she's nice. You want me to take you up there? Watch out for you?"

Beattie wanted that very much indeed. "It's too much trouble," she said.

He shook his head. "Missus, you're wet through, your little one's cold and frightened. If you don't mind a blackfella, I'll help you out."

"A black . . . No, of course I don't mind. You saved her life." Beattie smiled weakly. "I'd be honored if you'd take us."

Charlie bent down and smiled at Lucy. "You want to ride on my back?"

Lucy pouted and shook her head. But Charlie ignored her, scooped her up, and wrangled her onto his back. "Come on."

Lucy, glad to be off her feet, clasped her hands around his neck. Beattie picked up her box again—the clothes inside were soaked—and they started walking. Mud squished in her shoes.

"Must say, that's a fancy accent you got, missus."

"Please, call me Beattie. I'm half Scottish."

"Scotland. That's a long way. You're further from home even than me."

"Where are you from?" He walked very fast, and she had to hurry to keep up.

"Me? I'm from the Gulf. Top of Australia. I've worked all the way down to the bottom. Might head west next. Might stay a while. I'm fond of the soft light down here."

"Are you an Aborigine?" She didn't know if it was rude to ask, but she had never seen a person who wasn't white.

"Yeah. Well, my mum was. My dad was some whitefella that blew through. Ancient history."

"You've never met him?"

He was quiet a moment, then said, "Ancient history. I never think about it. I got no parents. Just me in the world now, looking after myself." But a sad expression crossed his brow, and she suddenly saw that he was older than she. Perhaps by ten years.

At length, they approached a white sign with the name Lewinford written on it. For the first time that day, she allowed herself to feel relief. They were here. At last.

Beyond the sign the road branched off to the left, and Beattie could see rows of houses, shop awnings, cars and carts parked on the dirt road.

"You want to head that way," Charlie said, pointing toward the town. "Then your first left is Mrs. Day's street. Hers is the house with the rosebushes out front." He crouched and gently let Lucy down.

"Can't you take us?" Lucy said. "I'm tired of walking."

Charlie shook his head. "Sorry, little one." He stood, nodded at Beattie. "Sorry, missus. I'm not welcome in Lewinford anymore. I was on my way out for good. I've got to go pick up my swag back at the creek and head down to Bligh for work."

"Not welcome? What happened?"

"I'm sure you'll hear about it." He smiled at her. "You take care of the little one." And then he rubbed Lucy's head. "And you take care of your mum."

"I will. And my daddy. When he's better."

Charlie was already turning away. "Good on you."

"Goodbye. Thank you," Beattie called after him.

He lifted one hand in farewell but didn't turn back.

Henry decided he needed a drink before he could face home. One turned into two or three . . . And it was dark before he finally returned to the house, twenty-four hours after he had left. He hoped Lucy was still awake: he missed her with every inch of his skin. She was the only reason he was coming home at all. He'd be happy to be done with Beattie, with her judgmental eyes and her long-suffering expression and her complete inability to run the household on a budget.

He was aware immediately that there were no lights on. Either they were both asleep or Beattie was trying to save money on their electricity bill. A twinge of guilt: so little money left in this week's pay packet. Perhaps their electricity had been cut off.

In his drunkenness, he fumbled with the key in the dark. Finally got himself in the door and tried the switch. The uncovered bulb above him lit up.

"Beattie?" he said. He knew he shouldn't be loud and wake Lucy, but she was so beautiful when she woke up. All warm and sleepy. He went to the main bedroom. The door was open.

He could see by the reflected light from the hallway that the bed was empty. Curious, he went to the kitchen. No sign of her.

Of course. She had probably fallen asleep next to Lucy. He crept to the child's room and opened the door. It was empty.

"Lucy!" he cried. Hearing the note of fear in his own voice frightened him further. Where was she? Had somebody taken her? Why wasn't Beattie here to protect her? He stumbled from room to room, leaving all the lights blazing. There was no sign of either of them. He raced into the garden, past the laundry. His shirts were still hung on the line, ghostly shapes in the dark.

"Lucy? Beattie?"

"They're gone."

He turned at the voice. The old woman who lived in the next house stood at her back door, clearly roused by all his shouting. He didn't know her name.

"What do you, mean?" he said.

"She's left you; she's taken the child." Her fingers were clenched hard around the door frame. She was afraid of him.

The anger was so intense that he nearly threw up. He choked it down. His hands felt heavy, his ears rang. "Where did she go?"

"If she'd wanted you to know, she'd have left you a note." In the dark, the woman's features looked severe. A bird of prey. But all the same, she shrank slightly from his thundering voice. "I saw her at the bus stop this morning. She told me everything about you."

"She knows nothing about me," he muttered, stalking away.

"The Lord is giving you an opportunity," she called after him, emboldened by his departure. "He's telling you that you can't go on drinking and gambling."

Henry slammed the door behind him, collapsed into a chair at the empty kitchen table. Silence gathered around him. A little moan escaped his lips. He put his head down on the table and listened to the dull thump of his own heart.

ELEVEN

B eattie picked Lucy up, holding her on her hip with one hand, the sodden box still tucked under her arm. She walked. Down the pitted dirt road past the pub, with its red iron roof and large, rough-hewn bricks. Past a grocer, a post office, a brick arched door. Past a baker, a bank, a used-furniture shop, and a row of houses: some wood, some stone, all with sloping tin roofs. She took the first left, as Charlie had told her, and identified Margaret's house immediately. Pale yellow weatherboards, a paved front path, roses growing in profusion. A moment's uncertainty: what if Margaret didn't take them in? Drizzle began again. Then she marched up to the front door under the shelter of the verandah and knocked briskly.

Within moments, a woman answered the door. She was much younger than Beattie had imagined—perhaps only in her late thirties—and she had a pretty face and a soft roundness to her.

"Oh! You're wringing!" Margaret said, opening the door wide. "And the child. Can I help you?"

"I've come up from Hobart. I lived next door to Doris Penny. She said—"

"Come in, come in. Do you have dry clothes? I might have some here to loan you. Shall I run a warm bath for the girl? What happened to you?"

Beattie was speechless. Margaret's kindness was too much to bear. As she stepped over the threshold, the bottom finally fell out of the box. A tumble of wet clothes cascaded onto the floor. She fought back sobs. "I'm sorry," she said, "I've had rather a long day."

"Then come in and take good comfort." Margaret bent to help her pick up her things. "Let me help."

Margaret's house, like Doris's, was tidy and full. Soft furnishings, knickknacks, paintings, even a sewing machine. A cross on the wall, pictures of Jesus and Mary, Bible verses cross-stitched onto cushions. As Margaret bustled about, Beattie followed her from room to room, haltingly relating her journey and the storm. Lucy was quiet. Exhaustion had hit her. Margaret took them into her bathroom, ran a warm bath. "I expect you'd like one, too?" she asked Beattie.

"We really should talk about—"

"Our first priority is to get you both clean and dry and fed. We'll talk when the child sleeps. You're not leaving this house tonight. I've a spare room."

So Margaret left them, and Beattie gratefully slid into the warm bath with Lucy, letting the heat melt the knots out of her muscles. She pulled Lucy against her, the child's back pressed against her breasts. Lucy's spine was bony: had Beattie not noticed before that she was growing thin? A delicious feeling—of relief, of the satisfaction of having done precisely the right thing—washed over her. She kissed Lucy's wet hair. "I love you, my girl."

"When will we see Daddy again?"

"We'll get settled here first. You must be patient."

Too tired to cry, Lucy slumped against her. Beattie wondered how long it would take for Lucy to forget her father, or at least to forget how madly she loved him.

Clean, dry, dressed in some spare clothes of Margaret's that were far too big, and fed on a hot meal of mutton stew, Beattie sat on the couch across from Margaret in a wing-backed chair. Lucy lay on Beattie's lap, and Beattie stroked her hair away from her soft white forehead while the girl drifted off to sleep. Beattie was exhausted, too, could barely keep her head up. But Margaret hadn't shown her the spare room yet, and besides, there were important things to sort out.

"So, how is Doris? Does she look well?" Margaret began, picking up an embroidery ring and a needle.

"Yes." Beattie's fingers itched to sew, too. She liked the way it calmed her mind. "Do you have another of those?" she asked.

Margaret smiled, kicked toward her a basket full of fabrics and threads. Beattie chose a scrap, some red thread and a needle, and began to stitch. Lucy breathed softly on her lap. "Doris said you might have work for me, that I might be able to earn my board."

"I always have work. I make clothes and repair clothes. I'm busy. You can certainly earn your board here helping out. But you would need to help with food costs, especially as you have a little one with you. You can apply for the government relief, though you have to go twenty miles up the road to the next town to do it."

Her heart sank. "Is there no other work in town?"

"Might be. I'll give you a little while to settle in." She smiled. "You needn't look so worried. You'll be safe here."

Beattie dropped her eyes, gazed at Lucy. She found herself crying. "Thank you," she whispered, though she wasn't sure if Margaret heard. Then she composed herself, looked up again. "The man who helped us, who rescued Lucy, he said he wasn't welcome in Lewinford. He was leaving."

Margaret narrowed her eyes. "What was his name?"

"Charlie."

"Charlie Harris?"

"I didn't ask his last name."

"He's trouble. Those half-bloods have got one foot in our world, one foot in theirs. It confuses them. They all belong together, somewhere, away from the whites."

"What kind of trouble?" Beattie thought about how gentle he had been with Lucy. She didn't want to judge Margaret, who had shown her such kindness. But the Charlie she met didn't deserve such censure.

"He was managing Wildflower Hill, a sheep farm on the other side of town. But all the while he was stealing from his boss. Now, Raph Blanchard may be a rogue himself, but a white man shouldn't have his things stolen by a black one, and that's that."

"I must say," Beattie ventured, "Charlie seemed very nice to me."

Margaret sniffed, dismissing the topic. "Even a stopped

clock shows the right time twice a day." She put aside the embroidery ring and fixed Beattie in her gaze. "This husband of yours, is he likely to come good and ask for you back?"

Beattie decided to be honest. "He's not my husband. He's somebody else's husband."

Margaret's mouth turned down sternly, and all the prettiness fled her face. "The child was born out of wedlock?"

"Yes. I was very young and very foolish."

"Is she baptized?"

Beattie shook her head.

"You'll need to fix that. There's a little church here on Maud Street. I teach their Sunday school. She can come along with me."

Beattie wasn't sure what to say.

"Good. That's decided, then," Margaret continued.

Beattie felt a moment's consternation. What precisely had been decided? But then she figured that Sunday school and a proper baptism couldn't hurt. They sat in silence a while longer, then Beattie finally said, "I'm so sorry, Margaret, but I can barely keep my eyes open."

Margaret smiled, and her prettiness returned. "You poor thing, you must be exhausted. Leave the child here a few moments, and I'll show you the spare room."

They walked down the narrow hallway to the laundry, where a set of stairs led up to an attic room. It smelled dusty and faintly damp. Margaret switched on the light. The roof was low and peaked, spiderwebs gathered in the corners. The floor was covered in old newspapers. There was a dresser and a single bed in the middle of the room with a thin mattress.

"It's not much," Margaret said, "but it's a roof over your head."

Beattie forced a smile. "I'll take it gratefully."

"I'll get you some linen."

Beattie cheered herself by thinking of cleaning up the cobwebs and saving for a rug for the floor. Margaret's linen was soft and pretty, and she was happy to lay Lucy down among it, curl up next to her, and finally sleep.

For the first few weeks, they kept busy and they ate well. Margaret taught Beattie to use the sewing machine, and Beattie took over all of the mending. There were two baskets of it, and more arrived every day. Nobody had money for new clothes, and old clothes needed to be made to last longer. After spending the mornings sewing, Beattie had the afternoons free for Lucy. They gathered up the old newspapers and scrubbed the floor of their room, cleared out the cobwebs, and Lucy even convinced Margaret to let them have one little painting—a scene of a boat on a river that Lucy had become fixated on—to hang on the wall. Margaret took Lucy to Sunday school once a week, and Beattie enjoyed the morning without her, using the sewing machine to mend some of their own clothes. She longed for a length of fabric to make herself a new dress but hadn't a penny. Margaret urged her kindly to take the bus up to the next town and sign on for government benefits, but Beattie resisted. She was determined to work for her money; she was done with relying on others. So she asked at every shop in the town, told everybody that she was look-ing for work, hoping something might come up soon.

At the beginning of the fourth week, something did.

Beattie sat on the couch, darning socks. Lucy played with peg dolls at her feet. It was the first day so far that she hadn't moaned about wanting to see Daddy. Margaret had helped—uninvited—by responding to Lucy's questions about her father with a stern "When God has helped your father to recover, God will help him find you, too." Lucy was both thrilled and terrified by the idea of God; Beattie was simply terrified by the idea of Henry finding them.

Margaret was pedaling her sewing machine and didn't hear the knock at the door. Beattie did and rose to answer it.

A middle-aged woman with an enormous bosom stood there. She wore eyeglasses, and her hair was piled high and tight on her head. "I'm looking for Beattie Blaxland."

"That's me," Beattie said, her heart thudding in her throat. What had happened? Had Henry sent her?

"I'm Alice. I'm the housekeeper at Wildflower Hill. We've lost a maid this morning, and I'd heard you were looking for work."

"I am!" Beattie said, reminding herself not to be so excited. The job wasn't hers yet. "Would you like to come in?"

Alice screwed up her nose. "I don't think so. When can you start?"

"Tomorrow afternoon? I work for Margaret in the morning."

"Can you make it ten? I'll need you to help with the lunch."

Beattie hesitated but decided she could simply get up

earlier to work for Margaret. "Yes, of course. I'll call at ten."

"No, no. I'll send the car. It's a long walk, and you'll be exhausted before you begin." Alice turned and marched briskly back down the stairs into a waiting car.

Beattie went back inside and explained the situation to Margaret, who wore a wary expression the whole time.

"I'm not much given to gossip," Margaret said, "but I do feel I have to warn you about Wildflower Hill."

"Warn me?"

"It's a place full of sinners."

Beattie tried not to sigh in exasperation. Margaret's constant talk about God and sin wore on her nerves. She wasn't sure if she believed in God: her father's atheism had made her skeptical. But if God were real, Beattie knew he'd be kinder than the God Margaret believed in.

"So Alice is a sinner?" Beattie asked, hoping she didn't sound impatient.

"Those who turn a blind eye to what's going on are sinners, for certain. You'd do well to remember that." Margaret smiled, touched Beattie's hand. "I don't mean to frighten you, love, but Raphael Blanchard who owns Wildflower Hill is bad news, and you'd do well to stay clear of him when you can."

"Thank you for your advice," Beattie said, reminding herself to be grateful. "Could I leave Lucy here with you while I go up to work?"

"Of course. We have a good time together, don't we, Lucy?"

Lucy responded by hopping up and giving Margaret a hug. Beattie was both relieved and discomfited. But it wasn't for her to complain. She had a home, food to eat, someone to help her care for her child, and now she had a job. With a little money of her own, she could buy a rug for the floor of their attic room or new shoes for Lucy. She didn't believe for a moment that Wildflower Hill was full of sinners; she had more important things to be afraid of.

The car turned in to their street on the stroke of ten. Beattie was waiting nervously outside the front gate, while Lucy watched from the verandah.

"There it is, Mummy!" she cried.

"Go back inside. Be a good girl for Margaret."

"I'll be a good girl for Jesus," Lucy said solemnly.

Beattie blew her a kiss and stepped into the car. It smelled of oil and leather. "Good morning," she said to the driver, a large man with a head that seemed carved out of stone. He didn't respond. Intimidated, she sat back and looked out the window. The town sped by. The narrow dirt road wound uphill, exposing a view of farmland under sunlight on both sides. They thundered over mud puddles with alarming speed. Within twenty minutes, they were turning between two tall stone gates and in to a long driveway. To the west was a small compound of sheds, stables, and a stringy-bark cottage. Up ahead, Beattie could see the homestead: lofty and looming, built of sandstone, with huge windows peaked like cathedral windows and tall chimneys standing out from the tiled roof. A mile behind it stood a forest of eucalyptus, fluttering their gray-green leaves against the morning sunshine, but the garden around the house itself was an English garden. Roses and poplars. The car pulled up near the front door, and Alice, the housekeeper, hurried down to greet them.

"Thank you," Beattie said to the driver as she climbed out.

Alice said, "Don't bother to speak to Mikhail, he knows ten words of English altogether. Come on, there's plenty to do. Mr. Blanchard's having guests for lunch."

Beattie was whisked in the front door, then Alice paused a moment in the reception hall. She jabbed her finger in three directions. "There, there, there . . . you are not allowed to go." Now she indicated to the left with a nod. "You will come in and go straight to the kitchen. I have you on kitchen and laundry duties. I'll take care of the rest."

"Yes, Alice."

"You'll work from ten until six daily except Sundays. Mikhail will fetch you and drop you home. During shearing season, there will be longer hours, but that's not until spring. As it is, there's only Mr. Blanchard and three staff here—me, Mikhail, and Terry, the farm manager—though Mr. Blanchard has guests most days and most evenings." She grimaced. "You won't see them. Keep your head down and stay in here."

"Here" was a long kitchen with floral wallpaper and flat wooden benches. There were built-in cupboards painted pale blue, and a large refrigerator that throbbed monotonously. A tall window at the end of the room let in white sunshine. Beattie went to the window and looked out over poplar trees to the gate, then down over green fields and hills, dotted with dirty white sheep.

Alice opened a door and pointed down the stairs. "Laundry

is down there. I'll leave the key in the gas for the copper so you don't have to come find me. I'll bring down anything that needs to be washed. Mostly sheets and towels for the guests. You can sew?"

Beattie nodded.

"If you see anything needs mending, put it aside and save it for quiet times. Usually, around three, it's quiet until five. You'll be paid twenty shillings a week, but you're on one day's notice. If you let me down, you're gone, and you won't be paid for that week."

Twenty shillings! Beattie knew it wasn't much, but she'd had nothing in her purse for weeks, so it sounded like a fortune. The sun from the window was warm on her body, and the warmth penetrated all the way to her heart.

Lucy liked praying. She had always prayed before bed with Mummy listening, but Margaret had shown her a new way to pray, without saying the words out loud. Just between her and God. And so sometimes she went up to her room, kneeled by her bed and put her head on her clasped hands, and prayed so hard that her ribs hurt for Daddy to get well and come back.

But still he didn't.

One day, while Mummy was at work, Margaret found her and asked her what she was doing. Lucy realized she had been crying and Margaret must have heard it. Margaret looked after her well, giving her little jobs to do, and pointing out the words in books, and giving her cuddles when she was feeling sad. Mummy was out a lot. She felt as though Mummy were shrinking in her imagination, and Margaret was growing bigger. Daddy was the biggest, but she had started to forget his face, like a jigsaw puzzle with pieces missing.

"I was praying," Lucy said. "But God isn't giving me what I want."

"What do you want? Some silly Christmas treat?"

The thought of Christmas without Daddy made Lucy cry harder. "I want my daddy."

Margaret came in and scooped her up, then sat with her on the bed, an arm around her waist. Margaret had a pretty face, much like Lucy imagined the Virgin might have looked.

"I don't want to have to tell you this," Margaret said, "but you need to know. You are innocent, you are still holy in God's eyes. But your parents did bad things. It's a waste of time to pray for them to change. You must worry about your own soul, not theirs."

"What bad things did they do?" Lucy gasped, shadows gathering in her mind. She thought of Jesus on the cross, dying for their sins. And them being so ungrateful. Why, she had never seen Mummy pray once!

"You'll understand when you're an adult. Now, you mustn't mention this to your mother. God wouldn't want you to."

Lucy nodded. "So if I can't pray for Daddy to come back . . ."

"You should pray instead for the strength to stop loving him, so it doesn't hurt anymore."

Stop loving Daddy? Lucy knew God wouldn't want her to do that. She decided she would keep praying just the same. She would be clever enough not to cry when she did.

* * *

Over the next few weeks, Beattie fell into a routine. She sewed for Margaret from five in the morning until ten, when she would kiss Lucy goodbye and climb into the car with Mikhail. On Sundays, after Lucy came home from Sunday school, Beattie would take her to the general store for an ice cream, and they would walk down to the creek—now a harmless trickle—and look for turtles. Beattie did not meet her new employer, Raphael Blanchard, though she came to know him through his clothes. Fine shirts and silk robes. It felt strange to be handling the underwear of a man she'd never met, but she kept this thought to herself. She did as she was told, never went anywhere in the house but for the kitchen and the laundry, and knew the satisfaction of stable work, a safe home, and money for food and shoes. It wasn't the life she had dreamed for herself, but it was a good life nonetheless. As each week passed without any contact from Henry, she began to feel sure that she had truly escaped him.

As soon as she'd saved some pennies for a stamp and an envelope, Beattie wrote a letter to her parents back in Glasgow. In truth, she had no idea whether they would accept her. Her mother had disowned her on that last awful day, but she hoped enough time had passed for forgiveness. After she posted the letter, she idly wondered if she should return home. But Scotland or England didn't feel like home now. Lucy had been born here, and the sunshine and broad sky were in her soul. It wouldn't be right to take her back to a miserable flat in a stinking city.

The reply came surprisingly quickly, though the return address was not her parents'. It was that of Mrs. Peters, the woman who had lived in the neighboring flat.

Beattie's skin prickled lightly, and she noticed her fingers shook as she picked open the envelope. Lucy was running about in the front garden, pretending to be a butterfly, and Margaret was sweeping the front verandah and humming a hymn. Mikhail would be here with the car any minute, but Beattie wanted time to hold still, all movement and noise to stop, as she concentrated very hard on what the letter had to say. Even so, only snatches jumped out at her.

> . . . *the new residents of your parents' flat passed me*
> *your letter . . . sorry to say I have no good news for*
> *you . . . your mother took the fever and went quickly . . .*
> *blessedly quick, she didn't suffer . . . your father*
> *wandered like a ghost for days . . . a fall down the*
> *stairs . . . nothing they could do to save him . . . certain*
> *that they thought of you often and well . . .*

Tears obscured the words on the page. Beattie drew in a sharp sob, determined not to upset Lucy. She sniffed back the tears quickly, hurried inside to hide the letter under her pillow. Outside, she could hear Mikhail's car pulling up, the peremptory bleat of the horn. Life went on, life had to go on. Her stomach clenched with regret, and she remembered Charlie

Harris, what he had said about having lost both his parents somewhere in the past. *Just me in the world now, looking after myself.* Palming away tears, she hurried back through the house and outside. There would be time to cry tonight, after her shift, curled up with Lucy in bed.

TWELVE

Beattie had been working at Wildflower Hill for six months before she met Raphael Blanchard. She had glimpsed him once, on her arrival, when looking at the upper story. She'd seen his profile at the window, but he hadn't seen her. She'd had an impression of dark hair, pale eyes, and youth, but nothing more. Meanwhile, Alice came down to the kitchen every day after lunch to catch the passing warmth of the stove, and she'd told Beattie bits and pieces about Raphael. He was the fifth son of a minor earl in England, and had been charged with expanding their business interests in the empire, but Raphael had little interest in business, much less sheep. He hired a farm manager and kept himself busy with his social life. Mikhail was the general handyman and gofer, and he drove out three or four times a day to pick people up and drop them home.

It was a fine winter morning. The sun had been late to get up, but now it shone clearly, lending its golden light to the trees and fields. When Beattie arrived at work, Alice was in the kitchen, sitting at the little table with her head in her hands.

"What's wrong?" Beattie asked, hanging up her coat and tying on her apron.

Alice looked up. Her face was flushed, and she held a crumpled hankie in her hand. "I'm sick," she croaked. As if to prove it, she succumbed to a coughing fit that seemed to go on for minutes.

Beattie fetched her a glass of water and put it at her elbow.

Alice brought her coughs under control and sipped the water. She blew her nose loudly. "Beattie, you'll have to serve lunch today. I can't be coughing all over the food."

"Of course. You only have to tell me what to do."

Alice looked at her blearily. "There's just one rule. Don't make eye contact with Mr. Blanchard."

"He doesn't like it?"

"Not for his sake, Beattie. For yours." Alice shook her head. "Just keep your head down. He'll only have one guest with him: Mr. Sampson, his lawyer. Wait until they are deep in conversation, then be invisible. Leave them their food, and leave the room. Two courses: soup and roast. I've already got the roast on."

They worked in the kitchen together that morning, while Beattie turned Alice's warning over in her mind. *Keep your head down.* He must be a tyrant, a terrible bully. How did Alice put up with him, if that were the case? She grew more nervous as the day wore on. After Henry, she'd hoped never to have to deal with a domineering man again.

At last it was time to take the soup up to the dining room. Alice gave her directions, and after forcing her hands to be still, Beattie finally emerged from the kitchen to see a little more of the Wildflower Hill homestead.

Directly opposite the kitchen was a room used for storage. Its door was closed. Stairs led up to the sleeping areas. Dark wood paneling absorbed the light. Behind the stairs were a sitting room and a large dining room. She found the door to the dining room, could hear men's voices from within. Perfect timing. She balanced the tray on her hip, opened the door, and slipped in quietly.

Head down. She caught the smell of cologne, under it a less pleasant musty smell. She registered the same tall cathedral windows in the room, and folding French doors opening to a damp, lichen-spattered patio. She didn't look at the men, and they kept talking as though she weren't there. A bowl in front of each of them—Alice had set the table that morning—and she was on her way out again.

But before she made it to the door, the conversation stopped abruptly, and an imperious voice said, "You're not Alice."

Beattie turned, tucking the tray under her arm. Was she still to keep her head down? It seemed rude, and she didn't want to be scolded for that. She lifted her gaze and smiled politely. "I'm Beattie, sir."

Raphael Blanchard would have been very pretty had he been a woman. He had thick, dark hair that curled around his brow and round, pale blue eyes with long lashes. His face was white, though shadowed with stubble, and his hands were long and flaccid. He bore the distinction of being both

thin—his arms and legs appeared almost wasted—and carrying too much fat around his middle. Beattie couldn't help but
be reminded of a doll she made once with Lucy: a stuffed sock
for a body, sticks for arms. She glanced briefly at his compan-
ion, an older man with a salt-and-pepper beard who smiled at
her kindly.

Raphael didn't smile, though. "Beattie, who are you, and
why are you bringing me my soup?"

"I'm your maid, and Alice is sick."

"Are you new?"

"No, sir, I've been here nearly six months."

"Six months! And I've never met you!" His eyes rounded in
surprise. "Alice has been hiding you, hasn't she?"

"No, sir. I work in the kitchen and the laundry. There's
never been any reason to come out before today." Slowly,
Beattie realized that Raphael wasn't angry at her. She relaxed
a little and smiled. "I'll be off now. Main course is roast beef."

"I look forward to seeing you again." His gaze roamed over
her face and body hungrily, and Beattie felt a prickle of revul-
sion.

Back in the kitchen, she confessed to Alice. "He saw me,
but he was very nice."

"Of course he was," Alice muttered. "Just don't let him be
too nice to you, if you know what I mean. That's how we lost
our last maid."

Beattie put the kettle on the stove to boil. In between
courses was always a good time for a cup of tea. "Go on. You'd
better tell me."

"She was a young fool. When he started proclaiming his

love for her, she believed him, even though I told her I'd seen it all before. He's never going to marry a maid! He wanted one thing, and when he'd got it, he sacked her."

Beattie stared at her in horror, remembering Margaret's warnings that Wildflower Hill was a place of sin. "He never!"

"He did. Now, don't you worry, after today you'll be back down here and in the laundry, and he'll forget about you quick enough. He's got plenty of other pretty young things to keep him busy. Mikhail's always running them here in the evenings. Let's have tea. I'm dying here."

Beattie made the tea, then sat with Alice. Strong, hot tea. Beattie gazed out the window at the rolling fields and pale distant sky and thought about Henry, about the girls at Morecombe House, about the relationships between men and women. Leaving Henry had taken a lot of strength, and she had been proud of herself, but it hadn't erased completely her feelings of vulnerability, her deep conviction that she was just a victim, waiting for someone to take advantage of her. She thought about the hungry look that Raphael had shamelessly given her; perhaps there was something inherent about *her* that made him feel he could do that. She decided that when she went back in, she would not simper and smile. She would lift her chin and show him that she was not a silly bauble to be toyed with.

So when she returned to the dining room, she did not keep her head down. She walked erect, keeping her shoulders square.

Raphael, who seemed to have been waiting for her return, broke off his conversation midsentence. "Ah, she's back. Can you believe, Leo, that Alice has had her hidden away downstairs all this time? Quite the beauty, isn't she?"

It had been a long time since anyone had said Beattie was a beauty. She'd not changed much—still small and thin, dark hair still refusing to hold a curl—but she suspected there must be an air of tired wariness about her that repelled the gazes of men.

The other gentleman had the good grace to sound embarrassed. "Any woman is beautiful if she has grace and compassion," he muttered.

"Beattie, this is Leo Sampson, my lawyer."

Beattie nodded at the lawyer, giving him a smile in acknowledgment of his kindness.

"Why don't you sit with us awhile, girl? We can leave our business talk until after we've eaten. Tell us about yourself. That's a Scots accent I hear."

Beattie cleared the soup dishes and, without meeting his eye, said, "Thank you for your kind offer, but Alice has asked that I return to the kitchen."

"Alice! She's my employee. As are you." A cold edge touched his voice. "Don't forget who pays your wages."

"I won't, sir, and I'm very grateful." She made sure her voice sounded strong; she tried to imagine what Margaret would do in such a circumstance. "But as God has been good enough to give me this work, I'd best show my gratitude by going and doing it." There, now she sounded too pious to be seduced.

Raphael fell silent—though she sensed he was angry—and she slipped quickly from the room, heart thudding, but glad that she could return to life in the kitchen and never have to see him again.

The following day, a Saturday, Mikhail didn't come in the car at ten, as he always did. Beattie waited for half an hour while Lucy bounced around her and asked her repeatedly if she was still working today.

"I don't know," Beattie said again. "I should be."

It was too cold to wait outside, so she decided that she would hear Mikhail when he came, and dragged Lucy back into the house.

Margaret looked up. "No car?"

"No car." Beattie's heart trembled. She'd lost her job, surely. Raphael Blanchard had taken exception to her refusing to sit with him. In trying to be strong and untouchable, she'd merely come across as condescending and rude. She sank into the sofa.

"Don't you worry," Margaret said. "You'd be better off out of that place."

Beattie thought of going to the post office and placing a telephone call to Alice but didn't want to spend anything: she had some savings and didn't want to start eating into them yet. Still, she didn't give up hope that the car would arrive. That Mikhail had been held up or there was some problem with the engine. But as midday came and went, as the afternoon grew chill, as sunset colors began to blush in the sky, Beattie was forced to admit that she *had* lost her job. She sat, tensed, in her chair, while Lucy tried to rouse her from her dark thoughts. But she couldn't even raise a smile for the child.

Margaret was muttering about starting the fire early when there was a honk from out front. Beattie raced to the door. The car was there. Mikhail was waiting. But it was five o'clock: the time she normally finished. Curious, she went down to the car and opened the side door. "What's happening?" she asked Mikhail.

"You come," he said.

"Why so late?"

He shook his head. He either didn't know the answer or didn't know what she was saying. She looked back over her shoulder at Margaret and Lucy on the verandah. "He's saying I have to go to work now."

"But it's nearly dinnertime, Mummy," Lucy protested.

Margaret's mouth was hard. "You be careful."

Beattie ran back up to the verandah to kiss Lucy good night, then turned to Margaret. "Thank you for taking care of her."

"Who's going to take care of you?"

"Perhaps there's a dinner on tonight and they need extra staff."

"I know what happens there at night."

Beattie swallowed hard. "What?"

"I suspect you're about to find out."

"I'll stay in the kitchen."

"Be sure that you do."

Lucy's face was pale, her eyes anxious. "Mummy? What's happening?"

"Never mind, dearie," Beattie said. "It's just work."

Margaret scooped Lucy up. "Come on, sweet pea. You can help me mash the potatoes."

Beattie returned to the car and climbed in. "Thank you, Mikhail," she said.

He grunted and pulled the car onto the road.

On the journey, Beattie's head was full of wild imaginings of decadent scenes. But then she had to laugh at herself. Margaret's idea of what sinners did and her own did not match up. She decided to reserve her judgment until she spoke to Alice. At this point, she was just grateful to be working.

Alice met her at the car, apologizing before she'd even opened the door. "I'm sorry, I'm sorry. Mr. Blanchard has changed your hours. He's hired another maid for morning work and laundry. No more scrubbing clothes for you." She smiled weakly as she led Beattie into the house. "But I'm afraid you won't be able to hide in the kitchen any longer."

Beattie's heart sank. "Oh, dear." She could hear music and voices, muffled behind the door of the sitting room.

"He wants you to work from five until midnight, just four nights, but for the same pay."

"Really? Fewer hours but the same pay?"

Alice nodded. Beattie was jubilant. Certainly, the night work would be tiring, but it would give her much more time with Lucy. "And what do I have to do?"

"We serve dinner together—Thursday to Sunday he usually has guests staying—and then you'll stay to help with drinks. There's a bar in the sitting room. They . . . play cards." Alice looked at her meaningfully.

"They gamble?" Just ordinary sinners, then.

Alice nodded. "Are you fine with that?" She knew a little about Henry, about Beattie's aversion to drinking and gambling.

Beattie almost laughed. Serving drinks at an illegal poker party. Five years on, she was back in the same job. "I'll do my best," she said.

Margaret waited a month before expressing her disapproval of Beattie's new job. The three of them were walking to the shops together. Lucy had run on ahead to the Garretts' long stone fence, which she loved to climb up on and walk along, arms spread out for balance. The morning was fine but very cold, and Beattie's breath made fog in front of her.

"How's it going, then, up at Wildflower Hill?"

"Fine, thank you." Beattie glanced at Lucy, her new winter coat and shoes. She'd found that Raphael Blanchard's guests would happily slip her a few shillings if she smiled at them the right way, and that she didn't mind Raphael's hungry gaze so much when it meant good clothes for her child. He'd not spoken directly to her again, apart from barking an occasional order at her. He'd certainly not tried to get her to sit and share confidences with him, and for that she was glad.

Margaret harrumphed.

"It's not as bad as you think," Beattie said. "They drink a little and play a few games of cards."

"And the women?"

"There are no women. It's like a men's club." Not entirely

true. Mikhail had brought two girls in just the previous night, but Beattie had studiously not paid any attention to them.

Another harrumph. "And what's your job there?"

Lucy was singing a tune, turning on her heel, and walking back along the fence. The morning sun warmed the leaves on the frosty hedges. Mrs. Garrett, who was gardening in a pair of tweed trousers Beattie had rehemmed just last week, called out a good morning to them.

Beattie dropped her voice. "I just bring food and drinks and clean up."

"In those clothes you've been wearing?"

Alice had told Beattie she was required to wear something fitter for company on her evening shifts, so Beattie had spent part of her savings on new fabric and had run up two pretty floral dresses with soft gathered sleeves. "You should see how the men are dressed. In their wing collars and waistcoats. Much finer than me."

Lucy grew tired of walking the tightrope and jumped down, ran to catch up with them. They were turning on to the main street now.

"I hear there's going to be a job going at the bakery," Margaret said. "Lizzie Flower is pregnant and sick all the time, and they'll need someone to help out in the shop if she goes. Why don't you stop in and ask them today? Better than coming home smelling like cigarette smoke and gin."

"I don't want to work at the bakery. I have a perfectly good job."

One more harrumph, and then Margaret fell silent. Beattie knew, though, that now she was a sinner, too, in Margaret's eyes. How long before she put them out on the street? Alice had mentioned the possibility of her staying at the homestead over shearing season in September to deal with all the extra work. Beattie hoped Margaret would keep them until then. Angry tears pricked her eyes, but she blinked them back. She refused to believe she was doing the wrong thing: she was looking after her child the only way she could.

Lucy woke. Something had prickled her in her sleep. She'd been having a dream, one that escaped the moment she tried to remember it. She turned over in the bed to see if Mummy was home from work yet, but she was alone. She stretched out, closing her eyes and praying in her head again as Margaret had told her. "Please take Mummy away from the sinners, please take Mummy away from the sinners . . ."

There was that prickle again. But it wasn't a real prickle, it was a prickle in her head. She realized she'd heard voices, and for some reason, they seemed important to her. She climbed out of bed and went to the door of the attic room, opened the door an inch, and listened.

Margaret's voice. Murmuring. Lucy could pick up only a word here and there. Meaningless words such as "long time" and "couldn't understand." Then a man's voice. That was where the prickle had come from. Why was there a man in the house? He, too, spoke quietly, but she heard him say her mother's name. She opened the door a little farther to lean out. The hinge squeaked, and the talking stopped instantly. Footsteps approached.

Lucy ran back to the bed and hopped in, screwing up her eyes tightly.

"Lucy?" It was Margaret.

She didn't open her eyes.

Margaret approached, sat on the bed. "I know you're awake. You left the door open."

Lucy opened her eyes. "Sorry."

"It's all right. You'd best come down to the sitting room. There's somebody here to see you."

"To see me? Does Mummy know? Is she here?"

"No, your mother's at work, and it's best she doesn't hear about this. Do you think you can keep it a secret? Just for a little while? We're working some things out, and we want it to be a lovely surprise for Mummy. All right?"

Lucy was curious, so she agreed. She took Margaret's hand and climbed out of bed again, came down the stairs and through the hallway. Margaret thrust her gently into the sitting room, where a handsome gentleman sat.

Lucy felt the prickle become a buzz. The gentleman's features seemed to swim and then solidify into a shape at once strange and achingly familiar.

"Lucy," he said, his voice caught on his breath.

Lucy rushed forward. "Daddy!"

THIRTEEN

It was rare for Raphael to have no guests on one of Beattie's nights, but it did happen from time to time. On such occasions, Alice would serve him his dinner, and Beattie would stay down in the kitchen to clean up, to mend clothes, or to review the grocery order for the coming week.

One Thursday night, two months after she'd started the night shift, she arrived to find that Alice had been given the night off to visit her sister in a town ten miles north. A note told her that Mr. Blanchard was eating alone, what she was to cook, and when she was to serve it. Beattie went about the dinner preparations with a growing sense of unease. It would be the first time she'd been alone with her employer, and even though he'd kept a respectful distance, she'd seen in his eyes that he desired her. She thought of going out to the shearers' cottage and asking Mikhail to stay close and keep her safe, but he would be unlikely to understand her, and no doubt it would upset Raphael.

She pulled out a dinner tray from under the bench and assembled the various parts of his dinner. Chicken breast stuffed with bacon and cream, baby carrots in honey, a pot of tea. She realized she was working too slowly and made herself hurry. Get it over with. In and out.

Raphael, if eating alone, took his dinner in the sitting room at the round wooden table he used for cards. She knocked quietly and entered. He was standing at the closed French doors, gazing out into the dark beyond. The sitting room seemed enormous now that it wasn't full of noisy men, though the drapes still smelled of smoke.

She silently slid the tray onto the table, hoping to escape unnoticed. But he had already noticed her, though he didn't turn or look at her.

"It's lonely here tonight, Beattie," he said.

"Yes, sir. Very quiet."

He turned and smiled. "Call me Raph."

Beattie was aware that even Alice called him Mr. Blanchard. "I wouldn't feel comfortable, sir."

"Would you feel comfortable sitting with me while I eat my dinner?"

"No, sir."

He shrugged. "I pay you. A little discomfort won't kill you. Sit."

Beattie hesitated, saw she had little choice, and sat opposite him. He slid into his seat and began to eat noisily, with his head bent close over his plate. She looked around the room, mentally straightening the painting that hung over the mantel, jiggling her knees under the table.

"So," he said through a mouthful of food. "Where in Scotland are you from?"

"I'm English, sir. My mother was Scots. I lived in Glasgow a little while."

"Alice tells me you have a little girl. No husband?"

"No, sir."

"Who was the father, then?"

Beattie didn't know how to answer, so she remained silent, bracing herself for his reaction.

He looked up, licked his lips. "Oh, go on. Do tell. Somebody dashing and dastardly, I imagine? Had his way with you, then abandoned you?"

Beattie stood. She could not let him think that she'd allow him to speak to her this way. "If you'll excuse me—"

"No, I won't excuse you. Sit down. I'll stop asking you about your naughty past." He poked his fork at her for emphasis. "Go on. Sit."

She did as he said.

He returned to his meal. "Now, let's find a topic of conversation that won't upset you. You live with Margaret Day?"

"Yes, that's right."

"And is she really as tedious and tiresome as she appears to be on short acquaintance?"

Beattie stifled a laugh, and Raphael smiled eagerly. "Ah, she *is*. Though you'd never say it. Are you all about God like she is?"

"Margaret is a fine model, sir." Anything to put him off her. "I'm a good Christian."

"Apart from having a child out of wedlock?"

"I do my best."

"Probably not good enough for Margaret. Here's the

thing." He pushed away his half-finished meal and wiped his mouth with his napkin. "I've been watching you these last few months, and I think you're very pretty. I'd rather like it if you'd come upstairs with me for a tumble in my bed. But I sense that you're going to say no."

Beattie was frozen.

"So I won't ask you that directly. Leo Sampson, my lawyer, told me explicitly that I wasn't to offer you money or threaten to fire you. I usually take his advice. So that leaves me in something of a bind. How *do* I get you? Because I want you."

"You can't have me," she said forcefully. "You should forget it."

He shook his head. "But I can't. I've tried. You're not like the others. They usually fall the moment I crook my finger."

Beattie forced herself to her feet and was halfway to the door when he seized her by the wrist.

"Don't run away from me, girl." His pupils were pinpoints in his pale blue eyes.

"I'm not running away. I'm walking away. At twenty shillings a week, you do not pay me enough to be insulted. Now let me go, or I will tell Mr. Sampson what you said." Her heart thudded in her chest: she really couldn't afford to be so principled. She needed the job.

Raphael pulled his eyebrows together: a cross child's expression. But he let her go. She hurried away, through to the kitchen, and stopped only when she had reached the warmth of the stove. She put her head in her hands but didn't cry. Simply, she couldn't be alone with him again. She would have to beg Alice not to put her in that position.

At length, she collected herself. She kept busy with little tasks, listening for his approach. He didn't come. At ten o'clock she went back to the sitting room, opening the door with trepidation. He was gone. She collected the dinner plates and hurried back to the kitchen. Nothing else to do except wait for midnight, when Mikhail would blearily come and get her for the drive home. Beattie put her head on the table, too tired to work, too wary to sleep.

Margaret had started behaving strangely toward Beattie: not meeting her eye, not falling into conversation with her, not walking to the shops with her anymore. Lucy was still close to Margaret; sometimes Beattie grew jealous at how well they got along. But she'd expected an increasing coolness—Margaret had made it clear she didn't approve of Beattie's job—so she didn't dwell on it.

But one morning Margaret seemed more agitated than ever.

It was a Sunday, after church, and Margaret wouldn't settle to sew or to read to Lucy. Rather, she paced back and forth between the sitting room and the verandah, humming tunelessly.

"Are you expecting someone?" Beattie asked.

"Perhaps," Margaret answered, glancing at Lucy. Lucy looked up at her and smiled, and Beattie had the distinct feeling that they were keeping something from her. Uneasiness prickled in her muscles. But she was tired from working late the night before and was easily distracted. She and Lucy were putting together a jigsaw puzzle at the dining table, and she was hunting for blue pieces.

The sound of a car out front. Beattie rose. "Is that Mikhail? He's very early."

"No, no," Margaret said, pushing her back into her seat. "I'm sure it's not your driver. Let me see."

Margaret disappeared out the front again. Beattie looked at Lucy, who was staring at her.

"What is it?" Beattie asked.

"I do love you, Mummy."

"And I love you." She smoothed Lucy's hair. "Why do you look so frightened?"

"But I love him, too."

For an innocent moment, she thought Lucy was talking about God or Jesus. But then she heard the voice outside, and freezing water hit her veins.

Henry!

She leaped from her seat and ran toward the door. She had to stop him before Lucy saw him. Margaret was walking him up the path, smiling at him. *Smiling!* How dare she? How dare she arrange this visit without Beattie's knowledge? She never should have trusted her, what with her cousin living right next door to Henry. She should have left Margaret's house months ago. All these thoughts raced across her mind as she hurried down the path and blocked their way.

"No!" she cried. "You're not coming near my daughter."

Henry smiled kindly. "She's our daughter, Beattie."

Beattie turned on Margaret. "Why did you have to interfere? You know what kind of man he is."

"I know what kind of man he *was*," Margaret said with a sanctimonious lift of her head, "but I have been hearing from Doris over the last few months about the kind of man he has *become*. And you have nothing to fear."

Beattie was so angry that she couldn't understand what Margaret was saying. She stood immobile on the path with her arms spread against Henry's entry to the house.

Henry spoke incredibly gently. "Beattie, if you are worried, I won't see Lucy today. I came to speak to you, anyway. Will you walk with me? Away from the house? Will you listen to my story?"

Lucy. Lucy *knew*. She had said as much. "You've already seen her, haven't you?" Beattie said, dropping her arms in defeat.

"I have been to visit three times."

Beattie gave Margaret a cold glance, but she shrugged it off. "I'll go inside to look after the child," she said. "You two talk."

Henry softly took Beattie's arm and led her down the front path and out the gate. A shining new Ford was parked on the street, and Beattie realized it must be his.

"How did you afford a car?"

"Things have changed for me," he said, leading Beattie past the car and down the street. "I work for the government now. In transport. I get good pay every week, and I spend it wisely."

The morning was cool, with a fresh wind blowing clouds in from the west. Beattie had forgotten her jacket, and gooseflesh rose on her skin under the sleeves of her blouse. She must have shivered because, a moment later, Henry had slipped off his jacket and had spread it over her shoulders.

She was startled and slightly afraid.

"Which way?" he said.

She guided him toward the main road. "So you don't work for Billy anymore?" she asked.

"I don't. Nor do I owe him money, and nor do I rent his cottage, though I've remained good friends with Doris. The first step was breaking his spell on me, putting that life behind me forever."

As they walked, she stole glances at him, assessing him. He seemed to be telling the truth: his skin and eyes were healthy, he looked well fed and strong. And his clothes seemed well cared for. They walked in silence for a while.

"Where are we going?" Henry asked.

"To the creek. There's a big flat rock there where Lucy and I go to sit and tell stories."

He followed her obediently. She turned the situation over in her head. What did he want? Turning up clean, sober, and rich: did he want her and Lucy back? Would that be such a bad thing?

At length, they came to the creek and the causeway where Beattie had nearly lost Lucy. She led Henry to the flat rock, and they sat down, still not talking. The creek ran past, gurgling, and the clouds grew darker.

"The day I left you," Beattie said, "it stormed, and Lucy and I walked for miles in the rain only to find this causeway flooded. We tried to get across, but Lucy was swept away. If it hadn't been for the actions of a kind man passing, she certainly would have drowned."

Henry went visibly pale. "And it would have been all my fault."

Beattie nodded. "Yes, perhaps."

"I was awful to you. Especially to Lucy. On the one hand declaring how much I loved her, and on the other taking away all her security. Taking food out of her mouth to gamble and drink. When you left me, I saw that clearly. But I'm changed now, and thanks to God's help, I have been sober and debt-free for six months. I intend to stay that way."

"And so now you want us back?"

Henry blinked rapidly, then glanced away. "I . . . ah, no, Beattie. Not both of you."

"Oh." Beattie swallowed her embarrassment.

"I . . . Well . . . Molly's come, you see. My wife." He smiled. "Molly's kept me straight and will continue to keep me straight. I owe her my life."

And even though her love for him had long since turned cold, a barb of jealousy pierced her heart. She didn't love him anymore; she didn't want him anymore. But she had hoped that he might miss her and regret what had passed. Beattie's heart hardened. "Well, you can't have Lucy. She's my daughter, I've taken care of her her entire life, even when you couldn't. You can't just walk back into her life now and expect me to give her up."

"I certainly don't expect you to give her up. I came to see you today to ask if you would consider letting her visit with us regularly. Perhaps one week out of every month." He saw that she was about to refuse, so he spoke quickly over the top of her. "We would pick her up and return her, she would be well taken care of and loved . . ." He ran out of words momentarily. "I would love her so well, Beattie, you've no idea."

That love between Henry and Lucy, which had so tortured her the first years of the child's life, was back, and she had to deal with it. If she said no, Lucy would go wild, try to run away, not speak to her for months. Damn Henry and Margaret for concocting this plan. They *knew* that if he saw Lucy first, Beattie couldn't say no.

"You went about this entirely the wrong way," Beattie said, helpless tears brimming. "You shouldn't have seen Lucy without my knowledge."

"I'm sorry, but that was Margaret's idea. She's got it in her head that you've fallen in with a bad crowd and—"

"I work because I have to. I do nothing that I'm ashamed of. I work to put food in my daughter's mouth and make sure she has new shoes. It may not be honest business, but it's honest work, and if I didn't do it, I'd be the worst kind of mother: with morals and no money. Children can't eat morals."

Henry was chastened, held back whatever reply he had thought of. Instead, he nodded. "I understand."

"Will you get lawyers? If I say no, will you spend your rich wife's money on taking Lucy away from me anyway?"

"I'm hoping it won't come to that, Beattie. You are a reasonable person, and I am making a reasonable request. You speak of what Lucy needs, and she needs a father."

Beattie was about to snap that Lucy didn't need another mother but then realized she would have sounded jealous. She *was* jealous. The thought of Molly looking after Lucy for a week every month was a knife turning in her heart. She took a deep breath, tried to regain her perspective. "This is all a bit of a shock," she said.

"I can give you some time to decide. A day or so? A week?"

"I'll need to meet Molly."

"I'll bring her the first time we come to pick Lucy up. You'll like her."

"She'll hate me," Beattie said with a grimace.

Henry shook his head. "Her forgiveness is vast, humbling. She is truly a remarkable woman. And she's longing to meet my girl."

Beattie put her head in her hands. The creek sang, the wind shook the branches of the eucalyptus that lined it. A crow growled, low and lonely. Her heart wanted to shout "No!," but her head was telling her quite a different story. What little girl wouldn't want to be with her beloved daddy from time to time, especially a good Christian daddy with a shining car and a rosy-cheeked wife at home? And to be honest, Beattie could do with a break from parenting from time to time. Having been solely responsible for Lucy for so long had bled her dry.

She lifted her head. "I don't need time to decide," she said, already feeling the anxiety and regret building in her breast. "The answer is yes."

When Mikhail picked her up that night, he was coughing wetly into his handkerchief.

"Are you sick?" she asked, not expecting an answer.

He folded away his handkerchief and pulled in to the

street. Along the way, he coughed, spluttered, sneezed, and generally looked miserable. Beattie was mostly lost in her own thoughts—Henry was returning the following Saturday to collect Lucy for the first time—but not so much that she didn't feel sorry for Mikhail. It was miserable to be sick, though more so when one lived alone, as Mikhail did in the shearers' cottage.

He dropped her at the door, and she climbed out of the car, then leaned back in the driver's side window to say, "Can I get you anything?" He looked at her blankly. She patted his arm. "Never mind. Get some rest."

Then she was caught up in work for a while. Raphael was having dinner with his lawyer, Leo Sampson, and two other men she hadn't seen. After their main course, she took a break while Alice served. As usual, she made herself a small meal and was about to sit down to eat when she thought about Mikhail.

Here in front of her, she had beef soup and hot toast with butter melting on it. Perfect food for a sick person.

"Alice," she said, "I'm going to take this over to Mikhail. He's sick."

Alice sniffed. "I wouldn't bother. He'll give you no gratitude."

Beattie was already up on her feet and finding a tray. "Still, everyone likes to be looked after when they're feeling poorly." She arranged the food on a tray, headed down the stairs through the laundry, and crossed the dewy house paddock to the shearers' cottage.

The old timber structure housed only Mikhail at the moment—Alice had a room downstairs in the homestead—but in about six weeks, it would house a half-dozen shearers from all over Tasmania, following the seasonal shearing work from place to place.

Beattie lifted the latch and let herself in. She crossed the large sitting room, past the narrow bench with the sink and stovetop, and stood at the top of the hallway. Only one light under a door. She moved down the hall and knocked loudly.

A moment later, Mikhail stood there. He looked bleary.

"I brought you dinner. Soup and toast."

Something softened in his face. He opened the door wide, and she walked in. In his room was a narrow bed and a table with a single chair. The room was large, enough floor space for three or four swags, and the lack of furniture made it echo as her shoes clipped on the floor. She slid the tray onto the table and turned to leave, but Mikhail said, "Wait one moment."

Beattie stared. She'd never heard Mikhail speak more than a single word at a time.

He pulled out the chair and offered it to her, taking his tray back to his bed to eat.

She sat down, waiting.

"Thank you," he said. "You very kind."

"I didn't think you could speak English."

"I am not stupid. I live here now since five year. I hear everything. But easier for me if Mr. Blanchard think I have no understand."

"Does Alice know?"

He nodded.

Beattie smiled. "Well, you certainly fooled me."

He smiled back. It was the first time Beattie had seen him smile, and it transformed his face. He didn't look so much like a creature formed of rock anymore. "Yes, I fool you." He indicated his soup. "You have good heart."

Beattie looked at the food and remembered she hadn't eaten herself. Mikhail seemed to sense what she was thinking and offered her a piece of toast. She took it gratefully.

"So why do you think it's easier if Mr. Blanchard doesn't know you speak English?" she asked.

"He will expect too much. He will talk to me and never stop. He will find some way to put me in the wrong. That is what he do with all his staff."

Beattie thought about her own dilemmas with Raphael. "Alice seems to manage him all right."

"Alice is only one. Everyone else, Mr. Blanchard he gives them fired before a year is over. I don't speak to him, he don't speak to me, I still have job. It is hard to find job. I keep it."

"I understand." She thought about Charlie, the man who had rescued Lucy all those months ago, leaving town. "I met a man named Charlie my first day in Lewinford. He was on his way out . . ."

"Charlie Harris. A good man."

"I heard he stole from Raphael."

Mikhail shook his head, slurping soup from his spoon. "Charlie was not thief. They say he stole cuff links! What use is cuff links to Charlie? No. He was given fired for telling Mr. Blanchard how bad is his business."

"I'm sorry?" She had trouble understanding Mikhail's syntax.

"Charlie is only one that I ever see who will say to Mr. Blanchard his business is bad."

"The farm? It's a bad business?"

Mikhail snorted a laugh, and it turned into a cough. Beattie waited patiently for him to catch his breath. Then he said, "Mr. Blanchard has no interest for sheep. You know this. He loses money every year. He can keep no staff. He has two thousand sheep. Maybe make twenty-five bale of wool a year. Not enough. This business, he is worth very little. I think soon Mr. Blanchard will be called home to England from his father. All the money will be gone." He shrugged. "Then nobody of us have job."

Beattie's heart stopped. If she had no job, no money, then what could prevent Henry from taking Lucy permanently? "Really? When do you think that will happen?"

He slurped more soup, rubbed his face with the napkin she had provided. "Who know? Maybe this wool clip, maybe next year's. We all hang on and hope for best."

Beattie realized she had been sitting in Mikhail's room too long, and Alice would be waiting for her. "I'd best go," she said, finishing her toast and wiping her fingers on her apron. "Thank you, Mikhail."

"You not say anything to Mr. Blanchard about me talking?"

"Of course not."

She hurried out, back across the paddock to the homestead. *We all hang on and hope for best.* Mikhail was right, it didn't do to imagine the worst. Not yet.

* * *

Saturday morning was overcast and threatening to rain, but Lucy was as bright as the sun, and as Beattie combed her red-gold hair into two plaits, she chatted merrily and wriggled to be free. Margaret bustled about making morning tea for the guests who were due soon, humming softly. The smell of tea brewing, of currant bun toasting. The clink of the best china—the plates with the green flowers—being set out. But all Beattie felt was a growing sense of dread.

Today they were coming for her little girl.

She knew she shouldn't worry: Henry loved Lucy and would be good to her. Still, the anxiety fluttered through her body, making her talk too fast, making her fingers fumble.

"Ow," Lucy protested. "You're pulling my hair."

"Sorry, darling," Beattie tied a bow at the end of the second plait, then stood back. "There, you look perfect."

Lucy twirled coquettishly. "Daddy will think I look so grown up."

The ache in Beattie's chest flared to life again. "I'm sure he will." The sound of a car arriving had her heartbeat echoing loudly in her ears.

"That sounds like them," Margaret said as she laid out the butter container and a stack of china plates. "Lucy, will you—"

But before she had finished her sentence, Lucy was running down the hallway to the door, squealing, "Daddy, Daddy!"

Beattie caught Margaret's eye and gave her a pained smile. Margaret, perhaps feeling guilty to have caused her so much anxiety, nodded sympathetically.

"She will be fine, you'll see," Margaret said.

"I won't be," Beattie replied.

Margaret made a dismissive noise. "Children aren't ours for life. Every parent has to let go sometime."

Beattie didn't point out that Margaret had no children and therefore couldn't know what it felt like. Instead, she followed Lucy down the hall.

The door was wide open, and Lucy was buried in her father's arms at the front gate. Beattie experienced both a pang of jealousy and a brief moment of joy that Lucy was so happy.

Henry let Lucy go and urged her forward. His eyes met Beattie's, and for a second, she saw a flash of the old Henry, the one she had fallen in love with. Then it was gone, and all she had were regrets.

Margaret was beside her, welcoming the guests in. "You're right on time," she said. "Lucy has been helping me all morning."

This wasn't entirely true. Lucy had begged to help but then done nothing beyond chatter and dance in the kitchen while Margaret worked, but still the little girl beamed proudly.

A woman in a long fitted coat—as gray as the cold sky— and hat and gloves walked a few paces behind Henry, her head down. On the verandah—he stopped and pulled her forward. "I'd like you all to meet Molly, my wife."

Not "Molly, the Irish wolfhound," as she'd once been known. Beattie might have laughed, but there was nothing about this woman that invited mockery. She had kind brown eyes and a shy smile.

"Hello," Molly said in a musical, Irish accent. "It's a pleasure to meet you."

Lucy looked at her warily but didn't say hello. Margaret greeted her effusively, but Beattie wasn't sure what the right protocol was for meeting the wife of the man she had stolen. She offered Molly half a smile and then hurried into the house.

Beattie assumed morning tea preparations while Margaret took their coats and settled them in the dining room. This morning her anxiety had been for Lucy: would Molly be nice to her? Or would she take out her resentment toward Beattie on the child? But now the anxiety was for herself. What if Lucy grew to love Molly? What if she preferred her to Beattie?

Beattie brought the tea tray to the table, and Margaret brought the toasted bun.

"Lucy, we have a lovely little bedroom set up for you at home," Molly said shyly, taking advantage of the quiet while tea was poured and butter melted. "With a toy pony you can ride on."

Lucy's eyes widened in excitement. "A toy pony? How big is it?"

Margaret indicated with her hand. "It's on rockers."

Lucy glanced at Beattie with awe. "Will you be upset, Mummy, if you don't get to ride the pony?"

Beattie shook her head with a laugh. "No, my love. Perhaps you can draw me a picture of it while you're away, to show me when you get back." Her throat tightened around the words. She took a sip of her hot, strong tea.

Henry, sensing her discomfort, turned to small talk. Beattie was lost in her own head for a little while, letting the conversation swirl about her. Her instincts told her to hold Lucy close to her, extract as much comfort out of her little body as possible in the short time they had left, but Lucy had climbed into Henry's lap and didn't look as though she'd budge. When Margaret rose to clear the table, Beattie pushed back her chair, too.

But Molly caught her gently around the wrist and, with her dark eyes locked on Beattie's, said, "I wonder if I might have a word with you alone?"

"I really should help with—"

"I can manage," Margaret said. "Off you go."

Beattie glanced around. "We could go in the sitting room."

Molly nodded, and Beattie led her to the sitting room and closed the door. Usually, the early-morning sun was caught beautifully by the large windows, but this morning they provided a view out onto the hedge shivering in the rainy wind. Beattie knelt to start the fire. When she had finished, Molly was sitting on the couch watching her.

Beattie sat opposite her. "What's on your mind?" She didn't want to know, not really. She expected a mouthful of recriminations.

Instead, Molly smiled kindly. "You're anxious."

"Yes, of course."

"I don't hate you."

"Why not?"

"Because what happened was a long time ago, and besides, it was partly my fault. I wasn't a good wife. I wasn't meeting Henry's . . . needs."

Beattie remained silent.

"In any case, it has all worked out. Henry and I are very

happy. Beattie, I'm not able to have children. That is why I can promise you that Lucy is important to me, and I will be so kind to her, I'll treat her as though she were my own daughter."

"She isn't your daughter," Beattie said.

Molly blinked rapidly, taken aback. "Of course. But she is Henry's. And I'm his wife." She gathered herself. "I'm trying to reassure you, not to threaten you."

Beattie sighed. "I know. I'm sorry. This is all rather difficult for me. I've not spent a night apart from Lucy since the moment she was born. And I'm still coming to terms with the fact that Henry is sober and secure."

"I swear to you that he is, and I swear to you that I will keep him that way," Molly said. "If I learned anything when he left me, it was what I needed to do next time to keep him. Put your mind at ease."

At that moment, Lucy burst in, her doll Henrietta under one arm and a cotton nightie under the other. "I'm ready. It's time to go, Mummy."

Henry stood behind her, smiling at her. "There's no hurry, little one."

"I want to see my pony," she said, matter-of-fact.

"Let me loan you a suitcase for those things," Margaret said, relieving Lucy of her load. "I'll pack for you."

Molly rose. "Fetch your hat and coat, Lucy, and we'll be on our way."

At the gate, Lucy showed the first and only sign of being anxious about separating from her mother. Beattie crouched for a cuddle, and Lucy pressed herself hard against her. "Will you be all right without me, Mummy?"

Beattie fought back tears. "Of course. I have Margaret to keep me company and work to keep me busy."

Lucy kissed her on the lips. "I'll draw you a picture."

"Please do."

Then Henry and Molly were helping her into the car and saying their goodbyes. Minutes later, the car was pulling away, turning down toward the main street, disappearing, gone.

Beattie stood in silence in the vacuum that followed, already missing Lucy, already aching to hold her.

Margaret touched her shoulder. "Don't worry, she'll be back."

Yes, that was so. But there would always be a part of her daughter that belonged to Henry, a part of her that would never return.

FOURTEEN

Beattie swore that she'd never get used to losing Lucy for a week in every month, but somehow after two separations, she did. She fought tears both times, and her heart leaped on both returns. But she found it didn't hurt so much the third time, that she didn't imagine fearful scenarios anymore, that she didn't try to memorize Lucy's face as though it might be the last time they ever saw each other.

Beattie never exchanged more than polite niceties with Molly, but Beattie began to warm to her nonetheless. She had a softness, a kindness, about her that was genuine. The jealousy still prickled Beattie—the worry that Lucy might grow to love her instead—but it was impossible to harbor resentments against Molly.

In fact, the worst part of the arrangement was that Lucy cried every time Henry dropped her off, asking if she could stay just a little longer. Within a few hours, she would be settled and clingy toward Beattie. But she never stopped talking about Henry, about her room in the house at Hobart, about the toys she had there.

September came, and shearing season was upon them. Wildflower Hill was about to be overrun with extra staff and extra chores. Alice asked that Beattie come and stay for the duration, to save Mikhail running in and out of town for her. Her wage would be doubled for those weeks.

So Beattie was left with the dilemma of what to do with Lucy. She couldn't expect Margaret to look after her the whole time, and as Beattie would be sleeping on a rolled-out mattress on Alice's bedroom floor, she could hardly have the girl with her. The answer was clear: Lucy would stay with Henry. Henry used his advantage to turn the two-week stay into a full month, and Beattie could do nothing but agree.

Beattie resisted thinking about the separation until the night before it came. But that night she couldn't sleep, lying in the bed next to Lucy with her outstretched hand on the little girl's back to feel her warm, breathing body. A month without her. At least Beattie would be busy with work. But she couldn't shake the awful sense of injustice: if she didn't have to work, she wouldn't have to give up Lucy. If Henry had simply done the right thing from the start . . . But no, she was forgetting that she had stopped loving Henry long ago, and that no matter how wealthy or moral he had become, she was better off without him.

She was exhausted when Henry came early the next morning to fetch Lucy. He didn't bring Molly, so Lucy was excited to have the front seat of the car. So excited she forgot to say goodbye to Beattie. Beattie watched the car go, then went inside to pack a box for her stay at Wildflower Hill.

Margaret watched her from the door of the attic room. She

seemed agitated this morning, but Beattie didn't know why. Their relationship had long since cooled, and Beattie mostly avoided her. Finally, she could stand it no longer. "What is it, Margaret?"

Margaret folded her arms. "You're going to stay there?"

"Yes, as we discussed. I'll still send you rent. You can enjoy the quiet without us both."

"Do you know what you're getting yourself into?"

"I presume it will be a lot of cooking and laundry." Beattie looked up. "Why?"

Margaret drew a deep breath through her nostrils and said, "Every time you come back from that place, you bring footprints of sin into my house."

"Margaret, really, I don't do anything that—"

"You don't have to *do* anything. It's what you don't do. Those who turn a blind eye to the corruption of others are just as bad in God's view."

"God would want me to pay for my daughter's well-being. I have to work."

Margaret dropped her head and said, so quietly that Beattie almost didn't hear, "I don't think you should come back."

"You're throwing me out?" She was at once relieved and horrified.

"If I turn a blind eye, then perhaps I'm no better than you."

"And being better than me is important, is it?" Beattie hefted her box off the bed and set it on the floor. "Very well, I'll pack the rest of our things and take them with me." Her heart was beating fast. Could she stay on at Wildflower Hill after shearing season? There would be room for her and Lucy in the shearers' cottage, though it would be nothing like the homey comfort of Margaret's place. Lucy would have to stay all day with Beattie in the kitchen. What would she do with the child at night when she was attending Raphael's gatherings? Perhaps Alice could help . . . She'd have to write to Henry to tell him to bring Lucy up to the homestead on her return. What would Henry think of the situation?

She glanced up at Margaret. No matter how she felt now, Margaret had provided them with a home when they needed it most. If she allowed herself to remember the warmth between them at the start, this cold change would hurt her too much. It reminded her too closely of the way her own mother had kicked her out, how Cora had never sought to reply to her letters. So instead, she said, "I'm sorry that I've become such a burden on you. But I thank you for giving me a chance when I first came to town."

Margaret wouldn't meet her gaze. She nodded curtly, then backed out of the room without a word.

Beattie was weary, so weary. Once again the struggle would start. Once again she and Lucy would be thrust into uncertainty.

For the next two weeks, there was no time to think about her situation. She was up at dawn making breakfasts, working right through the day, then slipping off her apron and combing her hair for an evening attending Raphael and his guests as they played poker and drank.

Raphael seemed largely unaware that shearing season was

going on. Everything was organized and run by Terry, the farm manager, an affable red-faced man who always smelled of sweat and horses. Raphael didn't set foot in the shearing shed, and his only acknowledgment of the frenetic activity on his property was when he grasped Beattie's hand as she served him a drink one night and said, "Your skin is quite red and raw. You have been working too hard for those ungrateful shearers."

She extricated herself and kept busy with her work. The busier she was, the less time she had to think. Every night she fell into bed, exhausted, around midnight. Woke six hours later to do it all again.

Then it was over. The shearers packed their belongings and moved on to the next farm, and quiet returned to Wildflower Hill. Beattie still hadn't found a place to live permanently. When she and Alice went out to the shearers' cottage to clean up, she decided to sound Alice out about the idea.

"Alice, I've nowhere to live anymore. Margaret kicked me out."

Alice, who was mopping the floor, didn't even blink. "You can stay here in the cottage."

"Do I have to ask Mr. Blanchard?"

"I'll tell him. It's easier for us if you're here. The room at the end of the hallway opposite Mikhail's is the nicest."

"There's not a chance that I could stay in the homestead, is there? Like you do?"

"Not with the little one. Mr. Blanchard doesn't like

children." Alice straightened up, slopping the mop back into the bucket. "You'll lose five shillings a week of your pay; six with the child."

"That's fine."

"And you'll have to buy furniture. A bed of your own."

Beattie nodded. There was a shop in town that sold cast-offs and old furniture, and she'd seen a rug and a bed for sale that she could afford out of her savings. She'd have to make do with fruit crates for chairs. Alice ate all her meals in the kitchen, and Beattie assumed she and Lucy could do the same. Perhaps it wouldn't be so bad.

Late that afternoon, she slipped out of the laundry for an hour and crossed the paddock to set up her new living space. Until she could get her bed, she borrowed a swag that had been left behind last shearing season and rolled it out on the floor to sleep on. It smelled faintly musty, of the man who had owned it, even though she had already washed it twice. Alice let her take a rickety bookshelf from storage under the house, and Beattie slid Lucy's favorite books onto it. Outside, the sun withdrew from the fields, blushing the sky pink. There was no fire, so she dared not open the windows to let fresh air in. The room smelled faintly of sweat and disinfec-tant. She picked a posy of wildflowers from around the edges of the cottage and put them in a cup without a handle on the windowsill. Then she sat on the rolled-out mattress and cried. There was no way to make this room look homely, or welcoming, or inviting to a little girl. Lucy would return from Hobart, from her toy pony and her embroidered linen, to this bare room. Beattie realized a terrible thing about herself: that she had tried as hard as she could and this was the best she could give her daughter.

A quiet knock at the door roused her. She wiped her face on a handkerchief and went to open it. Mikhail stood there.

"Mikhail?"

He searched her face. She knew he saw the tears, but he said nothing. "You play cards."

"I'm sorry?"

He reached into the pocket of his threadbare jacket and pulled out a deck of cards.

"Oh," she said. "No, I . . . I've never played." Though she had watched hundreds of games.

"Is easy," he said. "Night is very lonely and quiet. You play cards with me. I teach you."

So she stood back to let him in. They sat on upturned fruit crates and played on top of the bookcase. He patiently stepped her through the rules, and they bet matchsticks. The afternoon turned into night, and Beattie was grateful for his company, for ordinary human warmth when the future seemed so cold.

The next evening, as she was mending one of her slips by the fluttering light of a candle, she heard another knock. She rose and opened it, expecting Mikhail and his deck of cards. But it wasn't Mikhail, it was Raphael. And he was drunk.

"Beattie!" he exclaimed, putting out his arms to hug her. She sidestepped and he stumbled, righted himself, and shuffled into the room. "I'm so glad you've decided to stay with us."

She wanted to tell him she had little choice, and that in a perfect world she'd keep her daughter a million miles away from him, but instead, she gritted her teeth and said, "I'm very grateful, Mr. Blanchard."

He sat down on her swag, nearly losing his balance for a moment. He patted the blanket next to him, but Beattie shrank away, stuck her back to the wall by the window. She had never seen him anywhere near the shearers' cottage before and hoped that after this visit, he would never return again. At least Mikhail was just across the hall if she needed help removing him.

"When are you going to start calling me Raphael?" he asked, pouting like a child.

Alice had told her that he put all his staff—male and female—through this test. The moment they dropped the formal "Mr. Blanchard" or "sir," he fired them.

"It's not fitting, sir," she said.

He looked around. "It's very bare here."

She hoped he wouldn't recognize the bookshelf. "I'll get some furniture this week."

"If you sleep with me, I'll buy you a roomful."

Beattie's skin prickled. "No, thank you, sir."

He lay back on her pillow, sighing. "You are a stubborn thing. I'm determined to have you before I go."

"Are you going somewhere?"

"I might have to. My father is furious with me." He looked so vulnerable for a moment, like a little boy, that Beattie almost felt sorry for him. "Is your father ever cross with you, Beattie?"

"My father is dead, sir." Suddenly, she realized he was

talking about the business, how he'd run it into the ground as Mikhail had told her. Did this mean that her job would soon be gone, too? Her new living arrangements? There were no jobs out there; what would she do if she lost this one?

"Why is your father furious with you?"

Now his face became cruel and hard again, and the dim light drew dark shadows across his brow. "Because he's a fastidious old prick. Because he's made of ice and stone. Because he bought this place for me to keep me out of trouble, and I found more trouble. And I've not cared much about the business and lost a lot of money. Sheep! Who could be interested in sheep? I wasn't. I'm still not. And all signs point to rather a disappointing wool clip."

Beattie's stomach clenched at his lack of gratitude. Here he was, rich when so many were poor, the owner of a business, a large and beautiful house. And he would let it all go to pursue drinking and gambling. So many people would die for a chance like the one he was throwing away. *She* would die for that chance.

"What will happen to all of us if you go?"

He closed his eyes, and for a few awful moments, Beattie wondered if he'd fallen asleep. How would she get him out of her room? But then he opened his pretty blue eyes and sat up. "Beattie Blaxland, I'd do anything to have a chance with you."

"You didn't answer my question. What will happen to all of us? To Alice and Mikhail and Terry and me?"

He shrugged. "There are other farms. You'll find work."

"One man in four is unemployed," Beattie said. "It's almost impossible for women to get jobs."

He rose unevenly and came to stand next to her. He grasped her hand, and she couldn't wrestle it away. His fingers were icy. "I'll give you a bonus before I go." He laughed, forcing her hand onto the front of his trousers.

"Mikhail!" she shouted.

Raphael dropped her hand and stood back, narrowing his eyes. "I'd threaten to sack you, only it's going to be a miracle if you have a job at the end of the year anyway." He turned and let himself out just as Mikhail arrived at the door.

"It's all right, Mikhail," Raphael said to the big man, "her honor is still intact." Then he was shuffling off.

Mikhail waited until he was out of earshot, then said, "Are you well?"

"Thank you, yes."

"You should maybe put a bolt on door."

"Mikhail, he said he's probably going home soon, that the business has failed."

Mikhail nodded. "I hear him in the car talking to Mr. Sampson. He will know by beginning of November."

Two months. Should she look for another job? Move to Hobart with the hope that she could find work? Or should she hang on to this job and hope for the best? At least it was good regular pay. Better than the misery of the dole queue.

Mikhail nodded. "I see what you thinking, and I think same. Terry is talking of leaving. He have no farm manager soon. Alice is also asking other places. Me, I will do same. It is not so bad. We have long time yet. And maybe it won't happen. Maybe another year."

Mikhail, Alice, and Terry had no small children to take care of, though. They could easily follow the work around. Lucy needed stability.

"I hope you're right, Mikhail," she said. "Just one more year."

He tapped his pocket. "More cards?"

She smiled and nodded. "Come on. I'm determined to beat you at least once tonight."

Beattie was relieved to see Lucy's initial disdain for her new home quickly replaced with excitement. There were dogs and horses, rabbits and wallabies, miles of paddocks to roam in, and the big echoing kitchen to sit in, drawing with the new set of pencils Henry had bought her. The rug and the bed arrived in the first week, and Lucy settled back in to life with her mother.

Lucy was frightened of Mikhail at first but soon grew used to him. He came to visit every night, and Lucy fell asleep in the bed while Mikhail and Beattie played poker for match-sticks. Beattie found she had a knack for the game: years of watching men play helped, as did her gift for judging her opponent's hand through his subtle physical reactions. Soon she was confidently beating Mikhail at almost every hand. He began to call her the Matchstick Tsarina, until Lucy complained that her mother's name wasn't Serena, it was Beattie, and he should get it right.

Two days before Henry was due to collect Lucy for her next visit, Alice came to find Beattie in the laundry. Lucy was sitting on an upturned fruit crate, wrestling a peg doll into a tiny dress that she had sewn herself. Beattie was pressing Raphael's shirts through the mangle as the copper cooled beside her.

"Beattie, you have a telephone call," Alice said.

Beattie stopped and wiped her hands on her apron. "A telephone call? Are you sure it's for me?"

"It's Molly MacConnell."

Lucy looked up and beamed. "Mama Molly! Can I speak to her on the telephone?"

Mama Molly? Beattie's heart sank into her stomach.

Alice shook her head. "She wants to talk to your mother, dear. Not you."

Lucy pouted. Beattie stroked her hair off her face. "I'll tell her you said hello." She followed Alice to the long hallway, where the telephone sat on a polished table. She picked it up and said, "Hello?," trying not to sound too nervous.

"Beattie, it's Molly." Her voice was distant and small.

Beattie wound the cord around her fingers, leaning against the wall. Morning light through the transom fell in a pattern on the floor. The house was dim and quiet. "How can I help you?" she said.

"I hope you don't mind me calling, but I need to discuss something with you while Henry isn't around."

"Oh?"

"It's about Lucy."

Mama Molly. How long had Lucy been calling her that?

"Beattie, I know you love your little girl, and I know you are doing your best to provide for her, but . . . frankly, when we dropped her off last time, I was appalled. A bare room without even a bed—"

"We have a bed now. And rugs. Lucy loves the farm."

"Nonetheless, she's nearly five. Next year she'll need school. Here in Hobart, there are many schools. There's her church." Molly's voice grew urgent. "And a proper house with a room and a bed of her own, toys, books, everything she could need."

Beattie knew where this conversation was heading. "I see. So you think she'd be better off with you? With Mama Molly instead of Mama Beattie?"

Molly fell silent.

"*I* am her mother," Beattie said.

"Henry is her father. He has as much claim on her as you." Molly calmed herself. "Beattie, I don't want to argue with you. But surely you can see good sense? If we reverse the arrangement and she spends one week a month with you, then she will still get to run around on the farm from time to time."

Beattie was fighting tears. She knew deep down that Molly was making good sense, but to admit it was impossible. "Why did you have to call me when Henry wasn't there?" she asked. "Doesn't he want her?"

"Quite the opposite," Molly said. "He wants her all the time. He's been talking about engaging a lawyer, going to the court. I thought if I spoke to you, we could arrange something amicably, something that you could be happy about."

Happy? How could she possibly be happy if they took her little girl away? But then how could she hold on to Lucy in the face of this? Her job was uncertain, her living arrangements were inadequate, and Lucy spent hours of every day unattended.

"Beattie?" Molly said gently.

"Why must you be so kind?" Beattie said through tears. "Why can't you at least be cruel so that I can hate you?"

"Kindness is all we have to give others," Molly said. "You are Lucy's mother, and you will always be in our lives. Is it not better that nobody hates anybody?"

Now Beattie felt foolish, young, a naughty girl. "I suppose I have no choice," she said. "If I say no, Henry can afford a lawyer, and I can't."

Molly was silent, but Beattie knew what she was thinking: *You won't say no.*

Moments ticked past in the cool, dim hallway.

"All right, then," Beattie said at last. "You win."

"It's not a competition. What's important here is what Lucy needs."

For a moment Beattie wavered: Lucy needed her own mother, didn't she? More than anything else? But she wasn't such an idealist. "You're right, of course," Beattie said. "I'll let her know what we've decided."

Beattie waited until the morning they were to collect Lucy to tell her. She didn't want anything to spoil their last night together, snuggled up in the narrow bed. Lucy was excited about seeing her father again in the morning, demanding her hair be pulled into plaits, her pale skin flushed with happiness.

As Beattie sat her between her knees on the bed, carefully combing Lucy's silky red-gold hair into even strands, she finally said it aloud. "Darling, I need to tell you something important."

"Hm?" Lucy said absently.

"I spoke to Molly, and we all think it's best if you stay with her and Daddy and just visit me once a month." She hadn't meant to cry, but her voice broke and the tears spilled over.

Lucy pulled her hair out of Beattie's hands and turned to face her. "Mummy? Why is it best if I stay with Daddy and Molly?"

"Because there you have a room of your own, and you can go to school and church. And I know you love your daddy so much."

"I love *you* so much."

Beattie realized, through her own tears, that Lucy's little mouth was quivering. She hadn't expected this. She'd assumed that Lucy would be happy with the new arrangements. She put her hands gently on Lucy's white cheeks. "Don't cry."

"Don't you want me to live with you anymore?"

"Of course I do. I want you with me all the time." Beattie pressed Lucy against her hard. "But my life is so uncertain, and Daddy and Molly can give you things I can't."

"I will miss you." Lucy's voice was muffled against her shoulder.

"I'll miss you, too. But you'll come once a month for a week." Even as she said it, Beattie knew that arrangement wouldn't hold forever. Not next year, when Lucy was at school.

If Beattie even had a job next year.

And as Lucy cried against her, and her heart ached, and

she felt the full weight of her life's uncertainty, Beattie found herself growing angry. When she'd left Henry, she was certain she'd been taking control of her life. Being a woman who does things. And yet here she was, giving up her daughter for fear of having things done to her once more. She was tired of it, so tired that her bones hurt. All she wanted was a decent, secure, well-paying job, but there were thousands who wanted the same thing. She was one of a crowd of people who couldn't get ahead; she could never prove to Henry and Molly that she could look after her own daughter adequately.

Was there anything she could do to struggle out of that crowd; was there any pathway of thought she hadn't explored, any special skill or talent she could use? Her dressmaking skills meant nothing—but she had spent years working around men with ratlike cunning. What had she learned from that experience?

An idea glimmered. She felt giddy with fear. But she resolved to do what she had to.

It was late. Raphael and his lawyer, Leo Sampson, had already dined. It remained only for Beattie to bring them their brandy. She stood in the hallway, quite unable to open the door and go in. Her nerve was failing her. She wanted very much to open the brandy and take a long swig of it herself, for courage.

Do it, Beattie, do it. There wouldn't be a better time. She needed Leo to be there, and within a month Raphael himself might be gone. She strode forward, pushed open the door.

This time she didn't shrink about, hoping to remain invisible. She walked to the dining table, put the drinks tray down, and stood, erect, waiting to be noticed.

"Beattie?" Raphael said, his eyes roving over as they always did. "You're being rather a nuisance. We're busy talking."

Leo Sampson smiled at her weakly, embarrassed by Raphael's behavior. "Is there something wrong?" he asked.

"May I sit with you a moment?" she asked Raphael.

He raised his eyebrows, waved a languid hand. "If you must. Pour yourself a drink, too."

Beattie sat. She poured drinks for everyone, threw back the brandy quickly, forcing herself to relax. She couldn't let him see how anxious she was.

"Now, what's all this about?" Raphael asked.

"Do you want me to go?" Leo said.

"No, no, Mr. Sampson. I want you here very much." She smiled at him, then returned her attention to Raphael. "Mr. Blanchard, a few weeks ago, when you came to see me at the shearers' cottage, you said that you would give anything for a chance to sleep with me."

Leo's busy eyebrows shot up. "Steady on," he said, but Beattie wasn't sure if the warning was for her or for Raphael.

"Have you finally decided to concede?" Raphael laughed, leaning forward. "Was it the promise of new furniture?"

"I don't want new furniture. I only want to give you the *chance* of sleeping with me. If you'll give me the chance to get something I really want, too."

Raphael frowned, pushing his wet bottom lip out. A log on the fire cracked loudly and crumbled to ash.

Leo intervened, his face red with embarrassment and anger. "I don't think it's a wise idea for an employer and employee to discuss such things. This is unspeakable, it's—"

"Mr. Blanchard has raised this topic on many occasions," Beattie said. "I'm merely trying to resolve it once and for all."

"What do you want?" Raphael blurted suddenly. "Anything."

"This house. The stock and the land, too."

"You're mad. I'm not going to give—"

"Not as a gift. As a wager. Against my body."

Now he was laughing: cruel, merry laughter. And Beattie knew she'd already won the first round. He was going to say yes.

"Oh, dear, what a delight you are. Are we talking poker here?"

Beattie nodded.

"You will ante up a night of pleasure with me if I ante up the house? Good Lord, could you imagine if I lost? My father would have a conniption and die. With a touch of luck." Laughing again, bending over double. "It's beautiful."

"Well? Will you do it?"

"Of *course* I will!"

Beattie turned to Leo. "Will you witness it and make sure the transfer of the property happens if I win?"

Leo sat in stunned silence.

"Will you?"

"I'll do as I'm instructed by my client," he said gruffly.

"And I absolutely instruct you to draw up whatever papers are necessary to reassure Beattie that I take her wager seriously." He eyed Beattie. "Though I doubt you'll be able to witness Beattie fulfilling *her* promise. You'll have to take her word that she'll go through with it."

Beattie repressed a shudder. "I'll go through with it."

"Let me be clear," he said. "You have to do *anything* I want you to."

She nodded, and he clapped his hands together like a gleeful child. "Let me think, let me think. How are we to do this? Best of three games? I know, we'll play for buttons—that's all you can afford, isn't it, Beattie? Some buttons from the laundry? After three games, whoever has the most buttons wins."

"If that's how you want to play."

"Girl, have you ever even played poker before?"

She shook her head. "No," she lied, "though I've watched many games."

He laughed until he coughed, then calmed himself. "One week from tonight, then," he said. "Leo, get the papers ready this week. I'll want you to be here for the game. It will be quick, and you're welcome to stay for dinner afterward." He turned his attention to Beattie. "Off you go, then. Keep yourself nice for me. And thanks for providing me with so much amusement."

Beattie stood, locked her knees to stop them from shaking, and made her way to the door. Leo Sampson rose and grasped her wrist gently at the threshold. "You don't have to do this, you know," he said in a low voice.

"Leave her be, Leo," Raphael called after him.

She looked at Leo, smiled sadly. "Yes, I do."

"You really think you can win?"

She shrugged, and he let her go. "I'm tired of struggling," she said.

"I'll make sure it's all aboveboard. As aboveboard as such a transaction can be."

"Thank you," she said. "That's very reassuring."

Then she was out in the hallway again, the door closed behind her, letting her knees turn to jelly and gasping for breath. She allowed herself a moment's weakness, then straightened her back with steel. She and Mikhail only ever played for matchsticks. After her experience with Henry, she had grown to hate gambling. But if she was going to gamble once in her life, then she was going to gamble big.

Very, very big.

FIFTEEN

Within a day, everyone else at Wildflower Hill knew about the wager. Alice told her she was the most foolish girl she'd ever met and refused to speak to her. Terry laughed openly at her when she brought him his tray with dinner. "I don't know whether you're mad or bad," he said, his sun-reddened cheeks shining with amusement. "But I hope you'll give me a job if you win."

On the first night, Mikhail crept across the hallway to her room. "Come on, we practice. You win."

"Bless you, Mikhail," Beattie said.

What had been a leisurely pastime became terribly serious business. Sitting on the fruit crates, they played. Mikhail dealt hand after hand. Every spare moment they had that week, they practiced, passing the matchsticks back and forth between them. The little shards of wood were meaningless but by Sunday night, the buttons would be as heavy as gold.

Even though Beattie was sharp at the game, she began to realize just how dependent on luck she was. She knew when to raise the stakes, when to cut her losses. But the thing she could never control was what cards found their way into her hands. She lost sometimes, and nothing could be done to help it.

The night before the game, the last night to practice, Mikhail asked her outright, "If you win, you keep me on?"

Beattie was taken aback. She'd never thought of what she'd do with the staff. She had no money to pay them, and as she understood it, she wouldn't be getting the car that Mikhail drove. "I don't know," she said, guilt creeping into her heart. If she won, he would lose his job. "I don't think I can."

"Ah, is no matter," he said gruffly, dealing the cards again.

"You could stay as long as you need to, to find another job. Alice, too, though I doubt she'd want to stay."

"Is all coming to an end, anyway," he said. "You may be owning very bad business soon."

Beattie was crisscrossed by negative feelings: fear, self-doubt. This was madness. If she had any sense, she'd run away right now, head to Hobart, look for a job or join the dole queue . . . At this stage, she was sure she'd end up having to submit to a night of Raphael's vile desires like a common prostitute, then no doubt find herself without a job the next morning. If that were the case, then she didn't deserve to keep Lucy. Lucy would be better off with a mother like Molly.

Mikhail reached across the table and wiped a tear off her cheek with his knuckles. She hadn't even realized she'd been crying. "We win sometimes, we lose sometimes," he said. "No matter. We go on."

She smiled weakly. "Thanks, Mikhail."

"One more hand?"

"One more hand."

* * *

There are two types of women in the world, Beattie, those who do things and those who have things done to them.

Beattie's body felt it would shake apart from the inside. Her mouth was dry, her heart rattling her ribs.

Two types of women . . .

She stilled her hands to open the door to the sitting room. Raphael sat at the gleaming card table, shuffling the deck. He hadn't seen her yet, but Leo Sampson, who was on the sofa, looked up and offered her an encouraging smile.

Those who do things and those who have things done to them . . .

Deep breaths. She walked stiffly to the table, sat down opposite Raphael.

He didn't glance up, yet. "Just so you know, Beattie, Leo's looked at the deck, and he's checked up my sleeves for hidden aces." He looked up with a wild laugh, met her eyes, his pupils widening with desire. "Oh, you look beautiful tonight. I am going to enjoy this. Did you bring the buttons?"

"No, I . . ." She started up from her chair, but Raphael leaped to his feet.

"I'll get them. I'm terrified you'll run if I let you go now. You look sick with fright." He hurried out of the room, leaving Beattie alone with Leo Sampson and her own thunderous heartbeat.

"Beattie," Leo said quietly when he was sure Raphael was out of earshot, "I've got contracts here, and he's already signed them. I tear them up if you lose, but if you win, the house is yours. Perfectly legally."

Beattie tried to concentrate on what he was saying. "I see."

"He's only signed over the house, the land, and the stock. He'll take all the furniture, the car, everything." He grimaced. "Beattie, if you win, you might be better to sell the whole place and use the money more wisely. Buy a little cottage in town."

And have no job to pay for food. "Is this a good farm?"

"It's a bad business, but only because it's been run that way. The carrying capacity of the land is high. You could run seven or eight thousand sheep on it. Managed well, it could make you rich."

Beattie nodded. It would still take some time before she could convince Henry to give Lucy back. There was hard work ahead. "If I win it, I'll keep it."

Raphael's footsteps were returning. "I wish you luck, my dear," he said. "And if things don't go the way you hope, I wish you good courage."

Tears pricked her eyes. *Deep breath. Still your hands.* She was about to find out exactly what type of woman she was.

The world slowed down. Raphael poured the buttons onto the table with a clatter, divided them evenly between himself and Beattie. Different shapes and sizes. She spotted a red bow-shaped button from one of Lucy's dresses. She pushed forward three buttons, he the same.

Then he dealt the first hand of cards. She picked them up, closed her eyes before looking at them. Told herself to pretend she was in her room with Mikhail, just playing to keep the night away. Opened her eyes.

Two queens, a four, a six, and a two.

Raphael, with polished confidence, threw down one of his

cards and picked up another. Pushed one more button onto the pile. Sat back to look at her.

He had four of something. Was it a straight? Or was it four of a kind? Or was he hoping for a full house?

She threw down her useless cards, picked up three more: equally useless. Decided she wouldn't risk losing too much too early and met his bet.

She had two queens. He had four kings.

She had lost the first hand, and now he had eight more buttons than she did.

Raphael laughed as he collected his buttons. His pale eyes never left her face. She tried to hide her disappointment but knew it was written all over her. For the first time, she let herself imagine him making love to her. His cold fingers, his wet lips, his soft belly . . .

"Another hand, Beattie?" he said brightly.

She nodded, swallowing hard to wet her throat. What a fool she'd been. "Another hand." She put in three buttons, figuring it was the only way to even things up.

He dealt the cards. She picked them up quickly, wanting to get it over with. This time she had two aces, two fours, and a six. Her heart thudded in her throat. If she were playing with Mikhail, it would be so easy. Throw in the six, hope for another four or ace. Bet high.

And there it was. A four. She had a full house. She steeled herself, put another seven buttons forward.

He saw her, then raised it another seven buttons. Her nerve failed. She matched his bet and showed him her cards. He looked at them, then growled, throwing in his hand.

Relief flooded through her. She scooped the buttons toward her. She was ahead by twenty-six buttons.

Now it all rode on the last game.

Beattie had never felt more nervous in her life. Her stomach itched, and her blood seemed to scratch at her veins. The glimmer of possibility: that she would not only avoid Raphael's touch but would win the house. Her head seemed filled with light, and she had to remind herself to focus.

Raphael's eyes were glued to her again, angry and desiring all at once. He pushed forward three buttons. She submitted three of her own. The cards fell in front of her. She picked them up.

It was a nightmare hand. A pair of twos, a four and five of spades, and a king. She had no idea what to do. Raphael quickly upped the bet with another ten buttons, discarded two cards, and picked up replacements. Did he have three of a kind? If so, she was ruined. She hesitated, not sure what to do. Then quickly met his bet and decided to throw in the spades and hope for another king or another two.

And there it was, another king. Her blood was thrumming.

Raphael pushed in another ten buttons. He was so certain. She quickly did the numbers in her head. If he won, he would have twenty more buttons than she did. If she folded, they would be back to even, and nobody would have won. They would have to play a tie-breaking game.

Then he picked up another card and made a self-satisfied noise, and her heart sank. He glanced up at her, a smile curling on his lips.

And she saw it. A tiny movement of his pupils, shrinking.

She thought about all those times she had watched Henry play in Glasgow and what it meant when his pupils—so dark against the irises—shrank like that. Raphael was bluffing, trying to make her fold so she would be forced to play a fourth game.

She pushed ten buttons forward, then another five. Her body shook, doubt crushed her.

His face fell.

"Go on," she said. "Let me see them."

He laid down his cards. They were a hodgepodge: clearly he'd been hoping for a flush. She laid down hers.

"No!" he shouted, a spoiled child jumping from his chair. He knocked the cards off the table, and they flew about her and skidded into her lap. "No! No! No!" He accented every exclamation with a thump on the table. Leo rose and tried to calm him, but all the noise and commotion seemed to be happening a million miles away. Beattie sat in silence and shock. She had done it. She had *done something*.

And she was never going to have things done to her ever again.

Beattie stood at the crest of a hill, ten trudging minutes' walk from the homestead. Grassy fields undulated away from her, the darker green of eucalyptus forest skimming the farm's edges. Green hills: some in sunlight, some in lazy shadows. Silence. Silence for miles.

Miles and miles of silence. And all of them hers.

SIXTEEN

Emma: Tasmania, 2009

The driver of the car I'd booked wouldn't stop talking. I itched to be free. I needed to stretch my leg. My sore knee had been cramped up for over an hour from the airport, and two hours before that on the plane. I'd tried stretching it out on the backseat for a while, but the angle had made my back and hips twinge.

So I nodded and hmmed in the right places, but I longed for the journey to be over. To come to rest somewhere. Finally, we turned off the last unpaved road and in between the stone gates, up the driveway. I looked at the front of the homestead. I'd only seen it in pictures, when I'd never expected to own it. The aging sandstone, the peaked windows, the overgrown gardens. As soon as the driver drew breath, I blurted, "Thanks so much. Here," and threw a tip at him.

He folded it away while I opened the door and at last stretched my leg. It felt good. I stood up, taking a deep breath of the fresh country air. Apart from the rumble of the car engine, it was quiet. The driver went to the trunk for my cases and lugged them up to the front door for me. Lichen bloomed on the gray pavers.

He stopped, shrugging his shoulder toward a tree on the southern side of the house. "Possums," he said.

"Possums?"

"They're killing it."

I looked at the tree. A deadfall of gray-white branches lay under it, and spiky lomandra grew. "Possums are killing it?"

"They eat the new shoots. Look, one side is dying. You need to get a tree man out here to stick a collar on it."

"On the possum?"

"On the tree."

"Oh, I see." I didn't see. I didn't really care. I felt in my handbag for the set of keys Mr. Hibbert had given me. *I've had the electricity, gas, and phone reconnected. But nobody's been in there since before Beattie died,* he'd said. *I imagine it will be quite dusty. Will you need help cleaning it up?*

I'd declined. I didn't want to meet anyone or make any friends: too complicated. I planned to keep busy cleaning it up myself. I had a flight booked home in three weeks.

Now, as the car sped off, leaving only the sunlight and wind behind, I matched keys with locks and slowly got the front doors open.

Sunshine fell on the wooden floor of a long hallway. Dust danced in the light. The interior of the house was dark and airless. My lungs constricted. I left the door open behind me, my suitcases on the front step. Keys jangling, I stepped inside.

In front of me was a set of stairs: I could deal with those later. With my keys, I began opening doors room by room. A small front room full of boxes. A dining room where a white dust cover had long since slid onto the floor. I ran my finger along the dining table. The dust was thick. My nose was starting to itch. More boxes in the dining room, lined neatly against the wall by the fireplace. I drew the curtains for a view of the driveway and front gate. The window had been shut so long that it howled when I forced it open. Wind rushed in, dislodging dust. I sneezed uncontrollably for a few moments, then moved to the room across the hallway.

Perhaps it had once been a sitting room: there was a sofa, an upright piano. But now it was taken over by boxes. Cardboard boxes that were giving in to the weight of time, sagging and splitting; some plastic boxes with more recent things in them. I idly flipped the top off one. Papers, books, birthday cards . . . My heart caught. Here was a card I'd sent Grandma as a child. A picture of irises on the front; inside, my nine-year-old handwriting: *Dear Nana Beattie, happy birthday and I love you, Emma.*

Tears. Where had they come from? I slid the card back into the box and wiped them away. When Mum had called me to say Grandma was dead, it had been such a shock. Even though she'd been in her nineties, I'd always imagined Grandma as being invulnerable. Immortal. She'd seemed so strong. I'd always thought I'd see her again.

The tears and the dust set me sneezing again. I opened more windows, opened the doors onto the courtyard. Came through to the kitchen and let in light and air.

Then I braced myself: stairs were getting easier, but they still made me nervous. One foot in front of the other, holding on to the dusty banister. When I'd made it, I stopped for a minute to rest the joint. It throbbed dully. The carpet up here made the air seem all the more stuffy. I went from bedroom to bedroom, throwing open curtains and windows, letting the breeze in, marveling at how many boxes of stuff Beattie had. She hadn't actually lived in Wildflower Hill for decades before her death, but she had clearly used it as a place to send and store things. Perhaps she'd intended to come back one day and sort it all, or perhaps once it was out of sight, it was out of mind.

The last bedroom was the master bedroom. Despite the aging carpet and the patterned wallpaper, it felt roomy and sunny. The window looked out into the branches of the big tree that the driver had been so worried about. Across the paddock was a small wooden cottage, an old open shed, and the fallen-down remains of what might have been stables once. Beyond were fields, rolling down and away. Uninterrupted silence, except for the shushing of the breeze in the trees. Then the breeze dropped, and all that was left was the beat of my heart. Beattie had sold off all but five acres of the farm and all the livestock long, long ago. Once it had been two thousand acres, a thriving business. I couldn't even imagine two thousand acres, let alone the kind of work to take care of it. Grandma had seemed so ladylike in her old age, more concerned with designs and fabrics than farm life.

I pulled the dustcovers off the furniture. An iron-frame bed, an oak dresser with a corroded mirror, bedside tables, a bookshelf crammed with old paperbacks, a camphorwood chest for linen. I flipped open the chest. The smell of mothballs was overwhelming.

I closed the door on the master bedroom, making the firm decision not to use it during my stay. That would seem too much like I was settling in for a long time. It would be far easier to clean up one of the smaller bedrooms, live out of my suitcases for three weeks. I chose one on the western side of the house so it would be nice and dark in the morning. I opened the window and shook out the dustcovers, feeling overwhelmed by all the tasks ahead. Cleaning. Sorting. I'd envisaged all this differently. I'd thought I'd sort a couple of boxes, send most of it to the dump, give the place a bit of spit and polish, then leave it for the real estate agents. Easy. But none of this task was actually going to be easy, nor was it going to be quick. Perhaps if I were able-bodied . . . But then if I were able-bodied, I wouldn't be here in the first place.

A loud knock and a friendly shout from the front door shook me out of my self-indulgent misery before it started. Visitors? Already? I'd heard stories about country people but had hoped they weren't true. I didn't want endless visitors. I wasn't good with people; I couldn't make small talk. I always said the wrong thing, or misunderstood, or ended up seeming like a princess.

I left the bedroom and went to the top of the stairs, then stopped. I really didn't want to be going up and down if I didn't have to.

"Who is it?" I called.

"Mr. Hibberd sent me," a woman's voice called. "The door's open, can I come in? I know you've got a crook knee."

Mr. Hibberd. I'd expressly told him I didn't need help. But

before I could answer, she was in, one of my suitcases in either hand, standing at the bottom of the stairs. She was young—perhaps in her early twenties—with fair hair in a ponytail. She wore jeans and a blue T-shirt.

"Hi," she said, "I'm Monica Taylor."

"Emma."

"I know who *you* are," she said, smiling. "Everybody in town knows who you are."

"Are they all going to come and visit unannounced?" I regretted the unkindness in my words as I said them. When had I turned into such a cranky old lady?

Monica shook her head. "Okay, listen. Mr. Hibberd paid me to come down here this afternoon. My dad used to look after the gardens here when he was a teenager, so we have a family history of helping out. I've got a bunch of stuff for you in my car. Fresh linen, groceries, even flowers. I'm not here to interfere or be your best mate, I'm just going to drop off the stuff and go."

I sighed. "I'm sorry. It's the stairs. They make me anxious. I know I have to get used to them, and it's not as bad as it used to be . . ." I tried a smile. "I'm really grateful. Give me a second and I'll come down."

"No need. I'll just drop the stuff in the kitchen." She was back out the front door, and I made my way down—descending stairs always hurt more—and then met her in the kitchen. She insisted I sit down—"I'm being paid, just let me earn it"—while she switched on the fridge, unpacked a new electric kettle, washed up some dishes and cups, and put the groceries away. All the while she chatted. She'd never met

Beattie, but everyone in the town was proud of her for her independence, her spirit, and the way she insisted on stocking her world-class fashion line with Tasmanian wool. I listened, eyeing the kettle and longing for a cup of tea.

Monica seemed to read my mind. "Now, how about I make you a cup of tea and then get out of your hair?"

"Let's have one together," I said, still trying to make up for my lack of manners earlier.

Monica beamed, transforming her pale little face. "I'd love that."

So we drank tea together. She told me about how she'd had a job in Hobart, but she'd recently grown impatient with city life—I tried not to laugh, Hobart was *so* small—and had come back to Lewinford to live with her brother, who taught English at the local high school. She got by working odd jobs and a few hours a week in the local pharmacy. As she talked, I thought about the huge task ahead of me. If I wanted to be out in three weeks, I'd need help.

"Monica," I said, "if you're looking for work, perhaps I could pay you to come up here a few days a week and help me sort the place out. I'm going to sell it, but I'll need to empty it first. There are hundreds of boxes, and the place needs a really thorough clean."

"I'd love to!" she squeaked "That would be so much fun. I was wondering how you'd manage with your knee the way it is. You'll definitely need help. When do you want me to start? Now? I can muck out the kitchen for you while you go and have a rest."

As much as it made me feel like a nana, I had to admit that

having a nap on nice clean sheets while somebody else got my kitchen ready was very appealing.

"Okay, then," I said. "Go right ahead."

Around three in the morning, I woke to the sound of rain and remembered I'd left all the windows open to air the place out. At first I lay in bed listening. It was only light rain, surely not enough to gush in windows. But then it intensified, the wind picked up, and I knew I'd have to get up. And face the stairs.

I turned on every light, memories of the night I'd fallen coming back to me. Made my way down, then felt a rush of stupid pride. I went from room to room, closing windows and locking the dust back inside. Then up the stairs again and back to bed.

By now, though, I was wide awake and couldn't sleep.

I stared at the ceiling for a long time, listening to the rain, working out what time it was in London and what Josh might be doing; who might be at the dance studio; if the leaves had all fallen off the big oak across from our apartment yet. Then, because that hurt too much, I thought about nothing at all for a while. I became aware that the temperature was dropping, and then all at once I wasn't comfortable anymore. I needed a blanket.

I rose once again and made my way to the master bedroom and the old linen chest.

I flipped open the lid. The smell was intense. I pulled out the sheets folded on top and shook them out. They were discolored and old. No point keeping them, really. The whole thing—chest and contents—could go to the dump at the end of the week. Monica had said her brother, Patrick, would come and help them with any large or heavy things.

More sheets, no blankets. Right at the bottom, a scratchy gray one that stank so strongly of mothballs it nearly made my eyes water. I figured I could just put on another layer of clothes for tonight. I was about to put it back in when I noticed an old exercise book lying in the bottom of the chest. I flipped through it. The pages were blank. But just when I was about to toss it back into the chest, a photograph slid out of the book and landed on the pile of sheets.

I picked it up. Black and white. The lower left corner was water-damaged. The couple in it were dressed humbly but tidily—he in a suit, she in a fitted dress with a hat and gloves—standing in the street. The woman held an infant with a frilly bonnet on.

My eyes took a second to realize. The woman was Grandma. Unmistakably. Her round eyes, her wide cheekbones, and that smile that I'd inherited, which always looked fabulous on her but somehow looked goofy on me.

But who was the man with her? Not Granddad, who was much taller and thinner than this man. And what about the child? Mum and Uncle Mike had both been born in the fifties, but this picture looked to have been taken much earlier than that.

The smell of mothballs was making my sinuses ache, so I put down the photo and threw the linen back in the box to lock it away. I went down to the bathroom to wash my hands, then came back to pick up the photo and take it to bed. By the light of the lamp, I studied it some more. The man had his arm around Grandma's waist; they looked like a couple. A couple with a child. But I must be mistaken. Perhaps the man was a cousin or a close family friend. We knew little about Grandma's family back in the UK. I turned over the thought in my mind, then slid the photograph into my bedside drawer and turned off the light to wait for morning.

I must have dozed enough to dream. I was back in London, and the apartment was full of birds. The noise was deafening. I startled awake and realized that the bird noise was real. I had never heard so many birds at once in my life. I rose, opened the window, and listened, astonished, as the air vibrated with their morning calls from the trees behind the house. Why on earth did people talk about the peace of country life? This was louder than traffic.

Dreaming about London had made me melancholy. I got back into bed and screwed my eyes tightly shut and resisted imagining what Josh was doing. I wondered if he'd even heard that I'd left England, that my career was in tatters.

I sat up. Of course he didn't know. News of my injury had made the papers, but he never read anything but the business and finance section. *Josh didn't know.* And perhaps if he did know, he might take pity on me and . . .

Ouch. Was I desperate enough to settle for pity?

I checked my watch next to the bed. It was eight in the evening in London. I couldn't ring Josh, but I could ring

Adelaide. She wasn't my employee anymore, but surely she'd still be willing to help.

First I had to conquer the stairs again. At the top, my heart fluttered. When was I going to get over this feeling? I figured there was nobody around to see me, so I sat on the top stair with my bad leg out in front of me and slid down on my bottom. All the way to the lower floor. Like a baby. At least it beat the feeling of vertigo.

There was only one phone, and it was connected to a wall in the hallway downstairs. I really needed a portable phone, with an outlet upstairs, or my dreaded mobile; but I wasn't going to be here long enough to worry about it. I'd make do. I dialed London, Adelaide's familiar number, and waited for her to pick up.

"Hello?" She sounded breathless, as though she'd been running.

"Hi, Adelaide. It's Emma."

Surprise. "Oh, Emma! I was expecting somebody else. New boss."

"Who are you working for now?"

She sighed. "Alberto Moretti."

"No! The Flying Fascist? How on earth did you get that job?"

"His last PA quit the same week you left for Australia. And yes, he's just as bad to work for as people say. He rings at all hours of the day and night, he wants everything yesterday." She chuckled. "It's *so* nice to hear from you. Reminds me of the good old days when I worked for somebody who was normal."

"Was I normal? I'm coming to understand I was pretty self-absorbed."

"Yes, but in a nice way. How's Sydney?"

"I'm not in Sydney. I'm in Tasmania, six butt-jarring kilometers of dirt road outside a small town called Lewinford. My grandmother left me a house, and I'm cleaning it up to sell it." I told her the whole story, even about the mysterious photograph I'd found last night. I knew I was rambling: too embarrassed to tell her why I really called.

After a few minutes she said, "I'm sorry, Emma. I'm really going to have to go. I'm sure Alberto's trying to call me, and he'll be cross if he can't get me."

"Wait. I just . . . Have you . . . heard or seen of Josh?"

Adelaide paused, thinking. "Josh? No."

"Adelaide, I know you'll think I'm a fool, but . . . I don't know if Josh ever knew about my accident and—"

"He knew," she said quickly. "He phoned me when you were in the hospital having one of your operations. He'd seen it in the paper."

I softened inside. "He did? Why didn't you tell me?"

"He asked me not to. Didn't want to . . . I don't know."

"Get my hopes up?"

"Yeah," she admitted. "That's what he said."

It stung. I took a second to catch my breath.

"I really have to go," she said.

"If you see him," I said, "tell him I'm back in Australia. Give him my mum's phone number. I'll be back in Sydney in a few weeks."

"Why don't you just call him yourself?" she said gently.

"You were together a long time. I'm sure he'd be pleased to hear from you."

I bit back a bitter laugh. "I don't want him to think I have my hopes up." I gave Adelaide all my contact details and let her go back to waiting for her phone call. I went to the front door and stepped out into the cool fresh morning. The birds were still calling, the sunlight was lying flat across the damp fields, the sky was the blue of dreams. It was a scene out of a glossy coffee-table book, and I knew I should have felt overwhelmed by the peace and beauty of it. But I just felt empty and lost.

After breakfast, Monica arrived. While I was completely overwhelmed by the task of cleaning out the house, she was practical and organized.

"Do you want me to set up the master bedroom for you?" she asked as she packed a dozen eggs and a package of bacon I hadn't asked for into the fridge.

"No, I'm going to sleep in the one closest to the bathroom," I said.

"The master bedroom's so nice and sunny, though."

"You know what would be good? If you could see if any of these keys open the cottage across the paddock."

"The old shearers' cottage," she said, scooping up the keys. "I'll see. And I'll get your bedroom and bathroom set up. That way at least the places you'll use the most will be clean."

I left her to it and went down to the sitting room to start sorting through boxes.

I came to realize that Grandma never threw anything away, and it became difficult for me to do so, too. She had every letter, every card, she'd ever received. Some of them were in neat folders: old electricity bills dating back years, not even for this address. They were easy to throw out. But correspondence between her and my grandfather, when he was away and she was home with the babies, was far more difficult to put on the pile. I found myself getting distracted constantly, stopping to read, then reminding myself that I didn't have time for this. I started a "might keep" pile on top of the piano, and as the days went by, it grew.

We tried every key on the ring and couldn't open the shearers' cottage. I'd peered through the grimy windows, but they were covered over with old gingham curtains. I phoned Mr. Hibberd, but he couldn't help, either. "I gave you all the keys I had," he said. "Call a locksmith."

I didn't bother. I figured it was probably empty.

By the end of the week, we'd piled up twelve boxes of rubbish by the door and needed help carting it all to the dump. Monica had organized for her brother to come on Saturday. So I wasn't surprised, while opening the windows to air the main bedroom, to see a man standing at the foot of the sick eucalyptus tree, looking up. He didn't see me, so I went down to greet him.

"Hello," I said. "You must be Patrick."

He turned his eyes to me. "Hello, yes, that's right. I was just looking at your tree."

I don't know what I'd been expecting of Monica's brother: perhaps a meaty country bloke in a blue singlet with a workingman's tan. But Patrick was a tall man with straight blond hair grown almost to his collar, pale skin, and heavy-lidded green eyes. He was also older than I'd expected. I knew that Monica was only twenty-one, but I estimated Patrick was in his thirties, like me. His face was more interesting than handsome. At first glance, he seemed to have something Eastern European about his bearing, like one of the great composers. A little intense, a little scruffy. I couldn't help comparing him to Josh, who was so polished and so well made.

"Ah, the tree," I said. "Possums, I'm told. I'm not even sure what kind of tree it is." Why was everyone so hung up on this tree? There were a gazillion trees in the forest.

"It's a cabbage gum," he said. "Don't be walking under it when it starts dropping branches."

"Where's Monica?"

"She's just making me a coffee. I hope that's all right."

"Of course. You're going to help us take the rubbish away?"

"Yes, I brought a friend's pickup truck." He indicated a ute standing in the driveway. My eyes flicked back to his face, and his gaze darted away.

"Well, then," I said. "Time for a coffee."

I led him to the kitchen. Monica's chatter seemed to relax him, and I got to see him smile. Then he didn't look so serious, and I could see the resemblance between him and his sister. I left them to get on with the trip to the dump and went back to the sitting room, where I was determined to be ruthless with my "might keep" pile. I sat on the piano stool and pulled handfuls of letters into my lap.

The morning passed in quiet as I reread letters, knowing

all the while that three weeks was not going to be enough unless I could be merciless in what I threw out. I tried to tell myself that all this stuff had sat here, not looked at, for years and years, and it had never bothered me. Therefore, it couldn't bother me if it were all thrown away now, right?

But it was such a beautiful narrative of Grandma and Granddad's life together. The letters weren't in any kind of order, so I dipped in and out of history at random. Granddad had been an MP, always traveling back and forth to Canberra while Grandma stayed in Sydney with the children and her business. It was long before e-mails or even cheap long-distance dialing, so they'd written letters. Good old-fashioned letters, full of detail and affection.

I heard Monica and Patrick return and looked at my watch. Almost lunchtime. I knew I should offer them lunch, especially Patrick, who was doing this for free, but I'd nearly run out of the groceries Monica had bought earlier in the week. I figured if I just kept my head down in here, they'd go home instead.

Sure enough, a soft knock at the door a few minutes later. I glanced up. It was Patrick.

"We're heading off now."

"Thank you so much. I hope you don't mind if I don't get up. My knee . . ."

His eyes were very focused on me. "I need to ask you something, if you don't mind."

I tensed. He was going to ask me out. Unbearable. I tried silence as a ward against it, but he rushed in anyway.

"I volunteer playing the piano for a little dance troupe of

kids. In Hobart. A friend of mine runs it. The kids are really special. I don't suppose you'd be interested in coming down and offering them a few tips? It would make them so pleased to meet a real ballerina."

Relieved and perhaps a little disappointed that he hadn't asked me out, I couldn't get my head around his question at first. "Wait, you play piano for them? I thought you were an English teacher."

"I am. Well, I have to be. More jobs in English teaching than music teaching, especially as I was fussy about working in this area." He cleared his throat. "Well? Do you think you'd like to come down to Hobart for an afternoon and meet them?"

I didn't know how to answer. I knew for certain I didn't want to teach dancing to kids, so I decided to appeal to his sense of pity. "It's a long way in the car. My knee is very uncomfortable."

"Maybe if it improves, you'll—"

"I'm only here for three weeks. Sorry."

He nodded, smiled. "I completely understand. Let me know if you change your mind."

Then he was gone, and I felt guilty, guilty, guilty. Why couldn't I go and help kids learn ballet?

But I reminded myself I wasn't going to be here long enough to make friends, or help people, or do anything but get this house ready for sale. And it wasn't right to get people's hopes up that things could be different.

SEVENTEEN

I hadn't forgotten about the photograph, though I hadn't looked at it again since the night I found it. In my mind, it had recomposed: the man and Grandma had walked farther apart, Grandma's grip on the child was more casual, less imbued with maternal love. But when I pulled it out again, I could see that neither of those things was true.

The man's arm around Grandma's waist was possessive. *She's mine.* The child's arms around her neck said the same thing. Anyone could tell, just by glancing at this photograph, that they were a family.

So I stared at it for a long time, then decided that the woman in the photograph wasn't Grandma at all. It was a cousin, somebody with a close family resemblance. My brain almost managed to convince me. Almost.

Except that this *was* Grandma, and Grandma appeared to have had another family.

I imagined what my mother would say if she saw the photograph, and I decided not to tell her just yet. I'd take it home with me, show her in person. Perhaps in the meantime,

I'd turn up some other photograph, one that made it clear I was overreacting. Or a letter from a male cousin saying, "Oh, remember that time when we were walking down the street in Hobart and you were holding my baby and everybody thought we were a couple?"

This time I brought it downstairs and propped it up on the table in the long hallway, right next to the phone.

Monica couldn't come. She phoned just after eleven to say that she was sick.

"It's some stomach bug," she said in a weak little voice. "I've been on the toilet all morning."

I thanked her for her frankness and told her to get better soon. I had vowed to start on the little front room today, the one that was piled high with boxes. Starting it without Monica was going to be difficult. In fact, opening the door and peering in filled me with despair.

Surely, surely, I could just take all these boxes straight to the dump. Their contents had been sealed up for decades; did it matter if they never saw the light of day? But then I remembered the photo, and I wondered what other things might be hidden in the depths.

The room itself was dark and small, so I pulled the first two cartons out into the hallway and sat with my leg stretched out. Pulled open the lid and started.

As the hours went past, I often wondered if someday Grandma had intended to come here and sort these things out for herself. There was no apparent system at all: the first box was filled with old vinyl records, cookbooks, and birthday cards. The second box contained half a dozen paperbacks, a bundle of business correspondence from the fifties, and sleeve upon sleeve of photos, the kind of photos that aren't good enough to make their way into an album. Here was my mum as a blurry teenager; Uncle Mike just out of shot, one skinny arm outstretched for a basketball hoop. The idea of Uncle Mike as a skinny person amazed me, and I looked at it for a long time. And the others: my mum and my uncle in their teens. The passage of time. I remembered myself as a teenager, and it seemed recent. The time from the start of my career at seventeen to the end of it at thirty-two had gone in a blink.

And now what, Emma, now what?

Damn Monica. Why did she have to get sick? I wasn't good on my own. My thoughts turned in on themselves. I wished I had a radio. I wished I'd brought my iPod. Something to distract me. But I'd resolutely left everything behind. Three weeks. I was here only three weeks.

I cast a glance at the roomful of boxes behind me. Even if I were here only a short period of time, I could still make myself comfortable. Buy a radio, a portable phone, a proper vacuum cleaner rather than that primitive push-along carpet sweeper Monica so bravely used.

But wasn't that settling in? The thought made me feel trapped. This wasn't London. This wasn't my life.

As I wiped away tears, I realized I hadn't given in to them for a while. Was I growing accepting of my situation? I couldn't bear the thought.

Still, having a few comforts would be practical. I dragged

myself to my feet and decided I'd walk into town, buy those things I needed. The exercise would be good for me, for my knee.

The day was sunnier than I'd expected, and I chased the shade all the way down the road. My knee ached, but I kept going, concentrating on the muscles around the joint.

The driver who'd brought me to Wildflower Hill from the airport had driven me right through Lewinford, but I hadn't yet been in the town. The main street was lined with archaic shopfronts of stone. But off and around the corner was a large grocery store with its own carpark, and a complex of shops. Some were empty, one was for the local member; then there were a craft shop, a flower shop, an electronics store, a vet, a café, a newsagent, and a chemist.

I bought a tiny vacuum cleaner, a CD player, and a portable phone—the only one in stock, and its box was covered in dust—at the electronics store, then signed for them to be delivered and went next door to the florist. I'd always loved fresh flowers, and the ones Monica had brought were already wilting.

The florist herself was an ancient woman with knotted hands. I ordered two bouquets: one of white lilies because I loved the smell, and one of mixed colors for the kitchen. I tried to take pleasure in the feeling of nesting, even if it was only on a small scale.

"Anything else, dear?" the ancient florist asked me.

I shook my head, and offered my credit card, and watched her as she made the transaction. Then I started to think that perhaps she had lived in this town her whole life; perhaps she'd known Grandma. And perhaps she could tell me about the photograph.

"Actually," I said, "there is one other thing. My grandmother used to live up at Wildflower Hill in the thirties. I don't suppose you knew her?"

"Beattie Blaxland? You're her granddaughter?" She glanced at my name on my credit card to double-check, then smiled widely. "I'm so pleased to meet you. You're the ballerina?"

"I am. I was." A pang in my chest. "I injured myself. I can't dance anymore."

She clicked her tongue. "That's a shame. Lewinford is proud of you, and we were proud of your gran, too. Nobody ever saw her, though. I think she came down only once or twice in the last sixty years."

"So you didn't know her?"

"No, love. I grew up a long way north of here. Only moved here when I married."

"Your husband? Did he know Beattie?"

She shook her head sadly. "He died a long time ago. Before I had a mind to ask."

"Is there anyone around who might have known her when she lived here?"

"I dare say there are one or two. You should be asking Penelope Sykes. She runs the local historical society. She's recorded a lot of old stories on tapes and is busy transcribing them one by one. Here, I'll give you her number."

Clutching Penelope Sykes's number in one hand and with two bunches of flowers under my arm, I paused outside the café. The coffee smelled good, but even bad coffee smells good. I was spoiled forever by the cafés in London and in Sydney.

As I was deciding. I heard my name. I glanced around to see Patrick approaching from the car park.

"Oh, hello," I said, smiling.

"How did you get to town?" he asked. He was wearing jeans and a white T-shirt. I surmised from the time that he had just finished work. I couldn't remember any teacher I'd ever had in high school dressed so casually, but then my mother did insist on my going to expensive private schools.

"I walked. I had to buy a few things."

He indicated the open door of the coffee shop. "Are you having a coffee?"

"I . . . can't decide." I smiled weakly. "I'm a little fussy."

"They make great coffee. I stop here every afternoon."

I didn't know whether to trust him, and he could tell. But he didn't seem to take offense.

"Come on, I'll buy you one," he said. "Then I can run you home, if you like."

"Really? That would be nice. The lift home, I mean. And the coffee. They would both be nice." I realized I was rambling, stopped myself. Followed him into the café.

He bought two takeaway lattes, and damn him, he was right. The coffee was superb. Then he opened up his little Mazda for me and told me to wait in comfort while he went to fetch my electrical goods and canceled my delivery.

I sat gratefully in the car, my leg stretched out the open door while I waited. On the floor of the car, I saw a bunch of black-and-white leaflets held together by a rubber band. The word "dance" caught my eye, so I picked up the bundle and slid one out.

I realized straightaway that this was the dance troupe Patrick played piano for, the Hollyhocks. One glance at the picture alerted me to the fact that he hadn't told me everything about the "really special" kids: most of them had Down's syndrome. I felt so small. Such enormous, embarrassing guilt. And I grew angry at him for putting me in that position.

Patrick was back, loading my things into the trunk of his car. I pulled my leg in, took a moment to get comfortable. Then he was behind the wheel, pulling out of the car park.

"Was I right about the coffee?" he said.

"Why didn't you tell me the dancing kids were disabled?"

He glanced at me, then back at the road. "You're angry."

"I feel like you made a fool out of me."

"Look, Emma. I know you're injured. I didn't want to cause you any pain. I thought if I told you everything about the Hollyhocks, then you might feel pressured to come and see them. It's a long drive to Hobart, especially for somebody with a sore knee who isn't used to the distances." He offered me a smile. "Don't feel bad that you said no."

But I did feel bad. I felt like the worst kind of selfish diva. It would cost me only a mildly aching knee to go to Hobart, to meet these kids and talk to them about dancing. "I'll come," I said.

He was shaking his head already. "No, absolutely not. You said you couldn't travel."

"I'll be fine if I can take a few rest stops on the way."

"I won't hear of it, Emma. I'd feel like I imposed too much

on you. You're here only a short time, and Monica's off sick for a few days. You have so much to do."

"Really, I'll come. When do they rehearse again?"

He fought with himself silently, then said, "Every Saturday morning from ten until twelve. That's a flyer for their concert coming up in a couple of months."

"What time will you pick me up?"

He was reluctant, I could tell, but he also dearly wanted me to come. "If you insist . . ."

"I do insist."

"Around eight, then. That'll give us plenty of time for a short rest along the way and to get a coffee when we get to Hobart."

"Great. Fine."

He waited a few moments. Then said, "Are you sure?"

"Yes," I said quickly, wondering what I'd gotten myself into. "I'm sure."

I had no CDs to play, so I relied on the radio. I found a classical music station that played jazz in the evenings, poured myself a glass of wine, and sat down with a box to be sorted. This one was old, the cardboard falling apart ungracefully. Inside were old—very old—ledgers of the business here at Wildflower Hill. Thin exercise books with yellowed pages all covered in neat ink. I carefully tried to follow the transactions but wasn't at all sure what they meant. I recognized Beattie's handwriting in the columns, but there was also other handwriting. Not as measured as Beattie's. A man's handwriting, I imagined. But what man?

I shook myself. Imagination getting away with me again. Beattie hadn't run the whole farm alone; she would have had employees.

I pulled book after book out of the cupboard, thinking about the woman from the historical society. Would she want all these? Perhaps she could make sense of them. It seemed a shame to throw them away. But I wasn't at all sure I wanted to involve myself with a community organization. I didn't want visitors.

Then I found a folder held together with red ribbon. In it were dozens of contracts for the buying and selling of items. Furniture. Sheep. Even a contract for a piece of land that Beattie had sold off in 1934. And at the bottom of the pile was the contract for Wildflower Hill itself.

November 1934; the sale to Beatrice Alison Blaxland from Raphael William James Blanchard. For the sum of zero pounds.

I looked at this figure for a long time. Somebody named Raphael William James Blanchard had *given* Grandma Wildflower Hill. Only that couldn't be right, because Mum had told me differently. Wildflower Hill was a run-down business, losing money badly during the Depression. Beattie had inherited a small sum from an old uncle. The rest of the money she'd borrowed from the bank and had to struggle terribly to pay it off in those first years.

I itched to call Mum. Ask her if she knew who Raphael

Blanchard was. But I thought about the photograph and knew I had to be careful. Mum was drawn to drama like ants are drawn to honey. Besides, there were other ways of finding out who he was.

By the time I'd waited for it to be breakfast time in London and a decent hour to call, I'd convinced myself that the man with my grandmother in the photograph was this Raphael Blanchard, that they had a secret love child, that he'd given Beattie the property to keep her quiet . . . Of course, none of this fit with what I knew about Grandma, but the more wine I drank, the more plausible it became.

I phoned Adelaide. "Did I wake you?" I said.

"No." She yawned. "Um . . . yes. I don't have to lie to you anymore if you're annoying, given that you're not my boss, right?"

"Sorry," I replied. "I need help. I'm looking for information about somebody named Raphael Blanchard. I have no Internet connection here. Could you Google him for me?"

"Is he a dancer?" She yawned again.

"No. Why are you so tired?"

"The Flying Fascist had a party last night."

"And he invited you?"

"I handed out the canapés. Wait a sec, just sitting down at my computer now. What's the name?"

I spelled it for her. I heard keys tapping.

"All right. Which one?"

"Which one?"

"Raphael Blanchard the first, the second, or the third? Minor nobility."

Nobility? "In England?"

"Yes."

"The one who might have been in Australia in the thirties."

More tapping, more yawning. "That's the first. He lived in Australia from 1930 to 1934, in Tasmania, apparently. Am I looking up local history for you from London? Can you appreciate the irony?"

"Is there a picture of him?"

"Sure is. It's small . . . No, wait. Here's a bigger one."

I walked to the hall table and picked up the photograph of my grandmother with the strange man. "Describe him. Is he stocky, square-jawed?"

"Not at all. Bit of a pudding with wavy dark hair and girlie eyes."

I looked at the man in the photograph. There was no way he could be described as a pudding with wavy hair and girlie eyes. Still, I had difficulty letting go of the idea.

"Want me to fax this to you?"

"I don't have a fax," I said.

"Mail it, then?"

That would take too long. "I know. Could you look up the local high school's fax number and send it there? Lewinford High School. Mark it to the attention of Patrick Taylor and say it's for me." I heard myself and immediately felt guilty. "Sorry, Adelaide. I know I'm not your boss anymore, but—"

"It's fine, Em. I'll send it later today. You should get yourself set up with e-mail, though."

"I won't be staying that long," I said. "I'll be gone soon." Boy, was I tired of hearing myself say that.

* * *

Monica, recovered from her bug, returned to work on Thursday with the fax from her brother.

"So who is he?" she asked as she handed over the folded picture.

I unfolded it carefully. Disappointment. "Not who I thought it might be," I said. "Another mystery. This man apparently gave my gran the farm in 1934, but I don't know why."

"You should get on to Penelope Sykes."

"Yes, the florist told me that." But I was reluctant to go down that path, making new acquaintances, trying myself tighter to the town. Perhaps I'd find everything I needed to know right here in the house.

On Friday morning I was sitting at the kitchen table, eating toast and drinking coffee, when there was a knock at the door. Monica had her own key, so I knew it wasn't her. I rose reluctantly—I liked neither being interrupted while eating nor unexpected guests—and went to answer it. A small woman with tightly curled black hair stood there. She might have been in her fifties, but any gray was assiduously dyed out.

"Can I help you?" I asked, thinking of my coffee cooling on the table.

She held out a forthright hand to greet me. "I'm Penelope Sykes. I hear you've been asking about me."

"That's not strictly true; people have been telling me about you," I said. "I wasn't expecting you."

"I was on my way past. I'm driving up to my sister's in Launceston for the weekend. Is now a good time to chat?"

"Come in," I said reluctantly. "I'm just having breakfast."

Penelope studied each detail of the house avidly as we walked through to the kitchen.

"Have you never been to Wildflower Hill before?" I asked, wondering if it would be rude to drink my coffee without offering her one, knowing it would be.

"No, it's been locked up for decades. A lot of history in here."

"Coffee?"

She shook her head, and I warmed to her. I sat and resumed my breakfast. "There is a lot of history here. I have some books you can take, old records for the farm."

Her eyes widened. "I'd love that."

I shrugged. "They were going to the dump otherwise."

"Don't throw away anything like that. I'll take it. One day I'm going to write a book about Tasmania during the Depression." She sat opposite me. "My mother knew your gran."

"She did?"

"Not well. But she used to come and play up at Wildflower Hill some days in the school holidays. They lived on the neighboring farm for two years. Mum used to tell me there was a little girl who came every school holiday, and they used to play together all day. I can't remember her name, though."

"Would your mother remember?"

"She died four years ago."

"I'm sorry. Do you know anything else about the little girl?

You see, I've stirred up a bit of a mystery." I told her about the photograph, and she asked me to fetch it, which I did.

"This was taken in about 1929 or 1930," she said. "I can tell from the clothes but also the street scene. It's Hobart. There were street photographers who would take photos of passersby, then sell them at the end of the week very cheaply. But this shop here . . ." She jabbed her finger at a shop sign I hadn't even noticed. "MacWilliam farming supplies. They collapsed in 1931, during the Depression."

"So this child . . . ?"

"She's about a year old here, which would make her the same age as my mother. I wonder if it's the same girl she played with. She had red hair. They'd run about like savages, Mum said, completely unsupervised."

"Do you think she was Beattie's daughter?"

Penelope shook her head. "No. Mum said a black car would arrive at the end of the holidays and come for her. A man and a woman. Mum always assumed they were her parents."

I felt let down, though I wasn't sure why. "Oh. I see."

"I guess that Beattie was an auntie of some sort."

"Beattie didn't have any siblings."

"Then they must have been close family friends . . . Have you finished your breakfast? I'd love to see those books."

I drained the last of my coffee, and took her to the sitting room, and gratefully off-loaded onto her the books that were piled up on the piano. She gazed longingly at some of the letters, but they were too private and too much part of our family to give away. She promised to go through some of her materials at home and see if Beattie was mentioned anywhere else. She left just as Monica was arriving.

I put the photograph back on the hall table, feeling oddly disappointed.

EIGHTEEN

Saturday morning was overcast, threatening to rain, and I woke up with a scratchy throat and a headache. I thought about canceling my trip to Hobart with Patrick; I thought about staying in bed all day. But I would have felt too guilty. A hot shower cleared my head a little, and rather than my usual jeans, I put on the only dress I had packed. I brushed my hair out loose and hoped I looked nice but wasn't quite sure why I hoped it. I'd thought at the start that Patrick was attracted to me, but I hadn't really any evidence for it now. He was unlike most of the men I'd met. He wasn't polished and confident like Josh, nor was he rough and blokey like my dad. He was quiet but not shy. Gentle but not weak. Not that I was falling for him; I was still in love with Josh. I was just intrigued by him. He was different.

Patrick was dead on time, didn't say anything about my dress or my hair, and we drove away from Wildflower Hill just as the rain started. He seemed happy not to talk, so I watched the landscape speed by outside my window while the windshield wipers beat a rhythm. Sheep stood still and miserable in the downpour under dead crooked trees.

"Rotten weather," he said at last.

"I quite like the rain."

"No good for driving, though." Then he was quiet again.

I shifted in my seat so I could steal a glance at him. He had such a serious face, courtesy of severe eyebrows and a straight-edged nose. Then I turned my eyes to the windshield. The rain sheeted down, and Patrick slowed.

"I'm sorry, I'd planned to stop at a little town not far up the road for coffee. But it might take a little longer to get there in this weather."

I realized at that instant that he was being quiet because he was nervous. He was holding the steering wheel tightly, and his whole body was drawn up tautly.

"Are you okay?" I asked. "Wet-weather driving not your thing?" I tried to sound light, friendly.

He didn't smile. "Ah, you could say that." Then a pause. "Our parents . . . There was an accident . . . Monica was seven, I was seventeen. We were in the car. Dad lost control in the wet. He and Mum both died."

I was speechless with embarrassment for a moment, then my imagination conjured what Patrick must have experienced in those moments, and I was speechless with pity. "I'm so sorry," I managed. "I didn't know about your parents." Though, on reflection, I had wondered why Monica never mentioned her mother or father. "Take your time. My knee is fine at the moment." Then curiosity caught me. "So what happened afterward? Who looked after you and Monica?"

"We did," he said. "Or rather, I did. It was right at the end of my final year of high school, and there was talk of sending Monica off to our uncle's place in Melbourne, but we really wanted to stay together. We inherited the family home so we had somewhere to live. I got a part-time job, and we just managed. It was really tough. I worked whenever I could, I relied on the neighbors to pick her up from school when I was down at the university. I always felt guilty that she was growing up in such a strange way, but then she'd lost her parents, so I suppose it doesn't get worse than that. Not my fault."

"Of course. You did a brilliant job. Monica's a lovely young woman."

"I took the job at Lewinford High School when Monica was still there. Everything was easy for a few years then." He shrugged. "I did my best."

I tried to imagine what it had been like for him. No teenage tomfoolery, no going out on drinking binges with mates. Working and looking after his little sister instead. It went a long way toward explaining his nature.

I tried to remember what I was doing at the end of my final year. I was failing high school because I didn't pay any attention, thought I was above it all. I'd already been accepted into two dance academies in the United States and was waiting to hear from one in London. Mum had wanted me to study in Australia. We always rubbed each other the wrong way, Mum and I. She was too controlling, and I was too single-minded. There had been an enormous fight, perhaps the worst of my life. I told her I hated her. I was a child who thought she was a grown-up. Patrick had all the responsibility of a grown-up but

was little more than a child. As a rule, I tried not to be embarrassed about things I did in the far past, but that thought
made me squirm for the spoiled brat I had been.

"So how did you get involved with the Hollyhocks?" I asked.

"Marlon," he said. "You'll meet him this morning. He was
a drama teacher briefly at the school. It's his project, really,
and he used to have this ancient old battleax who played
piano for him." He smiled sheepishly. "Sorry, but she really
was a battleax. Used to shout at the kids. He asked if I could
replace her for a few months while he found somebody else,
and that was two and a half years ago."

He talked for a little while about the kids. It had started
out as a project between four mothers of children with
Down's syndrome, then it kept growing. Some of the children
were autistic, some blind, one was even deaf but felt the beat
of the music through the floor. They were drawn from all over
the southern parts of Tasmania. He told her about the concert
they put on last year and how the prime minister happened
to be in Hobart and turned up at the last minute to watch,
about how the dancing helped the kids with confidence, with
coordination, and how they made intense friendships with
each other. I felt myself growing apprehensive: he seemed so
natural and accepting of their differences. I was sure I'd be
awkward, say the wrong thing.

The rain eased as we pulled in to our first rest stop and
bought takeaway coffees. I walked around for a few minutes,
noted that the ache wasn't too bad, and urged Patrick to keep
driving while the weather held. We were in Hobart by a quarter past nine.

The Hollyhocks practiced in the theater of a private school looking down on the Derwent River. Patrick led me to wide double doors that were already open onto a large foyer. Beyond, a compact theater space waited. The seats were tiered, the stage on the ground. A tall, dark-haired man in tight leggings greeted us.

"Oh, how lovely to meet you!" he enthused, grasping my hand and shaking it firmly. "You look beautiful! That frock is *divine* on you! I've only seen you in pictures. You're twice as gorgeous in real life."

"Thank you," I said, readjusting to his extreme sociability. "And thank you for letting me come today."

All his sentences were punctuated with dramatic emphasis. "No, no, thank *you*. The kids don't know you're here yet, but they are going to *love* meeting a real live ballerina! My God! They will die! Especially Mina. Right, Patrick?"

Patrick's gentle voice was in deep contrast to Marlon's. "Mina Ballerina," he said. "She loves ballet."

"She's a *star*!" Marlon squeaked. "You're going to love her."

I took a seat in the front row while they set up the room. Patrick retrieved an electric piano from the backstage area and ran through some pieces on it. Marlon pranced about making up dirty lyrics until the first children and their parents arrived, when he became so dignified and circumspect that I wondered if I'd imagined my first impression of him. Slowly, the front rows filled up with parents, while children—from small ones to young adults—lined up with Marlon to have armbands attached to their wrists. Pink for left, blue for right. Ten of the eighteen had the almond eyes and square features of Down's syndrome, but apart from that, the children varied widely. I watched them getting ready. Some seemed brighter, more connected somehow. Others were off in a dream. Other children were alternately very focused or noisy or apprehensive and clinging to their parents. But when Patrick started playing the opening strains of an old love song from a musical that I couldn't place, they all snapped to attention and moved into their positions. Marlon started calling, "Move pink! Move blue! Turn! Arms up and . . . slowly."

I admit I didn't think it could be a pretty sight. I thought they would be clumsy, awkward, unable to follow instructions properly. But there was a childish grace about the dancers, a deep enthusiasm infused through their limbs and shining in their faces. It was beautiful. I had never felt more human. I blinked back tears—I didn't want anyone to think I felt sad or sorry—and let the slow, melancholy music wash over me.

As it finished, the parents and I applauded loudly. Marlon turned and gave a theatrical bow. "And now," he said, "our special guest. Guys, this gorgeous creature in the first row is a famous ballerina, Emma Blaxland-Hunter."

I wasn't sure what to do, so I smiled and gave a little wave. In seconds, the children were crowding in front of me, asking for autographs, calling out questions. I didn't know who to look at or answer first, but then an older, dark-haired girl with Down's syndrome slid into the seat next to me and took my hand. I turned to her.

"I'm Mina," she said.

"Nice to meet you," I replied, smiling.

"Mina Ballerina."

"Yes, I've heard of you."

"Could you teach me ballet?"

She spoke thickly through her tongue, but I could understand her perfectly, unlike some of the others. "I . . . I can show you a few moves, I guess."

"I already know all the positions. Let me show you." And she tugged my hand and pulled me out of my chair.

I found myself in the center of the stage with a crowd of children around me. Mina stood in front of me and went through the positions. I helped correct her arms on fourth position and her feet on fifth, though physically, she simply couldn't manage the last one.

"Show me something else?" she asked.

I glanced at Marlon, who smiled and shrugged. I had no idea what Mina was capable of. "How about the first arabesque position?"

"Is that more standing still? Because I'd rather learn a dance. I like *Swan Lake*."

"The dances from *Swan Lake* are very hard. I'd have to think about it. I'm not—"

"Can you dance for us?"

"I . . . No, I can't. I injured my knee. It doesn't work properly anymore."

Mina nodded reverently. "That happened to my friend," she said. "She had a car accident and she's in a wheelchair."

Marlon interrupted. "Okay, Mina. Let other people have a turn with Emma. Who wants autographs?"

A general chorus of "Me!" went round, and as I signed autographs, I tried to think about what kind of dance I could teach

Mina. I felt that I'd disappointed her. She clearly hadn't the physical ability for anything from the great choreographers: she could move her arms well enough, but her lower-body flexibility was always going to let her down. Yet she was keen and was clearly crazy for ballet. And having watched the first dance, I could see that she stood out in terms of her ability.

I watched the rest of the rehearsal, lost in thought. Marlon was wonderful with the children, firm and loving, occasionally cracking cheeky jokes to make them laugh. Patrick played beautifully and was patient and calm.

As the rehearsal finished and the children began to file out, chatting happily, Mina approached me again. "Will you come and see us next week?"

"I don't know," I said. "I'll try to. Patrick has to drive me, so I'll have to ask him."

"Will you teach me some ballet?"

"Mina, I'm really only here in Tasmania for a little while."

Patrick, who had heard his name, came over to join us. "Come on, Mina, your dad will be waiting out front." He led her off. I picked up my bag and hitched it over my shoulder.

Patrick returned. "She lives alone with her dad," he explained.

"He must be proud."

"He never comes in."

"Really?"

"Drops her off and picks her up. I've only ever seen him through his car windshield. She's the oldest here; she's just turned seventeen."

"She seems very keen."

"She's amazing. But I think she's sad sometimes. All the dances we do are to old show tunes or pop ballads. I think she really would like to do something more like real ballet."

I opened my mouth to say that I could help, but then I changed my mind. I'd be gone soon. Best not to raise anyone's expectations.

Monica and I were making headway. I was getting better at throwing things out. I didn't need to keep every birthday card Grandma had ever received, every drawing Uncle Mike had done in kindergarten. I had a week to go before my flight, and if I worked around the clock, I believed I was going to make it. Monica stayed longer hours. I sorted boxes until the early hours, then fell to sleep dreaming of more boxes filled with random, unidentifiable things.

Then Monica found the key. She was cleaning out the dining room, pulling out all the drawers in the oak sideboard one by one. The key wasn't hidden, it had just slipped to the back of the drawer and become jammed.

"Look," she said, standing in the threshold to the kitchen, where I was sorting business letters on the table. I glanced up. She held it out, told me where she'd found it.

"It's got to be for the shearers' cottage, right?" I said.

"It's the only door we haven't been able to unlock."

"Can you go and have a look?"

She nodded once, then took the stairs down through the laundry. I was skimming through an old letter to Grandma from a wool classer. I could barely understand what was being

said, whether the letter was important. It was dated 1938, so
Penelope Sykes might want it. I sighed, started a new pile.
Went to the next letter. I started thinking about a coffee
break.

Then Monica thundered up the stairs. "Emma!"

I turned; she stood at the top of the stairs, panting.

"Oh my God," she said. "It's full."

"Full?"

"Come and look for yourself."

I eased myself out of my chair. I'd learned that getting up
after sitting still for a long time was a killer. Then I followed
Monica carefully down the stairs and out through the laundry.

The sunshine was uninterrupted, but it was still cool. The
morning breeze moved gently, rustling through the tall gums
on the edge of the property. A pair of rabbits bounded away
from us. We let ourselves out of the gate and across the overgrown green field to the shearers' cottage, an old stringy-bark
cabin on the edge of the property. The door stood open. Cobwebs everywhere. And boxes. More boxes.

In every room, boxes.

"Jesus," I said.

"When does your plane leave?"

"Sunday at one." I turned to her. She was smiling, and although I felt overwhelmed at the thought of more boxes—so
many more boxes—I had to laugh. "I'm not going home, am
I?" I said.

She shrugged. "I guess you could just take it all to the
dump.

But I couldn't. I'd only just begun to realize that I was looking for something in these boxes. I was looking for the story behind Grandma buying a sheep farm for nothing, for who the little girl in the photograph was, for what Grandma did before she had Mum and Uncle Mike and settled down to life as a businesswoman and an MP's wife. I didn't want to miss anything.

I opened the lid to the nearest box and peered in. Mostly books. Perhaps it wouldn't take long after all. "I'll ring the airline, cancel my flight. Rebook it later, when I know I'm truly finished." That felt better; the sense that I was racing the clock had disappeared. "I'll get the house properly ready for sale, even if it takes another month."

"You want me to stay on?" Monica asked.

"Absolutely. I couldn't do it without you."

"Do you want me to clean out the master bedroom, then?"

"No," I said quickly. I was superstitious: if I moved into Grandma's old bedroom, that would mean I was staying forever. "I'm happy where I am."

The two rooms I loved best in the house were the kitchen and the sitting room. My bedroom was just where I slept, and I didn't tend to go up there until I was so tired that I couldn't keep my eyes open anymore. The sun in the kitchen kept me there during the day, and the fireplace in the sitting room kept me there at night. It wasn't really cold enough for a fire, but I loved the sound of it, the glow of firelight. In London

I'd only ever had central heating. My evenings involved listening to the radio, drinking a glass or two of wine, and reading old letters.

I was sitting on the couch, well into my second glass of red, reading one from Granddad to Grandma from an official trip he took to Hong Kong, when "The Waltz of the Flowers" from Tchaikovsky's *Nutcracker* came on the radio.

I had to stop everything and listen, even though it hurt me. My first professional role as a soloist had been Dew Drop in Balanchine's version, and this had been my moment. It was agony, here at the end of my career, to be reminded so brightly and sharply of the start of my career. My hopes. My dreams. My muscles and sinews seemed to twitch, remembering the movements, but I was still as a stone.

When it finished, I took a moment to gather myself, finished my glass of wine. I began to think about that first production. Balanchine's choreography called for children to play the roles of Clara and the Nutcracker, and he'd simplified the roles. I was no great choreographer, but I knew Dew Drop's dance inside out. Was there a way I could simplify it? Not for a child but for a girl with Down's syndrome?

I stood and flicked the radio off, tested my weight on my knee in the middle of the sitting room floor. Like me, Mina couldn't do anything complex or flexible with her legs. I hummed the tune and thought about some of the movements Marlon gave to the children. There was a lot of stomping and kicking. I tried to moderate these movements so they were more elegant, more like something Mina would think was ballet. Then I went through some of the arm positions, adding more to them so that they were telling the story that my feet couldn't. A vision flashed into my head: Mina, dressed all in pale colors, dancing in the center of the stage. The others, in white, around her, echoing her movements. It wouldn't be real ballet, not even close. But it would *feel* like ballet, especially to Mina, who longed for that music.

Then I sat back down. Did I really want to get involved? How long would I be here, anyway? If the boxes in the shearers' cottage were just books and knickknacks, I'd be tossing most of it out by the end of the week, be on a plane to Sydney a day or so later.

But Sydney wasn't where I wanted to be, either. Where I wanted to be was in my life six months ago. I bit my lip, determined not to cry or to feel sorry for myself. Determined not to feel the great emptiness.

Over the next few days, I kept refining the dance for Mina. All the time wondering if I was being an idiot. I didn't really know anything about her or what she was capable of. But I just kept getting this vision of her in my imagination: her pale skin, the lights on her, moving with childish grace to the sublime music. I was almost certain I'd made it simple enough yet still sufficiently beautiful and elegant to satisfy a girl who loved *Swan Lake.*

Finally, I decided I'd have to speak to Patrick directly, show him what I'd come up with. I was prepared for him to say it wouldn't work; I'd be disappointed, but it would be better than getting Mina's hopes up over nothing.

I didn't tell Monica where I was going, though I knew she'd find out. Patrick would tell her. She'd offer to drive me to town, and then she'd be there when I showed Patrick my ideas. Was I embarrassed about that? Perhaps. Was I hoping to be alone with Patrick?

Perhaps.

I told her I was going for a long walk and left her sweeping the shearers' cottage. She was singing along to a CD she'd brought with her, happy enough. Always happy. I found it impossible to believe sometimes, considering she had lost her parents so young. Patrick had done a wonderful job of keeping her stable under the circumstances. There was so much to admire about him.

I wasn't falling for Patrick. It was Josh whom I thought about at night before I went to sleep. I'd go over the first time we met, or the night we moved into the apartment, or any one of the wonderful, glamorous moments in our wonderful, glamorous life. Sometimes my thoughts were the fantasies of a teenage girl. I composed elaborate scripts of what he would say and do on the day he begged me back, imagined in keen detail the feel of him when he took me in his arms at the airport, how he might cry over the pain he'd caused me. Then I'd grow embarrassed for myself and stop, resort to tears of my own instead.

But still, Patrick intrigued me. He was like nobody I'd ever met. I felt good when I was with him. I turned up at the school just after three o'clock, and the secretary at the office directed me to the English department's staff room.

When Patrick saw me, he smiled and tripped over his words. "Emma. What are you doing here?"

"Hi. Surprise," I said, realizing I sounded like an idiot. "I wanted to show you something."

"Hang on just a second." He shut down his computer and stood up, pulling on a gray hoodie. "What is it?"

I explained to him what I'd been working on. He nodded, didn't show any real sign of excitement. I started to fade . . .

"'The Waltz of the Flowers'?" he said. "It sounds a little complex for her."

"You'll have to let me show you. But if you think it's too hard for her, that's fine. I just imagine she'd be beautiful at it."

He smiled, hitching his backpack over his shoulder. "Okay, I'll take you down to the music room, and you can show me."

We walked through the school as it emptied. He'd said that it was a high school, but there were kids from all age groups here. Patrick was tall, with a very straight back, and seemed quite oblivious to the older teenage girls who glanced at him under their eyelashes as he walked by. The music room was empty but unlocked. A low stage was set up in the corner, but it was covered in boxes full of musical instruments.

Patrick opened the cupboard and found a CD player. "I'm fairly sure we have that music on a CD," he said, rummaging in the cupboard.

Now I was starting to feel foolish. He was going to put a CD on, and I was going to dance to it. But not the dancing I could do, not the dancing I used to do, when I was in full flight. For one of the first times in my life, I felt awkward in my own body. Embarrassed.

He found the CD and put it on, and I steeled myself and thought about Mina. Went through the movements. Now he started to smile broadly, nodding.

"Yes, yes," he said. "Keep going. It's beautiful."

I wanted to say, "You should have seen what I used to be able to do." I wanted him to see me dance, to watch what my body was capable of, to know the grace and beauty that I could pull down from the sky. I stumbled to a halt, not meeting his eye. "Anyway, there's more of the same," I said. "And about six other kids could be involved. Is it worth my coming to another rehearsal?"

Patrick flicked off the CD player and steepled his hands against his lips, thinking. "I think that's up to you," he said at last.

"Up to me?"

"Mina will want to. Her father will be happy to let her. But it could take her a little while to learn it all."

"Oh. I'd have to teach her? I couldn't just show it to Marlon?"

He thought about this. "Perhaps not," he said slowly. "I think you would need to do it."

"Okay, well . . . I think I'll be around for another three weeks or so."

"Perhaps six?"

He was asking me to stay. Did I want to stay? It wasn't even a question I could answer. There was nothing for me back in Sydney.

"Yes, perhaps six weeks. I can't sell the place until March, anyway."

"If you could get us through to the Christmas concert . . ."

I wanted to say no. I didn't want to commit. Not to anything. But why not? Was I imagining that my knee would suddenly get better? That I would be off, back to London, to resume my career? Tears pricked my eyes.

Patrick stepped forward, gently touched my wrist. "I'm so sorry, Emma. This is too much to ask of you."

"No, no. I'm fine. I'm just thinking," I said, embarrassed by my sudden tears, surprised by the warmth of his hand on my arm.

"Mina will be fine. She doesn't need to learn a special dance."

"She does," I said, feeling it deeply. "I know what it's like to be young and obsessed with ballet." I forced air into my lungs, sniffed back the last tears. "I'm sorry. I didn't mean to cry."

"Tears come when they come," he said, withdrawing his hand. "Do you want me to run you home? I can pick up Monica."

"I'll stay," I said. "I mean, I'll stay here in Tassie. Until the Christmas concert. I'd like to help out."

"That's . . ." He looked like he was trying to hide a grin. "That's great, Emma. It's amazing."

The phone's ringing woke me early the next morning. Early? It was eight o'clock. I'd slept in. Too much wine.

I felt for the receiver on my bedside table. "Hello?" I managed.

"It's Penelope Sykes. I have something for you, and I

wondered if it might be all right for me to drop by this morning on my way through."

At least it seemed people were figuring out I didn't like drop-ins. "Sure. What is it?"

"I was flipping through those old record books when I found it. It's a letter. Personal. *Very* personal." A short chuckle. "You should probably keep it."

I sat up, my curiosity piqued. "I'd be grateful if you dropped it in."

"Good. I'm just leaving now. I'll be there in twenty minutes."

I showered quickly and got dressed for the day and tried to shake the hungover feeling. I knew that drinking a lot and alone wasn't good, but last night I'd fallen all the way into the pit and couldn't climb out. Today would be better, I promised myself.

Penelope was on my doorstep right on time.

"Will you come in for tea?" I asked as she handed me the letter.

"No, I'll be on my way. I don't want to interrupt you."

I realized I must have seemed unfriendly, perhaps even hostile, on her last visit. "It's no trouble," I said, smiling too much, feeling like a fool. "I've pulled out a few more things for you."

"Call me next week, perhaps, at a time that suits you." She tapped the letter softly. "There's no addressee, no date. But it was in the back of a book from 1939. I assume from the record books that it's your grandmother's handwriting." Then she was backing away, heading for her car.

I opened the letter, still standing in the doorway. A light breeze plucked at its corner. Penelope was right, it was Grandma's handwriting. It started midsentence, so it was only one sheet of a longer letter.

> *... but love isn't a thing to be told what to do, and I am not a woman to be told what to do. I love you, and whatever anyone else says, nothing can change that immovable fact. I feel as though I have loved you always, as though you were a star in the sky at my birth, waiting patiently for me. When I look at you, my ribs ache. My skin burns. I'm thinking of you now and flushing warm. Is there anything more natural and beautiful than such a reaction? Even if we turn off our minds, turn off our hearts, our bodies still draw to each other. It's primitive. If there is a God, it is what He wished for us. When you are inside me, we complete a circle that was never meant to be broken. I don't care what they're saying in town; they are small-minded fools who can't see beyond the surface. Be reassured, my darling, that you are mine and I am yours. They can't hurt us.*

I had to take a moment to catch my breath. The passion of the letter wasn't just in the words, it was in the strength with which the ink had been applied to the page. I knew this was my grandmother's writing—the same handwriting that had written me good wishes on all my birthdays, the same handwriting that had told my grandfather he had missed my uncle Mike's first steps—but it couldn't possibly be written by my grandmother. If it was in a book from 1939, then that was long before she met Granddad.

Unless it was to Granddad and had just found its way into the back of the old book somehow.

But even as I tried to rationalize it, I knew I was fighting a losing battle. This letter wasn't to Granddad. None of Grandma's letters to Granddad sang with that much passion. They were full of phrases like "thank you for being so reasonable" and "you are very good to send me such a lovely gift" and "when you're home, we should organize the Christmas holidays."

When you are inside me . . .

"Jeez, Grandma," I muttered. "You're full of surprises."

NINETEEN

Beattie: Tasmania, 1935

Two thousand sheep, an empty house, and a failing business. Mikhail had caught a rabbit, and now Beattie carved its stringy meat onto two plates. There were potatoes, too, from the vegetable patch. No dining table to eat on. In fact, Beattie kept the rooms without furniture locked up. The echoes drove her mad. Mikhail had moved his bed into Alice's old downstairs room and had helped Beattie maneuver her bed upstairs to the master bedroom. She'd bought a table for the kitchen. Every other room was empty.

She'd done her best in the two months she'd owned Wild-flower Hill. But how was she to tell Mikhail that her best wasn't enough? That she would have to sell and that they would both have to leave? He had nowhere to go.

Along with the house and the sheep had come the debts. The wool clip had not been enough to pay them off. Beattie's neighbor, the canny Jimmy Farquhar, had been quick to offer to buy some of her land. Under Leo Sampson's advice, she sold him three hundred acres. She used most of it to cover her debts, some to pay out her employees—Alice left immediately, but Terry and Mikhail had stayed on—the rest she put aside. There would be no more money for a year, until the next wool clip. She had to make it last. She couldn't spend it all on furniture and food. So she made do with nothing.

When Lucy came, it would have to be different. She would buy meat and porridge and honey, though Lucy would still have to sleep in Beattie's bed. Henry would think she was a fool for keeping the house. Leo Sampson thought she was a fool, too. Beattie was starting to suspect it was true.

Mikhail had stood by her. He did whatever was asked of him, whether it was walking into town, or helping Terry mend fences, or cleaning the kitchen, or just listening as Beattie complained about the horrific mess that the paperwork was in as she spent hours every day trying to sort it out. They were managing, they were getting by.

But today Terry had come to see her.

"I'm sorry," he said, and his pale blue eyes really did look very sorry, "but Farquhar's offered me a job next door. I have to take it."

"Why do you have to?" she snapped.

"Because you're going to run out of money before the next wool clip and put me off anyway. I've got to take the opportunity while it's there."

She couldn't blame him. He had been there for her in the past, but she couldn't keep prevailing on his goodwill. She knew uncertainty herself and would do anything she could to keep it at bay. But his resignation was the final straw for Beattie. Without a farm manager, the farm couldn't run. Without money, she couldn't attract a new farm manager. It was time to let go of this silly dream. Time to sell Wildflower Hill and buy a little house in Hobart to be near Lucy and look for a job doing something else. To settle for a modest life instead of a dream of being rich or powerful.

She carried the two plates to the table and went downstairs to call Mikhail. He was on his knees, fixing the wire cover over the vegetable patch. He was stiff when he stood, only in his fifties, but a lifetime of menial work was wearing him out. He would find it difficult to get another job. Beattie swallowed the guilt. *Tell him quickly, get it over with.*

"I come," he said. "I be just one more minute."

Beattie went up to the kitchen to wait for him. The gravy cooled on her plate. At last, he sat down across from her.

"Those possums are too clever. They find a way into vegetable garden," he said, picking up his fork.

"Mikhail, I've bad news."

He raised his eyebrows. "So? What is it?"

"Terry's resigned."

"Ah." He began to eat. "Farquhar got to him."

"You knew he'd offered Terry a job?"

"Terry mention it last week. Farquhar is very interested in seeing you fail, I say."

Beattie mulled this over. Jimmy Farquhar had always been nice to her, but she didn't doubt Mikhail's words. When she'd acquired Wildflower Hill, she'd made many enemies. It wasn't that Raphael was particularly well loved; it was the idea that a poor servant—a woman—could now own a large property. The details of the transaction had been secret, and rumors filled the vacuum, none of them generous. Beattie had constructed an elaborate story about an inheritance but so far had not seen anyone from town to tell it to. Now it looked like it wouldn't matter.

"I don't think I can go on, Mikhail," she said. "Everyone's telling me to sell: Farquhar, Leo, Terry . . . Perhaps they're right. I'm sorry. I know this will leave you with nowhere to go."

He ate in silence for a while. Then put down his knife and fork and considered her in the dim evening light of the kitchen. Electricity was a luxury she couldn't afford. "You are give up?"

She smiled tightly. "Yes, Mikhail. I am give up."

"I think you should not."

"I can't see any other way."

"You hire good farm manager, you keep going. You be boss. Then you never work for another man again. That is good, yes?"

"I can't afford to hire another farm manager. I'll run out of money before shearing season."

"Sell some more land. Farquhar will buy."

"But how will I know if I can trust a new farm manager? I don't want to sell off another chunk of land on such a risk. Terry knows the farm backward."

Mikhail pushed out his bottom lip while he thought, which made him look ridiculous, like a petulant child. Beattie almost laughed. Then he said, "Charlie Harris."

It took her a moment to remember, then the events of the day she left Henry came back to her. Charlie saving Lucy's life.

Mikhail continued. "Nobody knew Wildflower Hill like Charlie. He is very clever man. He knows what is good for business. Mr. Blanchard not like him because he is too clever. You like him."

"How would I even find him?"

"He went to Bligh."

"That was years ago."

"Maybe he is still there. Write letter. Postmaster will find him if he is still in town."

Beattie was tempted. The idea of having someone brilliant run the farm, somebody who could make it work, was so appealing. If she sold the property, she would be wealthy in the short term. But if she could make the farm work, she would secure herself for life.

"All right," she said. "I'll write to him, but if I've heard nothing in two weeks. I'll have to ask Leo to find me a buyer."

Mikhail nodded and returned to his meal. If he was worried about his future, he hid it well.

A week passed. Nothing. Then Leo Sampson phoned one morning just as Beattie was putting clean sheets on her bed in readiness for Lucy's first visit. She'd put off Lucy coming to see her until things were settled at the farm; now she realized that settlement might never happen.

"There are rumors in town you're going to sell the farm," Leo said.

Beattie jammed the phone between her shoulder and ear and pinned her hair again. She was growing it longer, and it kept slipping out of its pins. "I'm thinking about it," she said warily. "Why?"

"I've had an offer."

Beattie's heart picked up its rhythm. "You have? From whom?"

"He doesn't want to be named."

"It's Jimmy Farquhar, isn't it?"

"Do you want to know how much?"

"Go on."

Leo read out the figure. It was a lot of money, but it was nowhere near what the property was worth.

"It's an insult," she said. "It must be Farquhar."

Leo was silent.

"He's preying on me when he knows times are bad. He poached my farm manager."

"I think you should take it," Leo said. "You'd be securing your future."

"I'd be *selling* my future," Beattie said. "And my daughter's."

"This is more than you could have imagined a year ago, Beattie."

"But I've imagined more since," she said, then sighed. "I'll consider it. I'm not a fool."

Just as she hung up the phone, there was a knock at the front door. Nobody ever came to visit, so she went to it curiously. With trepidation.

On the other side was a tall, dark man in a white button-down shirt and dark trousers. Under his hat, his hair grew almost to his shoulders in loose curls. It took a moment for Beattie to recognize him as Charlie Harris.

Beattie couldn't help but smile. "You came," she said.

He grinned back at her, lifted off his hat. "Got your letter, missus. Can I come in to talk to you about it?"

Two black and white dogs flanked him, but they sat respectfully back as she opened the door wide. She knew that other women in town would be much more circumspect: an Aborigine calling when she was alone. But this was the man who had risked his own safety to pull her daughter from a raging flood.

Besides, she already knew she was different from the other women in town.

Beattie led Charlie to the kitchen and put the kettle on the stove. He took a dish of water outside for his dogs, then returned and folded his tall, lean body into a chair. There was an easy languidness about him.

"I hope I haven't put you to any trouble," Beattie said as she spooned tea leaves into the pot, stopping herself from measuring out the length of his legs with her eyes.

"Not at all. I love Wildflower Hill. I'm keen as mustard to come back. Wouldn't have walked all the way from Bligh if I wasn't."

"I need to explain a few things."

"You sure do. Last time I saw you, you had nothing but a soggy box and a little red-haired girl. Now you've got more than a soggy box."

"Raphael Blanchard ran this business into the ground. He needed to sell, and an uncle of mine in Scotland died and left me a small inheritance." There, that hadn't been a hard lie.

"I see. And the little red-haired girl?"

"She's with her father at the moment. Due for a visit at the end of the week."

She made the tea, slid the tray onto the table, and watched as Charlie dumped three teaspoons of sugar into his cup. He took a slurp like a man dying of thirst, then seemed to remember his manners and settled back in his chair to sip politely.

"I must be honest with you, Mr. Harris. There's no more money. I sold off three hundred acres to pay debts, and now I'm running out fast. I'm on the verge of selling the whole lot. If you agree to come and work for me, I'll sell off enough to pay your wage and hang on a little longer."

"Don't sell anything," he said, shaking his head. "This is a fine property, missus. You shouldn't be selling it to anyone."

"Call me Beattie," she said. "But I'm afraid that I've not got enough money to pay you until the wool clip comes in."

"How are you paying Mikhail?"

"I'm not. We eat what we grow."

He shrugged. "I can do the same."

"It isn't right, Mr. Harris."

"Call me Charlie." He smiled, and she noticed a deep dimple in the dark skin of his left cheek. It made him look boyish.

She smiled in spite of herself. "It's not right, Charlie, to hire somebody and offer to pay him nothing."

He leaned forward and put down his teacup, seemed to be searching for words. "I watched Raphael Blanchard put the boot into this business," he said. "He was a bloody fool. You can carry a lot of sheep here. You shouldn't be selling a thing. You should be going to the bank and borrowing enough money for two thousand more sheep, at least. This farm will take seven thousand, easy. You could be making a hundred bales of wool a year. Then we can worry about what you'd pay me."

Beattie knew the right thing to do was say no. But the last wool clip had been twenty-two bales of wool. It had fetched a good sum, then been eaten up by Raphael's debts before Beattie saw a penny. Fifty bales would keep the farm running longer than a year, would buy them furniture. A hundred might even make her rich enough to have Lucy back permanently.

"But I'd need help. I can't do it alone," he said.

"I can't afford to hire more help, and I can't expect everyone to come and work for me for free."

"Mikhail can help. Can you ride a horse? You can help."

"No, I've never even been close to a horse."

"I can teach you. The three of us and the dogs, we can turn this place around, make it into the kind of business it should be. When you spent your uncle's inheritance on it, isn't that what you intended? You wouldn't have wasted the money. You wouldn't have bought it just to off-load it at the first hurdle."

Beattie felt a pinch of guilt for her lie. "Of course not," she said.

"Then if we're all willing to get our hands dirty, I reckon Wildflower Hill can be a fine business. It'll be tough, but we can do it."

Beattie certainly wasn't afraid of hard work. She was far more afraid of losing her newly gained power. With a deep breath, she reached across the table and shook his hand firmly. "You're hired, Charlie Harris," she said.

* * *

Beattie was exasperated with herself the morning Lucy arrived. She was so nervous. It was her daughter's first visit since she'd acquired Wildflower Hill. What if Lucy didn't like the new house? It made Beattie sad: once, Lucy had just been part of her, in her life daily. Well, with hard work and Charlie Harris, Beattie was going to get her back. Hard work and sacrifice. Beattie had to take a deep breath every time she thought about the loan she had just applied for. The bank manager had shown her a list of her quarterly interest repayments and when they were due. Terrifying. In fact, there wouldn't be enough money for the final one of the year, but by then she hoped to be close enough to having sold her wool clip to put the bank off for a month or so. Even so, she had to be more careful than ever with money. She and her two staff had already switched to bread and dripping for breakfast: jam was officially no longer affordable. Luckily, Mikhail had a green thumb, and his seedlings were sprouting everywhere in the garden.

Henry's new car, a blue Chevrolet, hummed up the long earth driveway just before lunchtime. Much later than she'd thought. She hoped that Henry and Molly weren't expecting to stay for a meal. There weren't even enough chairs, let alone food. Beattie had been stockpiling for Lucy's visit so her daughter didn't have to go without; she didn't want to give it all to Henry and Molly on the first day. Especially as they had so much already.

She waited at the front door. The car engine cut off, leaving only the sound of the rustling gums. Lucy climbed out, her red hair gleaming in the sun, and Beattie spread her arms, expecting a running hug. But Lucy was more circumspect. She approached almost warily, awkwardly. It had been a long separation.

Beattie knelt and put her arms around Lucy, ignoring her hesitation. "My darling, I have missed you so much."

Lucy melted and clung to her tightly, her warm little heart beating hard. Beattie looked up to see Henry and Molly walking up the driveway. Henry wasn't wearing a hat, and Beattie noted his hair was growing thin. She stood, hoisting Lucy onto her hip—even though the child was far too heavy to comfortably do so—and smiled in greeting.

"Welcome to Wildflower Hill," she said.

"We've been here before," Henry said dourly.

Beattie realized that Henry was jealous. Perhaps he even wished that he was still together with her; perhaps he fancied himself as the owner of a farm this big. "But now it's mine," she said. "Come in."

Of course, inside there weren't many opportunities to impress. She allowed Lucy to run about upstairs and downstairs, opening and closing doors to empty rooms.

"So tell me about this uncle who died and left you the money to buy this place?" Henry said, peering around.

"Great-uncle. On my mother's side."

"You never mentioned him before. I didn't know you were still in touch with your mother."

Thankfully, Molly interrupted. "Where will she sleep?" she called from upstairs, having peered into all of the empty rooms.

"With me for now. I haven't enough to buy a new bed just yet."

Lucy galloped down the stairs and put her arms around Beattie's middle, but Henry turned his mouth down in disapproval. "She's not a baby anymore, Beattie. She needs her own room."

"I don't mind," Lucy said.

"Of course you don't, my darling," Molly said to her. "You've a good heart."

"So this uncle?" Henry continued.

"Great-uncle Montgomery. He lived in Inverness. I only met him once." She wondered if she were blushing.

"And you're here by yourself?" Henry asked as Molly headed back down the stairs.

"No, I have Mikhail, who helps me with the house and the garden, and Charlie, who manages the farm."

"They live here?" Molly looked horrified.

"Mikhail has a room downstairs, and Charlie has set up in the shearers' cottage." He'd been insistent. It wasn't right for him to sleep in her house; nor would anyone else think it was right.

"You can afford two staff, but you can't afford furniture?" Henry asked.

"Not until the next wool clip."

"When will that be?"

They'd arrived back at the front door. She wasn't going to tell Henry that no more money was coming for a year. That in fact, she might be trying to sell wild rabbits for a few pennies just to make the gas go at night. Winter was still months away, but already she dreaded it.

"Soon," she told Henry. "But Lucy will be comfortable and well cared for. I cared for her by myself for many years, Henry. You needn't doubt me now."

Henry, chastened by the memory of his loose past, put his head down and headed for the car. But Molly hung back.

"Lucy," she said to the little girl, "could you go and give your daddy six kisses to say goodbye?"

Lucy ran off, and Molly turned to Beattie. "I need to tell you something, because I know you'll hear it from Lucy, and you'll be upset."

"What is it?" Beattie tried to make her voice sound warm.

"She doesn't call me Mama Molly anymore. She just calls me Mama."

Beattie opened her mouth to protest, but Molly kept on talking.

"I know that you are her mother, and I don't aim to replace you. But Lucy is starting school next year, and it's too complicated to explain to everyone—teachers, neighbors, friends—what the real situation is."

"Complicated?" Beattie said. "Or shameful?"

Molly blushed. "Both. I admit it. The child was born out of wedlock. In Hobart, where we live, where she will go to school, I am the person who acts as her mother. Why tar the poor child with the stigma of being so different from her little friends? It isn't her fault that her origins are . . . less than savory."

Beattie wanted to retort but restrained herself. After all, she had known Henry was married when she'd had an affair with him. It seemed a million years ago.

"In any case, I am Mama and you are Mummy, and the child knows what is what," Molly said, pulling her gloves on.

"Hurry up!" called Henry from the car.

"He's in a very bad mood," Molly said, waving him away. "We'll see you in a week. Call us if you need us to come earlier."

Beattie didn't tell her the phone was no longer connected. "I'll see you then."

Lucy came running back, and Beattie's heart beat uncomfortably with indignation. How dare Molly? How dare she offer such reasonable explanations for her actions? Beattie knew that Molly longed for a child of her own, that Lucy calling her Mama was as much about her own desires as the child's.

"Are you all right, Mummy? You look cross," Lucy said.

Beattie leaned down and kissed her head as the car pulled away. "Not with you, my love," Beattie said. "Let's go inside our new house."

Lucy woke up early. Too early. Mummy was still asleep beside her, curled on her side with one arm over Lucy's tummy. Lucy tried to snuggle back down to sleep, but the bed was strange, the birds were noisy, and she needed to wee.

She rose and pulled on her pink dressing gown, the one that Molly had knitted for her. Molly didn't make pretty clothes the way Mummy did, and the dressing gown was lopsided. Lucy tiptoed out of the bedroom, remembering what Daddy and Molly always said: "If you're up early, go and make your own breakfast. Don't wake us up."

The hallway was cold, and she pulled her gown around her tightly. She stopped by the toilet, then went downstairs. She loved Mummy's big new house, with all of its empty rooms. She wondered if Mummy would let her set up a tent in one of the big rooms and sleep on the floor with blankets one night.

Lucy found the kitchen and cut herself an uneven piece of bread, poured honey on it with a spoon, and went to the window. Down in the paddock, she could see a man saddling a horse. He had dark skin, but nowhere near as dark as the maid of Mrs. Bainbridge across the road back home. She was so dark that she made Lucy think of licorice.

Lucy watched for a while. She had a toy pony back home, but she longed to touch a real one. Last time she'd been here, she'd been told off by a man for going near the horses. But the dark-skinned man looked friendly. Besides, Mummy owned the farm now, so he probably had to do what Lucy said. She opened the door to the laundry and descended the stairs, then let herself out into the paddock.

The grass was still dewy, and the sun rimmed the clouds with gold. The sky was the color of a strawberry milk shake. The man was about to climb on the horse, and then he'd be gone, so she called out, "Hello! Wait!"

The dark-skinned man turned and smiled at her, waited for her to approach.

Her bed socks grew damp from dew. Up close, the dark-skinned man was handsome, with big dark eyes that seemed very kind. "My mummy owns the farm," she said to him. "I want to pat the horse."

"Of course," he said. "But you must be gentle."

The horse put his head down, and Lucy carefully rubbed his nose. The horse's ears flicked backward and forward.

"There, he likes you," the man said.

"My name's Lucy," she said.

"My name's Charlie. We've met before, a few years ago."

Lucy turned to look at him. "I don't think so. I have a very good memory."

"You were small, crossing a swollen creek with your mum. The water caught you, and I had to jump in and pull you out."

She stretched her mind back as far as it would go, but struggled to turn up the memory. A brief flash of being in the water and of being frightened came to her, though not fully formed. "Really? It's a good thing you did, or I might have drowned." She patted the horse's mane, then stood back to look at him. "Why is your skin so dark?"

"Why is your hair so red?"

She shrugged, and he shrugged back. Lucy laughed.

"You better get in out of the cold," he said, pulling on his hat and mounting the horse. "Your mum will be worried."

"No, she won't."

Charlie laughed. "She might." He whistled, and two dogs shot out of the stables and raced toward him. Then he was galloping off, leaving Lucy standing in the damp field.

Had he really pulled her out of a creek when she was little? Surely she'd have remembered that. Perhaps he was lying.

Molly said that Mrs. Bainbridge's maid couldn't be trusted because she was black; perhaps it was the same with Charlie. Though he seemed nice to her. Sometimes Molly said things about people that didn't seem quite right, though. One time Lucy had heard her arguing with Daddy—the only fight they'd ever had—and Molly had called Mummy a name. She couldn't remember it now, but she knew it wasn't a nice word.

"Lucy!"

She looked around and up to see Mummy standing at the bedroom window beckoning her.

"Come up! It's too cold to be down there at this time of day."

The sun broke over the clouds, illuminating the dew on the grass. Lucy made her way back inside, pretending to be a horse all the way.

Beattie pinched the bridge of her nose and put down her pen. Her neck was aching with tension, and her scalp was tight. She looked over the figures again, couldn't make them add up properly.

The interest on the loan was going to kill her.

But Charlie had sourced two thousand of the finest-quality merino sheep from the farm he had last worked at on Friday. Too late for regrets now: she had already signed the paperwork.

Still, it was a beautiful afternoon. The sun was bright on the window of the study—a tiny room with a crate for a chair and a desk knocked together unevenly by Mikhail—and the wildflowers were blooming all over the hills behind the house. Perhaps she just needed to get out of the study, out into the fresh air, and clear her head.

A knock at the study door. She looked up to see Charlie standing there.

"Hey, missus," he said. He insisted on calling her missus, no matter how many times she'd reminded him to call her Beattie. She'd given up.

"Charlie. How can I help?"

"It's been two weeks, and you still haven't got on that bloody horse."

"You said yourself you don't need me yet."

"I'll need you before summer's over. Me and the dogs can't do it all."

Beattie didn't want to admit to him that she was terrified of getting on the horse. Horses always seemed to her so big and unpredictable. "Well, there's still plenty of time to learn."

"Not plenty of time to get good. Listen, missus, you can't run a sheep farm and not ride a horse. That's the way Raphael Blanchard operated, and look what happened to him. The sheep need to be moved around a lot. We've got two thousand more coming this week. You're going to have to help me, or you're going to have to hire somebody else."

Beattie looked at the row of figures, felt the familiar stab of heat to her heart.

Charlie crouched, leaning his arms on her desk and his chin on his arms. "Missus?" he said quietly. "You frightened?" He smiled broadly—he had such an infectious smile.

Beattie laughed. "Not frightened. Uneasy."

"Everyone is, first time. But Abby's pretty calm. She'll be kind to you." He stood, pointed at her skirt. "You got something else to wear? Get changed, meet me down at the stables."

He strode off. Beattie closed the book, peered around the threshold to watch him walk away. He had such an easy grace, was so comfortable in his body. Beattie knew she was going to be awkward, ridiculous, trying to ride that horse. She felt embarrassed already.

She changed into a pair of trousers she'd run up for gardening and grabbed her hat from by the door, then made her way through the clucking chickens wandering in the garden—Mikhail was planting herbs today—and across to the stables. Abby, the big chestnut mare, was waiting. Charlie leaned against the horse gently, talking softly against her cheek. His own horse, the gray stallion Birch, waited tied up to his stall.

Beattie swallowed down hard. "I'm ready," she said.

Charlie patted Abby's flank. "Left side is the near side, right side is the off side. Stay on her near side, that's what she's used to. Let's saddle her up."

Slowly, with great patience and good humor, he took Beattie through all the steps. Sliding the bit into the horse's mouth, fastening the throat latch, smoothing the saddle cloth, and tightening the girth. He showed her how to talk softly to the horse to calm it, and he steadied her as she climbed up. It felt so high. She wanted to lean forward and clutch the horse's mane for dear life.

"No, no," Charlie said, "you've got to relax, missus. Hands down, heels down. Feet forward. You've got to be able to see your toes. Don't jiggle. Relax. Take a deep breath."

Easier said than done. Abby started to get twitchy, so Beattie forced herself to be still and sit properly. Charlie calmed the horse again. Beattie took deep breaths.

"Gentle now," he said to Beattie, "nudge her with your heels. Gentle, gentle."

She did so, and the horse began to move.

"Walk on, Abby," Charlie said, rubbing the horse's nose. "Walk on."

"How do I tell her where to go?" Beattie asked, panicked.

"Use the reins, of course." With fluid ease, Charlie mounted his horse and was alongside her a moment later. "We'll take it slow," he said. "Just around the paddock."

Beattie thought she would never get used to the feeling of being up so high, so dangerously perched on the animal. But Charlie was patient with her, never forcing her to do more than she was comfortable with. They walked the horses around the paddock twice, then returned to the stable.

"That's it?" Beattie asked.

"That and a lot of practice," Charlie said, dismounting and lifting his hands to support her hips as she attempted to climb down. He was strong and steady. She was awkward, clumsy, came down with a clatter. Abby whickered softly.

"Don't you laugh," Beattie said to the horse.

"Every day, missus," said Charlie. "Twice around the paddock, then three times, then four. And when you're used to it, faster and farther. I need you out mustering with me by autumn. Think you can manage that?"

Beattie blew out noisily. "I suppose I have to."

His dark eyes grew serious. "Yes, missus. I suppose you do."

TWENTY

Every day she practiced riding the horse, and slowly, she got used to it. The days were long, the new sheep settled in—crowding under the trees for shade in the hottest part of the afternoon. On the last day of February, she rode out with Charlie for the first time to muster stock from one paddock to another. In truth, the dogs were of more use than she was, but Charlie said nothing. At the end of the day, her legs ached, and her wrists were burned pink where the sun had found them between gloves and sleeves. But she slept better than she had in a long time.

Charlie and Mikhail were her two rocks. Mikhail managed the house, Charlie managed the farm, and Beattie tried to make sense of the paperwork. She spent almost nothing. They lived off the garden and tried to eat the eggs rather than the chickens. Once a fortnight she walked into town for supplies: porridge, honey, milk, soap, flour. She enjoyed the walk; it gave her time to think and relax away from the farm. She was so consumed by the numerous daily tasks that she often didn't have time to reflect on anything.

The general store had new owners, and Beattie was hopeful. She never actively listened to the gossip in town. She suspected half of it was about her acquiring Wildflower Hill, and the other half was grim yet enthusiastic speculation about the possibility of war in Europe. But she had overheard two elderly women expressing their distaste for the young woman who ran the store.

"Too young and too ambitious," one had said.

"Tells her husband what to do," the other replied.

Beattie dreamed she might find an ally. Behind the long glass cabinet that served as the front counter stood a small, round woman with blond curls. She smiled up at Beattie when she walked in. Beattie smiled back. It was the first time anyone in town had smiled at her in a long time.

"Hello," she said. "Welcome, I'm Tilly."

"I'm Beattie Blaxland, from Wildflower Hill."

"You're Scottish. That accent . . ."

"Yes."

"My mother was Scottish. I was raised by my aunts, though, in South Africa."

"How did you end up all the way down here?"

Tilly laughed. "I might very well ask you the same thing. I married an Australian man."

They chatted briefly as Beattie selected her purchases and eked out her pennies as though they were diamonds. Tilly asked her a few questions about the farm, how far away it was and how big, and commiserated with Beattie about the difficulties of working and also taking care of a house.

"I think our husbands expect too much of us." Tilly laughed as she wrapped up a box of milk powder.

"Actually," Beattie admitted, "I'm on my own now."

"Oh, I'm sorry. Did your husband die?"

"He . . . It didn't work out." Her face flushed.

Tilly smiled again, a little tighter. "That's bad luck. It must be difficult on your own. I feel for you."

Beattie grasped at this morsel of sympathy, the only one she had ever received from someone in town. "It's very, very difficult," she said softly. "Thank you for your kindness."

Then, like a lizard slithering out from behind a rock, a red-faced, oily-haired man in his thirties emerged from the storeroom. He looked Beattie up and down with narrow, cold eyes.

"Oh, here he is," Tilly said with a laugh in her voice. "Frank, this is Beattie."

He nodded once, with a tight smile. Beattie noticed Tilly had grown anxious. The idea that she bossed her husband around was patently ludicrous: the jealous rumblings of elderly women with too little to occupy themselves.

"It's a pleasure," Beattie said, picking up her parcels. "I must be on my way."

She pushed open the door. As she did, she nearly ran into Margaret Day coming the other way. She hadn't seen Margaret since the older woman had asked her to leave many months ago.

"Hello, Margaret," Beattie said, buoyed by her successful exchange with Tilly.

Margaret gave her a cold stare, brushed past her. The shop

door swung closed, and Beattie stood outside, her feeling of goodwill draining away. She dared to look over her shoulder, through the shopwindow, and saw Margaret leaning over the counter talking to Tilly. Tilly looked up, saw Beattie through the window, and looked away. No smiles this time.

Beattie wanted to run back inside and shout, "Don't listen to her! She's a pious fool!" But she didn't. She set her chin and started the walk home. She didn't need allies; she could manage on her own.

The long weeks when Lucy was away only pained her at nighttime, when she lay in her bed alone and had many dark hours to contemplate how she'd mismanaged her life. The days were busy and full, left her tired and yet satisfied. Only with the evening came the regrets.

In March it was crutching season. Charlie taught Mikhail how to use a pair of shears, and he chipped in, too. It was an intense time: up early, the predawn sky bruised with rain clouds, the black crags of dead trees standing still in the mist. Then endless days of mustering stock and wrangling them in and out of the sheds. Beattie fell into bed every night exhausted. But it was all worth it when they sold the crutching to a Launceston wool trader for much more than Beattie had hoped. A little extra money. She walked into town and bought a few feet of heavy pink cotton from Tilly Harrow's store. Tilly had hardened toward Beattie but, like everyone else in town, was still happy to take her money.

With the cotton, Beattie hand-sewed a dress for Lucy.

She'd forgotten how much she loved fabrics and sewing, seeing the neat lines of seams and pleats appear under her needle, and wondered what happened to the wool that she sold. If she could get a little of it back, made into cloth, she could wear her own farm on her back. The thought gave her a feeling of intense pleasure, of being independent, strong. That night, for the first time in many, many months, she pulled out a piece of paper and sketched a design for a jacket that would be perfect made of wool. In the magazines for sale in the Lewinford general store, she had seen the long lines and wide bindings of the latest fashions. She lost herself in it for hours.

Easter finally came, but Henry refused to bring Lucy until after the Easter Sunday service. Beattie never made it to church; there was too much else to do, and anyway, Wildflower Hill with its unbroken silence and earthy smells felt much closer to God than the damp little church hall in town. Sometimes when she walked out at dusk—the distant mountains had shaded to blue, the dam was a silver mirror, the cool shadows spread from hollows to cover the grass and trees— she couldn't believe she had ever lived in damp, crowded cities and been happy.

Finally, on Sunday afternoon, her little girl came back.

Charlie was wrestling with some fencing wire beside the driveway—they hadn't money for new fencing, and he'd become an expert at patching it with old cutoffs—when Henry's car rounded the bend and came into view.

Beattie's heart soared. The long months of waiting were over. For two weeks now, she would have Lucy's little body snuggled against hers in bed at night, would fall asleep with the warm smell of the girl's hair in her nostrils.

The car beeped—surely not Henry acting unprompted; she could imagine Lucy and Molly urging him to—and then pulled to a stop at the top of the driveway.

The door opened and Lucy climbed out. This time Beattie didn't wait for her. She folded Lucy into a tight embrace. When she stood back to look at her, Lucy's face was awash with tears. "I missed you, Mummy," she said.

"I missed you, too. More than you could know."

Molly and Henry were climbing out of the car now. Molly, beautifully dressed as always with her hat and gloves, froze when she saw Charlie.

Henry approached Beattie and handed her two books. "Make her keep up with her reading," he said gruffly. "She's not doing well at school."

Lucy blushed.

"Yes, Lucy, you must read better so that your mother can write you letters while you're apart," Molly said gently, her eyes darting back to Charlie nervously.

Beattie tucked Lucy under her arm. "Molly, have you met Charlie? He's my farm manager."

"Charlie!" Lucy exclaimed, spotting him for the first time and racing over.

Charlie, who sensed the situation, pulled up so Lucy couldn't hug him, holding out the wire and a set of pliers in warning. "Hang on there, little red-haired girl, I've got sharp things here."

"*That's* Charlie?" Molly said under her voice. "I've heard Lucy talk of him endlessly. I'd no idea he was black."

"He's barely black," Henry said with a shrug, not bothering to adjust his volume. "And what does it matter, anyway?"

Beattie was torn between embarrassment that Charlie could hear them talking about him so openly, and amusement that Henry was so unmoved by Molly's discomfort.

Lucy remained with Charlie, talking animatedly about horses and school and Easter eggs. Henry put Molly back in the car, and they drove off. Beattie was surprised: it seemed Molly's good and gentle heart didn't have a place in it for anyone who wasn't white. Selective kindness rather than the genuine variety. It wasn't often that Beattie had opportunity to feel morally superior to Molly, so she enjoyed the feeling while it lasted.

"Come on, darling," Beattie called to Lucy, "I've got a little present for you."

Lucy dashed toward her, wrapping her arms around Beattie's middle. "What is it, what is it?"

"I made you a dress. Pink. Your favorite color. Come inside."

Beattie led Lucy upstairs to the bedroom. The little pink dress was lying on the bed. Lucy immediately stripped out of her skirt and blouse. She had lost much of her baby fat—in fact, she had started to look quite different, taller, managing her own buttons. A child rather than a big baby. As Lucy stepped into the dress, Beattie realized that it wouldn't fit her.

"Oh," Lucy said.

"Lucy, you must have grown two inches!"

Lucy grinned proudly. "Mama always says I eat like a horse."

Mama. All at once, Beattie felt a sense of having lost something precious. Her daughter was growing up somewhere else. With someone else as her mother. She had changed so much in the months since Beattie had last seen her and held her. She would continue to change, no doubt, constantly and constantly, like the face of the sea. Then one day, perhaps, she would change so much that Beattie wouldn't know her. Not in the intimate way a mother should know her child.

"Mummy? Are you sad that the dress doesn't fit?"

Beattie took her hands. "No. I can make the dress bigger. I'm sad that you are growing up without me."

Lucy blinked back at her.

"Are you happy with Daddy and Molly?"

"Yes. But I liked it better when I saw you more."

"I liked it better, too."

"I don't like school."

"But Molly's right. Once you can read and write, we can write letters to each other and not feel so far apart."

"All right. I'll try a little harder."

"That's my girl."

The bank manager increased the interest on Beattie's loan just as the first cold finger of winter traced itself across the fields. Much of Beattie's life in the last few years had been consumed with worrying about running out of money, but she had never been so responsible for finding it. She spent long hours over the bookwork, making budgets, going back through old records for past wool clips, and estimating this year's clip, which was now only four months away. The cold season was not a time to be eking out pennies, and she felt particularly sorry for Mikhail and Charlie, who were men and needed much more food than she did. She knew, herself, from the long days spent mustering and treating sheep for foot rot, that a hard day's work could make her ravenous. To serve them thin vegetable soup and bread and dripping on such evenings seemed almost cruel.

But they never complained. And so the three of them became like family, bonded through hardship, sacrifice, and a common sense that they were achieving something together. Beattie knew she occupied a privileged position: she would reap most of the benefits of their hard work. So she vowed to herself that she would repay them, would never take so much for herself that a gap would open up between them and break their bond. After Lucy, they were the people she cared most for in the world.

Beattie decided it was time to open up the sitting room, even though there were no chairs to sit on. The big fireplace was in there, so she had sewn cushions out of scraps for the floor and bought a secondhand rug from town. While Beattie went over her books for the day, sitting in the windowsill, trying to catch the sun's warmth through the cool glass, Mikhail cleaned out the fireplace. Beside it was a neat pile of wood that he'd chopped earlier that day. Beattie was very much looking forward to firelight and warmth that afternoon and hoped that Charlie would join them. She couldn't understand why he refused to spend more time in the house. She had lived in the shearers' cottage; she knew that it was cold and rough. He worked so hard, and she wished for him just a little comfort.

She wished, also, to spend a little more time with him.

That feeling had crept up on her. When they were out working together, there wasn't time for conversation. They were often working opposite ends of a paddock, calling to each other over barking dogs or bleating sheep or across the muddy ditches. But she drew such comfort from his presence. The more familiar they became, the more she longed for a deep familiarity: to know him better, know about the mind and the heart at work in that lean, graceful body; to draw him closer to her somehow. He was patient and kind, hardworking, strong . . . He was many admirable things. Perhaps she had come to admire him a little too much.

"There. I am all done," Mikhail said, scooping up his bucket and his brush. His face and hands were sprinkled with soot.

"We can light a fire tonight?"

He shrugged. "I hope so. If room fills with smoke, we will know I need to try again."

Beattie laughed. "You go and clean yourself up. Thank you for that."

He tilted his head to the side, wincing. "I have very stiff neck. Too old for these jobs now," he joked. He left the room limping, as he had done since he'd speared his foot on a piece of old fencing wire the week before.

Beattie eyed the fireplace. It was only afternoon; not cold enough for a fire yet. Though she would have to test the chimney . . . Smiling to herself, she stacked the wood in the fireplace, carefully arranged some kindling, and lit it. For the next quarter of an hour, she tended to the fire, poking it and making sure it wasn't going to smoke the house out. Then she pulled up a cushion on the floor and sat on it, gazing at the flames.

Her heart relaxed a little. Yes, money would be tight over the winter, but then the shearing season would come, and she had budgeted so beautifully that when the money came in, they would be fine. She could pay Mikhail and Charlie, she could meet her interest payments, she could even buy some furniture. She closed her eyes and tried to imagine what this room would look like this time next year. A sofa, a side table, a lamp . . . Yes, she could reconnect the phone and electricity: Raphael had spent so much money having the lines run out here, and now they were idle. Upstairs, there would be a room for Lucy. Beattie would miss the girl in her bed, but she was getting far too big to share. Beattie still wasn't in any hurry to open up the other rooms in the house. She'd rather have the ones she used looking nice. Winter would give her time to sew, here by the fireplace. Ah, yes, when the money came, she could buy an electric sewing machine.

She warmed herself on her fantasies while the afternoon deepened. Outside, she could hear Charlie coming back to the stables, calling to his dogs, and she thought about making dinner. She went up the hall and knocked gently on Mikhail's door.

"Come in," he called.

She opened the door. He lay on his bed, on top of the covers, looking stiff and in pain.

"I'm about to start dinner," she said.

"Not for me tonight," he said. "I am not well."

She was concerned. "What kind of not well? Just stiff from cleaning the fireplace?"

He shook his head. "I don't know. I think I have fever."

She advanced toward him and put a hand on his forehead. It was warm but not alarmingly so. "Just get some rest, then," she said. "Charlie and I will eat on our own."

But Charlie said it wasn't worth making a proper dinner if Mikhail wasn't there, so he ate some bread and honey and went back to the shearers' cottage. Beattie returned to the fire and used the light to work on some cross-stitch. She stayed up for hours, her hands aching and her eyes straining in the firelight, enjoying the fire as the wind rattled outside.

At last she couldn't stay awake any longer and put aside her sewing. She lit a candle to show her the way and left the fire to die. When her foot struck the first stair, she realized she hadn't checked in on Mikhail again. He was probably asleep. She rounded the bottom of the staircase and listened outside his door.

There was a groan. Had he heard her footsteps? She leaned close to the door to listen. His breathing was labored. She paused, not wanting to go in uninvited, but worried that he was sick.

"Mikhail?"

The groan again; he was trying to call to her. Her pulse quickened, and she opened the door.

By the flickering candlelight, a grim scene confronted her. Mikhail was where she had left him, on top of the covers, but his body had arched into a rictus. His fists were curled tight at his sides, his back bent like a violin bow. He looked at her with pleading eyes, his jaw clamped tight and his lungs struggling for breath.

"Oh, God!" she exclaimed, thinking back to his stiffness that afternoon, his fever. "Oh, God! Charlie! Charlie!"

She ran from the room and through the kitchen, calling Charlie even though she knew he wouldn't hear her at this distance. She felt intensely the farm's isolation from the world, from help. Not even a phone to call a doctor. Icy moonlight spread across the dewy grass, threatening to slip her up. A few moments later, she was hammering on Charlie's door in the shearers' cottage.

"Charlie, come quick! It's Mikhail."

He opened the door, sleepy-eyed and shirtless. "What's wrong?"

"I don't know."

Charlie felt around on the floor for a shirt, pulling it on but leaving it unbuttoned. He was ahead of her in a second, finding his way through the dark to the house. The wind had whipped up, sending clouds scudding across the face of the moon. She hurried after Charlie, her heart thudding and hot, her breath fogging in the cold night air.

She waited outside Mikhail's bedroom door. She didn't want to see him again; his posture had terrified her. Charlie took the candle in and spoke gently to the older man, who moaned through his frozen mouth but couldn't make any words. Then Charlie emerged, closing the door behind him, and looked at her gravely.

"He's in a bad way. It's lockjaw."

Beattie's heart tightened. She'd heard the word before, only ever in dark tones. "What can we do?"

"We have to get him some medical help."

"Can you ride to Farquhar's? Use their phone?"

"It's not that much farther to town. Farquhar might not help us. He doesn't like you."

Beattie knew it wasn't the time to be affronted. "How do you know?"

"Why would he like you? Your farm's better than his, and he knows it. He's got a swamp on his." Charlie managed a smile. "Town is better. Dr. Malcolm. Abby's not going to like going out in the dark, but at least there's moonlight."

"Abby? You're not taking Birch?"

"I'm not riding to town, missus, you are."

"Me? Why me? You'd be quicker." Safer.

"Everyone in town thinks I'm a thief. They're not going to help me."

"But surely they won't still think that. Nobody liked Raphael." Even as she said this, she remembered Margaret's opinion of Charlie all those years ago. *A white man shouldn't have his things stolen by a black one, and that's that.* "I really have to ride to town in the dark?"

"Abby's a good girl. You can trust her. She can hear and smell things we can't."

Beattie glanced at Mikhail's door. She dropped her voice very low. "Will he die?"

Charlie's eyes were dark pools of emotion. "I don't know, missus. I've seen one fella die from lockjaw and another two come through just fine. While you're gone, I'll clean up that wound on his foot and keep him calm."

Beattie nodded.

"There's a torch in my room over at the cottage," he said. "The battery's getting weak, but it will help you get Abby saddled in the dark. Take it with you, too. Just in case."

Abby took a while to settle, unused to being ridden in the dark. She snorted and shied at shadows, and it took all of Beattie's nerve to keep her voice calm and reassuring enough to settle the horse down.

The wind was high, sometimes rattling, sometimes howling through the treetops. The moon shone, then disappeared through clouds, then shone again. Mad shadows flashed across the road; it felt as though the night were moving and shaking.

Beattie hung on for her life and urged Abby forward. Her hands burned with cold on the reins, her nose and eyes streamed. Her body buzzed with fear for Mikhail, with extreme alertness for herself. She didn't want to have a fall and end up injured, too. The road disappeared underneath her, Abby found her stride, and they galloped along the hard-packed dirt toward town.

All of the little houses were in darkness. It must have been after midnight. She found her way to Dr. Malcolm's house, tied Abby loosely to the fence. Her nose and cheeks were icy, her ears aching.

It took nearly five minutes and a lot of knocking to rouse

anyone. The porch light went on, the door opened. Dr. Malcolm was there in his robe, his wife shadowing his shoulder.

"What is it?" he asked, not bothering to hide his irritation.

"One of my men at Wildflower Hill. He has lockjaw."

Dr. Malcolm fought within himself, sighing through his nose. "I can't come out," he said at last.

"But he might die."

"Lockjaw, you say?" He rubbed his chin, mouth screwed up reluctantly. "I'll give you penicillin. And a barbiturate to ease the rigors. Call me in the morning if he's no better, and I'll come then."

She was too tired, cold, and distressed to feign politeness. "We don't have a phone," she pleaded. "That's why I just rode all this way in the dark. You're a doctor. You have to help us."

He wavered. Beattie felt certain he was about to change his mind when his wife put her hand on his shoulder and snapped, "It's one o'clock in the morning. He's not coming now. Which of your men is it? The Abo or the commie?"

Beattie fought down her anger. "Mikhail is not a communist," she said.

"He can only speak Russian."

"He speaks English perfectly well."

"I'll give you those medicines," Dr. Malcolm said, shrugging off his wife, "and I'll come out first thing tomorrow to look in on him." He turned to his wife. "You go back to bed. I'll just be a few minutes."

His wife gave Beattie a look—perhaps it was one of superiority or perhaps pity. Either way, Beattie had to glance away to stop her blood from boiling over.

The doctor prepared two small jars with a few tablets in each and gave her instructions. Then he put her back outside in the cold—unable to meet her eyes—and went back to his warm bed. Beattie untied Abby and started the freezing dash home.

Beattie left Abby at the stables still saddled, and ran up through the laundry and into the house. She dreaded what she would see when she got inside. She expected Charlie to say that Mikhail was dead, that he had stopped breathing. She braced herself for the worst.

Charlie heard her and met her in the hallway. "He's in a bad way," he said on one rush of breath. "He's just had a fit, couldn't breathe. He's breathing again now—"

"He has to have two of these and one of these." She shoved the pill bottles into his hands. "I'm sorry, Charlie, I can't do it. I don't even know if he can swallow and . . . you should do it."

Charlie looked at her and nodded. He took the bottles, his warm desperate fingers brushing hers briefly. He turned and headed toward Mikhail's room, closing the door behind him.

Beattie waited in the hallway, her face in her hands. Tears threatened, but she didn't let them spill over. Mikhail had been so good to her, so loyal and so hardworking. She couldn't bear the thought that he might die. The image of him, his body twisted and stretched, haunted her. She lowered herself to the floor with her back against the wall and put her head on her knees to wait.

It might have been half a hour later that Charlie emerged, the candle burning low in the holder, and sat with her.

"Well?" she said.

"He's settled. I think the pills might be helping. His body's softened a bit." He drew his long legs up and wrapped his arms around his knees. "The doctor wouldn't come?"

"He says he'll come in the morning." Beattie shrugged, trying to stop her face from contorting with tears. "His wife called Mikhail a communist."

"Ah. Her loss. Mikhail is a good man."

"The best of men."

A pause. "What did she say about me, then?"

"Nothing," Beattie lied.

Charlie's lips twitched as though he might laugh. "Sure," he said. "She always holds her tongue, that one."

Beattie couldn't help but laugh. Then she grew serious. "Charlie, do you ever get tired of people around here thinking ill of you?"

"You don't think ill of me," he said plainly.

"No," she said, her throat constricting slightly. It felt as though she were saying something she shouldn't. "No, I don't. Far from it."

"I've had to worry about worse things than what Doc Malcolm's wife thinks." He nodded at her. "So have you."

Beattie leaned her head against the wall. "It's true, I suppose." She glanced at him while he wasn't looking at her, then away before he saw her. "I know nothing about your life, Charlie."

"Not much to tell, missus."

"Are you ever going to start calling me Beattie?"

He spread his hands. "Wouldn't be right."

"I'd like it."

"You might regret it. If someone in town heard it, I guarantee you'd regret it."

"I wouldn't. I'm not ashamed to call you my friend. Why, without you and Mikhail, I wouldn't have survived this long. And I'd be proud to tell people that." She was immediately self-conscious about the vehemence in her voice.

Charlie's eyes met hers in the dim candlelight. He seemed to be about to say something, then looked away. Something stirred inside Beattie, something that she hadn't felt in many years, since she was a foolish teenager in love with Henry. With a thrill of alarm, she realized it was desire. Charlie's long, lean body, folded up so close to hers; his creamy dark skin; his dark curls and black eyes . . . But she admonished herself, decided that she was tired and worried about Mikhail, that her mind was playing tricks on her.

"Are you going to go get some sleep?" he asked her, shaking her out of her train of thought.

"Are you?"

"I'm going to stay right here."

"Then I am, too," she said.

He climbed to his feet. "I'll go unsaddle poor Abby. You keep an ear out."

Beattie waited, reorienting herself. The spear of longing had unsettled her. She had long ago given up thinking about men; had presumed that nobody would want sullied goods such as her. She had been so consumed with caring for Lucy, with fending off poverty, that desire had waited in the wings. That Charlie should arouse it was unexpected. She examined her feelings cautiously, for surely nothing could come of them.

He returned, slipped inside the bedroom, then came back quietly to sit. "He's asleep. The fever seems to be going down."

"His body?"

"A little more relaxed." He smiled. "I think he's going to make it."

Beattie's heart was warm with relief. "I hope you're right." She was growing tired, her head heavy on her knees, but was determined to wait out the night for Mikhail. She rose and lit a new candle. The wind rattled the windowpanes, but they were safe and inside. "Keep me awake," she said to Charlie, lowering herself to the ground again. The candle wax smelled warm in the dark. "You said there's nothing to know about you, but I bet there is."

Charlie nodded once. "Sure, missus, if you really want to know."

So he told her. He told her of the random glimpses of childhood he remembered, far, far north in the warm and wet part of the world, where the sea was green and the sky blue enough to make his eyes ache; of realizing early that he wasn't the same color as his beloved mother and how that made his community wary of him; of white men coming to take him to a special school for other kids like him, his mother weeping and saying it was for the best; being confused and disoriented, realizing and not realizing at the same time that he would never see her again.

"You can't imagine it, missus," he said, "all around you,

people are saying something is good for you. And all you got inside you is a feeling so bad . . ." He trailed off, his voice buckling under the weight of emotion.

She reached for his fingers with her own, but he shrank away a little, and she recalled her hand reluctantly. The night wore on, the deepest part of the night when secrets come to the surface. Every nerve in her body ached to reach for him again, but she didn't. It wasn't right, and she had to remember that he was her employee. When his story wound down, he asked her about her life, and she told him about her childish dreams of making clothes, of her love for fabrics and design, her fantasies about making something out of the wool they grew here at Wildflower Hill. She was encouraged by his interest, and somehow other truths slipped from her grasp: about Henry, about Lucy, even about Raphael and how she'd become the owner of Wildflower Hill—this made him laugh without stopping for a full ten minutes.

Somehow, in among the words and stories, dawn broke. So, too, did Mikhail's fever. Dr. Malcolm came soon after; Charlie disappeared back to his cottage. The spell of the night had passed, and practical needs reasserted themselves. Mikhail would be well in a week or so.

But Beattie feared her heart would not be the same again.

TWENTY-ONE

If Beattie hadn't had Charlie to organize shearing season, she would have fallen apart.

Five shearers came, moved into the cottage, and demanded huge breakfasts and dinners. Faced with spending the last of her money on paying either them or the bank, Beattie chose them. She wrote to the bank saying her interest payment would be late—until after the wool clip—and hoped for the best.

There was no money for extra stockmen, so Beattie and Mikhail were pressed into service. Beattie spent the mornings mustering and the afternoons cooking; Mikhail managed the gates and drafted the sheep into the pens; the dogs worked so hard that they dropped in the afternoons and slept like the dead. And Charlie ran the whole show. He knew where every person was at all times, he called out orders in his slow, gentle voice, he managed the mobs of sheep from one side of the property to the other, and he made sure that the shearers did their eighty sheep each a day.

Lack of room in the shearers' cottage meant Charlie had to sleep in the house. He rolled out his swag on the floor of one of the upstairs rooms. When Beattie climbed into bed at night, she often found herself thinking of his proximity. Just down the dark hallway, two doors down . . . his long body stretched out, his warm skin . . . But then she either banished the thought or fell asleep from exhaustion and the next day tried to deal with Charlie as though she'd not thought such things of him at all. He certainly gave no indication that he was thinking such things of her.

It was the fourth night of shearing. Beattie was wearily climbing the stairs for bed when she saw Charlie emerging from the bathroom, his hair wet, dressed in a loose shirt and denim pants.

"Good night, Charlie," she called as he headed toward his bedroom.

"Good night, Beattie," he replied as the door closed behind him.

Beattie. Not "missus." To hear his lips speak her name was a soft and unexpected pleasure. Her heart felt warm, and she couldn't help smiling.

Then finally, finally, money came in.

The wool classer had declared the fleeces very fine, yet they still had good weight. The resulting payment, when it was sold on, was far greater than Beattie had budgeted for. The bank, which had been sending her increasingly terse letters of demand, was paid out. More important, Beattie was able to pay Mikhail and Charlie, lining each of their pay packets with a generous bonus.

"I can't take this extra, Beattie," Charlie said. "You own the business, you take all the risks, so the rewards should go to you."

"You took many risks yourself," Beattie countered. "You worked for me for months without real payment."

He pushed the envelope back into her hands. "Give me what I'm due and not a penny more. Buy stock. What am I going to spend money on? Buy stock and make this business even stronger, so I have a job next year and the year after. That's how you can repay me."

Beattie heeded his advice, organizing another fifteen hundred sheep to come in November.

At last there was money for furniture. She opened up the dining room, put in a table big enough for six, moved two sofas into the sitting room. She bought a bed for Lucy and put it in the room next to hers. There was money for rugs and for curtain fabric. For the electricity and telephone to be reconnected. Wildflower Hill transformed, just in over a month, into a proper home. Lucy came at the start of the Christmas holidays, and for the first time since they had left Henry all those years ago, Beattie knew she could give her daughter everything she needed.

Beattie had thought it through carefully. She would hire a governess to teach Lucy her lessons, someone who could also help in the kitchen and with the household chores. Lucy would grow up learning about the farm, how to run it, how to ride and muster and do all the million jobs that Beattie and Charlie managed. Then, when she was a young woman, she could work alongside Beattie in the business and inherit it—and her own financial stability—when Beattie was gone. Beattie knew she could offer Lucy more than Henry and Molly: more than a life circumscribed by town, school, and church; more than being a well-behaved girl in training to be a well-behaved woman.

But Beattie was wary of approaching Henry and Molly directly, so she phoned Leo Sampson and asked him to come out and meet with her to discuss it.

She hadn't seen Leo since he'd handed her the keys and papers to Wildflower Hill over a year ago, hadn't spoken to him on the phone since she'd refused to sell another portion of Wildflower Hill to Jimmy Farquhar. He was as pleasant and practical as she remembered him.

"I must say, Beattie," he said, dropping his battered leather briefcase on the dining table, "you have made a real success of this place. I didn't think you could do it."

"I had good advice from Charlie Harris," she said, sitting opposite him. "He's been wonderful."

Leo frowned.

Beattie wasn't going to endure petty prejudice in her own home. "You, too, Leo? You don't believe that nonsense about him stealing from Raphael? You of all people know what kind of man Raphael Blanchard was."

"I do, and I also know what a good man Charlie Harris is. But they speak ill of him in town, and a number of them are saying . . ." He struggled with words for a moment, then said, "That you shouldn't have him here."

"If I didn't, I'd have gone under a year ago."

"Yes, and don't underestimate the jealousy people feel about that. You were a maid. Now your business is doing almost as well as Farquhar's. That you have in your employ a black man who's considered a thief . . ." He trailed off. "Look, Beattie, I know how hard you've worked here. But you must also work on your relationship with the folks in town. There isn't much goodwill there for you. And like it or not, you are part of the community. Your business relies on goodwill as well as good sales."

The doors to the courtyard were open, letting in the smells of earth and wildflowers, the summer wind. Beattie sighed deeply. "Thanks for your concern, Leo," she said. "But I want to talk to you about something other than business."

He pulled out a fountain pen and a notepad and adjusted his glasses. "Go on."

"I want my daughter back. I know that Henry and his wife are prepared to hire a lawyer against me, so I wanted to consult you first."

He scribbled on his page, then looked up at Beattie. "They are prepared to take you to court over her custody?"

"I'm sure of it."

He cleared his throat, seemed to be taking a long time to answer. Beattie's heart sank slowly.

"Go on," she said. "Tell me."

"If I may . . . as I understand it." Again he cleared his throat. "Henry was married to Molly when you fell pregnant with Lucy?"

"Yes."

He drew a tally mark on his page. "You ran away with Henry to another country to escape his wife?"

"Yes."

Another tally mark. And slowly they built up. She'd taken Henry's daughter away without his knowledge. She'd assisted at Raphael's gin and poker parties. She'd wagered her body to win the farm.

"Yes, yes, yes," Beattie said irritably. "But not everyone knows about those things."

"They will find out. If Henry puts a lawyer on it, they will find out. They'll ask Margaret Day, they'll talk to Terry over at Farquhar's, they'll find Alice, and she'll be only too glad to fill in the details."

"But Henry was just as bad. I had to leave him because he drank and gambled and let us starve."

"Can you not see how many marks I have on this page?" He picked up his pen and made one more, longer and darker than the others. "Beattie, you don't know what they're saying about you in town," he said gently.

"Then you'd better tell me."

He couldn't meet her eyes. "There's talk that you and Charlie are lovers."

Beattie's whole body grew warm. Embarrassment tingled into desire. "Who is saying that?"

"One of the shearers apparently mentioned that Charlie sleeps in the house."

"Terry slept in the house when Raphael lived here."

"Raphael wasn't a single woman of questionable sexual morals."

Beattie's throat blocked up.

"The chances of you getting Lucy back under the circumstances . . . You should consider letting Charlie go."

"I will not let him go," she said through gritted teeth. "If I lose Charlie, this business won't be worth passing on to my daughter. We are not lovers. He is my employee."

"I have no doubt you're telling the truth," Leo said.

Beattie had a sudden realization, and the words bubbled out of her quickly. "You aren't to talk of this to anyone. If Charlie thought he was making my life difficult in any way, he'd be gone in a second."

Leo spread his hands. "This entire meeting is confidential."

Beattie fell silent. Thoughts and feelings chased themselves through her mind and her body.

"Just be aware that, if you proceed, it will be difficult. You'd be better off asking Henry and Molly nicely if you can spend more time with Lucy. Buy your own car and get down there to Hobart on weekends. Keep it amicable."

She'd considered buying a car but had bought more sheep instead. She felt keenly the difficulty of balancing Lucy's present against Lucy's future.

Then she grew grumpy. Why should she have to ask anyone nicely—especially a woman who wasn't even related to Lucy—to spend more time with her own daughter? It was so unfair.

"I want her back, Leo," Beattie said, her voice catching.

"Then follow my advice," Leo said. "Give it another six months, make sure you're stable, hope for the rumors to go away."

"Six months is a long time in a child's life."

"She'll still be a child in six months or a year. Imagine: one more good wool clip, and you'll be quite wealthy. Wealthy people always have more power."

Six months or a year. Her heart didn't want to listen to Leo's advice, but her head had already submitted. One more year. One more wool clip. Then she'd be in a better position.

"Proceed with caution," he said, sliding his notebook back into his briefcase. "And for God's sake, make some friends in town."

When the new stock came, it was clear that Beattie could no longer be Charlie's off-sider. He needed a man, a well-trained one, to work with him. She hired a stockman named Peter to come in peak seasons, and she spent more time inside the house with her bookwork and her new sewing machine. It was hard to get used to not being around Charlie as much, but her body thanked her for it at the end of the night, when there was no sunburn to tend to nor callouses to treat on her hands.

Autumn gilded all the leaves on the row of poplars that lined the driveway. Beattie didn't fear winter's approach this year; in fact, she barely noticed it. Rain had made mud of the paddocks, green of the hills, but she was comfortable inside. Lucy slept upstairs in her warm bed but was due to return home to Hobart in two days.

Beattie worked at her sewing machine under the window of

the sitting room, letting down the hems of Lucy's school uniforms. The little girl grew taller by the moment. Beattie and Henry had an agreement: he would keep up with the shoes if she took care of the uniforms. She hummed to herself as she sewed, the squeak of the pedal on the sewing machine keeping a comforting rhythm. On the wireless, a man talked about Germany. It seemed everyone wanted to talk about Germany these days. It made her glad that she was so far away from Europe. Then she sensed movement behind her and looked around.

Charlie stood at the threshold, a grin on his face.

Beattie smiled in return. It was always a pleasure to see him. "Hello," she said.

"I have something for you." He pointed at one of the sofas. "Sit down and close your eyes."

"What is it?"

"Go on."

Beattie switched off the wireless, moved to the sofa, and closed her eyes.

"I've been tracking this down for weeks now. You might see a few calls to Launceston listed on the phone bill. But I think you'll like it."

Curiosity prickled all over her skin. Then something large and heavy dropped into her lap. She opened her eyes. It was a bolt of black cloth.

"Wool," she said, running her fingers over it. "Fine wool."

"Your wool," he replied.

"You mean . . . ?"

"I talked to the selling agent, and he put me on to the

manufacturer who bought most of our last clip. Look, the wool is sold at auction, and sold on and sold on . . . Well, there's no way of knowing for sure if it's all yours. But it's Tasmanian wool from this region. Might be a bit of Wildflower Hill in there."

Beattie unwrapped a few feet of the cloth and bunched it in her hands. She felt a sense of promise, of possibility, that she hadn't felt since she was a teenager.

"Sorry, black was all they had."

She realized she hadn't said anything to Charlie yet. "Thank you," she said, breathless. "It means so much to me."

"I know. I remember you telling me that night Mikhail was sick."

She gazed up at him, and for a moment their eyes locked. Then his gaze slid away. Her pulse hammered in her throat. He had gone to so much trouble . . . why? How else could she read it but as a sign of his affection for her? Perhaps his desire?

"Anyway," he said, slouching toward the door.

"I'll make you something," Beattie called.

"Nah, don't worry about me. Keep it for yourself."

Then he was gone. Beattie pulled out a few more feet of the fabric and held it up to her face, her mind already drawing patterns. She had a grand idea.

All through April and May she worked and never made a single thing for herself or Lucy. Instead, she designed two skirts and made ten of each in varying sizes. Then she embroidered twenty tags and sewed them into the seams: *Blaxland Wool*. The feeling of pride that seeing those tags in the skirts gave her was unutterable. She lovingly folded the skirts between tissue paper and stacked them on the sofa.

Leo Sampson's words came back to haunt her: *like it or not, you are part of the community.* He was right, she did need their goodwill. She especially needed the goodwill of Tilly Harrow, who ran the general store, if Beattie wanted her to stock these clothes for sale.

One fine, clear Friday morning, she walked down to town to speak to Tilly directly.

After Tilly had heard Margaret Day's gossip, she had cooled considerably toward Beattie, so Beattie hadn't tried to engage her again or even smile at her. Better to be rejected wearing a stony face rather than a grinning one. But today she applied a smile as she waited at the counter.

"Morning," Tilly said in a vague tone, not quite meeting her eye.

"Tilly, I need to ask you a very big favor."

Tilly's mouth twitched downward.

Beattie stumbled on. "I've made these . . . They are fine work, made with local wool." She pulled out one each of the skirts: the long slender one and the flared one. "I need somewhere to sell them and wondered if I could leave them here to sell on consignment."

This time Tilly's mouth went in the other direction. It seemed she found Beattie's request amusing. "You're not serious?" she said. "There's not a person in town who'd buy something you made."

Beattie folded the skirt back into its tissue paper, keeping her dignity. She realized hotly and clearly that she never should have come here. That she should have taken a bus down to Hobart and gone to a larger store, where women were more interested in fashion than in the designer's shady past. She turned to leave, but then her annoyance got the better of her. "What have I ever done to you, or to anyone in this town," she asked, "to be treated so poorly?"

Tilly blinked back at her, perhaps considering this question for the first time: a pack animal suddenly asking itself why it did what the others did without question. Then her face hardened again. "There are plenty of people who are honest and work hard, who are justified to dislike people who don't."

"I'm honest. I work hard."

"That's not what I've heard." Tilly sniffed.

Beattie wanted to shout and stamp and knock over the neat jars of sweets and postcard racks on the counter. She took a deep breath, said, "You know nothing about me," and left.

Next wool clip, she was going to buy a car and go to Bligh for supplies, or up to Bothwell. In the meantime, Mikhail would have do the shopping, because Beattie was never going to speak to anyone in town again.

In the end, it was Molly who helped Beattie sell her skirts. When she and Henry dropped Lucy off for the winter holidays, Molly found them piled up behind the sofa.

"What are these?" she asked, unfolding one. "And why do you have so many?"

Beattie explained that she had designed and made them—a

fact that astonished Molly—and that she hadn't had any luck placing them in the local shops.

"I have a friend at church who works at FitzGerald's in Hobart," Molly said. "I can take them to her if you like." She closed her mouth quickly after she spoke, as though she might have regretted offering to help.

Beattie was desperate enough to overlook any of the unspoken discomfort between them. "Would you?"

"I . . . Yes, of course." Molly's eyes flicked to Henry, who shook his head slightly with exasperation. "I'll ask for you."

"Thank you. I don't know what they're worth. Ask your friend to do with them what she thinks is best. And to call me if she needs to." Beattie loaded Molly's arms up with the skirts. "Keep one for yourself."

She waved them off cheerfully, with her arm around Lucy's shoulders.

"Why are you smiling so much, Mummy?" Lucy asked.

Beattie cuddled her tight. "Honest work, darling," she said. "Always its own reward."

Beattie kept the last of the wool for a special purpose: she was making Charlie a coat. The old gray coat that he wore when out mustering was falling apart where the sleeves met the shoulders; she had repaired it three or four times already. But she imagined him in a new coat, one handmade by her, with raglan sleeves and a fly fastening, lined with sheepskin to keep him warm through the long unforgiving winter. But it was to be a surprise, so she had been measuring him with her eyes the last few months. When he came into the kitchen at night, smelling faintly of horse and perspiration, she judged the distance across his shoulders, the line from the nape of his neck where his dark curls sat, the length of his strong arms.

Watching him so closely for so long prodded the bruising ache of desire inside her. What did it matter? Everyone in town already thought badly of her. She had nobody left to offend. What did it matter if she wanted him? When he had gone to all the trouble of getting her the wool, he had been letting her know, surely, that she was special to him. As the weeks went by, she searched every word, every expression on his face, for evidence that she was right. And sometimes, for just a flash in an unguarded moment, it was there.

So the coat became much more than a coat; it became a potent symbol of her desire for him. At night, after he had gone to bed, Beattie stayed up and worked on it, hand-stitching the lining and the pockets. As she sewed, Beattie allowed herself to imagine the moment that she gave it to him. Each stitch became alive with the knowledge that she was falling in love with him. She sewed that love into the coat.

Finally, as midwinter closed in, making daylight a fleeting thing, it was ready. And she readied herself to give it to him.

She caught him at the bottom of the stairs, his determined footsteps heading toward the kitchen, the laundry, the stables. Out to work with his threadbare gray coat on.

"Charlie?" she said, surprised that her voice sounded so smooth.

He turned, tilted his head slightly to the side, and gave her his customary gentle smile. "Good morning, Beattie."

She hurried to the bottom stair, holding the coat out in front of her.

He took it from her hands; his eyes ran over it, and a look crossed his face—she couldn't describe it. It might have been sadness. She didn't know what she'd done to make him feel sad, though.

"Don't you like it?" she asked.

His smile was back in place. "It's brilliant, Beattie. Thanks." He slipped out of the gray coat, hung it over the banister, and slid his lean body into the new coat.

It fit him perfectly. She was impossibly proud of her handi-work; it hung on his tall frame as well as if she'd measured him with a tape instead of a hungry gaze.

"Bloody brilliant," he muttered, holding his arms out to admire the sleeves. "It's the nicest thing I've ever owned." He looked up at her, nodded. "Thanks."

"You're welcome." She wanted to touch him, smooth the material over his shoulder. Her hand itched. An enormous moment of choked silence. "Charlie, I—"

"Beattie, don't be worrying too much about me," he said. "Don't be making me nice things and fussing over me. I'm not . . . I'm not the man to make a fuss of."

In none of her fantasies about this moment had Charlie ever said that. She swallowed hard. Was he warning her off? She couldn't bear to go on not knowing. Forcing herself to be brave, she said, "You are worth making a fuss of. You are one of the best men I have ever known." *The best. Not one of the best.*

Again the sad expression. Beattie's fantasy was falling apart.

The coat was meant to bring them together, not separate them awkwardly.

"I'm just your farm manager. I'm your employee."

"Without you there would be no farm."

"I'm not that special." He looked at her squarely. "I shouldn't be that special."

Without doubt, he was warning her off. She felt such a fool. He had seen through her as though she were made of brittle glass, had seen the silly desire she nurtured for him, and was telling her to put it away before it embarrassed them both. Beattie blinked rapidly to keep tears at bay. She forced a little smile. "Well. I can't stand here talking all day. I'd best get on with the bookwork."

He pulled on his hat and nodded, then turned and left. Gorgeous in his new coat, forever out of her reach.

On the first day of August, Beattie took a call from the women's-wear department at FitzGerald's in Hobart. They had sold all her skirts and wanted to know if she had any more. And they had forty-eight pounds waiting for her to pick up.

Taking on the extra business seemed a good way to try to get Charlie out of her mind.

TWENTY-TWO

1938

Christmas wouldn't be the same without Mikhail.

The room swirled with laughter and music. Peter and his brother, Matt, the stockmen, were singing a drunken goodbye song; Lucy was jumping up and down near the Christmas tree, demanding to know what "the big green present" was. And Mikhail stood by the empty fireplace with his arm around his fiancée, grinning as widely as he had for the entire six months since he'd met her. Mikhail was marrying Catherine—a widow with two grown children—and they were moving to Launceston to be near her elderly parents. Beattie would have to learn to manage without him.

"Come on," Beattie said, flipping up the lid of the piano. "Rosella, will you play us a song to stop those men from singing so terribly out of tune?"

Rosella was her new neighbor. She and her husband had leased Jimmy Farquhar's farm at the start of the year and become good friends to Beattie. Their daughter, Lizzie, was the same age as Lucy, and they spent every moment of the holidays together, racing around in the paddocks, building cubbies and making mud pies.

As Rosella sat and started playing Jingle Bells and everyone joined in, Beattie curled her arm around Lucy, and her eyes moved from face to face as she counted her Christmas blessings. Two fabulous wool clips and a growing side business in designing women's work wear had brought her the financial security she had long dreamed of—the piano, the little utility truck, the glass Christmas decorations. It had even bought Henry's grudging respect and, with that, his permission to allow Lucy to spend a full term that year with Beattie, learning with a governess. Though Lucy was so distracted by what was going on in the paddocks that she'd learned hardly a thing, and Molly had noticed.

"She must start regular school again come January," Molly had said, her pale hands fluttering near her throat. Molly knew she was losing Lucy; Beattie had no sympathy. It would be a wrench to send Lucy back after so long, but Beattie knew that—slowly and irrevocably—she was winning.

What her financial success hadn't bought was a calm heart. Charlie still worked for her, and he had moved back to the shearers' cottage. Yes, he had let her buy him a proper bed, a little desk, a cupboard for his things. But he kept her very much at arm's length. Indeed, there was little need for them to see each other. He ran his side of the business, and she ran hers. There had been no other gestures of affection since he'd brought her the bolt of cloth. He was just across the paddock but may as well have been a million miles away. She tried not to mind. She usually managed to keep those warm imaginings of him at bay. But she still hadn't met a man who could compare to him.

Charlie saw her eyes roaming the room and smiled at her. Just a friendly smile with no hidden meaning. But that small offering of affection—guarded as it may have been—imbued the Christmas music with an air of melancholy, as though somewhere in hearing range, another, sadder tune played against it.

The song came to a close, and Beattie asked everyone to be quiet so she could say a few words. "Mikhail," she said, "when I had nothing, you were here for me. You stood by me in the worst times of my life, and for that I am forever in your debt."

Mikhail waved her away with embarrassment. Catherine stood on tiptoe to kiss his weathered cheek. Everyone applauded, somebody called for more brandy, and Beattie realized that Lucy was up far too late.

"Good night, little red-haired girl," Charlie said affectionately as Lucy called out her good nights from the threshold.

Beattie took Lucy upstairs and tucked her in. "It's nearly eleven." Beattie laughed. "Don't tell Molly."

Lucy giggled. "Naughty Mummy."

Beattie sat on the bed, enjoying the cool dark of Lucy's bedroom after the bright warmth of the sitting room. "Do you miss Molly?"

Lucy nodded. "I miss Daddy the most. But then I miss you when I'm with Daddy. It's not fair. No matter where I am, I miss somebody."

Beattie smoothed the girl's red-gold hair away from her forehead. "I'm sorry, darling."

"You know, sometimes I make up this story in my head. And in it, Molly dies and you and Daddy realize you still love each other. Then we're all in one place."

Beattie had to stifle a laugh. "You shouldn't wish Molly to be dead."

"I don't wish it, not at all!" Lucy cried. "I just think of it sometimes. And I know it would be sad and I'd miss Molly, but if you and Daddy and I were all together, maybe I wouldn't mind so very much."

Beattie smiled at her in the dark. "I'm sorry, Lucy, but it's just a story. Daddy and I will never be together like that again."

Lucy nodded sadly. "I know." She thought for a moment before adding. "But you loved him once, didn't you?"

"Yes, of course," Beattie said, trying to remember what that had felt like.

"Because I asked him the same, and he said he'd loved you very much, too. Once. And that my smile is the same as your smile."

For some reason, this thought made Beattie feel melancholy. Yes, they had loved each other. Foolish love. And they'd made this gorgeous child, then done nothing but fight over her since.

"But Molly heard," Lucy continued. "And she got so angry. I've never seen her so angry."

Beattie wasn't sure how to explain the situation to her daughter, so she said nothing. The girl was only nine. Perhaps when she was twelve, Beattie would tell her the whole story. And hope that Lucy didn't judge her too harshly.

"Time to sleep now," Beattie said.

"One more thing, Mummy. Daddy has Molly now, but you don't have anyone."

"I don't need anyone. I manage fine by myself."

"That's good," Lucy said, turning on her side, "because I don't want another daddy."

Beattie patted her shoulder and rose, drew the curtains tight to block out the patient starlight, and returned downstairs.

Matt, Peter, and Charlie had headed back to the cottage, and Rosella and her family were packing up to go. They were going to put Mikhail and Catherine up for the night, as the bus to Launceston ran close by their back fence. The sight of Mikhail's bags by the front door made Beattie's eyes prick with tears. In among the whirl of movement and voices, she found him.

"Goodbye, old friend," she said, grasping his hand firmly. "I will miss you."

"Ah, you will forget me in no time."

"Never. Never." She squeezed his hand hard.

He bent his head and kissed her knuckles softly. "You are best boss I ever have," he said.

"Come on, Mikhail," Catherine was calling. "Our lift is leaving."

"I come, I come!" he said gruffly. Then leaned in close to Beattie so nobody else could hear and said, "Is greatest happiest to be in love."

"I'm very pleased for you."

"I hope for you such happiness, too."

Beattie smiled unevenly. "Well, I . . ."

"I am not supposed to say anything. He says this to me one, maybe two years ago now, that I am not allowed to mention it. But I always hope that Charlie and you would be in love."

Beattie's face felt warm. "Charlie told you not to say that to me?"

Mikhail nodded gravely. "Charlie is very concerned for your reputation." He snorted a laugh. "I say that Beattie doesn't care much for reputation. You don't need it. You have brains and money. And you are always very beautiful." He stood back, smiled over at Catherine. "Though not quite as beautiful as my wife-to-be."

Catherine gestured to him urgently. Rosella's daughter, Lizzie, was grizzling with tiredness. "Time to go, time to go," Catherine said.

"Goodbye," said Mikhail.

"Not forever," said Beattie.

The noise withdrew, the door closed.

Beattie returned to the sitting room, collected glasses and plates, and dusted cigarette ash off the table. Slowly, carefully, tidying the room, patting the cushions. She switched on the wireless. Christmas carols. Such a lovely change from the daily talk about Hitler and Churchill.

What had Charlie said to Mikhail, and why? Did he have feelings for her after all, and had he hidden them in some misguided attempt to protect her from the town's opinion? Now she was confused. She had spent so long convincing herself that her feelings of love were nothing of the sort, that they were just the folly of a lonely woman. What was she supposed to do now?

But Charlie was estranged from her. At one stage, that night when Mikhail had been sick, they had been close. Just a half inch of air between them. That long night of stories and secrets was years ago now; since then their roles on the farm had crystallized, and they'd moved away from each other. He was over at the cottage with the boys; she was at the house with her books and her sewing machine. There was surely no way to bridge that gap. She cursed him for taking that decision away from her, for deciding that the opinions of a handful of fusspots in Lewinford were more important than her feelings for him.

And now it was too late.

Before he left, Mikhail had taught Beattie how to drive the little utility truck, with its rumbling engine and wide tires, and so she took Lucy back to Hobart herself in the middle of January. The girl cried on arriving at Henry's house, but Beattie wasn't sure if the tears were about leaving Beattie or about having missed Henry. Henry hugged Lucy savagely. There was still no denying the bond he had with her.

"Thank you for returning her safely," Molly said, touching Lucy's shoulder lightly. "We've missed her so much."

"And now it's my turn to miss her," Beattie said. "Walk with me a few moments?"

Lucy and Henry went inside, and Molly went out the front gate with Beattie and walked down to the big gum at the bottom of the street. A hot wind had been blowing from the west for days, making Beattie's skin dry and cracked.

"I want to have Lucy back more often. I want her for half the year," Beattie said plainly. "She works well with the governess."

Molly was already shaking her head. "It's too disruptive for the child. She needs to be more settled at school. She doesn't go to church when she's with you. She runs wild."

"She doesn't run wild," Beattie said, wondering if that was a lie. Lucy certainly had a lot of unstructured time on the farm. "She's learning about the farm. She can ride a horse so well now, and she helps with the chickens and the garden."

"That's not a life for a young girl. She needs boundaries. She needs manners, she needs to be able to fit in. And she's getting quite freckled." Molly frowned, glancing up at the sun. It was fierce today, baking everything. "Henry won't hear of it, I'll warn you now. He did nothing but grumble the whole time she was away. He was unbearable. He loves that child more than you know."

Beattie didn't push it further. Parting from Lucy was always hard enough, without stirring up any old ill will.

Beattie dropped in on two of the boutiques she made clothes for in Hobart to collect money and new orders. She had stopped supplying to FitzGerald's when she realized she couldn't keep up with the demand. She was only one woman. So she concentrated on fewer designs in fewer sizes, charged four times as much, and took special orders if necessary. She found wool loaned itself best to practical clothes, not the frivolous dresses she had loved to design as a teenager. She began to appreciate the beauty of simple lines. In her head she had dozens of designs, and she sometimes idly sketched them. But without a team of seamstresses, there wouldn't be time to make them all, so she focused on keeping the business ticking over slowly.

Heat shimmered on the road, and Beattie drove home with the windows down. The car seemed empty on the way back without Lucy's chatter. She always experienced the girl's absence like a slow ache that wouldn't go away. It had been nearly ten years since that day she had realized she was pregnant. Ten years gone in a blink. Why was she waiting, hoping for Henry and Molly to be kind to her? Surely by now she was wealthy and powerful enough to rise above any ideas they had to discredit her.

She drove up through hills and valleys, parched under the yellow sun. The road ran out and dirt took over. She slowed. Lewinford was approaching. She decided to stop. This time she wouldn't let Leo talk her out of it. If they wouldn't share Lucy, then she would have to get her back permanently.

Beattie was almost a curiosity in Lewinford these days. Normally, she drove an hour north for her supplies, to a town large enough not to care about who owned Wildflower Hill and why. When she parked her mud-splattered utility truck outside the post office—across from Leo's little stone cottage—one or two curious locals stopped to see who owned it.

Beattie climbed out proudly, pulling off her gloves and tucking them into her handbag. Tilly Harrow's slit-eyed husband, Frank, was sweeping the footpath in front of the shop. He stopped to scowl at her. She shrugged off the attention. She was dressed well—her own designs—and her dark hair was arranged perfectly behind her ears. She knew she looked good: fit and well from hard work and good living. Let them die for the fact that she was now a wealthy woman.

A hot wind buffeted Beattie's hat, and she raised her hand to hold it on. She crossed the road and rang the bell. Leo answered and ushered her inside into the cool.

"Beattie, what a delight! You look marvelous. Come in, come in."

He showed her through to a narrow study with polished wooden floorboards and an oak desk that didn't quite fit the room. It was shoved tight up against a window that looked out into a gully of overgrown bushes. Leo's beard was almost entirely gray, and his fingers were yellow from nicotine. His office smelled strongly of tobacco.

For a little while they talked, but then he asked her how Lucy was. Beattie came to the point. "That's why I'm here. I want full custody. I'll take him to court if I have to."

Leo nodded. "That might be expensive."

"I can afford it."

"And you might not win. You might end up with reduced access. The courts won't look favorably on you. He's married, you aren't."

"A girl should be with her mother."

Leo seemed to be about to say something, then stopped

himself. "My warnings from last time we still hold," he said instead.

"I know. But I want to do this. I have a past, and I'm not proud of it. But Henry does, too. I could call on witnesses, if necessary. Billy Wilder, Doris Penny, the women who owned the store where he ran up all his debts. People back in Glasgow, if I have to. I was only eighteen! He was thirty."

Leo sat back, considering her. At length, he said, "Put all of this into a letter. Take your time. Write it slowly and carefully, and list names of people who could help. When I have it, I can set this in motion."

She stood and leaned across to shake his hand. "Thank you. I'm glad to have you on my side."

Beattie woke late in the night. It was so hot that she'd left the window open, and she saw that she had kicked off her covers. Was that what had woken her? The heat?

No, it was something else. She became aware of the faint but distinct smell of smoke.

She startled, leaped out of bed. She leaned out the window and sniffed the air. Smoke on the wind, and the wind was hot and fast.

She pulled on her robe and hurried downstairs, opened the back door, and descended through the laundry and into the paddock. She had a view of the fields behind the house to the north, the rising slope of the ridge. The smoky sky glowed amber. The eucalyptus forest was on fire.

Beattie froze for a few moments, watching the leaves on the

trees behind her house rattle harshly in the wind. The wind was coming from the northeast. That meant the fire was coming this way.

She yelped, began to run for the shearers' cottage. "Charlie! Charlie!" she called, her voice seized by the wind. In snatches, a terrifying sound like trains roaring past. Was that the fire? Abby and Birch were spooked already, kicking against the stable, alerted by the smell of the smoke. "Hang on," she called to them. Her heart thundered. Charlie would know what to do, wouldn't he?

He met her at the front door, his face soft from sleep. He opened his mouth to ask what was wrong, then his own senses told him.

"Jeez, Beattie," he said, breaking into a run. The dogs were at his heels. "Saddle up Abby quick and run down as far as you can to open up the gates. Take the dogs, but don't bother driving the stock, they'll have to figure it out themselves."

"Aren't we going to get in the car and run?" she asked.

He turned to her, his eyes glittering in the dark. "You want to lose everything?"

She shook her head.

"Then we stay."

Beattie's heart thumped loosely under her ribs. She dashed to the stable and, with shaking hands, saddled up a skittish Abby. Birch tore off the minute the door was open and galloped south. Beattie could barely mount Abby, who was tossing her head and dancing from side to side. Beattie soothed her and spoke to her softly, even though she wanted to shriek with fear. What on earth would she do if she lost it all? The house? She could never rebuild it. The stock? Even if she bought new stock, what would they eat on a burned-out farm?

"Oh, please, please, God," she said, screwing her eyes tightly shut. She urged Abby forward, whistled to the dogs, and began to ride over uneven ground in the firelit night, opening gates, eyes on the wind. Her robe got caught on barbed wire, ripped. Large, thin pieces of ash began to flutter over her. First one or two, then dozens. It was raining ash. Thundering footfalls from behind her as a family of kangaroos raced through the farm, heading south, away from the fire, leaping fences as though they weren't there at all.

Abby had had enough. She put her head down and threatened to buck. Her head was darting, her nostrils wide as she snorted her fear. She shied wildly at shadows and at nothing, then sidestepped away from a thrashing branch. Inexperience made it difficult for Beattie to stay in the saddle.

"Whoa, whoa, girl," Beattie said, but she could feel herself slipping. She dismounted quickly, and Abby jerked her head and the reins slipped from Beattie's hands. Abby was off in a second, galloping away.

Beattie turned. Dread chocked her. Flames were roaring down the mountainside. She didn't know what to do.

Charlie. He was at the house alone.

She turned to the dogs. "Go!" she said, pointing after Abby. "Go on."

They looked at her; they seemed uncertain.

"Go now. Go!" She began to run back toward Charlie. She didn't care if every damned sheep she owned was destroyed; she was going to stay by his side.

The ash that fell now was alight, sizzling into smoky life-lessness as it hit the ground. She ran harder than she'd ever run, until her thighs burned with pain and her heart hammered her ribs. In the distance, she could see the stables were alight. Embers must have gotten under the eaves. Against the red sky, the silhouette of Charlie moved on the roof of the house. She put on an extra burst of speed.

Suddenly, the wind dropped. Quiet, eerie by contrast.

"Charlie!" she called. "The wind's stopped."

He turned to see her running toward him. "It's going to swing around," Charlie said. "Hang on."

Sure enough, moments later, the trees began to shake again. The thinnest branches were buffeted in circles, then ripped off and cast away. A fresh shower of ash rained down on them.

She was at the laundry and could see that Charlie had the hose up on the roof, putting out embers as they pelted the house.

"It's heading east," Beattie cried, relief flooding her despite the choking smoke. "The wind's changed direction. It's going to skim right across the top of us."

Up on the roof, Charlie was swearing.

"What is it?"

"The pump's failed."

"I'll bring water."

"No, forget the buckets. Check the pump!"

Beattie looked at the pump dumbly. She had no idea. Embers swirled around her.

"Check where the hose is connected," he called.

She could hardly focus. The hose was turned over on itself,

blocking the flow. She unhooked the fold, hands shuddering, and water burst out all over her. The hose had disconnected altogether.

"Hurry, for God's sake, Beattie!"

She fumbled for the hose, fitted it back on the pump, pressed down on the clamp as hard as she could.

Up on the roof, the sound of water. "That's it!" he said. "That's it!"

His silhouette up there, against the flames, made her heart clench. What if he slipped and fell? Or what if flames caught him? If her house was still there but Charlie wasn't in it, it was hardly worth saving. With sudden clarity, she realized that she loved him. That all of the concerns about what people thought were ridiculously small and petty. Why should either of them let anyone else's opinion dictate their lives?

"Be careful, Charlie," she shouted. "Please, please be careful."

He didn't answer. The fire wasn't drawing any closer, and she allowed herself cautious hope. She clutched the collar of her dressing gown to her throat. The rain of ash eased. The wind was definitely driving the fire in another direction. But what was to stop the wind from changing again?

Moments passed, her heart kept beating. The wind died down. Ash settled and didn't catch.

"I reckon you can turn the hose off now, Beattie," he called. "But I'm staying up here."

"Then I'm coming up, too."

"You stay down there."

She didn't listen. She turned off the hose and ran into the

house. Up in Lucy's room was a ladder into the attic, which led out onto the roof parapet. Through there she could climb up onto the tiles. Charlie sat there, the hose dormant at his side. He had his arms around his knees, and his face was streaked with soot.

"I said not to come up," he said.

She put her hands on the gutter to pull herself up, but he stood carefully and waved her down.

"I'll come down there," he said. "We can watch the fire."

He slid down off the roof and onto the parapet beside her. From there, they could see out over the fields and to the trees beyond, the orange glow reflected in the smoke.

"Is it going to miss us?" she asked.

"Looks like it. Unless the wind changes again."

They watched in silence for a long time. The stable burned and fell in on itself with a great exhalation of ash and embers. Gradually, the roaring of the fire in the distance grew quieter. Beattie realized that she was still clenching her fists tightly. She released them slowly. Charlie stood next to her, close enough that she could feel the heat of his body. She stole a glance at him and felt a sense of vertigo, of falling out of her own skin.

He sensed her gaze and half turned, seemed afraid to meet her eyes.

"Thank you," she said.

He shrugged. "It's my job."

"That's the second time you've saved something precious to me."

He didn't answer, but this time he allowed his eyes to meet hers fully. Adrenaline flashed through her.

"Charlie . . ." she started.

A long silence. Her stomach twitched. Her whole body was singing out to be pressed against his. She glanced at his lips—a half moment—then away. But the thought of those lips touching hers ignited her skin.

"Beattie," he said in a tone so reasonable and patient that it warned her he was about to rebuff her, "you should go to bed. I'll stay up here and keep watch."

"I'll stay with you."

"Absolutely not."

Beattie wanted to cry with frustration, exhaustion.

"No point in both of us being tired tomorrow. There will be work to do. You go and sleep. I'll let you know if the wind changes again. You can trust me."

"I know I can," she said, and she meant it.

She woke four hours later to a grim dawn, a stinking black mess on the mountainside. Beattie stood at her window for long moments, horrified by the smoking bodies of trees. In the daylight, she could see how close it had come to Wild-flower Hill. She wondered, with an ache that surprised her, how her neighbors had fared.

She glanced down, and there was Charlie, sitting beneath her window. His dogs were back, lying exhausted on either side of him.

Beattie pulled on her torn and sooty robe and hurried down. "Charlie?"

He turned to see her, and the weariness in his face made her ribs contract. Her darling Charlie.

"Hey, Beattie," he said with a weak smile. "The fire went east. Made a fair mess up there, but we didn't lose much. Just the stables and a view."

Fear, exhaustion . . . many unnamable feelings. She had come so close to losing everything. She began to sob. He stood, awkward at first, a hand reaching out and then withdrawing.

So she fell against him and he caught her. His body against hers was hard and strong. His arms gingerly went around her, patted her back. "There," he said. "We're all right."

She lifted her head to look into his eyes. What he saw there must have terrified him, because he took a step back.

"Beattie, I—"

She lifted her hand, pressed fingers to his lips to hush him. "I think I might die if you don't kiss me," she said.

The moment stretched out, her body tensed for his response. Then he took her hand away from his mouth and used it to pull her close again. With a soft groan, she let herself be folded into his arms, let him push back her hair, and let his hot mouth kiss her throat, her ears, and finally, her lips. His body was so hard against hers, his embrace so firm and strong. The whole world slipped away from her, and she existed only for that moment, only for the searing passion between them. His hands moved to her robe, slowly slipped it from her left shoulder. His lips were against her skin a moment later; warm, reverent. She pressed herself against him, feverish.

"Come upstairs with me, Charlie," she muttered.

"I'm covered in soot and ash." He laughed, extricating himself and standing back. Then his face was serious again. "Beattie, are you sure about this?"

"I am certain," she said.

They lay in the sunshine filtering through the open curtains for a long time afterward, a tangle of limbs and shed clothes. The window let in the warm morning air, the acrid smell of smoke and crushed eucalyptus. Charlie's fingers idly moved in patterns around Beattie's left shoulder as she listened to the thump of his heart under his hard chest.

"I need to tell you something, Beattie," he said, his voice gruff from lack of sleep and smoke.

"Go on," she said.

"I've been in love with you a long time."

She smiled, though he couldn't see her face.

"What are we going to do now?" he asked.

"Forget about the world and love each other," she said.

He fell silent, and next time she looked, he was asleep.

TWENTY-THREE

Henry sat in the car, the engine running, wondering what the devil was taking Molly so long. They'd pulled over in Lewinford on the way back from taking Lucy to Beattie's, and Molly had insisted on stopping for something to eat on the way home. She never seemed to stop eating lately, was straining at her skirts. Henry had tried not to notice how fit and fine Beattie was looking by comparison.

Not that he would ever take Beattie back. Those feelings had gone cold many years ago.

Why must Molly drag her feet so? Could she not remember that he was always in a terrible mood when he had to say goodbye to his little girl? The child was the only thing that made him happy in the world: the rest—money, a good job, a faithful wife—were empty things. Only Lucy made his heart truly glad.

Henry cut the engine and climbed out of the car. He crossed the road and pushed open the door to the general store. Molly stood at the counter in rapt attention. The young woman and young man behind the counter were talking to her, taking turns, in quiet voices.

"Molly? Are you ready to go?"

Molly turned. He saw her face was pale.

"What is it?" he asked impatiently. She was always overreacting to something.

"I've just heard the most despicable thing about Beattie," she said.

Henry's back prickled with irritation. He didn't love Beattie, but she was Lucy's mother, and anything that dragged Beattie down dragged Lucy down, too. "Get in the car, Molly," he said.

Molly gathered her purchase and scurried ahead of him. He gave the couple behind the counter a glare and headed out into the sunshine again.

Molly waited in the car, her hand in a box of chocolates.

"I wish you wouldn't listen to gossip. Molly," Henry said as he started the car and pulled onto the dirt road. "It's beneath you."

"I think we should know what kind of a woman is looking after our child when we're not there, Henry. We'd be bad parents if we didn't."

Henry winced. *Our child.* "Lucy is as much Beattie's daughter as mine."

"Yes, but you've chosen as your wife a good churchgoing woman. I'm a good mother to Lucy. But the man Beattie has in mind for Lucy's father is horrifying."

A small barb of jealousy. Where had that come from? He didn't want Beattie; he was absolutely sure of it. "What do you mean?"

"They tell me she has taken a lover."

Henry glanced at Molly. She was licking her fingers. "Go on."

She paused for drama. "Charlie. The black man."

Henry watched the road unfold under him, silent for a long time. In truth, he didn't care if people were black or white or green. Charlie seemed a low sort of fellow but decent enough. Henry felt strangely displaced by the news. Was it the imaginings of the fellow touching Beattie in the way that Henry had once touched her? Or was it Molly's warning that Charlie would not be a good father for the child?

"I see you think the way I do," Molly said. "It must be stopped."

"Beattie can choose to love whomever she wants," Henry said, but his voice came out choked.

"I think it's appalling," Molly continued, as though she hadn't heard him, and he began to doubt that he had ever said anything. "Imagine him kissing our little girl good night."

It seemed to Henry as though his whole body were rumbling.

"I know that some of those dark fellows can be all right," Molly conceded, "but I'd rather not have one quite so close to something I hold so dear." Her voice dropped to a whisper; he almost didn't hear her over the engine. "They say he's a thief."

"Be quiet," Henry commanded, at a loss to understand

the currents of fear and anger that infused him. "I wish you'd never said anything."

Molly sat back in silence for the rest of the trip home.

Charlie had finally moved into the house, though he insisted on a separate room. Lucy's bedroom was between Beattie's and Charlie's, and Beattie told herself that for her daughter's two-week visit, they would simply sleep apart.

Simply, it was impossible.

She had grown too used to the proximity of his warm skin, to the passionate touch of his fingers. Late at night, when she was sure the child was sleeping, Beattie crept down the hallway and knocked lightly.

He answered the door warily, eyes black in the dim light. "Are you sure, Beattie?" he asked.

"You always ask that, and I am always sure," Beattie said.

He stood back to let her in, then closed the door behind them. She fell into his arms, surrendering her mouth to his lips, his tongue. His narrow bed waited for them. The stars beyond the curtainless window glowed soft and eternal. Charlie had quickly learned precisely the best way to meet her needs; by comparison, Henry had been positively clumsy. Charlie always left her spent, her ears ringing, and pulled tight against his hard chest, muttering to her words of love.

But it was more than physical attraction. She sometimes felt as though her soul and his were magnetized to each other, always pulling together. They were made of the same stuff. He was the safe harbor she had been searching for all these years.

"We should get married," Beattie said idly, after, when midnight was drawing close.

"I don't know, Beattie. Folks in town wouldn't like that."

"We can't just go on the way we are." She sighed. "As though it's a secret. As though we're afraid of their opinions."

"According to that lawyer of yours, we ought to be afraid of them."

Beattie conceded. "All right, but as soon as Lucy is mine, then we won't keep it secret anymore." She had spent weeks wording the letter for Leo Sampson as precisely as she could. She'd felt guilty, enumerating Henry's faults one after the other. But she had to remind herself that she wasn't making any of it up: he *had* run away from his wife, he *had* drunk and gambled away their security, he *had* taken Molly back when she'd inherited money. In truth, Beattie didn't think him a bad father; she knew that nobody could love Lucy more. But she had to say whatever would make the court decide that Lucy was better off with her mother. Her *real* mother and not Henry's fretful, childless wife. Now Leo had the letter, and the papers had been signed and were ready to submit as soon as Lucy returned to school. Leo had told her it would take months to get through the courts.

"Imagine, Charlie," Beattie said. "You and I could marry, Lucy would be with us. Wildflower Hill would be ours."

Charlie laughed. "You know I don't care about owning anything, Beattie."

"But you should. Imagine if I died tomorrow and somebody else took over the property. You've done so much for it, and you get only the smallest rewards."

"I'm happy with what I've got," Charlie said. "It doesn't pay to dream too big. Especially for a blackfella."

Beattie sat up, gazing down on him. His dark hair was spread about him on the pillow, his strong bare shoulders. "Dream as big as you like with me, Charlie," she said.

"If you don't mind, Beattie, I might still take care."

She bent to kiss his forehead. The smell of his skin filled her nostrils. "Everything will be fine," she said. "You will see."

Beattie took a long time to identify the feeling that itched in her stomach on the drive down to Hobart. It was guilt.

She was taking Lucy home, but everything was different this time. Yesterday Leo Sampson had sent papers to Henry and Molly's lawyer. Sometime this week they would know that Beattie was going into battle for Lucy's custody. That Beattie had committed to print all of their faults as parents.

Today they didn't know. Today Molly came to the front gate waving when she heard Beattie's car. Today was the last time they would be civil to each other.

"Oh, my dear girl." Molly sighed, closing Lucy in a hug.

"Hello, Mama. I patted an echidna!"

Molly looked over the top of Lucy's head at Beattie. "Henry's been called in to work."

"Tell him I sent my best."

Molly smiled tightly, and Beattie grew afraid that she could read Beattie's mind. "How are you?" Molly asked.

"Well. We're looking at a good wool clip this year, and the boutique is selling my designs quicker than I can make them." She told herself to stop talking so fast.

"And how is Charlie?"

Words got stuck on her tongue.

Lucy intervened. "Charlie showed me how to tie five different knots!"

"That's lovely, dear," Molly said, "but you should be careful about getting too close to a black man. They aren't quite the same as us."

Beattie's spine grew hot with anger, but she knew better than to jump too quickly to Charlie's defense. "Lucy takes people for who they are," she said, "no matter how they appear on the outside."

"Because she is a child," Molly said smoothly, "and surely in time she will learn."

Beattie knelt to hug Lucy, who looked confused and hurt.

"Charlie's not a bad man, is he, Mummy?" she asked.

Beattie kept her voice low. "Charlie is a good man, and you are a good girl. I will see you in three months."

"Thirteen weeks."

"Exactly." Beattie pushed away the intense sadness she always felt saying goodbye. Come July, Lucy might well be coming to stay with her permanently. "Goodbye, my darling."

"Bye, Mummy," Lucy said. She waited with Molly at the gate while Beattie got into the car and drove away.

* * *

Peter and Matt came back for crutching season in April, as green was reappearing on the scorched hillside. Charlie became profoundly uncomfortable about the extra people on the farm.

"Don't worry," Beattie assured him as he pushed her away gently in the kitchen one night, "they're over at the cottage. They don't even take their meals in the house. They'll never know."

"Last time they were here, I slept in the cottage. They'll have noticed I'm not there anymore."

"And they'll think nothing of it. Mikhail lived in the house for years, and nobody ever said a word about it."

He took her hands in his, brought them to his lips. "I'm only worried about you. About what people think."

"I don't care what people think."

He struggled with words for a moment, then said, "You can only say that because you've never really been hated."

"I have. Most people in Lewinford think I'm colored scarlet."

"Yeah, but at least they don't think you're colored black."

Beattie fell silent. Charlie dropped her hands. "Let's keep our distance till after dark."

"Then we can get nice and close?"

He smiled. "As close as you like."

Winter came and they were left alone again. Long nights by the fireplace, lost in each other's arms. He told her he loved her over and over, against her skin, against her hair. Her heart became so entwined with his that she began to fear: nameless fear, the fear of anyone who loved too intensely. The only way to make the fear go away was to focus her entire mind and imagination on Charlie and let the rest of the world slip away.

Henry phoned the day he got the letter from his lawyer, to spit blood and threats at her. She didn't mind. Leo Sampson told her the court hearing for Lucy's custody was held over until August. She didn't mind. The new postmistress in Lewinford refused to serve her when she wanted to send a package of clothes to the boutique in Hobart. She drove to the next town and didn't mind. She was in love—mad love, love that blinded her. She didn't see what was coming.

Not at all.

When Lucy came home from church, she took off her shoes in her bedroom and placed them in the wardrobe. She flopped on her bed where Bunny and Horse were waiting. She picked up a book and began to look through the pictures. A knock at her door, and Molly's voice calling, "Lucy?"

Lucy stopped reading. She didn't want to let Molly in. Molly was acting strangely. Like she was afraid of something. Like she was afraid of Lucy.

But Molly let herself in anyway. Lucy drew herself up into the corner of the bed, winding Bunny's ear around her fingers.

Molly smiled at her, and for a moment Lucy felt like everything was normal. But it wasn't normal. Molly and Daddy had been talking a lot lately, in quiet tense voices. Whenever Lucy came in the room, they hushed quickly. Lucy knew there was something going on, and she knew it had something to do with her.

"Can I talk to you, darling?" Molly said, sitting on her bed and smoothing the covers under her hands. "It's important."

Lucy nodded, though she wanted to say no. "Where's Daddy?"

"He's in the sitting room. He said I should talk to you, seeing as we're both girls." She smiled again, and Lucy thought she didn't look like a girl at all.

Lucy shrugged. "What is it?"

"It's about Beattie, about your mother."

Lucy waited, her breath caught in her throat. She didn't want to hear that Mummy was sick or dead.

"She's done a bad thing," Molly continued. "She wrote a very bad letter, and now Daddy is cross."

"Did she write it to Daddy?"

"No, she wrote it to Daddy's lawyer, but that's not the point. She said some things in it that aren't true. What do we call a person who says things that aren't true?"

"A liar," Lucy said quietly.

"Yes, that's right. Your mother . . . She has done some things that a lot of people are unhappy about. Things that God wouldn't like."

Lucy wasn't so sure about God. She was still terrified of Him, but only when she was at home in Hobart. At the farm, she wasn't quite so worried what He thought of her. "What kind of things?" Lucy asked.

"It's too grown-up to explain."

This wasn't the first time Lucy had heard accusations about her mother, so she didn't think to question them.

"But she's far too close to that black man."

"Charlie? He's nice."

Molly's mouth turned down at the corners. "He only *seems* nice. He's actually a thief. Everyone in Lewinford knows that he stole something from a wealthy white man." Molly took Lucy's hand. "You must tell me, darling, have you seen anything while at the farm? Anything . . . wicked? If you have, you must let me and Daddy know. It will help us a lot as we get the lawyer to make his case."

"No," Lucy said, shaking her head hard.

"Tell me what she does. Who she speaks to."

She kept shaking her head.

"Where does she sleep at night?"

"In her bedroom. Next to mine."

"And when she gets up in the morning?"

Lucy was frightened by Molly's hard eyes. "My mummy does nothing wicked. She gets up and has breakfast in the morning with me and Charlie and—"

"Charlie? He's there at breakfast?"

Lucy went still. Her heart thudded in her throat.

Molly's eyes grew round. "Lucy? Does Charlie sleep in the house?"

Lucy nodded, not sure why Molly should find this so shocking.

Molly looked away, her face reddening. "I'm sorry to tell you this, but your mother has sinned."

"She's not a sinner."

"Does she go to church?"

Lucy couldn't answer.

"Henry!" Molly called. "Henry, come here."

Lucy waited on the bed, her heart thumping. She wished she hadn't talked to Molly. She wished she had kept her mouth shut. Then Daddy was there, and she knew she could trust him. She leaped from the bed and buried her face in his chest.

"What's going on?" he asked in a gruff voice, and Lucy could hear his words rumble around in his chest. She refused to look up.

"Lucy says Charlie sleeps in the house. Has breakfast with them in the morning. I'm sure you can imagine the rest."

A pause. Daddy's hands were still on her back.

"Well?" said Molly. "You want your daughter to have a black man and a fornicator for parents?"

"Molly—"

"I tell you, if we lose, that will happen. Instead of you, she's going to have that man for a father."

Lucy grew alarmed, stood back to gaze up at Daddy. "I want you to be my daddy," she said. "Not anybody else."

"Tell her," Molly said. "Her mother is too steeped in sin."

"Molly . . ." he said again, but couldn't finish his sentence.

"We need to keep her away from that farm."

Lucy kept her eyes fixed steadily on Daddy. Whatever he said was right and true. Molly was upset and acting strangely, but Daddy wouldn't let anything bad happen to her.

Daddy's eyes turned down, and he smiled at her crookedly. "How would you like to go on a little trip, my girl?"

* * *

Beattie caught a fever that flattened her in the first week of July, the day that she was supposed to drive down to Hobart to pick up Lucy. She rang to tell Lucy she might be a day or so late—all the while dreading Henry or Molly answering the phone. But there was no answer. There was nothing for it: she could barely stand, let alone drive. She went to bed and hoped to feel better the following day.

Next morning, and still she couldn't rouse anyone on the telephone at Henry's house. She figured their telephone was playing up and was worried that Lucy would think she'd been forgotten.

As she picked up her handbag to go out to the truck, she lost her balance and stumbled against the wall. Charlie saw her and came to steady her. "You're still sick," he said.

"My ear is very sore," she said. "I can't seem to find my balance."

"You can't drive. You're too sick, and it's too foggy."

"I can't stay here. Lucy has been expecting me since yesterday."

"She'll wait."

"You don't understand. She'll think I've forgotten her or I don't love her. I don't want her to think that, not even for another hour. Certainly not another day."

Charlie's grip on her arm was firm.

"You could drive me," she ventured.

He smiled bitterly. "Beattie, I've seen the way Molly looks at me."

"I don't care about Molly."

"You probably should."

"You're my employee. It wouldn't be unusual for you to drive me somewhere." She touched his hand softly. "Please? My little girl is waiting for me."

"You can't get them on the telephone?"

"Something's wrong with it."

He sighed, reaching for his hat. "All right, but I'm waiting in the car when we get there."

It was the first time they'd driven anywhere together. Away from the farm, the fog rolled back to reveal grass silvered with ice. Beattie's throbbing ear and constant sense of vertigo couldn't detract from how lovely it felt to be speeding down the road, past winter-bare trees and wide rolling fields, with the man she loved. A sense of injustice pricked her. Other women could enjoy such simple pleasures. Molly could go driving with Henry, Tilly Harrow with Frank . . . but Beattie and Charlie's love was so much purer and stronger than either of those couples'. Once this business with Lucy's custody was sorted out, she was going to marry Charlie and laugh at all the disapproving faces in the township.

They arrived outside Henry's house just before eleven. Beattie eased herself out of the car, waiting for the dizziness to pass before letting herself go through the gate and up the path. She knocked.

No answer.

A prickling feeling of dread was suddenly upon her. No answer on the phone, no answer at the door. She knocked again, louder. Then went around the side of the house. She heard the car door slam. Charlie was coming to help her, but she barely registered. The edges of her vision blurred into black. Something was wrong, and she felt it coldly and sharply.

Knocking at the back door, no answer. She found Molly's mop bucket by the back door and upturned it under the window to Lucy's room. Climbed up as Charlie arrived to steady her. Her breath fogged the glass.

"What can you see?" he asked.

The curtain was open a crack, but it was enough to see in. To see the empty room.

No bed. No toys. No wardrobe. All gone.

Her heart seized, refused to beat. Then she was falling, falling into Charlie's arms.

"It's empty!" she cried.

"Shh, don't worry. Not yet," he said.

He helped her around the side of the house. Henry's neighbor was pegging her laundry.

"Can you help?" Charlie called.

The woman looked up, saw Charlie with his arms around Beattie, and scowled. "What is it?"

"Did you see them leave?" Beattie asked desperately. "The man and the little red-haired girl?"

"About three weeks ago," she said grudgingly. "Why?"

Three weeks ago? How could she not have known? "I'm the girl's mother," she said, her blood fluttering loudly in her ears. "I need to know where they've gone."

"He said he was heading north. That's all." She picked up her laundry basket and turned her back.

"Please!" Beattie called.

"I don't know anything else," she replied as she closed the door behind her.

Beattie felt the bottom drop out of her world. Sobs heaved in her throat.

Charlie folded her in his arms.

"Where's my baby, Charlie?" she sobbed. "Where have they taken my baby?"

TWENTY-FOUR

Beattie woke in the grainy predawn light and wondered for a moment where she was. Then she remembered: the threadbare sheets, the smell of old tobacco smoke in the curtains and rugs . . . She was in the only hotel in Hobart that would accept a white woman staying with a black man. And she was still trapped in the nightmare of Lucy's disappearance.

She rolled over and saw that Charlie was already awake, looking at her with his soft eyes.

"How long have you been awake?" she asked.

"About an hour," he said. "I wanted to be right here when you woke up. When you remembered."

She smiled weakly. The previous day had been a long blur of running around, asking questions of neighbors, the local pastor at Henry and Molly's church. Henry's employee, Molly's friend from FitzGerald's. She and Charlie had tracked all over Hobart, asking questions and getting no answers. Most people knew nothing at all; Pastor Gibbins said they had simply stopped coming to church. Some knew a little, but it was all the same information. They had talked of going north. Nobody knew how far or where. But they were all surprised to hear that Beattie was Lucy's mother. In fact, she suspected some of them didn't believe her at all.

Finally, Charlie had tried to convince her to go home, but she had refused to leave town without her daughter. Foolish, of course. Her daughter was probably nowhere in Hobart. They had tracked about looking for a hotel, then fallen into exhausted sleep.

Now Beattie was faced with the decision about what to do next.

"You'll be better off at home, Beattie," Charlie said, climbing out of bed and pulling on his jeans. "We've done everything we can here."

"This is my fault," she said, lying on her back and putting her arm over her eyes. Her heart thudded heavily under her ribs. "If I had just talked to them about custody rather than taking them to court . . ."

Charlie slipped on his shirt and came to sit on the bed, deftly buttoning it up. "You said yourself that Henry was prepared to get a lawyer first."

"I just want to know she's all right."

"Of course she's all right. They dote on her, they're not going to hurt her."

Beattie took small comfort in this but couldn't articulate to Charlie how lost she felt, not knowing where Lucy was. Not knowing when she would hold her again. She tried to stop herself from crying, but it was impossible.

"Well, then," Charlie said softly, crooking his finger to

brush a tear off her cheek, "if the lawyer got you into it, per-haps he can get you out. Let's go home, Beattie, and you can drop in on Leo Sampson on the way."

Beattie nodded, pulled herself together. "You're right. They can't have just disappeared. He'll help me find her."

The drive back to Lewinford was so different in tone and intent from the drive down that it was almost agonizing. Beattie leaned her head on her hand against the window and watched the landscape slip by, contemplating the miles and miles between her and Lucy. By the time Charlie stopped the car outside Leo's office, she had started to fear she might never see her daughter again.

The usual crowd across the street craned their necks to see her. When she climbed out of the passenger side, they craned even farther to see who was driving, but Charlie steadfastly kept his hat on and his window wound up.

"Come in with me," Beattie pleaded, leaning back in the door.

"No, Beattie. The last thing you want is for me to parade around next to you while those folks are watching." He kept his hands firmly on the steering wheel.

She closed the door and steadied herself. Her face felt hot even though the air was bitterly cold, and she was aware that she still was not well enough to be out. Her left ear ached and rang faintly.

Deep breaths. She pushed open Leo's door.

Leo was filing in his tiny office; a redolent pipe waited for him on his desk. He turned and saw her, smiled . . . then read her expression, and the smile turned to a frown.

"What happened?" he asked.

"They've taken her," she managed before breaking once more into sobs.

With a generous brandy in her hand, she told him the whole story. He took notes, nodded sympathetically. Outside the window, the hedges shivered.

"I'll be in touch with their lawyer fortwith," he said. "He might know where they've gone. Beattie, you need to go home, and you need to rest. You look very unwell."

"I can't rest until I know where she is."

"I think you're going to have to accept that it may be some time before we know where she is. Rest. Is there . . . someone who can look after you at the farm?" This last was delivered in a quiet tone.

"Charlie's there."

He nodded, smiled a little sadly. "I'm glad." He tapped the page of notes in front of him. "I'll call you the moment I hear anything."

The icy air outside made her cough. She stopped, trying to catch her breath. Then found herself pitching forward.

The cold grassy path hit her hard, but the hands around her waist, pulling her up, were gentle.

"Beattie? Are you all right?"

"Charlie, I'm not well."

"Get your hands off her, you black bastard."

Beattie looked up to see a slit-eyed Frank Harrow standing a few feet off.

"I'm helping her," Charlie said.

"You shouldn't be touching a white woman like that."

Frank pushed his way in, bumping Charlie aside and steadying Beattie under her elbow.

Overwhelmed by Lucy's loss, Beattie could not endure his rudeness. "Get your hands off me!" she shrieked at Frank, shrugging him off violently. "How dare you speak to Charlie like that?"

An audience was forming, drawn by her raised voice. Two outside the general store, one from the post office, three neighbors of Leo's.

"Are you going to let him touch you like that? Like he owns you?" Frank spat.

"Come on, missus," Charlie mumbled, "we'd best get back to the farm."

Missus. The name was an insult to her, a symbol of the time before they had loved each other. She was not going back there, and Frank and his army of bigots weren't going to make her.

"He does own me," she said boldly. "He owns my heart. And I own his."

Muttered disapproval. Charlie was in the driver's seat, slamming his door, revving the car.

"So don't you dare say a word against him again. He's a better man than you." She looked around, raising her voice. "He's a better man than any of you."

She steadied herself on the car, found the handle, and let herself in. Gratefully slid into the seat.

"You shouldn't have done that," Charlie said, his voice icy.

She turned to him. "Charlie? You're angry with me?"

He pulled onto the road, not answering her.

"Say something," she said to him.

"You wouldn't want to hear what I want to say," he replied. "Now you're going home to bed, and I'm going to get the doctor from Bothwell. We can't do anything about Lucy, but I'm going to make bloody sure she has a mother to come back to when it's time."

Beattie turned to the window again, letting hot, silent tears make their way down her face.

Beattie was sick for nine days. An infection in her ear kept her flat on her back, fighting a high fever. She slept for long stretches, punctuated by vivid dreams about Lucy and Henry. Charlie made her soup that she didn't eat, made sure she had clean linen when she sweated through her sheets, and had the doctor come to see her.

On the ninth day, feeling clearer, she sat up and ate properly for the first time. Charlie sat on the end of her bed, watching her closely. He was quiet, had been quiet the whole time. She presumed he was still angry at her for what she had said to Frank Harrow. Why shouldn't she have said it, though? She cared nothing for their opinions.

She tore up a piece of bread and dipped it in her soup. "I've been thinking about Henry telling his neighbor he was heading north, and I remembered that Billy Wilder, an old friend of his, moved up to Launceston. I think I should get in touch."

The corner of Charlie's mouth twitched. "Beattie . . ."

"North could mean the mainland, too, but it wouldn't be

like Henry to go where he knew nobody and had no job. He's essentially a coward so—"

"Beattie," he said more forcefully. "Leo Sampson called two days ago."

She froze, her bread halfway to her mouth. "Why didn't you tell me?"

"I wanted you to get better."

Her stomach shivered with fear. "It's bad news, isn't it?"

He spread his hands apart. "Leo spoke to Henry's lawyer. He and Molly and Lucy have gone to Scotland."

Scotland. The distance froze her. Lucy was in Scotland . . . or still on her way there. Beattie's stomach twitched as though the umbilical cord had never been cut, as though Lucy's distance were threatening to pull out her insides. She put her hands over her belly.

"I'm sorry, Beattie," Charlie said.

"I have to go find her," Beattie replied, putting aside her soup and throwing back the covers.

Charlie grasped her firmly, smoothed the covers over her again. "Not so fast. Think this through."

"My daughter is on the other side of the world. I have to go and get her." Beattie's voice was tense, high. She hadn't expected it to come out that way.

"Listen, and try to be calm," Charlie said. "Henry said he'd contact you with an address as soon as they've settled somewhere. You're going to have to wait."

"Why should I wait?"

"Because if you run away to Scotland now, you won't know where to find them."

"He'll be in Glasgow somewhere. I could find his mother . . ." Even as she said it, she knew she sounded desperate and foolish. There were no guarantees Henry would contact his mother, and she could wind up in Glasgow with no idea how to find Lucy. "But it's not fair," she wailed. "He can't just take her. He can't dictate the rules. She'll be missing me. She'll be wondering what's going on. She'll be confused."

"Lucy is nearly ten. She'll understand."

"What have they told her about me?"

Charlie fell silent.

"Charlie?" she said, examining him closely. His eyebrows were drawn down hard. "Are you angry at me?"

"I told you nothing good would come of us being together."

"This isn't our fault." But was Charlie right? If Molly had heard any town gossip, she might have thought that Lucy would end up with Charlie as her father. Was that the catalyst for them to run away to Scotland?

Beattie sagged back into her bed. Charlie lay down next to her, on top of the covers, his cheek against her pillow.

"I'm sorry, Beattie," he said, his hand twining in her hair.

"It's like I can feel the weight of all the cities and seas between us." She touched her chest. "Sitting here on my heart."

"Let me take some of that load," Charlie said.

"You can't," Beattie replied. "The burden is mine."

Beattie suspected that she wasn't recovering from her illness as day after day passed with leaden limbs and a weary head.

Then she came to understand that this was an illness not of the body but of the heart.

The awful thing was that life went on as normal. She was used to being separated from her daughter, so nothing actually felt any different. No mourning in the empty bedroom, no sense of loss at the absence of childish laughter. In many ways, life was the same as it had been before. Weeks slipped by, yet still the feeling of heaviness pervaded her. Charlie was her sole comfort, but he had work to do to prepare for shearing season. Beattie had work to do, too, designs to sew, but she could barely lift her head.

Because her imagination told her terrible things. Now that Lucy was in Scotland, would Beattie ever get her back? Her mind circled and circled around the problem. By the time Beattie got over there, what things would Molly and Henry have told her? How could she rip Lucy away from the father she adored so much? How could she be away from Charlie for such a long time to fetch Lucy? What would people make of a white woman and a black man traveling any distance together? What would happen to the farm if they were both away?

She came to understand that she was stuck in an impossible place. The anger turned inward, and she blamed herself. If she hadn't set in motion the custody hearing, they wouldn't have felt the need to run . . .

Then, finally, a letter arrived.

Charlie brought it up from the postbox when he came in for lunch. It was one of the first days of spring, and he'd been mustering with the dogs. Peter and Matt weren't due for another two weeks, then the shearers would arrive the week after. With Beattie so preoccupied, Charlie had been doing everything.

He solemnly handed her the letter in the kitchen, where she was making lunch. She tore the envelope open with shaking hands and unfolded the letter. Charlie read over her shoulder.

Henry's handwriting, not Molly's.

Dear Beattie

We have bought a townhouse in Glasgow and have settled in well. Lucy is very happy with her new school and church, but it will be easier if you don't contact her for a month or so to allow her to concentrate on forming new attachments here.

Beattie had to look away and take a deep breath before continuing.

I hope you understand why we took such drastic measures. Faced with a choice between keeping our daughter close to God and letting her be witness to iniquity, we did what any loving parents would do.

That sentence was definitely dictated by Molly. Beattie felt a squall of fury rise up in her and was terrified to realize that she would be happy to kill Molly at that moment.

Our return address is on the back of the letter if you wish to write, though I won't pass on any letters to Lucy until I'm sure they won't upset her.

Beattie crumpled up the letter and threw it on the ground.

"Steady on, you're going to need that," Charlie said, retrieving the letter. "You'll need the address to write to Lucy."

"I'm not going to write to Lucy," she said.

Charlie looked at her wordlessly.

"I'm going to Scotland," she said. "I'm going to turn up on their doorstep and demand my child back."

He nodded. "When will you go?" he asked.

"Tomorrow. This week. As soon as I can."

"We're three weeks out from shearing season."

"You can manage without me."

He pressed his lips together tightly.

"I don't care about sheep. I don't care about anything but getting my daughter back."

"And if you don't? If they won't let her go?"

"I'll make them let her go."

That night Beattie was sorting her papers on the floor of the sitting room. The fire was warm, the wireless crackled, Charlie drew up plans for the shearing season. Beattie had dug out her passport and was consumed with a sense of purpose. She had phoned a shipping company that could give her a berth to London in two days. She had to finish up some important bookwork before then. From London she'd make her way to Glasgow, show up on Henry's doorstep before he could protest. How dare he? How dare he take her child away and then try to control how and when Beattie saw her?

The piece of music on the wireless finished. An announcer's

voice came on, smooth and rich. He was talking to another man, but Beattie was only half listening. There had been talk in the last month of an increasingly aggressive Germany, but it seemed so far away, so removed from her simple life down here at the bottom of the world.

She became aware that Charlie had stood and turned up the wireless.

"What is it?" she asked, looking up from her bookwork.

"Did you hear?" he said.

She shook her head.

Music burst once more from the wireless. "We missed the news. Germany invaded Poland."

Beattie didn't admit that she wasn't even sure where Poland was. "Is that right?"

Charlie shook his head. "You don't understand. England had a pact with Poland."

Beattie's heart grew hot.

"We're at war, Beattie."

He begged her not to go. The night before, he held her against his warm body all night. She barely slept, waking over and over with a swirling ache inside her. To be apart from him for so long . . . But she held true to her purpose. She would get Lucy, she would bring her home, they would live as a family.

Deep down, she knew this fantasy had many things wrong with it, but she refused to acknowledge them. To make this journey, she had to be single-minded. She couldn't sacrifice a moment of her focus.

He dropped her at the dock just after midday.

She turned to him, her eyes fixed on his. "Goodbye, my darling," she said.

He tried a smile. "You'll be back soon. I'll keep busy."

She nodded, tears pricking her eyes. She pushed herself against him, and their last kiss was searing, passionate. "I love you," she said.

"I love you, too," he replied. "Forever."

She took her suitcase and waved him off, watching until the car disappeared around the corner. At the end of a long gangway, a large ship painted red, black, and rust waited. Gulls flapped overhead. The sour smell of the harbor rose up from the barnacled wood. Off to the side, a tiny wooden office shed. This was where she was to meet the booking agent and pay for her fare. She felt giddy at the idea of getting on the ship, of the long journey and the cold distance between her and Charlie. It was as though she could feel Charlie drawing away, farther and farther. And Lucy so far now. Both of them in opposite directions, and she alone at the center of the world.

Beattie walked up to the office and pushed the door open. It was empty. She glanced around outside but couldn't see anybody hurrying to help her. A cloud passed over the sun. Inside, two wooden chairs were pushed up against the wall. She sat down, pulled out a notepad and pen, and began to write Charlie a letter, one she could build on over the coming weeks. Furiously, she poured out her feelings. They would get married, they wouldn't care what anyone thought, because this love was greater than worldly matters.

"Miss Blaxland?"

She looked up, quickly shuffling the letter into her notebook. "Yes?"

A man stood at the door. He had dainty features apart from very dark eyebrows. "I'm Alan Jephson. We spoke on the phone."

She stood and offered her hand to shake. "When do we set off?" she asked, sounding braver than she felt. "I'm keen to get settled in my cabin."

He didn't quite meet her eye. "I'm sorry, miss, but we're not going to be able to take you to London after all. We're all in a bit of a flap this morning and—"

"Not take me to London? But I booked it."

"Things have changed since then. We had word this morning that the Germans have torpedoed an unarmed British liner off the coast of Scotland. The *Athenia*. Over a thousand civilians on board." His mouth clenched, and Beattie didn't know if it was fear or sadness. "We don't know what to do. We're waiting for orders."

"But . . . you have to go. I have to get to Scotland. When will you know? Whose decision is it?"

He looked shocked. "Miss, do you not understand? You'll be traveling into a war zone. We don't know what those Jerries are capable of. You'd be taking your life into your hands. A hundred people died, including a little girl."

A little girl. Like Lucy. She started to cry.

"There, there," he said, handing her a big white handkerchief. "This silly war has all of us in a flap. You'll see, it'll be over by Christmas. Storm in a teacup. Save your traveling until then."

Beattie thanked him for his handkerchief and left the office, picked up her suitcase, and made her way back up to the street. She gazed up over the buildings. The big hump of Mount Wellington sat behind the city, striped with sun and shadows. What was she to do now?

Dragging her feet and her suitcase, Beattie went into every shipping office she knew, even the one where Henry had once worked. At each one she heard the same story: wait and see.

But she didn't want to wait and see. She wanted to act now, while she had the courage and the anger. Her frustration intensified as the day progressed, until she was snapping angrily at shipping clerks who were only trying to preserve the lives of their crew at a frightening time.

By the time she'd received her last refusal, it was too late for the bus back to Lewinford, and besides, she thought she might pay someone to drive her directly to her door in the morning. She tried to phone Charlie, but he wasn't answering. He was probably out in the last shred of dusk, pushing sheep into paddocks, ready for shearing season. Thoughts of Charlie made her smile, and she fell asleep early and slept deeply.

Charlie whistled the dogs back home, fed and watered Birch, and returned to the house.

It was strange to be here alone, rattling around the empty

house. Even though Beattie was slight, her warm presence filled the place. Everything seemed a little cold without her.

Dusk had faded to dark, and he was pulling leftovers out of the refrigerator when a knock came at the door.

Curious, he went to answer it.

Six faces looked back at him, none of them friendly. He recognized Frank Harrow, his wife, Tilly, two of the old coots from the pub, and another two men whose faces were only vaguely familiar. His heart picked up its rhythm. "What is it?"

"The lady of the house not home?" Harrow asked.

Charlie shook his head.

"We saw you leave town with her and come back without her. Been wondering what you did with her."

"She's gone away a little while."

"Where? How long?" Tilly demanded.

"That's her own business."

"It's our business if we think you done away with her," one of the old fellows said, and Charlie realized they were drunk. The danger of his situation pressed itself upon him suddenly, and he tried to close the door.

"No, no, wait on," Harrow said, pushing the door open again with his foot. "Where you going, blackfella?"

Charlie knew nothing he could say would make a difference, so he said nothing.

"The lady's gone missing, and you've got the whole farm to yourself. You sure you haven't done something you shouldn't?" Harrow said.

"We all know he's done something he shouldn't," one of the

unfamiliar men said. "Climbing aboard a white woman like that."

"I'll thank you to keep it clean," Harrow said. "My wife is here."

"What do you want from me?" Charlie asked.

"Simple. You leave now, and we won't hurt you."

Charlie nodded. What did it matter? He'd just sneak back tomorrow, around from the north. And remember to keep the doors locked next time. If he was going to keep the farm ticking over while Beattie was gone, he had to be more careful. "All right," he said.

Harrow looked taken aback. Perhaps he'd been hoping for a fight. Charlie shut the door behind him and pushed his way through them and down the path. They jeered at him, even the woman. He'd never thought women could behave like members of a pack, and it turned his mind to Beattie, her softness, her grace.

Smack! Something hard and heavy hit him in the back of the neck. His legs crumpled underneath him, and his ears rang loudly. Consciousness receded, then sprang back. Voices in the distance, and one up very close.

"In the dirt where you belong, blackfella," Harrow said.

Charlie kicked him as hard as he could between the legs, and then Harrow was kneeling beside him, spitting venom and curses. Harrow dragged himself up onto Charlie's chest.

Charlie felt the blade but never saw it. Hot pain. Harrow was stumbling away, still cursing. Charlie felt at his stomach, pressed his hand against the searing pain. His fingers came away black with blood.

Still disoriented, he couldn't stand. He lay on his back, looking up at the stars. In the distance, a car engine. They were leaving. He had to get to Beattie's car and drive himself to the doctor. But his energy was flowing away from him; he couldn't gather his limbs.

The car engine again, this time closer. They were coming back. Headlights washed over him. A silhouette of a man approaching.

"You got to help me," Charlie.

The man leaned over him. Not Harrow. Leo Sampson.

"Charlie? Oh God!" Leo saw the blood and recoiled.

"You got to help me," Charlie said again, and his own voice seemed to be coming from far away.

"Did they do this to you? I heard them talking about you in the pub. They all left together, and I followed." His voice was panicked, tripping over words.

"Get me a doctor, Leo?"

Leo bent to help him up, but the pain was excruciating. He yelped.

"Just leave me here. Bring somebody back, quick as you can," Charlie said. Each thump of his pulse seemed weaker than the last.

"I will," Leo said, climbing to his feet.

"Leo, if I die—"

"You're not going to die."

"If I die," Charlie said as forcefully as he could manage, "don't tell Beattie how it happened. She'll blame herself."

"But the police should know. They should be brought to justice."

Charlie shook his head, impatient. "There's never any justice for men like me. You know that."

"But you deserve justice, Charlie. You're a good man. One of the best."

"Just promise me. Don't tell Beattie. Don't tell anyone. I'd save her that pain at any cost."

Leo nodded gravely. "Yes, yes. I promise." He touched Charlie's shoulder, then turned and ran for the car.

The stars looked on patiently, so Charlie gazed back at them. They had seen his birth; they had witnessed his greatest love. It was only right they should be here now.

The car dropped Beattie off at the bottom of her driveway, and she hefted her suitcase up the dirt path. She had cried all the way up from Hobart, quietly in the backseat, and hoped she had made peace with her decision. After the war, she would go to see Lucy. In the meantime, she would play by Henry's rules: she would write letters, send presents, call long-distance when their phone was connected. When the Germans were defeated and travel wasn't so fraught, she would head over there—perhaps even on an airplane, if she had a good wool clip this year—and negotiate with them reasonably.

Leo Sampson's car was parked in her driveway. She frowned. She hadn't been expecting him. She hurried to the front door, pushed it open. "Charlie?" she called.

Leo appeared from the sitting room. He looked as though he had been up all night. "Beattie," he said. "I didn't know where you were."

"Charlie didn't tell you?"

He approached her, took her hand. "Come into the sitting room."

She pulled her hand away, fear icing her skin. "No. What is it? Why are you here? And where is Charlie?"

Leo licked his lips.

"Leo?" Beattie said, her throat blocking up with terror. "Tell me!"

"There's been an accident."

"No." Her face crumpling, her chest heaving. "No, no, no. Not my Charlie?"

"Beattie, I—"

"What happened?"

"I'm not . . . I'm not certain. I had driven up to see you, and Birch was there, all saddled up, reins dragging. He led me to . . . Maybe a snake spooked the horse. Charlie was . . ."

She gazed back at him. Mute. Willing him not to say the thing she knew he was going to say next.

"I'm sorry, Beattie, Charlie's dead."

"Where is he?" she gasped. "Can I see him? Is he . . . ?"

"His body is at Dr. Malcolm's. You don't want to see him, Beattie. Remember him in life." Leo shook his head, pinched the bridge of his nose. "I can make arrangements for him to be buried right here in the house paddock, if you like."

Buried? Buried? Charlie in the ground. Her hands scrabbled at her face, her sobs so loud they terrified her.

"I'm so sorry," Leo was saying, trying to gather her against him for comfort.

But she didn't want to be held, not by anyone who wasn't Charlie.

Leo backed away. She collapsed at the bottom of the staircase, sprawled herself out, and banged her head on the corner of the closest stair. A scream trapped inside her. Time telescoped—minutes, hours. Emptiness. Emptiness. Year after empty year, waiting ahead of her.

TWENTY-FIVE

Emma: Tasmania, 2009

A warm breeze moved through the bushes outside the double doors of the school hall, and in the distance I could see the masts of boats down in the harbor, colored flags flapping. I waited on a long wooden bench while Patrick and Marlon set up inside, to enjoy the turn toward summer. Blue skies, warm sun on the grass and on the water. One by one, cars arrived and the children were dropped off. One or two came up to hug me, and I was taken aback by their artless affection. Mina came last, in her father's white Lexus. She got out, closed the door, and he drove off. I walked down to the car park to greet her. Her dark hair was pulled back in a ponytail, and her cheeks were flushed in her pale face.

"Hello, Mina," I said.

"Did you come back?"

"I did. I'm going to teach you some ballet."

Her face broke into a broad smile. "Really?" She grabbed my fingers in her warm, soft hand and squeezed them hard. "*Swan Lake?*"

"*The Nutcracker*. Is that okay?"

She nodded, not releasing my hand, and we went inside.

Marlon took them through his usual warm-up, then Mina and I split off into a back room with the stereo and the *Nutcracker* CD. It took her a little while to understand that she'd been singled out, that I wasn't going to invite Becky or Zack or any of her other friends. But once she figured out the situation, she devoted herself with intensity to the task. I was hugely surprised—embarrassed though I was to admit it—by the way she applied herself to learning the movements, and even more surprised by how well she copied them. I saw in her real grace. After about half an hour, though, she flagged.

"I'll learn some more later," she said, abruptly stopping in the middle of a movement.

It took me a second to adjust my focus. I wanted to say, "You'll never learn if you give up that easily," but had to remind myself that she wasn't a ballerina; she was a girl with Down's syndrome. And she had done brilliantly.

"Well done," I said. "It's a great start. You are going to be the most beautiful Dew Drop anyone's ever seen."

She took my hand and shook it solemnly. "Can I go back with the others now?"

I watched the rest of the rehearsal from the stalls. Actually, I watched Patrick's back quite a bit more than I watched the rehearsal. He had a straight back, nice square shoulders. A little on the skinny side but not bony. Josh worked out; he had the muscles of a docker even though he spent all day inside an office, where he had to lift nothing heavier than his BlackBerry. For the first time ever, this struck me as funny.

Rehearsal finished, and Patrick and I had to wait outside for twenty minutes with Mina because her father was late. I took her through her steps again on the grass, but she had trouble concentrating without the music, so I let her be. Finally, the Lexus arrived. He beeped, and Mina walked down to the car park with a quick "goodbye."

"He never comes to watch rehearsal?" I asked Patrick quietly.

"Never."

"Concerts?"

"Never."

The door slammed and they drove off.

"Bastard," I said.

Patrick sighed. "We don't really know what goes on inside families. Best not to judge."

"Does she have a mother? Siblings?"

"Her mother died when she was little. No siblings."

I turned the thought over in my mind for a while. Then Patrick said, "Are you hungry?"

"No," I said, before I realized the ramifications of his question: hunger in company meant a lunch date. "I mean, yes. A little. We've got to eat, after all. Did you want to go and get some lunch?"

"If you like."

"Sure. Why not?" I said, wondering if I sounded at all nonchalant.

We wound up in a café at Sandy Bay. The coffee was a disappointment, but it was nice to look at Patrick's front instead of his back. I found it hard to believe that I'd once thought him more interesting than handsome. In fact, his face was appealing. His eyes, in particular, were an unusual shade of green, and the outer edge of his lids creased upward in an exotic way.

"So how did it go with Mina?" he asked after his first sip of coffee.

"She did great. So focused. I didn't realize she could be capable of that."

"All of the kids are different. They have a varied range of abilities," he said. "Nothing surprises me about them anymore." He smiled. "So she likes her dance?"

I nodded. "Real ballet," I said.

"It looked great, what you showed me."

I squirmed a little. "Very simplified. Dew Drop was my first role. It's quite demanding, in reality." I realized I was bragging, but couldn't stop myself. I wanted him to know what a big deal I had been when I could dance. But my desperation to impress made me sad, and I fell silent.

He let me sit there quietly for a few moments, then he said, "Emma, I've seen you dance."

I lifted my head to meet his eyes. "You have?"

"Monica has a DVD. You were a hero of hers when she was a teenager. Everyone knew about you because of the connection your grandmother had to town, and the newsagent stocked a couple of DVDs with you in them. I must have seen you dancing Giselle about a hundred times."

I glowed with pride. "I had no idea Monica was a fan."

"She made me swear not to tell you, in case you thought she was a dork."

I laughed at this. "She wanted to dance?"

"She tried it for a while when she was small, but she never really got the hang of it. Tall and gangly, like me." He made a fuss of stirring his coffee, not looking directly at me. "You dance beautifully."

"Danced," I said. "Past tense." I thought about my changing body. Already the edges of my muscles were softening, and a comfortable layer of fat was creeping over everything.

"Sorry," he said. "I don't want to make you feel sad."

Then our lunch came and we got off the topic of me, which was both a blessing and a disappointment. I did want to hear more about how beautifully I'd danced, especially from him. But the thought aroused in me such a keen sadness, of things lost that couldn't be found again.

Patrick dropped me home around 3:30, and I found myself alone and disconsolate, with a wishing feeling in my chest. Trouble was, I wasn't at all sure what to wish for anymore.

My grandmother had kept every sketch and every pattern of every item of clothing she had ever made, and they were all filed at Blaxland Wool's head office in North Sydney. Usually, there was a display in the foyer of the building, behind glass and under white downlighting. So the last thing I expected to find in the boxes was a tracing-paper pattern.

I nearly tore it, vigorously emptying a box I thought contained only cockroach-stained Georgette Heyer novels. It was Sunday, very early. I'd been awake at the first caw of the crow. A dream had woken me. My mother was in it, but she wasn't really my mother; a big tidal wave was coming, and I had to find a photograph in a box to prove who she was before the wave hit. I'd woken up just as the sky had grown dark with the coming wall of water.

It unsettled me.

So here I was, pulling out a folded pattern, thinking about how it would go in the collection back in Sydney. Then I unfolded it to look at it, and it was clearly for a child. A little girl. It was a small dress.

Curious, I kept digging. In the bottom of the box, I found eleven similar tracing-paper patterns. All for a child. Little tops and skirts and pinafores.

My grandmother had never designed children's wear. She was known as an icon of women's work wear. I laid them all out and looked at them for a long time. Yes, she could have made these things for a neighbor or a friend or . . . But I kept thinking of the little girl in the photograph. Were these for her? Who was she?

And why wasn't I just calling my mother to ask? She might be able to clear it up in seconds.

Or not. If Grandma had a secret first family, Mum would be upset if she found out. And then she'd want to come here.

Carefully, I refolded the patterns and put them on top of the piano.

I admitted that I wasn't just cleaning out boxes to find Grandma's story. I was on a hunt for evidence. I slowed down to half speed, scrutinizing every notebook, every letter, every business record. I examined old invoices for sheep bought and wool sold, to see if they yielded any clues. They didn't, but I kept looking.

* * *

With her usual almost supernatural prescience, my mother called that evening to see how I was doing.

"Oh, fine," I said vaguely, sitting on the bottom stair and stretching my knee out. "There's still a lot more to do."

"I expected you home today."

"Ah. You didn't go to the airport, did you?"

"No. But I changed the sheets on your bed."

I felt guilty, but it wasn't new for me to feel guilty where Louise Blaxland-Hunter was concerned. "I'll be a few more weeks. Maybe six."

She sounded horrified. "How much is there to do?"

"I'm going slower than I thought, and I really quite like it here. I've even made friends. Don't be shocked."

Mum laughed.

"I'll definitely be home for Christmas, though," I said.

"That will be lovely. Our first Christmas with you in a long time."

"Hey, Mum, could you send down my stuff, please? The things I brought with me from London?" I could use my laptop, perhaps even my mobile phone. And I did have other clothes apart from jeans and T-shirts.

We chatted for a while, and then—foolishly—I ventured a question. "Mum, how much do you know about what Grandma did when she lived down here?"

"She ran the sheep farm. She kept the books, but she used to go out mustering, too. I never believed her until I saw her ride a horse one time at a friend's property. She must have been fifty by then but very comfortable in the saddle."

"I can't imagine it."

"She was graceful." There was a smile in Mum's voice.

"Anything else? Did she have any friends? Boyfriends?"

"I doubt it, love. She wouldn't have had time. Besides, Granddad was her first love."

"Really? She was in her thirties when she met him."

That little thinking pause that my mother did. A few moments of silence that weren't mute so much as calculating. "Why do you ask?" she said smoothly.

"No reason," I said, not nearly so smoothly. And she was on to me.

"Em, if you know something I don't . . ."

"I don't know what you mean," I said.

"Why are you asking about Grandma's past?"

"Because I'm here in her big old house and thinking about whether she lived here alone. Thinking about if she was lonely."

"Are you lonely? Do you need me to come down there?" she said. "Do you need some help sorting things out? Really, you shouldn't stay too much longer. You belong up here with us in Sydney. I can help you get through it quicker. I can be on a plane tomorrow, bring your things down with me."

I was well used to her persuasions; I'd heard them a thousand times in London.

"No, Mum, I'm fine. Just send my stuff down. I'm enjoying being by myself. I need the time to think. Don't come." *Please don't come.*

She smelled a rat, though, and I wished I'd said nothing.

At least not to Mum. I wondered whether, if I prodded Uncle Mike the right way, I might get better information.

It took until Thursday for my things to arrive.

"What have you got there?" Monica asked curiously as the courier van backed down my driveway.

"My things. Clothes, bits and pieces I brought from London." I peeled open the tape and flipped open the first box, kneeling gingerly.

"You're settling in, then?"

"Not really, I . . . well, for a while." I pulled out the clothes on top and set them aside on the floor of the hallway.

"Let me turn over the main bedroom for you. Have the nice room."

I shook my head. "All the rooms are nice. I'm fine where I am. Look, my laptop." I pulled out the laptop and rested it on the floor. "I thought maybe I could get connected to the Internet."

"I can call the phone company," she offered. "You'll need a modem."

"That would be great," I replied. I found my mobile phone. Dead as a doornail. I rummaged farther for the charger but couldn't see it. I couldn't even remember bringing it from England. It was probably still plugged into the wall there.

Monica took the phone from me. "I'll take care of it," she said.

I smiled at her, thinking of what Patrick had told me: her

teenage case of hero worship. "You are so fabulous, Monica. But I really should learn how to do some of this stuff myself. I always had a PA, so that meant I never had to be organized or figure out how things work. I just danced."

"That's good, though."

"In some ways. In others, it meant I was allowed to fall out of the world. That made it much harder to cope when I had my accident." From the kitchen, I could hear the kettle whistling. Monica had put it on before the courier arrived.

"I'll get it," Monica said. "Tea or coffee?"

"Coffee," I replied. "Make it strong." The front door was still open, and a wide strip of sunlight crept into my lap as I unpacked the box. A flock of cockatoos screeched past, but then there was silence in their wake. I was growing to love the silence, the absence of traffic noise particularly.

In the box, I found a plastic bag with the Blaxland Wool logo on it. Curious, I opened it up. Inside was my tiara from *Swan Lake*, the one I'd told Dad to throw away. He never was good at taking instructions, I suppose. Years of being bossed by Mum made him immune. Monica returned, and we sat together on the floor drinking coffee.

"What does it say about me," I asked, "that my whole life fits in four boxes, while my grandmother's takes up a whole house?"

"It doesn't say anything," Monica replied. "You had a different kind of life."

In the next box, I found a photo of Josh and me in a cracked frame. I wasn't prepared for it. I pulled it slowly out into the light.

"Who's that?" Monica asked.

It took a moment for me to speak. "That's Josh," I said. "That's my ex."

"Your ex?"

"Yes, only I didn't want him to be ex. He left me right before my accident."

"You still love him?" There was a frown in her voice, and I glanced up to see that she was scrutinizing me very closely.

"Well, yes," I said. "Perhaps. He's always on my mind." Though I was beginning to forget. Forget the way his face moved when he smiled, forget the way his skin smelled when he came out of the shower, forget the exact timbre of his laugh . . .

Monica grew quiet, and I wondered why my talk of Josh upset her so. We drank our coffee in silence as I pulled out some of my dancing awards. Mum hadn't been selective at all: she had literally sent all of my things.

"Can you think of a place I can put these?" I asked her.

She shrugged. "Not really."

"You're usually so good at that kind of thing."

She climbed to her feet. "I'll go clean up the kitchen," she said shortly.

I looked at the photo of Josh on the floor, then back at Monica. She was acting as though she were jealous. Then it all clicked into place. She *was* jealous: on behalf of Patrick. I didn't know what to say, so I said nothing. I was torn between wanting to reassure her and not wanting to lie. I *did* still love Josh. At least I thought I did. I couldn't broach the topic, so I pretended I hadn't noticed her anger.

But I did curse myself for going against my instincts and making friends with people down here. People were so complex and unpredictable.

Myself included.

I knew if I waited until around eight o'clock on Saturday night, I'd have a good chance of getting Uncle Mike while he was sauced. He loved his beer but was prudent enough to partake only on weekends.

Uncle Mike lived alone. My auntie Donna had left him when I was still small, and since then he'd had a string of "lady friends" but hadn't settled down with anyone.

"Uncle Mike?" I said when he picked up the phone. "It's Emma."

"My favorite niece!" he boomed. "Just having a few beers. Why don't you pop over?"

"I'm in Tasmania," I replied.

"Still? Louise didn't tell me that."

"There's a lot more work involved in clearing up this place than I'd thought."

"You should pay someone to do it for you, sell the place, and use the money to get yourself a nice little flat in Sydney. I'm seeing a lady who's in real estate. She can help you find something."

I let him talk and offer me advice for a while, warming him up, I suppose. I did love my uncle Mike, but he was a terrible know-it-all. Finally, he drew breath long enough for me to speak again. "Hey, Uncle Mike, what do you know about Grandma's life down here in Tassie?"

"Sheep," he said.

"Beyond that, I mean. Her personal life. Did she live alone?"

I heard a faint scratching noise and surmised this was Uncle Mike rubbing his stubbly chin: a good sign. He usually did this right before he revealed something he shouldn't. "Well," he said slowly, "I don't really know. Why do you ask?"

"I'm finding bits and pieces in the boxes down here that make me wonder if she had a special . . . friend."

"Look, I wouldn't be surprised. Not that I know anything for sure, but when I was about sixteen, I eavesdropped on an argument between your nana and granddad."

"And?"

"I just remember him saying to her, 'You're not telling me something, Beattie,' and she was completely silent. Then he said, 'If something you've done in the past is going to come back and bite us on the bum, I need to know.' But she said nothing; wouldn't answer him."

My granddad never would have said the word "bum," so that was an embellishment, but the rest of it pricked my interest. "Really?"

"Can't remember the exact words, but it was definitely that she hadn't told him something about her past, and he was worried. He was tense. That was just before the 1966 election, and his seat was pretty marginal. He only just hung on that year."

"So, what did you think he meant?" I asked.

"Don't really know, Em. Earlier that year, Mum had gone away for a while. Just off on her own, down to Tassie. Dad didn't tell us what was going on, but Louise and I kind of understood that it was a trial separation. She came back, and they seemed fine and got on okay. Haven't really thought of it much since."

I turned this over in my head. Granddad accusing Grandma of past secrets. A photo of a child in her arms and a collection of children's dress patterns. A lover. A farm given to her for free by minor English nobility. For the first time, I realized I wasn't involved in idle speculation. Grandma really did have a secret past in this house, but I couldn't pin all the pieces together.

TWENTY-SIX

Beautiful weather came. Clear, clear skies, sunshine, warm breezes, and wildflowers everywhere. God's own weather, if you believed in that kind of thing. All at once it seemed a crime to be inside. Patrick had come by to take more things to the dump and help shift all the remaining unpacked boxes into the front storeroom. He'd been tense, and he said it was because the school where the Hollyhocks practiced had said they couldn't have the hall for the next two weeks, and this was going to make their rehearsal time for the concert much shorter. I wondered if Monica had said something to him, if he couldn't meet my eye because he knew that I was in love with somebody else.

The house was almost completely cleaned out; it was certainly in salable condition. It looked like somebody lived there. Monica was in the process of cleaning up the cottage properly. A few boxes still remained in the little front storeroom, but the weather was too glorious to be inside during the day. I saved sorting them for nighttime and made a start on the gardens instead.

The garden beds around the front entrance were my first project. I had almost zero gardening abilities but had watched Josh tend to his pots on the terrace and had gotten the basic idea. I trimmed and weeded with the sunshine in my hair, thinking about nothing for long stretches of time. A pile of green waste piled up behind me, and I wished I had a cat or a dog to lie on the path in the sun and keep me company. I heard the phone ring somewhere in the house, but with my knee, I couldn't rush about for phones anymore, so I let it go.

I was contemplating clearing up the deadfall under the cabbage gum when a car eased up the driveway. I stood and stretched my leg, recognizing Penelope Sykes's car. Another unannounced visit. Or perhaps that had been her on the phone. Immediately, I felt ashamed of myself. Why did I always think the worst of everyone? Why couldn't I just be friendly? I overcompensated.

"Hello!" I said, waving as she got out of the car.

She smiled cautiously as she approached. "I did try to call."

"I'm just about to have a cuppa. Would you like one?"

"I won't stay."

I was determined that she *would* stay, that I would make a better impression on her. "I insist," I said, taking her elbow.

Penelope allowed herself to be brought inside and seated at the table while I made tea.

"I've got something for you," she said, sliding a book across the table to me. "I was putting away all those records you gave me in my prewar file, and I found this. Had forgotten I even had it."

I picked up the book. It was printed on thick, shiny paper,

with a slightly crooked cover. Self-published. The title was *Life of a Godly Woman*. I winced.

"It's as boring as it looks," Penelope said, carefully pouring milk into her teacup. "But you should read between the two Post-it notes I've put in there."

"What's it about?"

"A woman named Pamela Lacey wrote it. Her aunt Margaret Day lived in Lewinford from 1929 to 1945. She kept a diary and passed it on to her niece when she died. The niece wrote it up like a biography. Fictionalized it a bit, I'm sure: names changed to protect the innocent . . ." Here she raised her eyebrows dramatically. "I had a quick skim with your grandmother in mind and . . . Look, I don't know, but there's a character in there who sounds like she might be based on Beattie. Young Scottish lass comes up from Hobart, desperate and poor, winds up owning a big sheep farm."

My blood electrified. "Yes! It must be Beattie."

"I can't tell you how much of the story has been embellished, Emma, and Pamela Lacey is no longer around to ask. If it is Beattie, she's a pretty minor character . . . dealt with in a few pages." Penelope sat back, sipping her tea. "And it's not a flattering portrait, I should warn you of that."

I was sorry I'd encouraged her to stay. I really needed to sit down and read the book that instant, not make small talk—something I wasn't particularly good at anyway. Still, we spoke about the house, my plans, the weather, and she was soon on her way. I saw Penelope to her car, the book tucked under my arm. Then I found a patch of soft, overgrown grass between the poplars. The breeze had picked up, and the clouds were racing across the sky. The whole world seemed to be moving, but I sat very still as I read.

The Scottish lass, as she was known, arrived one evening soaking wet with a tiny red-haired child in tow, asking for help. The book did not make it clear whether the child was Beattie's, but her father came for her two pages later, so perhaps she wasn't. Or was. Depending on my mood. The Scottish lass was involved in alcohol, drugs, illegal gambling, and possibly orgies—the word was never used, but "the worst imaginable congress between desiring adults" was referred to—before she seduced the owner of a local farm to sell it to her cheaply.

Well, the author got that bit wrong. Beattie didn't get her farm cheaply; she got it for free.

I didn't know what to make of it. The writing was so over-wrought and sanctimonious that the events didn't sound real. It did make me wonder if the man who gave Beattie the farm was the lover referred to in her letter, but the dates didn't match up: Raphael Blanchard went back to England in 1934; the sexy letter was probably written in 1939. So did Grandma have more than one lover? Was the little girl in the photo her daughter? Who was the man who came for the little red-haired child? I wanted to believe, like Mum, that Granddad was the first. The only.

But the worst mistake we can make about old people is to forget they were young once.

I read the same seven pages again and again, looking for information between the lines and letters that simply wasn't there. I started to understand that I might never know what

Grandma's secret was. That bothered me. I should have been around more when she was alive. I shouldn't have taken her for granted. But I was off in London having my Terribly Significant Career, and even if she'd said she wanted to tell me something important, I might not have listened.

I was listening now, that was for sure.

Patrick came by Wednesday afternoon after school to pick up Monica. She usually walked, but there was a thunderstorm brewing somewhere behind the warm horizon. I was glad to see him but cautious about showing it.

"Wow, you've done great things with the garden," he said.

"It's therapeutic," I said, showing him the mountain of branches and weeds.

"You'll need somebody with a trailer to help you with that. Do you want me to ask around?"

"It's fine. I have to get better at that stuff. Looking people up, sorting out problems." I noticed he hadn't taken off his sunglasses. "I wanted to talk to you about Mina, anyway," I said, "so I'm glad you're here."

"What is it?"

"Two weeks without a rehearsal. She might forget it all, and time's running out. Do you think her father would drop her off up here on the weekend? She could stay the whole weekend if she wanted to . . ." I trailed off, realizing I didn't know the first thing about taking care of somebody like Mina. "If that's not a mad idea."

Patrick smiled, pushing his sunglasses up on top of his

head. It made a piece of his hair stick out at a right angle to his face. "I think it's a lovely idea. But her dad won't drive this far. I might be able to convince him to let me pick her up and drop her home, though."

"That's hard work for you."

"I don't mind. I'm quite used to driving the distances." He slid his sunglasses back on. "Can I call you back about this? I'll see what I can do."

"Certainly, let me know."

I was growing to love gardening, which surprised me, as I'd never been outdoorsy at all. The long garden bed that ran down from the driveway to the laundry was my latest project. I'd started with the grass and weeds, careful to avoid the thorns on the overgrown roses. I found it hard work, physical work, and didn't mind at all. I lost myself in it, and I liked the way it made me stop thinking. I didn't think about my knee or Josh or my mother; there was just me and the sun-warmed soil.

Monica came to find me around three o'clock. "How's it going?" she asked.

I surveyed the heap of weeds behind me, then looked back at the garden bed. "Feels like I'm getting nowhere."

"Do you want to come and see? I've finished in the cottage."

I climbed to my feet and peeled off my gardening gloves. "Really? Finished?"

"Come and see."

I hadn't been into the cottage since it had been emptied of boxes. I remembered a dark, cobwebbed space. Monica threw open the door, and I didn't recognize the place. It was clean from floor to ceiling, mold scrubbed away to reveal golden floors and walls.

"This looks fantastic," I said.

"Come in farther, there's something interesting to show you." Monica tugged my sleeve lightly. It was the first time since I'd told her about Josh that she'd been her usual friendly self.

I followed her to the biggest of the rooms, and she crouched down under the tiny window to show me.

"Look," she said. "All the shearers who came here have carved their initials."

I bent to look. She was right. A collection of initials. It made me smile. "Are they in every room?"

"Just this one and the one across the corridor. Some are in love hearts with a sweetheart's initials."

This pricked my interest, so I went to the other room to look. But there were no BBs for Beattie Blaxland. Still, it got me thinking. Was Grandma's secret lover one of the shearers? That would account for her talking about the opinions of the township.

"You know what you should do," Monica was saying, thumbing a smudge she'd missed off the window. "You should spend a little money decorating the cottage, then let it out for holidays. Farm tourism is big."

I was already shaking my head. "I'm going to sell the whole lot in March. That can be somebody else's problem."

"You're definitely going to sell?"

I looked back at her and laughed. "Definitely. Probably. I don't know. I can't stay, I'll have to get on with my life at some stage."

"In Sydney? Or back in London?"

I took a moment to answer.

"With Josh?" she continued quietly.

I decided to tackle this issue head-on. "Why does it upset you so much that I have an ex-boyfriend in London?"

"Whom you still love?"

I spread my hands, not elaborating. Waiting for an answer.

Monica sighed. "I'm sorry, have I been obvious?"

"Yes."

"It's just me being silly. I thought you liked Patrick. You know, *liked* him. And I was quite invested in that thought, so . . ."

"You were jealous on his behalf?"

"I guess so." She smiled. "Sorry."

"It's all right."

"It's just . . ." She trailed off. I waited. "I shouldn't say anything . . ."

I waited again. I had discovered over the years—accidentally—that silence made people talk more.

"It's just that Patrick likes you."

"Likes me? Or *likes* me?" I asked, feeling like a teenager.

Monica shook her head. "He's going to kill me."

"I won't say anything." Okay, that was weird. A little thrill ran through me. Patrick, with his exotic eyes and his straight back. I was right: he did find me desirable, enough so to tell his sister. The thought sparked off all kinds of unconscious reactions in my body. I actually laughed softly, like a giggling schoolgirl.

"Anyway," Monica said, "forget we had this conversation. I'm sorry if I've embarrassed you. Do you want a hand with that garden bed?"

"I'd love it," I said.

We worked through the rest of the golden afternoon together in silence.

Mina's father insisted on meeting me, so I drove down to Hobart with Patrick to pick her up. We pulled up outside a huge, glassed mansion at Battery Point.

Patrick frowned, checked the address on the piece of paper, then turned off the car. "That's a big house," he said.

"Is it just the two of them?"

"As far as I know." He climbed out of the car, and I followed. We went up to the front door and rang the bell. I stole glances at Patrick in the yellow midday light, but he seemed oblivious to them.

At length, the door opened, and Mina's father stood there. He was a tall man with a ruddy complexion and thin black hair. He didn't smile. "Good afternoon," he said, offering his hand to shake. "I'm Reynold Carter."

"Emma Blaxland-Hunter," I said, shaking his hand. "And this is Patrick Taylor."

"You're the ballerina," he said expressionlessly. "Come in."

Patrick and I exchanged glances as we followed him into

the house, down a polished parquet hallway and into a large, heated sitting room. Mina sat demurely on the sofa, a little suitcase at her feet.

"Patrick! Emma!" she said in an excited voice. She remained still under her father's gaze, though her feet twitched happily.

"This is a lovely home," Patrick said, his eyes going to the window to take in the view down to the Derwent River.

I noticed a laptop set up at a desk by the door. I would have thought a man like Reynold Carter would have a fancy office, not a corner.

"Now, Mina can look after herself well enough," Reynold said. "Don't do too much for her. Her independence is important to me. And to her, of course."

"I'm just looking forward to spending some time with her," I said, touching the girl's hair. She smiled up at me affectionately.

"Yes. Well." He cleared his throat. "She hasn't stayed away from home overnight, so call me if you have any problems." He was already turning away, his eyes going to the computer screen. "Excuse me a moment."

Patrick picked up Mina's bag while her father clicked a few keys. He returned, not meeting our eyes. "I'm sorry. I trade shares online. The U.S. markets are still open. Saturday mornings are a busy time for me."

"That's your job?" I asked, aware that I shouldn't pry but curious nonetheless.

"I was a stockbroker before Mina's mother died," he said,

matter-of-fact. "I had a nanny for her for a while but then decided she was better off with me at home."

"Daddy works all day and all night," Mina said.

"But I'm here, aren't I?" he said defensively.

She put her arms around his waist and cuddled him. "I love you, Daddy."

"You be good," he said, kissing her on the top of her head, then extricating himself. "Call me if you need me."

We helped Mina into the back of the car. She was excited and chatty now. Her father didn't come to the door to wave her off, and I found myself growing angry at him. Sure, he had provided her with a big house, but Mina clearly needed love. She was such an affectionate, sunny girl.

Then I remembered Patrick's advice to me. *We don't really know what goes on in families. Best not to judge.*

I noticed that Mina's excitement bordered on anxiety as we drove through the big front gates at the driveway up to Wildflower Hill. I decided to ask Patrick to stay for the afternoon, because Mina knew him better, and I wanted her to settle in. He waited downstairs, playing the out-of-tune piano, while I took Mina up to her room. It was the one next to mine, and Monica had turned it over the day before. Fresh sheets, and wildflowers in water on the dresser. Mina put her suitcase on the bed and sat next to it thoughtfully.

"Are you okay?" I said.

"This house is dark and old," she said.

"It is. Over a hundred and fifty years old. Are you scared?"

"No," she said. "Which is your bedroom?"

I knocked on the wall. "Right next door," I said.

She smiled. "Okay."

Downstairs, Patrick was picking out the melody to "The Waltz of the Flowers."

"That's your song, Mina," I said. "Let's go and dance."

Mina was happier, less worried, downstairs in the sitting room. She marveled over all my dancing awards, which I'd lined up on top of the piano. I pushed the couch back up against the wall and the coffee table under the window to clear a space, and we danced.

She had forgotten a few of the movements from last time, but she held herself beautifully, with a straight back and strongly pointed feet. We went through the whole piece three times, with Patrick picking out the tune, then we found the CD player, and Patrick and I sat back on the couch while Mina performed for us.

She took my breath away. When I'd first met Mina and the others, all I'd seen were their similarities. But now I was seeing through to the young woman underneath: the liquid eyes, the clear skin, the fine dark hair, her dimpled elbows and soft white hands. When Mina danced, she was beautiful.

Patrick leaned over to speak quietly in my ear. "You have done a brilliant job with her. And with the dance. The movements are perfect for her."

"She's the one doing all the work. She has natural grace." Monica's words came back to me, that Patrick *liked* me. I felt the heat of his arm against mine, and I let myself enjoy it.

"Stop talking and watch me!" Mina demanded, midway through a *relevé*.

We laughed and returned our attention to her. Her eyes shone with happiness, and it was such a lesson to me. Mina would never be able to dance ballet properly, but she danced anyway. And she loved it.

Patrick and I applauded loudly when she was done, and she theatrically bowed and blew us kisses.

"Now I'm tired," she said.

"Good," I replied. "That means you worked hard. Real ballerinas work very hard."

She fetched Snakes and Ladders out of her suitcase, and we sat on the floor in the sitting room and played together. My knee ached, but I didn't mind so much. Around dusk, Patrick said he had to go home.

Mina looked uncertain again, like she had when she'd first arrived.

"It's okay, Mina, I'll be here with you," I said.

"Is this house very safe?" she asked. "Are there locks on all the doors?"

"Absolutely," I said.

I saw Patrick off at the door. He was reluctant to go, I could tell. Perhaps I was a little reluctant to let him go. I felt a pang of regret as he drove away. The evening cool crept across the fields and hushed through the blue gums. I went inside to make dinner.

Mina helped me, sitting at the table, shelling peas, while I cut up chicken to go in the pasta bake.

"What is my daddy doing now?" she asked.

"I don't know. What does he usually do on Saturday afternoons?"

"He works on the computer," she said.

"Well, that's probably what he's doing now." I sat down with her. "Are you missing him?"

She smiled at me. "A bit."

"You'll see him tomorrow. We've got more rehearsing to do before then." I reached across and squeezed her hand. "Would you rather go home? I can call Patrick to come and get you."

"No. I'll be fine," she said. "Ballet dancers have to work really hard."

"They do."

"Then I'll stay and keep working."

Around midnight, the wind picked up, and I could hear thunder rumbling in the distance. It was enough to make me get up and close the window in my bedroom. I got back into bed, then realized I could hear a knocking sound.

I sat up. It was coming from the wall adjoining Mina's room.

I climbed out of bed again and went next door. "Mina?" I said, opening the door.

She looked up at me in the dark. She was by the wall knocking, just as I'd shown her yesterday. I switched on the light and saw there were tears on her face.

"Sweetie, what's wrong?" I said, hurrying over to her.

She said something, but all her words were jumbled up behind her tongue. I took her hand in mine. It was cold and clammy. She was terrified. "Do you want me to call your dad to come and get you?"

She nodded, sobbing.

I led her to my bedroom and put her in my bed. "You wait here, where it's warm and cozy. I'll call Daddy."

She nodded again.

I went downstairs and switched on all the lights. I found the phone number that Patrick had written down for me and dialed it. It rang and rang. Six times. Seven. Eight. Nine . . .

Finally, he answered. "Hello?"

"Mr. Carter, it's Emma Blaxland-Hunter here."

"What is it?" Not friendly. Not at all.

"Mina's got herself all wound up about the storm, and she wants to come home."

Silence. I waited.

"Mr. Carter?"

"I'm not coming out in the middle of a storm."

At first I was too shocked to speak. Then I said, "But she's crying with fear."

"We all have to do things that we don't like. She'll have to stay there. Call me in the morning if she hasn't settled down."

"But—"

"She'll be fine," he said. Then hung up.

I stared at the phone for a few moments before replacing it. I couldn't quite believe what had just happened, and I burned with fury. *Burned.*

Somehow I had to go upstairs and tell this beautiful, fragile girl that her daddy wouldn't come and get her. I thought about calling Patrick but couldn't bear the thought of making him come out in the rain. I took the stairs carefully, as always, breathing deep to get my anger under control. She was sitting up in my bed by lamplight, staring at the window.

"Mina?"

She looked around.

"He can't come, sweetie. It's too stormy."

She nodded.

"Hey, I know what might cheer you up."

She watched me as I went to my dresser and opened the top drawer. Inside, I found my *Swan Lake* tiara. I carefully pulled it out and brought it over to her.

"What's that?" she said, brightening, finding her voice again.

"It's so special, Mina, you have to be careful with it."

She took it from me reverently and gazed at it.

"It's a special tiara. I wore it when I was dancing Odette."

"Swan Lake," she breathed.

I took the tiara from her and put it on her head, encouraging her to go and look at herself in the mirror over the dresser. Her fears were forgotten as she twirled in front of the mirror, the tiara sparkling in the reflection.

"Come back to bed," I said. "There's room for both of us in this one. We're not worried about the storm."

"We're not," she said, marching back to the bed and snuggling up next to me, the tiara still on her head.

I switched out the light, and her soft hand found mine in the dark. "Good night, Emma," she said.

"Good night," I replied.

I lay awake until I was sure she was sleeping. Her hand uncurled from mine. The storm passed overhead, and she didn't stir.

TWENTY-SEVEN

I found myself awake early, cramped and hot in my bed. Mina slept on peacefully. The tiara had fallen off her head and lay on the pillow beside her. I picked it up carefully and placed it on the bedside table. Soft morning light glowed beyond the curtains. I thought about my garden and decided to get up and do some more work down there. I pulled on jeans and a long-sleeved T-shirt and went downstairs.

The sky was clear, washed clean by the storm. The grass and rocks were still damp. I picked up my bucket of tools on the way and set them down near the old rose bed. I was slowly making my way through, cutting, pulling, digging. I'd no idea if the roses would grow again after being pruned back so savagely, and I realized with a touch of sadness that I would never see them bloom, either. Somebody else would own the house then.

I put down my trowel for a moment as I thought of this. Somebody else parking their car in the driveway, somebody else moving their things into the bedroom, somebody else cooking in the big echoing kitchen.

Told myself I was being sentimental and kept digging.

The sun rose fully, and I went inside to check on Mina. She was awake and dressed and in the sitting room looking at my awards. I made her breakfast, then asked if she wanted to do some more dancing practice.

"No," she said, "I want to help you in the garden."

So I gave her a sturdy pair of gardening gloves, and we went back outside into the fresh morning light. I didn't want her in the rose bed; I was too worried about the thorns. So I told her to collect the fallen twigs from around the sick cabbage gum and put them in a pile near my weeds.

Mina was much more relaxed than the previous night, and she chatted happily about gardening, about how she and her dad had planted a little vegetable patch and grown their own tomatoes. I was still angry at her father for not coming to get her the night before, and for not taking an interest in her dancing, so I wasn't persuaded by one gardening story.

"What do you do with your time, Mina?" I asked. "If your dad is working on his computer."

"I work three afternoons a week at a supermarket. Packing shelves," she said.

I was taken aback. "Really?"

"I make some money that way, to give to Dad to help. And I have a friend who comes three mornings a week to help me learn things. Her name's Mrs. Pappas."

"Like schoolwork?"

She shook her head. "No, I finished school last year. Mrs. Pappas teaches me how to go on the bus and stay safe and things like that."

"You can go on the bus by yourself?"

"I did once. That was fun. But I nearly forgot my stop." She giggled, throwing a handful of twigs on the pile. "Then I remembered the chocolate shop, and the stop was right outside it."

"Ah, hard to forget about chocolate."

She didn't answer, and I looked around to see her peering between two spiky bushes under the cabbage gum.

"What is it?" I asked.

"I don't know."

I rose slowly and came to join her. I expected to see an animal, maybe a dead one. But it wasn't an animal. It was a shape. I frowned. "It's a cross."

"Like at a church."

"Yes. Something must be buried here." Or someone, though I didn't want to say that and freak Mina out. "Let's see if we can make our way through to it."

Mina and I hauled branches and deadfall out of the way, and I savagely hacked back the sedge. Finally, we got there. I crouched carefully. The cross was about thirty centimeters high. I used my trowel to scrape off the decades of accumulated dirt. Letters. I didn't want to pull the cross out, so I got in close to uncover the other letters.

From top to bottom, written vertically: C H A R L I E.

"Does it say something?" Mina asked.

"Charlie," I replied. A shock to my heart. Somebody was buried here? Surely not. Surely people were buried in cemeteries.

The sound of a car engine. I looked up to see Patrick

turning in to the driveway. The sun flashed off his windshield. Was it that late already?

"Patrick!" Mina exclaimed, running down to greet him.

"We haven't practiced," I said, dropping my tools. I was aware that I was filthy with soil and sweat and that my hair was unwashed.

"We've been gardening, and we found a cross," Mina told him.

"Can I see?" he asked, and Mina led him over.

"'Charlie,'" he read. "I wonder who Charlie was."

"I'm hoping a pet," I said.

Patrick straightened up and looked at me, raising one eyebrow. "A pet? You think? On farms, animals die all the time, and nobody gets sentimental about it. I can't imagine someone planting a tree and raising a cross over the grave of a pet. It's obviously some kind of memorial. To a person."

He was right, and I knew it. The cross had been deliberately placed there. I just found the idea that there was a body buried in the house paddock a little creepy.

"Go and pack your things, Mina," I said to her.

"Okay." She hurried off inside, and Patrick smiled at me. "You have dirt on your face," he said.

"Where?" I asked, my hand going to my left cheek self-consciously.

"Here." He grasped my fingers gently and moved them to the other side of my face, then let go.

Warm tingles. I brushed off the mud. "So you think it's a person buried here?"

"It might be. Dig it up and see," he joked. He glanced up

at the branches that spread above us. "I wouldn't stand here for long if I were you. Some of these branches look as though they are dying."

"The possums," I said. "I suppose I'd better do something about them. This tree is more important than I thought."

That night, after a long shower that washed away all the mud and sweat of the day and left me pink and clean, I was thinking about the cross. In truth, I hadn't stopped thinking about it all day. I was clean and dry, so I didn't want to go down into the dew-soaked evening to look at it again. Instead, I opened up the main bedroom and went to the window there. I pushed the sash open. The moon was just off full, and white light fell on the dewy fields. The cabbage gum was right there. This was the only window in the house that faced it.

The scene awoke a stirring of memory within me. I concentrated, trying to grasp it. Then realized: this was the painting in Grandma's house. The one she'd told me always made her feel calm and happy. Of course it was, I could see it from up here. The curve of the hill and, behind it, the distant rocky outcrop, just the same. This tree was special to her. She'd planted it where she could see it every day, and when she'd left, she'd had it painted so she could still see it.

Patrick was right, the tree was some kind of memorial. I'd always thought the tree was planted too close to the house, but perhaps that was the point. To keep somebody close. Somebody named Charlie. Tears pricked my eyes, even as I wondered if my imagination was overreacting.

I stood there a long time, breathing the night air, watching the silver moonlight create shifting shadows over the fields. My grandmother loved somebody named Charlie. He was the man in the letter, for certain. But he'd died. I felt the world swing away from me a moment. If he hadn't died, Grandma might have married him. Never met Granddad. Never had Mum or Uncle Mike. History would have erased me. And yet I wished things had worked out differently for Grandma's sake. It's a terrible thing to lose the man you love.

The following Saturday, back at the school hall, Mina was brilliant. She remembered the whole dance, and Marlon began to put the rest of that part of the show together. Six other children danced around her—very simple, slow movements—and it all started to look wonderful. Marlon pretty much memorized Mina's dance in one viewing, changed a few moves she was having trouble with to make them more practical, and I felt a bit useless. I sat and watched and realized my knee didn't ache so much from the long drive down.

Spring started looking toward summer. The concert approached. The gardens grew tidier. The last of the boxes was emptied and packed away. Monica had nothing to do, so I let her go with great regret. She promised she'd come to see me once a week, and she did, but it wasn't the same as having her around all the time. I missed her. Patrick was distracted and busy. I grew lonely.

I walked a lot. I even ran sometimes. I tried to dance, but it was a thin impersonation of the kind of dancing I'd once been capable of. I felt fully and clearly the truth that my body would never move like that again. The flexibility was gone, and pain always waited if I wasn't careful. It still made me cry.

We were three weeks out from the concert, and Marlon called four nighttime dress rehearsals.

"You don't have to go," Patrick said. "It's an extra drive to Hobart for you."

"My knee's pretty good now," I said. "And I'd love to see Mina in her costume."

The summer evenings were divine. The light stayed on the land late, and the air was sweet to breathe. Nothing like fumy London in summer. As we climbed out of the car at the school, everything smelled beautiful: cut grass, distant flowers, food cooking. I took deep, grateful breaths.

On the other side of the car park, Mina's father was dropping her off. I craned my neck to see him, scowling. "I don't suppose he'll come to this year's concert, either," I said.

"Best not to get involved, Emma," Patrick said.

Mina waved, excited by the night and the hall lights and the glittering difference of it all.

I walked over to take her hand, leaned into the car, and said to her father, "You should come in, Mr. Carter."

"No time," he said gruffly.

"Are you going to be able to make it for the concert this year?"

He glared at me. "Nobody's business," he said.

"Emma," Patrick said, caution in his voice.

"She's a beautiful dancer. It seems a shame for you to miss it."

"Close the door please," he said. "I'm in rather a hurry."

I did as he said, and Mina looked up at me with an expression of confusion. "He's very busy," she said.

"I know, honey," I replied, stroking her hair. "I just don't want him to miss out on seeing you dance."

We went into the hall, and when Mina ran off to join her friends, Patrick turned to me and said sternly, "You shouldn't have said anything."

"He's a selfish bastard."

"You don't know that."

"He wouldn't come out and get her from my place during the storm, even when she was sobbing with terror."

Patrick shrugged. I prickled. "Sorry," he said. "But Marlon told me that right from day one. We can't really know anything about these families, and they are all coping with difficulties in different ways. He's doing his best to bring in a good income while still working at home. That's admirable."

"But he's too busy to spend time with her. You can't be too busy for love." As I said it, I had the horrible feeling that I had been. That my whole life, until my forced retirement, had been *precisely* too busy for love. I hadn't seen Grandma before she died; I wouldn't visit my mother; even Josh had grown sick of my not being there for him and had run off with his assistant.

And now? Was I reformed? Only because I had to sit still so bloody often. I thought of the initial unfriendliness I'd shown Monica, Patrick, Penelope Sykes . . . everyone, really.

Patrick was called away to deal with some crisis, and I took my seat in the front row to watch.

The lights were dimmed, and the stage lighting came on. Patrick had explained that they started dress rehearsals so early to get the children used to the lights. I saw why. Some of them were completely stagestruck, forgetting moves and wandering about instead. Marlon remained beautifully patient despite the disaster that was happening onstage. I stifled a chuckle.

Then Mina's music came on, and she emerged in her costume: a blue leotard with a soft, silky skirt over it. She was barefoot, as I'd advised her to be. She took center stage, the lights softened, a white spotlight hit her. I tensed, wondering if she would be distracted, like the others.

Then she raised her arms in a perfect arabesque and started to move.

I admit, I was invested—deeply so—in Mina's performance. But it was one of the most beautiful things I had ever seen. Not just because she nailed every move, not just because she looked like a pale blue angel up there surrounded by six other white angels who moved slowly in a circle around her. But because she was a girl who had been given so many challenges in life and had overcome them with such grace and spirit. I cried all the way through it and wondered how her father could bear to miss it.

Patrick dropped me off just after ten. I put the kettle on and slipped off my shoes and was thinking about climbing straight into my pajamas when there was a knock at the door.

Curious, I went to open it.

Patrick was there. "I'm sorry, I forgot to give you this." He handed me a plastic package with a phone charger in it. "From Monica. She ordered it for you. Only came in today."

"Thanks," I said, taking the package. The kettle started whistling. "Come in for a coffee?"

He glanced away from me. He was uncomfortable for a moment. Then he seemed to find his voice. "Sure."

In the kitchen, I plugged my mobile phone into the charger and made coffee. We sat at the table and talked about the rehearsal, about Mina, then somehow got on to the weather. We were talking like people who really wanted to talk about something else but weren't quite brave enough. I did admire him. I admired his lean body, his green eyes, his long fingers around his coffee cup. I also admired his gentle humor, his kindness, his courage. But I was afraid to do anything other than admire him. I was afraid to get closer to him, though I wasn't sure why.

"I should go," he said, finishing his coffee. "School night."

I laughed. "I'll see you on Saturday morning. Not that I'm needed anymore."

"Of course you're still needed," he said. Gently, earnestly.

I didn't believe him, but I would go anyway. I'd grown fond of Mina. I'd grown fonder of Patrick.

I saw him off at the door. He walked halfway to his car, then turned around and came back. I waited in the threshold. Moonlight suited him. He came to stand right in front of me and said nothing. I said nothing.

Then he leaned in and kissed me. Warm lips, warm body.

I pressed myself against him, curious hands running over his back, feeling the shape of him under his clothes.

He stood back, said, "Good night," and went back to his car.

I couldn't stop smiling, even after his car had disappeared out of sight.

Next morning, late, I came down for breakfast. While I waited for the toaster, I switched on my newly charged mobile phone. It beeped at me. I had four new messages.

Already my heart was beating quicker.

I dialed the message bank number, noticing that my hands were shaking.

"Emma? Are you still on this number? Call me." *Josh.*

As I listened to the four messages, a narrative unfolded. *Call me. Need to talk to you. Sarah and I have split; it wasn't working. She's not you. Call me, babe. I miss you. Call me. Call me.*

Call me.

Dreams solidified into reality. Everything that had gone between—my accident, the inheritance, life at Wildflower Hill—grew as light and pale as tissue paper. There was no battle with conscience, there was no wondering if I was being a fool. There was only his voice, as I'd imagined it a thousand times, telling me to come home.

I called him. I called London. I called my old life.

TWENTY-EIGHT

Beattie: London, 1965

B eattie dropped her little case full of toiletries on the crisply made bed while Ray wrangled their two large suitcases through the door of the hotel room. They dragged on the thick brown carpet.

"Can I help you with those?"

"What kind of a husband would I be if I couldn't manage my wife's suitcase?" He laughed.

Beattie sat on the edge of the bed and watched him bring the cases in. His pale hair was growing thin, but still without a streak of gray, as though years of public life and political responsibility hadn't worried him at all.

He sat next to her. "Tired?"

"I feel fine."

"Thirty hours on a plane and you feel fine." He touched her hair. "My Beattie."

"When do you have to go?"

Ray glanced at his watch. He was in London for a conference. Usually, Beattie didn't accompany him, being so tied up with her own business back in Sydney. But she was slowly letting go of Blaxland Wool's reins, as the company got too big for her to manage solo. That and the fact the children were now teenagers and quite happy to be left with an indulgent auntie for ten days.

"Welcoming drinks are at six P.M. But I don't have to go. They won't miss me."

Beattie yawned. Maybe she wasn't fine after all. "No, you should go. I'll order room service and read a book."

"Don't go to sleep too early. You'll be out of sync for days."

"I'll wait up for you."

She folded away their clothes while he showered and shaved, got his papers together, tightened his tie. Then he wasn't her Ray anymore, with his goofy smile and taste for silly but gentle practical jokes. Now he was the Honourable Raymond Hunter MP, member for the federal seat of Mortondale, and shadow minister for health.

"I won't be too late," he said, kissing her cheek.

"Thanks, darling." She tried a smile but could feel the corners of her lips were frozen.

He tilted his head, examining her. "There's something wrong, isn't there?"

"I miss the children," she said quickly. *And there's more than that, but I can't tell you.* She met his blue eyes evenly. "I'll call your sister to see how they are, and then I'll feel better."

"Tell them I said hello."

After he'd gone, Beattie opened the window and let in the traffic noise and the cool autumn chill. She climbed up on the high bed and picked up a book but couldn't really concentrate on the words in front of her. The last time she'd been in

London was just before she and Henry had run away to Tasmania. But Ray knew nothing about that. She hadn't meant for her past to become a secret, dark and buried and shameful, but somehow it had. What Ray didn't know was that she had another motive in coming to the UK with him. For the first time in twenty-five years, Beattie hoped to see her daughter.

Charlie's death had been an agonizing rupture in her world. But shearing season was coming, and there was no stopping it. Leo Sampson helped her all he could, and Peter and Matt took control of the procedings. Beattie stayed upstairs in her room, crying for hours, sitting under the window so she could look down on the cabbage gum sapling she'd planted over Charlie's grave. At night she dreamed that she was chasing him as he disappeared down a dim hallway, or was waiting for him to come back on Birch from the southern end of the farm. Waiting and waiting as the sun set and the sky turned cold and black. Then she would wake and feel his loss anew. Her arms and legs ached so much that she thought she was coming down with an illness, but no illness ever eventuated. She remained almost cruelly healthy. Heart in pieces, body robustly ticking along.

Somewhere in the world, there was a war raging. Somewhere in the world, her daughter was being raised by another mother. But Beattie could not pick herself up long enough to deal with those worries. Months went by in a kind of awful stasis as the cloud of grief set in and would not lift, like the winter fog that sat in the valley behind the ridge. She saw no sunlight.

Christmas approached, and Beattie found a little satisfaction in sewing a winter coat for Lucy and posting it to Scotland. With it, she included a long letter, explaining to Lucy that Charlie had died, and that was the reason she hadn't written. A long silence followed, not unexpectedly.

Easter came. By now Beattie had written six or seven letters, sent them off, and waited. No reply ever came.

Her anger kept her awake at night. She knew that Molly and Henry would have a telephone, but they hadn't given her the number. How dare they? All she wanted was to hear her daughter's voice. It would give her so much comfort. Beattie couldn't wait for this silly war to be over. The moment it was, she was going to Scotland, she was going to find them. In the meantime, she kept writing letters, pouring out her love for her daughter. And kept sending them into the silence.

Beattie knew her business was faltering. Peter and Matt were young, not really up to the task of managing the farm. Her last wool clip had been the best ever, so she wasn't worried about money, but she was letting the bookwork slip, organizing things too late or not at all. She had lost her heart for this business. Once the agricultural rhythms had seemed about new life, renewal, growth. Now she looked around her and saw only death. A gray pall had settled over everything, and she knew she had to get away.

She advertised for someone to lease the business from her and began to pack her things.

One morning as she made her usual pilgrimage to the

letter box to see if there was anything from Lucy—there wasn't—she found a letter with an Australian government crest on it. She frowned. She feared the tax office or perhaps even bad news from abroad. But the letter had nothing to do with taxes. It seemed the advisory war cabinet was ratifying a proposal to create five hundred positions for woman telegraphists in the air force. They needed a uniform—wool skirt and blazer—and wondered if Beattie might tender a quote for the work.

Beattie read the letter twice by the letter box, then twice again in her sitting room. A warm tingle in her heart, like the first shoots of spring after icy winter. It was ridiculous. She could design a blazer and skirt, but she couldn't make five hundred uniforms single-handedly.

And yet all they had asked was for her to tender for the work. She would have to budget in hiring a dozen employees, buying a dozen sewing machines. She would have to do nothing but design, manage, and oversee the production.

The morning slipped by as she worked at her desk, drawing, scribbling, tearing up, starting again. It had been so long since she'd felt any enjoyment in life that it was almost like being drunk. Pleasure, real pleasure. When she had roughed out six or seven designs, she turned her mind to the quote, estimating prices, crossing her fingers that she wasn't too high or too low. Her stomach rumbled, reminding her she hadn't eaten. She looked up to see that the shadows outside had grown long. She had literally worked on the idea all day.

She couldn't remember when time had sped like that last. Each moment since Charlie's death had been excruciatingly long. She knew then what might save her: work. But not work on the farm—there were too many memories for her here.

It took six weeks for Beattie to hear that she'd secured the contract. By then she was already packed and ready to go. She'd had a broker find her a little place at Haymarket in Sydney, with a space big enough underneath for a small workshop.

Rain fell the morning she left Wildflower Hill. The new tenants arrived and were trying to move their furniture in through mud and puddles. Their three little boys ran around inside, squealing with excitement. It made Beattie glad to know that the house would hear laughter and feel love again. She climbed into her car and didn't look back at Charlie's grave. She knew it would have made her cry.

It was in Sydney, four years later, that she met Ray. Beattie had been invited to a fund-raising ball for the War Widows Guild. Normally, she liked to keep to herself. She wasn't reclusive so much as wary. Where she lived now was vastly different from Lewinford. Nobody knew that she was a single mother of dubious morals. Nobody saw her sending the endless letters to Scotland, to her illegitimate daughter or her ex-lover and his wife. Nobody except Leo Sampson knew of her efforts to find Lucy through the tortuous and expensive legal system, or how the endless dragging on of the war had made all her efforts doubly difficult. Nobody knew, certainly, of the tears she cried into her pillow at night, realizing that her child would have changed vastly since she last saw her. Realizing that she barely knew what Lucy looked like anymore, and that the long absence had dulled her need to see the girl. In many ways, the Lucy she knew was gone forever. By now a tall and strange teenager would have taken her place in the world. One who, if Beattie guessed correctly about the poison Henry and Molly had filled her ears with, would be hostile toward her if they met.

The ballroom of the Wentworth Hotel was ablaze under the dazzling chandeliers. Dozens of tables had been set with fine china and silver for a five-course meal, but Beattie was far too nervous to think of eating. She was due to give a speech. She had become something of a minor celebrity in Sydney since her designs had been picked up by a large American chain store. Nearly 60 percent of her business was in exports. She no longer designed for government and business but for department stores and fashion boutiques. Her practical but beautiful designs were in demand as women saw themselves as newly powerful and capable. And Beattie—young, single, wealthy—had become a symbol of those qualities herself. *The Australian Women's Weekly* had run an article on her just after Christmas, and she found she was even recognized on the streets from time to time.

The well-heeled guests drifted in. Women in long embroidered gowns, fox fur stoles, and suede bags; men in two-piece flannel suits, gold tie clips and chains, and silk cravats. Beattie had chosen to wear one of her own designs, a short skirt with box pleats, a V-neck silk blouse, and a short bolero over the top. She wore a silk flower on her shoulder and high heels trimmed with bows. The room filled with the smell of cigar smoke, and Beattie found it hard to catch her breath. She asked a passing waiter for a glass of brandy and surprised him by downing it in one gulp.

"Thank you," she said, returning the glass. "That's a little better."

Finally, it came time for her to speak. The lights in the room dimmed, and she leaned on the lectern for dear life and took a deep breath.

She'd been asked to talk about her success, how she'd arrived, where she'd arrived. But so much had to be left out of this account. Yes, she was a poor immigrant from Scotland who had struggled, making money working for Margaret Day, sewing buttons back on people's jackets. But she mentioned nothing about the child she'd had to support, the drunken gambling husband she'd had to flee, the lecherous boss she'd had to outsmart. Yes, she had worked her hands raw mustering sheep in long winters only to return home to tiny serves of wild rabbit meat and parsnips for dinner. But she mentioned nothing about the man who had taught her to ride a horse, who had loved her and supported her through the difficult times. To narrate her life this way was to blend out all its contrasts, to make it far duller. But she could hardly stand up here in front of wealthy Sydney society and admit to having an illegitimate child, winning the farm in an unsavory bet, conducting a passionate affair with a black man. She wondered if those unpalatable truths would ever make their way into the light, or if the people of Lewinford were happy enough, now that she was gone, never to mention her again. Small enough in their outlook never to hear of her success on the world stage.

She finished talking, feeling all the while like a fraud, and the audience erupted into enthusiastic applause. She was taken aback; she had thought she was boring everybody.

"Thank you," she muttered. "Thank you."

The band struck up as she left the stage, and the audience surged to the parquet dance floor. Beattie returned to her table, to a plate of melting ice cream. She was suddenly ravenous, ate the ice cream, and felt a little sick. The other guests at her table leaned toward her, smelling of expensive colognes and hair cream, told her how much they loved her speech, then spun out to the dance floor. Beattie sat alone, wondering when it would be polite to leave.

"Miss Blaxland?"

She looked up to see a tall man with fair hair and kind eyes looking down at her. He wore a beautifully cut striped wool suit.

"Hello," she said.

"May I ask you for a dance?"

Beattie's eyes went to the dance floor and back to the man. She couldn't dance. The events of her life had never taken her to the ballroom. The other women were elegant, knew what they were doing.

"I'm sorry. I don't feel much like dancing," she said.

He hesitated, no doubt wondering if her rejection was general. "Can I get you a glass of champagne, then?" he asked.

She felt sorry that she'd turned down his offer to dance, and he did seem rather sweet. "Certainly. I would like that."

She waited until he returned, wishing she'd dashed off when she'd had a chance.

He sat with her, offering her a champagne glass. She sipped from it slowly, aware that on an empty stomach, the bubbles would go straight to her head.

"May I introduce myself to you properly?" he said with a steady, direct gaze. "I'm Raymond Hunter, member for Mortondale."

"My pleasure," she said.

"I enjoyed your speech very much."

"I thought I was boring everybody."

"Not at all. I think we were all enchanted. At least I know I was."

Don't drink too fast, Beattie. She put down the glass and took a deep breath. "Well," she said. "How long have you been in parliament?"

"Three and a half years." He smiled. "Though it feels like dog years sometimes."

She laughed softly. Encouraged, he told her a few stories about life in Canberra. She was disarmed by his self-deprecating humor and found herself laughing as loudly as the crimson-faced dowager who'd had too much to drink at the next table. Her keenness to get away softened, and when he asked if he could call on her the following night and take her to dinner, she didn't say no.

Nor did she say yes.

"Ask me tomorrow when I've had nothing to drink," she said, offering him the empty champagne glass as evidence. "I'll give you my phone number at work."

He respectfully copied down the number with a black fountain pen, then saw her into a cab at the entrance to the hotel. She smiled all the way home, flushed and still laughing at some of his jokes.

Beattie had learned the hard way to separate her living space and her working space. In the first two years in Sydney, she had lived directly above the workshop and found herself at work from the moment she woke till the moment she slept. Now she took the tram down to Castlereagh Street every morning, to her little workshop with the desk and phone in the corner and the sound of the electric sewing machines running all day. Ray phoned her just after lunchtime, just after she'd convinced herself he wouldn't call, and made herself unexpectedly disappointed.

"So?" he said.

"Yes," she answered.

Almost despite herself, she found herself with a new beau.

TWENTY-NINE

Beattie never intended to keep Lucy secret from Ray. It had happened almost by accident, not by design.

They had two dates together before he had to return to Canberra for parliament. He hadn't so much as held her hand, let alone kissed her. It wasn't time yet for sharing her shady past with him. He was gone for two months, wrote periodic letters full of humorous observations, and promised to take her out again when he got back. She got on with life, didn't really think of him.

It was nearly Easter when he came back, and he surprised her with his interest. With the way he spoke, as though they were already a couple. He took her to a restaurant on Pitt Street and told her about how much he'd missed her. She was flattered. That was all.

Or was it? She was so relaxed in his company. She liked him—truly liked him, for his kind eyes and his boyish humor.

At her door that night, he kissed her softly on the lips. Her reaction surprised her. She pressed her body close to his, returning his kiss with passion. It had been so long since any-one had held her like that. But he pulled away gently, laughing.

"I have a surprise for you on the weekend," he said.

"What is it?"

"If I told you, it wouldn't be a surprise."

So she waited the week out, thinking of him idly in her spare moments. But still not taking him particularly seriously.

Ray sent a card on Friday that told her to be ready to leave Saturday morning, to pack things for an overnight stay. She did as he asked, curiosity piqued. An overnight stay: did that mean he wanted to sleep with her? Perhaps her fierce embrace the other night had given him the impression that she would. Would she?

He arrived just before nine in his big Dodge, wearing a trilby and a knitted cardigan. He was handsome, with his rangy athletic body and his fair hair. Despite this boyishness, he was a person with much authority and public responsibil-ity. She wondered if he behaved differently in Canberra. He loaded her suitcase into his car, and they took off.

"Where are we going?" she asked.

"Up to the mountains," he said with a smile.

The autumn air was clear and cool. Pale bluish mist sat in the valleys. They wound up the mountain road. The sun was bright on the hood of the car and on the yellow leaves of the trees lining the road. She was comfortable to sit in silence, watching the scenery speed past. Just being with him was so easy. She glanced at him while his eyes were glued to the road.

"I can see you looking at me, Beattie," he said.

She laughed.

"Out of the corner of my eye," he added.

"What are we going to do up the mountain?" she asked.

"My parents live at Katoomba. I'm taking you to meet them."

Her heart cooled. "Really?" He was taking her to his parents? Were things that serious? She hadn't told him anything about her past. Should she?

"Don't sound so worried," he said. "They're very nice."

"I . . . hadn't imagined that you'd want to introduce me to family quite so soon," she said.

He glanced at her sharply, then turned his eyes back to the road. "Have we not been seeing each other since January?"

"Well, yes. But you were away in Canberra for two months."

"I feel a bit of a fool, Beattie. Do you have your eye on someone else?"

"No," she said quickly. "Of course not."

"Then it can do no harm to meet my parents, and they have a guest house adjoining their property where we can stay. To get out of the city. Mountain air is invigorating." He recovered from his consternation quickly and began yodeling.

Beattie laughed, and this encouraged him to continue. She laughed harder, until her belly ached and tears ran down her face.

His parents were very kind, as he'd said. The day passed with a long lunch and a longer walk, until finally, Ray and Beattie retired to the guesthouse in the late cool of the evening.

"There are two bedrooms, you'll see," Ray said as he unlocked the door. "But only one bathroom. We'll go up to my parents' house for breakfast. After you."

She walked ahead of him into a tiny cottage with a low ceiling. It smelled faintly of old ash and old books, and Ray strode directly to the fireplace to light a fire. There was a large settee in front of the fire, and a wall lined with bookshelves.

"There's a bottle of port in the cabinet there," Ray said, indicating with his shoulder. "Will you join me for one?"

"Certainly," Beattie said. She found the bottle and poured two glasses, and they sat back to watch the fire.

Ray had his arm along the back of the settee, behind her shoulders. Her skin prickled faintly with desire.

"Can I ask you something, Beattie?" he said, turning to face her. His skin was golden in the firelight.

"What is it?"

"This morning in the car, I sensed you were reluctant to be with me."

"No, not at all. I really enjoy your company."

"I mean reluctant to be with me . . . as in a relationship. As in getting to know each other with a view to . . . more."

Beattie blinked back at him. It was time to tell him. *Tell him, go on.* About Lucy. About Charlie. About how she got Wildflower Hill. But she was aware that Ray was a man who had known her for months before he'd kissed her, had graciously extricated himself from her passionate kisses. How was she to admit not one lover but two?

She couldn't. Simply couldn't. Lucy was out of her life at least until the end of the war. Perhaps it didn't matter so much if she didn't say anything about her now, in the firelit room, with Ray's eyes locked on hers.

"You are a lovely man," she said.

"But . . . ?"

"No buts."

"So I've not made a fool of myself by bringing you to meet my parents?"

"Not at all." She reached for his hand, clasped it in her own.

"You deserve better than me," he said. "Somebody who isn't away half the year."

"I don't mind," she said. "I'm used to my own company."

"But you won't see anyone else while I'm gone?"

She shook her head. "I promise, Ray. You're the one for me."

Beattie knew that eventually, it would all come out, because eventually, she would see Lucy again. But it didn't seem to matter so much when he was away, and when he was with her, she was too busy to think about it. The war finally ended, and in the same week, something finally came from Scotland.

One of her own letters marked "not at this address."

Beattie was devastated, furious, bewildered. How long had it been since they had moved without telling her?

Ray noticed that evening at dinner that she was distant and preoccupied, but she told him it was something to do with work and he wasn't to worry. She cursed herself for not telling him the truth. He was a kind man, he would understand. He would tell her it was all right and that he didn't mind.

But it wasn't only his opinion she feared. He was an elected member of parliament: his career depended on his being clean, honest, trustworthy. A terrible sadness washed over her. She was bad for Ray. She ought to get out of his life and let him get on without her, let him find some young virgin to woo and marry, a woman who would never embarrass him publicly.

He chose precisely that moment to stand up from his chair, put aside his napkin, and go down on one knee in front of her.

Other people in the restaurant stirred, murmuring excitedly.

"No, Ray, no," she whispered, but he didn't hear her.

"Beattie—"

"Not here," she said.

But it was too late. They had an audience. Tears pricked Beattie's eyes. He looked so hopeful. He reached for her hand, but she snatched it away. Shot out of her seat and ran for the door.

Out into the evening air, the traffic noise and the cigarette smoke of passersby.

He found her, sobbing, on the front step of her house. Somehow in the mad dash, she'd lost her key: the final straw.

"I'm the one who should be crying," he said from the front gate.

She looked up. "I've lost my key."

He held it up. "Found it on the floor of the restaurant. Luckily, I was down there on one knee, so I spotted it easily."

"I'm so sorry, Ray."

"Can we talk inside? It's rather cool out here."

She gestured for him to come forward, and he opened the door to let them in. She switched on the lamps on either side of her couch and drew the curtains closed. Her heart thudded dully.

"Now, I take it you don't want to marry me?" he said, settling in the wingback armchair by the empty fireplace.

"It's not that simple."

"So you *do* want to marry me?"

Marriage. The last time she'd thought of it, she'd been with Charlie. When he'd died, she'd supposed it would never happen to her.

"Why now?" she asked.

"The war is over. Life is going on."

For some reason this thought made her terribly sad. Life was indeed going on. And it looked like her life was going on without her daughter in it. Lucy would be sixteen now. Her childhood was over. What Beattie longed for was little Lucy again, with her light body and trusting eyes. She longed for something that was impossible.

"I'm not what you think I am," she said.

"Yes, you are," he countered.

"I'm . . . My past is not so . . ."

"You've had lovers? I could tell that when I first kissed you. I've had lovers, too. They aren't here now. I'm here now."

His answer surprised her. "Your reputation—"

"Beattie, we're both in our thirties. Nobody in the government is expecting me to take a virgin bride."

She couldn't meet his eye.

"We can have a long engagement. As long as you like. There's no hurry. But I see myself growing old with you, my dear. Please let me believe that this dream might come true."

She dissolved into tears.

"Ah, there. You're going to say no again, aren't you?"

"Yes. I mean, no, I'm not going to say no. I'm saying yes," she said.

He strode to her and caught her in his arms, pressing her close. "I will take such good care of you, my love. I will never let you down."

Beattie intended to tell him so many times. Before their engagement party; after their engagement party. Before the first time they made love; after the first time they made love. But she kept putting it off. In the meantime, she wrote to anyone she knew in Glasgow, asking if they could help her find the MacConnells. She ended up with sixteen different addresses of Henry MacConnells in the greater Glasgow area. Wrote to them all. Had not a single response.

She intended to tell Ray before their wedding, which was July the following year. But then an election was called, and suddenly, he wasn't happy, easygoing Ray anymore. He was always busy, he was tense in private but all charm in the public eye, he was perpetually exhausted. Beattie asked if he'd rather put off the wedding, but he said he wanted to be married before the election, so she went ahead with plans for a small registry office wedding, all the while dreading it. Dreading it.

You have to tell him.

She hadn't counted on the letters.

Two of them arriving on the same day. Same stamp. Same lack of return address. Different handwriting on the envelopes. One hand she recognized as Molly's.

Beattie was at home, taking a rare day off. She was barefoot, hoping to occupy the sunbeam that hung about in her sitting room for most of the morning. With the letters in her hand, she returned to her couch, but the sun didn't seem so warm now.

She opened the first, unfolded it slowly. Molly.

> *Dear Beattie,*
>
> *We are aware of your attempts to find us, and ask respectfully that you do not contact us again. We are all happy and well as we are, and have no desire to be reminded of our difficult times in Australia. Lucy is growing into a fine young woman, and it is important that her friends and potential suitors continue to believe that I am her natural mother. I know that you care about her enough to let her go.*
>
> *Yours, Molly.*

Beattie was about to scrunch up the envelope with rage when she realized there was something else in it. She tipped it up, and two small photographs fell out in her lap.

She caught her breath. It was Lucy. Tall. A young woman. She looked directly at the camera, unsmiling. Henry's customary expression. The other photo was a family portrait of the three of them. Molly had aged terribly, and Beattie knew it was the guilt. Well, damn her, may she feel the guilt forever. *Ask respectfully that you do not contact us again . . .* How dare she? And what kind of a mother did Molly think she was to let her daughter go so easily?

She turned her attention to the other envelope. Perhaps it was from one of the other MacConnell families she had contacted, apologizing for not being who she wanted them to be. But it wasn't. It was from Lucy herself.

Dear Beattie . . .

Beattie pinched the bridge of her nose. Not *Dear Mummy*. She knew in that instant how things were going to go.

> *Would you please allow me to get on with my life in*
> *peace? I have received all your letters and haven't cared*
> *to read them. I appreciate all you did for me as a child,*
> *and Daddy has told me to admire you for taking me*
> *away when he was steeped in sin. When he brought me*
> *here he was merely doing the same thing and I am very*
> *grateful to him. And to Molly, whom I consider to be my*
> *mother now. I like Scotland and have no desire to return*
> *to you or the farm or any of it. Leave me be.*
> *Lucy MacConnell*

The rejection, petulant though it sounded, hit Beattie like a physical blow. Her stomach ached. She put aside the letter and picked up the photograph again. This unsmiling stranger had written the letter. Lucy, her russet-haired angel, was long gone.

The stars had aligned cruelly. Lucy didn't want to know Beattie, and Beattie didn't want Ray to know about Lucy.

So, helpless to fight the tide, Beattie said nothing to Ray. And something that never should have been a secret became just that.

Beattie felt a cool touch on her cheek. She opened her eyes with a gasp.

"Only me," Ray said. "You left the window open. It's freezing in here."

Beattie reoriented herself. That was right: they were in London, in the hotel. Ray had been to his welcome dinner. She'd sat down to read and remembered little after that.

"I slept like the dead," she said.

"It's traveling across time zones," he said. "You'll take a day or two to adjust."

"How was your function?" she said, watching him close the window.

"Not as dull as the dullest meeting I've ever been to, but close."

She sat up, brushing her hair away from her eyes. "Ray, you'll be busy the next few days, won't you?"

"I certainly will."

"I wondered if you'd mind if I headed up to Glasgow tomorrow and stayed overnight."

"Glasgow? I didn't think you had any relatives there still."

"I don't," she said quickly. "I . . . I'm interested to see how it's changed since I left. A long time ago now." So long. Here she was, nearly fifty-five years old, hair streaked with gray, skin growing thin. Lucy was thirty-five. The private detective had told her that Lucy had two children of her own. Beattie was a grandmother, a thought that filled her with curiosity rather than joy.

"It's a long way," he said, unthreading his tie.

"I'll take the train."

"No, no. Get a car to run you up there."

"Then I'll feel like I have to make conversation. No, I just want to read my book and drink a cup of tea."

He patted her hand. "Have it your way. As long as you're happy."

She turned away so he wouldn't see her face.

A miserable London morning dawned. Gray streets, black taxis, black umbrellas, sodden leaves in the gutters. Ray left while she was still packing a few necessities. She couldn't concentrate, kept forgetting what she was doing.

Finally, she made her way to King's Cross station, her shoes filling with water, and bought a ticket for the ten o'clock train.

"There's a delay on the line," the man behind the counter told her. "We're running twenty minutes late."

She took her ticket and sat on a bench while the activity of the station whirled around her. People in overcoats and dripping umbrellas brushed past. She closed her eyes, thinking of home and sunshine. An image of Wildflower Hill on a clear day came to mind, Lucy in the garden with Mikhail, sunshine in her hair. Beattie hadn't missed Tasmania in long time; Sydney had firmly become her home. But all these thoughts of Lucy had made her long for the lingering quiet, the smell of the eucalyptus, the cool sunlit days.

When the first set of tenants had moved out of Wildflower Hill in 1951, Ray had urged her to put the place on the market.

"You're too busy to manage it," he said, "and we can't move there permanently. I'm an elected official. My job is here, among my constituents."

"I know, I know," she said. By this stage she had two children in nappies, both of them hanging off her ankles at inconvenient times. They had money for a nanny four days a week, but she was still far too busy to think about taking anything else on. And yet she couldn't face the idea of selling Wildflower Hill. Not the least reason being that Charlie was buried there.

But she could hardly admit that to Ray. No man liked to think that he wasn't his wife's greatest love.

Still, what was she to do with the thousands of sheep? She contacted Leo Sampson, who suggested she divide the property. Wool prices were skyrocketing: she would have no trouble finding a buyer. Keep the house itself and the paddock it stood in, along with the shearers' cottage and the new stables. Sell the rest. The new owners could build their own house at the southern end of the property.

Within a week Leo had called back. "Now, you might

not like this idea," he said, "so I need to know you're sitting down."

Sitting down? She had two children under two. She couldn't find a chair under the piles of unfolded laundry, let alone a moment to sit. She glanced around the large, sunny room and realized that she couldn't even see Mikey. He'd pulled one of his disappearing acts.

"Go on," she said.

"The Harrows have asked about buying the farm."

"The Harrows? Tilly and Frank?"

"Yes. I know you don't like them, nor do I, but—"

"Name a price they can barely afford. Wool is booming. They'll pay," she said. "If they accept it, why shouldn't I take their money?"

Leo hesitated.

"I really must go," she said before she changed her mind. "I've lost one of my children."

"I'll see what they say," he replied. "Take care, Beattie."

"And you."

"Boo!" said Mikey, jumping out from behind a curtain. Baby Louise began to cry.

The children had changed them. There were not long hours for leisurely discussion anymore. In truth, they were probably both too old and too set in their ways for children, but the chorus of urgent voices had eventually persuaded them. They were a happy couple with public lives; they needed offspring to cement the image. A boy for him and a girl for her.

Having Mikey had been so different from Lucy's birth twenty years before. This time around, doctors interfered, nurses tried to separate her from her baby and return him to her every four hours, when he was too distraught to feed properly and had to have a bottle forced into his mouth. Beattie had told Ray she wanted to leave the hospital immediately.

"But shouldn't you listen to them?" he said. "They have so much experience with babies. We have none."

She'd convinced him, returned home with Mikey. He thrived on her breast milk and slept in a crib right next to their bed until he was six months, just as Lucy had done.

Both her babies were fat and happy, and she hadn't wanted more, but Ray had taken himself off for a vasectomy without consulting her. She didn't know why she minded so much; she didn't tell him everything. But it was the first in a long string of infelicities that weakened their relationship. The fact that he was away so much, leaving her to single-handedly care for the children and run her business, didn't help. He never quite valued her work as highly as his own.

He still loved her. She still loved him. But the prospect of their growing old together no longer seemed romantic. Some days it seemed a trial.

Leo Sampson contacted her just before shearing season. She'd had to hire staff and cross her fingers, and so far everything seemed to be going smoothly. So she dreaded bad news.

"The Harrows have agreed to your offer," he said.

"Really?" she asked. "I get to keep the house paddock?"

"They're going to build a lean-to down on the southern boundary near the dam. Are you happy for me to send you the contracts?"

"I'm delighted!"

Their bungalow in Edgecliff was getting too small for them, so they put the windfall toward a purchase they'd been wary about making so far: a ramshackle but sunlight-filled house at Point Piper.

They had been there nearly a year when Tilly Harrow phoned her. The nanny, a Yugoslavian immigrant named Ivona, was playing a rowdy game of horsies with the children in the living room. Beattie was in her office, under the window with the view over the harbor, trying to catch up on some long-neglected correspondence. The phone rang, and she was tempted not to pick it up, but Ray was away, and she didn't want to miss him.

"Hello?"

"Beattie Blaxland?"

Wary now. "Yes."

"My name is Tilly Harrow. I don't know if . . . you remember me?"

Oh yes, Beattie remembered her. She remembered all of them, the way they had treated her, the stories they'd told about her. They had played their part in her losing Lucy, of that she had no doubt. But she said none of this. "Of course I do, Tilly."

A long silence. Beattie wondered if the line had gone dead. Then a long, shuddering breath. Tilly was crying.

"What's wrong?"

"Can you help me? We've been running this farm a year, and it's not going well for us. We just did a muster, and we've somehow lost a thousand sheep. Is that even possible?"

"Are they dead?"

"I don't know."

"Tilly, I'm very busy." Beattie tapped her pencil on the desk, wondering how to extricate herself from the conversation. "When I ran the farm, I always had good help. Good advice. Who's managing the place?"

"Frank."

"But does he have some expert advice? A man who knows the land?"

Tilly's voice dropped to a whisper. "He won't take advice. It hasn't rained, and the dam's drying up. The sheep won't lamb. I don't know what to do. We can't make the repayments."

Beattie felt a twinge of guilt. She had asked a terribly high price and was living in a house bought partly with those proceeds. "Tilly, I'm sorry you're in trouble. But you simply must convince him to hire somebody to help. That's the only suggestion I can give you."

Tilly drew a shuddering breath. "I'll try."

Three years of bad rainfall plagued the Harrows. As Leo Sampson told it, every rain cloud skidded past the farm to rain on their neighbors, on the town, everywhere but in their dams and on their fields. In early 1955, Beattie heard that

Frank Harrow had hanged himself and Tilly had moved back to South Africa, a broken woman. Beattie found that she couldn't feel sorry for him or for Tilly.

Perhaps the land had a way of finding its own justice.

Still the train hadn't come. A slow bloom of adrenaline uncurled in her heart. What if it was a sign? What if she shouldn't go?

Beattie stood and returned to the ticket counter. The rain had eased, and weak sunshine broke through clouds to gleam in oily puddles. "Any news on the Glasgow train?"

"Another twenty minutes, at least. Go and have a cup of tea."

She walked back out to the street and hesitated outside the entrance to a café. Her reflection looked back at her. She was well dressed, of course, and still slim. But any trace of the old Beattie—break-of-dawn Beattie—was gone. She was a respectable middle-class woman, the head of a fashion empire, the wife of an MP. What on earth was she thinking she would find in Glasgow? Heartache: yes. Public scandal: perhaps. Her daughter's love returned: probably not. It had been too long. If Ray found out now that she'd kept a secret from him for over twenty years, it would tear them apart.

Beattie turned away from the station and her silly plan.

"You're here?"

Beattie looked up from the armchair under the hotel window. "Yes."

Ray crossed the room and kissed her. "That's a nice surprise. Shall we go out for dinner?"

"I think I need to go back home for a while."

He looked at her curiously. "We'll be going home at the end of next week."

"I'm sorry. I mean Tasmania. I . . . I want to go back to Wildflower Hill."

"You know we can't move. I represent the people of Mortondale; I can hardly do my job from the back of beyond in Tasmania."

She looked at him, and for a moment, he seemed a complete stranger. Had she really been married to him for over twenty years? Shared a bed with him? Had children with him? How could she have shared so much with him and yet never have told him about the twin losses she had endured—first her daughter, then her soul mate? Then he seemed familiar again: her Ray, the man who had been so good to her for so long.

"I think I need to get away by myself," she said quietly.

"Without us?"

"You go away all the time."

"For work."

"I'll do some work. The children are big enough, not so hard to take care of." She hated herself for the pain in his face. "I'm sorry, Ray, but it will be good for us, I know it."

"Are you thinking of leaving me?"

"No," she said quickly, and it was true. "But I need some time and space to think, to be by myself." To put some memories to rest at last.

"If that's what you need, of course. Of course." He touched her hair tenderly. "I do love you, Beattie. So very much. I'm glad you're here and not in Glasgow."

Beattie didn't trust herself to speak without crying, so she said nothing.

THIRTY

Wildflower Hill was both terribly familiar and not quite as she remembered. It seemed bigger. The trees were much taller, the cottage was farther away from the house. But the way the light changed across the fields, the way the leaves on the gums rattled, the way the starlings and sparrows chattered and sang at the twilit ends of the day was exactly the same.

The poor house was dim and neglected. The old fridge had given up long ago, and the laundry was still home to a boiler and wringer; she was used to the ease of her Rolls Razor twin-tub machine. For the first two days Beattie managed with the inconveniences but then told herself she was being foolish: she was a wealthy woman. She made two phone calls to Hobart for some appliances to be delivered. Then she got busy cleaning up the place, sewing new curtains, taking care of small repairs.

The misgivings were enormous. On the one hand, she was fixing up Wildflower Hill because it had once meant a lot to her and it deserved to be taken care of well. On the other hand, she was making herself comfortable here . . . just in case. After years of hard work—running a business, raising children, being the perfect politician's wife—Beattie was grateful to have a break from it all and be herself. She felt she grew younger in the first few weeks she was there. Was she thinking about leaving Ray?

Well, perhaps she was.

She spoke to him every night on the phone, her voice smooth and calm over her tumultuous feelings. Her children clamored to speak to her. Mikey was jovial and full of sunshine, as he always was. Louise was more circumspect, with dark irony underlying her words. They knew. They knew she was away to consider her future. And they weren't happy.

The guilt burned most intensely at night, when she had time in the dark to think about all her children. Not just Michael and Louise but also Lucy. Sometimes she entertained fantasies of a reunion, but then she told herself not to be a fool. She wasn't the first woman in the world with a secret illegitimate child, and she would hardly be the last. Nevertheless, her thoughts turned more and more to her own mortality, to the fortune she would leave behind. How could it be fair to leave it to Michael and Louise and not to Lucy? What would they all make of such unfairness? How dimly must Beattie be remembered in Lucy's mind? Most nights she fell asleep pondering these questions, questions that were too hard for her to answer.

Right outside her bedroom window was Charlie. He was the first thing she saw every morning when she opened the curtains, the last thing she saw in the evening when she drew them again. Really, there was only a tree. But he was there nonetheless. She could *feel* him, see him as though he were right in front of her. He hadn't changed at all. His hair was still thick and black, his body still lean and strong. If she closed her eyes at those moments, she could smell him, too, and she experienced a longing so intense—a longing to be young again, to be in the time before it had all gone bad, to be in love and to have her little girl with her—that it caused shooting pains throughout her body. How unfair that she should have to grow old! She cared nothing for her business, for her wealth, for the mansion they had built on the harbor. She would trade it all to be back in 1939: frozen in one moment there, forever.

One fine morning, Beattie decided to venture into town. She had run out of the groceries she'd brought up with her from Hobart. Even though twenty-five years had passed since she'd been there, she still felt her pulse quicken as she neared Lewinford.

The town was bigger, the road paved. A lot of the old buildings were still the same. The post office, the general store, the pub. Leo Sampson's office was now a bric-a-brac shop; he had died in 1959. Beattie took a deep breath and went inside the general store.

It was like stepping back in time. The wooden shelves, the long glass counter, the sacks of flour stacked up on the floor. But instead of Tilly Harrow and her pursed, disapproving lips behind the counter, there was a middle-aged man with a florid complexion. He smiled at her broadly. "Hello, stranger," he said.

She was wary about smiling. As soon as he found out who she was . . . But then she shook her head. A long time had passed. "Hello," she said. "I'm down from Wildflower Hill."

She waited, realized she was tensed against him rejecting her.

"Wildflower Hill? You're the new tenant?"

"The owner, actually," she said.

His eyes rounded. "Really? You're Beattie Blaxland? You . . . Wait here. I have to get my wife." He dashed to the stairs, called out loudly, "Annie, come down here! You'll never believe who's come to town!"

Beattie flushed with pleasure. Moments later, a tall fair woman had come warily down the stairs.

"What is it?" she asked.

"Look," the man said, "it's Beattie Blaxland."

Annie smiled, reaching out to take Beattie's hand. "Why, so it is!"

"I take it you like my designs?" Beattie said proudly.

"Your designs? Oh, yes, I like them well enough. But we know of you from before you were famous."

"You do?"

"Come upstairs," Annie said. "Let's have tea."

Beattie could have laughed. It was so vastly different from the reception she used to receive in town. She followed Annie behind the counter and up the stairs to a cozy, floral sitting room.

Annie put the kettle on to boil and came to sit with Beattie.

"My father . . . I'm sorry, I should say my stepfather. He used to work for you. Mikhail Kirilliv."

"Mikhail! He was your stepfather? You're Catherine's daughter?"

"I am. I can't believe you remember Mum's name." She smiled broadly. "They were very happy for many years."

"Is he . . . ?" Beattie couldn't bring herself to say the word.

"Dead? Oh yes. Mum died in 1958, and he said that he wanted to come back here. He missed the place so much. By then he was very old and not well, so we brought him down with us. At the same time, the business here was up for lease, and we fell in love with the area. Dad died in 1961, right back there in the bedroom." She indicated with a wave of her hand. "Went very peacefully. Would you like to see some family photographs?"

"I would."

Annie went to a crowded bookcase and pulled out two photo albums. "Here, you look through these. I'll go and make the tea."

Beattie started with the more recent photographs, turning the pages carefully. Mikhail—stooped and white-haired but unmistakably Mikhail—smiled out from the photographs. Annie and her husband were in many of the photos, and children who grew up from one page to the next. Beattie picked up the other album. The pages were falling to pieces. The photos were held in by white tabs that had long ago lost their stickiness. The photos slid into the cracks between pages.

She tried to sort them, glancing at them. Was astonished to see one taken in the sitting room at Wildflower Hill.

It must have been from right before Mikhail left. The Christmas tree was up. She remembered now, Catherine had had a camera and had taken some pictures of the property on his request, so he could remember it after he left. Focusing intensely now, Beattie pulled the photographs out one by one to look at them.

There he was. There was Charlie. A figure on a horse, his hat obscuring most of his face. Still, Beattie's heart skipped a beat.

"Find something you like?" This was Annie, returning with the tea tray.

She held out the photograph. "It's Charlie Harris."

"Dad spoke about him a lot. They were great friends. Take it if you want. I've no use for it."

"Really?" Her face felt warm.

"Of course. Take any of the old ones from Wildflower Hill."

"No, no. I'll leave you with your stepfather's memories. But I will take this. He was . . . rather special to me." There: her heart was beating too hard. A few ounces of young blood still ran in her veins.

Annie poured tea, and Beattie asked her about other residents of town whom she remembered. Annie recognized none of the names. Beattie passed the morning in memories, then decided she had better get her groceries and head home.

"Annie," she said, an idea forming. "There will be nobody at Wildflower Hill for a while, but I'm going to send down some boxes to store. If I give you a key, could I ask you to go up there from time to time, check on the place, store the boxes for me if I ship them to you? I'd pay you."

"If it's a paying job, I'll pass it on to my son," Annie said. "He's seventeen and in need of some part-time work. He can keep the dust off and keep the gardens neat for you, too, if you like."

"That would be wonderful," Beattie said. Perhaps next time she came down, the house wouldn't look so neglected. *If* she came down again. "What's his name? I'll write him some instructions."

"Andrew," she said. "Andrew Taylor. He won't let you down."

When she arrived home, Beattie pinned the photograph of Charlie to the wall next to her bed. For some reason, having the photograph made the visions of him go away. She was sad about that but didn't take the photo down. Her sorrow was less frightening trapped between the four white borders of the picture.

Beattie came to understand that she'd come to Wildflower Hill to grieve. Not just for Charlie and Lucy, whom, frankly, she had grieved over a great deal already. She was grieving the loss of her youth, the closing down of possibilities as life became what it was rather than what it might have been. As time passed and the only sounds were her thoughts and the quiet land, she found the grief lessened, that she began to see more clearly how blessed she had been. A loving husband, two spirited children, a chance to pursue her creative dreams. Charlie had stopped appearing below her window, and to her surprise, she began to feel restless for Sydney, for Ray and Mike and Louise. The relief was enormous.

Then one night, two days before she was due to return home, she had a dream.

Lucy was in it. She was about eight: liquid eyes, pale freckles on her face, warm sweet breath. The child stood directly in front of Beattie, who was crouched to tie the belt around her waist.

"My darling," Beattie said.

"Who are you?" the child asked.

"I'm your mother." The pain of her not knowing this was excruciating.

"And will you be forever? Until the stars go out and the silence comes?"

"Yes! Yes, I—"

Beattie woke up before she could say the words. Crying, she got up. The early-morning dark was cold. She pulled on her robe and went down to the study.

There, she wrote a letter. She poured out her feelings, all the things she wanted to say to the little girl in her dream but could never say to the grown woman Lucy had become, the one who had told Beattie to leave her in peace. As she wrote, she sobbed until her ribs hurt. Finally, she sealed the letter into an envelope. She even addressed it—that unvisitable address forever burned into her mind—though she didn't intend to send it. Writing it had been enough. She debated what to do with it. It wasn't right to burn it or to throw it away, so she slid it away carefully with some other mementos that weren't for Ray's eyes and prepared to return to her life in Sydney.

* * *

On the morning of her departure, she locked up the house and went to stand under the cabbage gum. It had grown beautifully—tall and strong like Charlie—and it made her happy to think that it would be here long after she had gone, watching over Wildflower Hill.

A taxi turned up the driveway, its horn beeping.

"Goodbye," Beattie said. "Goodbye, my love."

And left Wildflower Hill forever.

THIRTY-ONE

Emma: London, 2009

The flight was hell. The man in the seat across the aisle snored like a chain saw. I drifted in and out of sleep, and the edges of reality became blurred. I was suspended, literally in the air, between two worlds: my new life in Tasmania, my old life in London. Neither felt quite real.

At Heathrow, I felt all my nerves start to hum. What if it had been some grand hallucination and Josh wasn't really coming to meet me? But there he was, waiting outside customs. He ran toward me, and I fell into his arms. Real Josh. Flesh-and-blood Josh. Not the Josh who had inhabited my fantasies the last few months.

"Em, Em," he said, mouth against my hair. "God, I've missed you."

I didn't trust myself to speak, so I breathed in the warm, woody scent of him. At length, he released me, and I stepped back to look at him.

Really look at him.

It was strange: I'd remembered him being more handsome,

having kinder eyes. He glanced at his watch. "I've got the morning off work. Let's get you home."

The word confused me momentarily. "Home? Oh, you mean your place?"

"What did you think I meant?" He laughed good-naturedly. Perhaps not so good-naturedly. "Jet lag's gone to your brain."

I followed him to the cab rank, and we made our way back toward the city.

"Good flight?" he asked.

"Terrible flight. I—"

His mobile phone rang. "Excuse me," he said. Then took the call. I stared glumly out the window at the glum London morning. He pocketed his phone again and said, "Where were we?"

"Terrible flight."

"Sorry to hear that. It's a long way between here and Tim-buktu."

"Tasmania."

He laughed. "I know. I'm joking."

I sighed. "I'm just tired, Josh. Sorry. I'll feel better after a long sleep."

He'd moved into a serviced apartment in a Georgian ter-race at Limehouse. It was immaculate, modern, tasteful. All the things I loved. Or had loved. His keys clattered onto the granite kitchen bench as I wheeled my suitcase in behind me.

"Home sweet home," he said.

I felt awkward, though I didn't know why. We'd lived to-gether for months, flossed our teeth in front of each other.

He'd been uppermost in my thoughts the whole time I was away . . . Well, perhaps not the whole time. But a lot at the start.

"I need a long shower," I said, thinking an extended period in the bathroom would fix me. Give me time to adjust to the fact that it was true, I really was back.

"Go ahead. I'll make a few phone calls."

I found my robe and some clean underwear in my suitcase and shut myself in the bathroom. There was no window, just a bright electric light. I stripped off and stepped under the hot water.

I tried to tell myself that jet lag always did my head in: other people got tired, but I got confused and anxious. Given a few days and some restorative sleep, I would lose my shyness with Josh, and things could go back to the way they had been. I sat on the floor of the shower with the hot water gushing over me and closed my eyes.

A light knock at the door and Josh's voice. "You all right in there?"

"Yes. Fine."

He opened the door, stood there fully dressed and smiling at me. "You still look good, Em."

"Don't," I said, laughing. "Unfair advantage."

He loosened his tie and dragged it off. "I can even the playing field if you like."

I stood and turned off the shower and reached for a towel to cover myself. He had his shirt off, now—that chest, those arms . . . spectacular—and was trying to pull the towel off me. He caught me, pressed me hard against him, and kissed me. A deep, hot kiss. My body was melting in his arms, my towel pooled on the floor. But one little part of my brain was telling me to slow down. To slow *right* down.

"Wait," I said as Josh began to fumble with his fly.

"What's wrong?" he asked.

"Not yet. I . . . Not yet."

He stood back; I picked up my towel. "Is there something wrong?" he asked.

Yes. "No. At least, I don't think so."

"Is this about Sarah and me? Because I promise you that is over."

"But when did it start?" I asked. "No, don't tell me that."

He couldn't quite meet my eye. "I'm sorry, Emma, but I'm hoping that the past can stay in the past. I've missed you so much. You're the girl for me."

"Then give me a couple of days to find my bearings."

"You want to sleep in the guest room tonight?"

"It might be for the best."

I was wide awake at two the next morning and watched cable television until dawn, when Josh got up.

"I would have kept you company," he said, kissing me below my right ear. He smelled divine.

"No point in both of us being tired."

He switched on the coffee machine, yawning. "What are you going to do today?"

"I thought I might see if I can catch up with some friends, let them know I'm back in town."

"Ballet people?"

"Maybe. If it doesn't make me too depressed."

He came to sit with me, slowly pushed up the leg of my pajama pants to reveal my scarred knee. "I'm so sorry about this," he said, running a thumb over the deepest part of the surgery scars.

"It's been hard," I said. "Impossible."

"You won't dance again?"

I shook my head. A children's cartoon had come on, so I reached for the remote to switch off the television. "I'm afraid not."

He gently covered my knee again. "I'll try to finish early. Keep your mobile switched on. We can meet somewhere for dinner, like old times."

I saw him off into the foggy morning and returned to the couch. I found myself wondering what Patrick was doing and then shouted at myself to stop. I was *not* going to sit here in London thinking about Wildflower Hill, as I'd sat at Wildflower Hill thinking about London. I'd made my choice.

I'd called Patrick straight after I'd booked the flight, I'd called him to say I had to return to London indefinitely and to wish him luck with the concert.

"Mina will be disappointed," he'd said. And damn him for saying the only thing that could make me feel guilty. Apart from that, he hadn't begged me to stay. He made no sudden declaration of love. What would I have done if he had?

The fog rolled off the river and lifted to reveal a clear autumn morning. I dug around in the bottom of my suitcase for my old address book, to look up old friends. *Friends* was perhaps a bit of a stretch. Old acquaintances, people I'd air-kissed and promised to call sometime in the past.

First call: answering machine.

Second call: rang out.

Third call: no longer at this number.

I kept going, determined to find somebody.

Fourth call: a human being.

"Hello, is Miranda there?" I said, knowing I sounded desperate.

"This is Miranda."

"Hi, it's Emma Blaxland-Hunter."

A short pause. "Emma?"

"I know, I know. It's been a long time."

"I thought you moved to Australia."

"I was there for a while, but now I'm back. I'd love to catch up some time."

"Well, certainly, but I'm catching a plane this afternoon to Switzerland for a season of *The Firebird*. I won't be back until Christmas Eve."

I was speechless for a moment. That was my life once. Jetting about, turning up at new theaters in new cities, being dressed and made up, taking to the stage under the blazing lights, giving my body over to the music.

"Perhaps I'll give you a call then," I managed.

I continued on through my book, came across another Miranda, and suddenly wasn't sure which one I'd been talking to. I sighed. Put the book away. I knew Adelaide would be down at the rehearsal studio, running errands for the Flying Fascist. She would be glad to see me, at least. It was time to climb out of my pajamas and enjoy the life that I'd so longed to get back to.

The last time I'd been at the studio had been the night of my accident. The smells of the place—hair spray, glass cleaner, perspiration—almost overwhelmed me. I spoke briefly to the receptionist and then headed up the stairs, *those* stairs, to find Adelaide.

Instead, I ran into Brian, the artistic director.

"Oh, my!" was the first thing he said. "You've packed on the weight!"

I was so taken aback that I couldn't speak for a moment. Then I said defensively, "I haven't been able to do anything with this wretched knee." His words weren't even true: yes, I was heavier than I had been, but I had been far too thin before. Bony. We all were.

"Let me see," he said. I had to lift up my skirt to show him the scars from the operations, and he inspected them eagerly. "It was perfect timing, really," he said, smoothing my skirt down. "If you had to have an accident, that was the time to have it. Right at the end of your career."

"I'm only thirty-one."

He shrugged. "I saw you dance. You had two years left if you were lucky."

"Emma!" An excited voice from down the hallway.

"Adelaide!" I left Brian muttering darkly into his clipboard and gave Adeladie a hug.

"When did you get back?"

"Yesterday morning. Can you come out for lunch? I have so much to tell you." I dropped my voice low. "Josh asked me to come back."

Adelaide's eyes widened in surprise. "He did? And you came?"

"It was all I'd dreamed of for five months." The words left my mouth hollow.

Adelaide checked her watch. "Alberto's in rehearsal until twelve-thirty. Would an early lunch now suit?"

"My body clock is so out of whack that it hardly matters," I said. "Now is fine."

Outside on the cold street, the scent of roasting chestnuts mingled with the traffic fumes. I'd not remembered London being so noisy, so full of smells and movement. I found it unnerving, disorienting. I blamed that on the jet lag, too. I'd get used to it again.

We wound up at the little café we'd always have our Monday-morning briefings at. It was almost empty—a little too late for morning tea, a little too early for lunch. The only other patrons were a man in a tracksuit eating a fig tart, and a thin woman reading the *Daily Mail*. We ordered and sat down in a warm back corner, as far as we could from the speakers that pumped out jazz music.

"So," Adelaide said, pushing a curl of black hair off her face. "Josh."

"Yes. Josh."

"How did it happen?"

"He split with Sarah. He called me. I came back."

"And that's . . . okay with you?"

"Of course." But I felt awkward around him. And I couldn't bring myself to sleep with him yet. Didn't tell her that. "Though I admit," I said, "it's all a bit sudden. Let's talk about you for a while. I can't bear the scrutiny."

Adelaide was comfortable to change the topic and told me lots of stories about life with the Flying Fascist, of whom she had come to feel strangely fond. As our meals arrived, she prompted me to tell her what I'd been doing in Tasmania— something Josh hadn't yet asked me—and I felt a little swirl of melancholy while I told her. It felt an awful lot like homesickness.

In Adelaide's company, at last I started to relax, not to feel so strange and surreal. The Moselle helped, I was sure. Soon enough, she had to get back to work and walked me out to the street to wait with me for a cab.

"Do you think you'll stay?" she asked.

"I guess so."

"Hm."

"Hm? What does that mean?"

"It's just . . . When we were talking then, you only mentioned Josh twice."

"So?"

"You mentioned somebody named Patrick eleven times."

I laughed it off, was about to tell her that she must have misheard, when a cab came tearing around the corner and we both stepped out to hail it.

"Bye, Emma," she said, kissing my cheek. "See you soon. Maybe for the wedding." She winked, but the mention of a wedding made my stomach go ice-cold with fear.

I was just tired. That's what I told myself in the cab. I was tired and not thinking straight, and that was why being back here in London didn't feel as fabulous and exciting as I thought it would. Jet lag and two glasses of lunchtime wine conspired against me. I sat on Josh's couch, trying to concentrate on the television, but fell asleep with the sun on my cheek.

Later, I wasn't sure how much later, I woke to a tickle on my leg. Somebody's warm fingers were drifting up under my skirt, creeping between my thighs. My head felt hot, and I was woolly and disoriented. I opened one eye to see Josh lying next to me on the couch. His hand slid up and inched under the elastic of my knickers.

I pushed his hand away. "No, Josh," I said.

"No?" He made a sad puppy-dog face.

I laughed. "No. I've got the worst jet lag I've ever had. You'll have to give me a few days."

"So you're too tired? Is that why you're saying no?"

I sat up. "I don't know. Probably."

"And you're sure this isn't about me and Sarah?"

I thought hard about the question and realized I didn't care a great deal about what he'd done with Sarah. Although at the start I had, I'd cared very much. Should I be worried? I didn't know how to answer that question. "No, I think I'm over that," I said carefully.

"Then what's the problem? You're here, we're back together. Let's pick up where we left off." His voice dropped low, and he murmured close to my ear, "I've missed your beautiful body."

What the hell was wrong with me? I'd dreamed of him saying these things to me, doing these things to me. But right here with him, I felt awkward. Embarrassed.

"I'm sorry, I'm sorry," I said. "I feel strange. I don't feel like myself. I'm sure by the weekend I'll be feeling better. When we can spend some extended time together, I won't feel so odd."

"That reminds me," he said, sitting up and straightening his tie. "Saturday night we're going to a dinner party at Hugh's place. I hope that's okay with you. It's his fortieth birthday, been organized for months."

Hugh was Josh's boorish best friend from work. "Are they expecting me or Sarah?" I asked.

He couldn't see the humor in the question. "You, of course. I've told everyone you're back, that we're back together. You needn't be narky about it."

I didn't point out that I wasn't narky. He'd gone to the cabinet for a bottle of bourbon. We followed the same routine we'd had in the last days of our relationship. We had a drink and cooked together, I talked about my day, he talked about his. But this time I listened to what he was saying, trying to make an effort. I knew that I'd been bad at listening before our split, that I'd been too self-obsessed to care much about the minutiae of his day. I was determined this time to get it right.

I realized, with a terrible sense of disappointment, that Josh didn't have all that much interesting to say.

* * *

Two days passed and not a single old friend returned my calls, so I learned that way that they weren't really my old friends. I didn't blame them, I blamed myself and I blamed the scene. We were all trying to get ahead, we were all pretending to like each other, when in truth, we would have climbed over each other's corpses for bigger and brighter successes. Those people were never my friends, and I was never theirs.

So what was a friendless girl to do? I headed to the library. I caught the tube up to St. Pancras and went looking for information I couldn't get at home in Australia. I thought Raphael Blanchard might be accounted for in some obscure book in the British Library.

I checked my bag and coat and registered for a reader pass. Once I had my books, I found a seat in the deafening quiet of the reading room and began to leaf through. He was one of three Raphael Blanchards, but I managed to track down a reference to him in a book from the 1950s about minor nobility from the Warwickshire region. I was secretly hoping I'd find out Raphael's nickname was Charlie, that Grandma had had an affair with him and that was how she'd gotten the farm for free.

Page 181 rewarded me, but not in the way I'd hoped.

The Blanchard family made an unsuccessful attempt to develop agricultural interests in the colonies. Raphael Blanchard was sent by his father to purchase a large sheep farm in Tasmania (far southern Australia, once a penal colony). The business did not prosper and he returned to

Warwickshire in 1935. Rumours circulated that he had lost the farm in a game of poker, but the family maintained that Raphael returned to England for his health.

I would have laughed out loud, only I was in a library. Instead, I sat there with a stupid grin on my face. Grandma won Wildflower Hill in a poker game? She'd always been violently opposed to gambling, from what I could remember. Could it be true? After all, she did get the farm for free.

I wanted to ring my mum and tell her, but that would mean admitting to her that I was in London, and she wasn't going to take that well at all.

Instead, I asked if I could photocopy the page. I took it back to the apartment with me to wait for Josh to finish work.

My body clock was totally out of its usual rhythm. I couldn't keep my eyes open during the day and was wide awake before dawn. Josh kissed me goodbye every morning to go to work, and as the week went by, he got less and less patient with me. I didn't melt into his embraces, I wouldn't have sex with him, I pushed him away if he got too close. He kept asking what was wrong with me, but I didn't know, so I couldn't tell him.

On Friday morning, I woke early. A moment or two passed before I knew where I was. I was expecting to hear birds. Then I opened my eyes and I wasn't at Wildflower Hill. I was in a serviced apartment in London, with the heating humming softly. I felt desolate: I wanted birds.

I felt so far from home.

I got up and pulled on my robe, quietly opened the door to Josh's room. I needed warmth and comfort, but I hesitated. My eyes adjusted to the dark as I stood there, and I could see the outline of Josh's well-muscled shoulder. He was easily as gorgeous as I remembered him, but I observed this fact as I might observe it in a movie. It didn't feel like it belonged in my life. Tears pricked at my eyes. I had made such a cock-up of things. I had let people down. Now I was starting to suspect I had chased an empty fantasy to the other side of the world.

I calculated the time back home in Australia. Three-thirty in the afternoon. Patrick would be home soon. I wondered how preparations were going for the concert. Perhaps I could donate them some money or something, send flowers for Mina over the Internet. I felt a desperate urge to make contact.

I left Josh to sleep and went to the kitchen. I turned on the lights, blinking at their brightness, and picked up the phone. Fog pressed against the window. Daylight would not come for hours, if it came at all. But where the phone was ringing, it would be full, bright afternoon.

Monica picked up on the second ring. "Hello?"

"Oh, hi, Monica. It's Emma."

Silence, probably icy.

"Is Patrick home?"

"Not yet."

"It's okay, I'm glad I got you anyway. I probably owe you an apology," I said.

"No, you don't."

I hesitated.

"You owe Patrick an apology," she said. "And Mina. And Marlon. And the rest of the Hollyhocks. But you owe me nothing, and I wouldn't accept it anyway."

I felt almost sick with shame. "Look, I know you're angry. But I told Patrick that I was leaving, and he understood."

"Did he? Because I don't. You promised you'd be here to help with the concert, and now you've pissed off to England three weeks before the big night."

"It's more complicated than that," I said. "I left London under such difficult circumstances. All I've wanted was to be back there."

"That much was obvious," she interjected. "Our little town wasn't good enough for you."

"That's not true," I said, but it was true. At least I'd thought it was true once. "I don't expect you to understand, but I didn't intend to hurt anyone."

"I really don't care what you intended, Emma," Monica said. "But you did hurt a lot of people. Now I'm getting off the phone before Patrick gets home, because I don't want him to know that you called. And I'll thank you not to call him yourself."

"Why not?"

"Because he needs a chance to get over you, so whatever you need to do to assuage your guilt, just stay away from my brother." Her voice was dark, passionate. "He deserves the very best, and you're not it."

The line went dead, and I found myself staring at the

phone, throat choked up with emotion. She was right. Patrick did deserve the best. Somebody wonderful. But I couldn't bear the thought of him being with somebody wonderful, somebody who wasn't me.

"Em?" This was Josh, sleepily leaning in the threshold to his bedroom. "Everything okay?" The downlights created unkind shadows on his face.

I replaced the phone in its charger. "I think so, yeah. Just trying to sort something out back in Tassie."

He crossed the room and took me in his arms, mouth hot on my throat. I could have wept. I gently pushed him away. "Tomorrow night, I promise," I said. "I'll feel more in the mood after the party. I've been stuck here in the apartment waiting for you to get home every day. It doesn't make me feel romantic."

"You're in London, for God's sake. Get out. Shop. Do things."

"I know. I'm not myself."

"I hope yourself comes back soon," he said. "Because she's the one I asked to return to London."

I laughed as though it were a joke, but we both knew it wasn't.

I was cheered by the preparations for the dinner party. Josh and I had to go out and choose a couple of bottles of fine wine—I insisted on Australian wine—and then I had the chance to dress up, put on some makeup, and straighten my hair. We sped off in a cab through nighttime London, and I had my first sense of the thrill of being in a big international city, in a place where things happened. I snuggled up with Josh in the back of the cab, didn't turn away his hot kisses on my throat and ear. Maybe the jet lag was over. Maybe I hadn't made the wrong decision in coming back.

Hugh and his wife had recently bought and renovated a garden flat in Kensington. Hugh was a few years older than Josh and in many ways was like a big brother: someone to aspire to. He and Olivia had a toddler who had already been dispatched to bed before the guests arrived. There were eight of us in all, four couples. I forgot the names of the other people straightaway, but they formed their own subtribe in the garden to smoke under the fairy lights. Josh and I stayed in the kitchen with Hugh and Olivia.

"This place is brilliant," Josh said, high color in his cheeks, as he surveyed the view onto the busy street from the bay windows.

"Ground floor," Olivia said, grimacing. "Hardly ideal."

"But you have a garden," Josh said.

"Could have had the rooftop garden if Hugh had earned a tiny bit more last financial year." Olivia held her fingers a few millimeters apart. She was laughing, but I sensed there was truth in her words. I didn't warm to her.

"I earned more than you," Hugh countered lightly.

Olivia looked at me and Josh, swirling the champagne in her glass. "Don't have children if you want a rooftop garden, you two, that's the lesson to be learned here."

The French doors opened, and the other two couples came in, dragging with them the smell of their extinguished cigarettes, though they didn't realize they had. The little flat was bright and warm, with Coldplay on the stereo. I drank two glasses of champagne a little too quickly and felt a flush come to my cheeks. Josh had his warm arm around my back, and it was all going to be fine. I could see that now. We would get married and have one child because we couldn't afford more. I'd start my own ballet school and work too hard, Josh would stay at the stock exchange and work too hard, then we'd have a garden flat and a dinner party just like this when Josh turned forty. It would be easy.

Then why did the thought of it make me feel so flat?

We all took our places at the long dinner table, and Olivia served the first course. She was a little drunk and clearly displeased with how little Hugh had helped to organize the party. Josh and I raised our eyebrows at each other, suppressing laughter. One of the other guests, an elegant Indian woman with long black hair piled on top of her head, got up to help Olivia, offering around a bottle of wine. She came to where I was sitting, and said, "And for you, Sarah?"

There was a pause. The music kept playing, but the voices had all stopped. Nobody could look at me.

"I'm sorry," she said smoothly. "I mean Emma."

"It's fine," I said, offering her my glass.

Josh leaned in to me, whispering frantically. "We all went out together a few times when I was with . . . her," he said. "I'm sorry."

"It's fine," I said again, but it wasn't fine. It *wasn't*. He had been cheating on me. He had dumped me. He hadn't come near me while I was going through my operations. Was that the kind of man I wanted to marry and have a middle-class, only-child, garden-flat life with?

Olivia was tapping her glass, getting our attention. "A toast," she said. "To Hugh on his fortieth."

"To Hugh," we all chorused. I gulped my wine. I was well on the way to being drunk.

The evening wore on. I was half in, half out of the proceedings. I could make conversation just fine but found myself listening in to other people's conversations, passively observing. A large, rough-faced man at the end of the table spent half an hour bragging to Josh about his real estate. Josh was enraptured, so I watched them as if from afar.

"How do you get such low prices, though?" Josh asked. "Nothing is on the market that cheap."

"I don't wait for the market," the man said. "If you know where and when, you can pick up amazing deals. Outside bankruptcy hearings, for instance. Always people desperate to sell there. Picked up a holiday house in Brighton from a bird outside court one day. She was very keen to off-load, if you know what I mean. She cried the morning I went over with the contracts."

Josh laughed. He *laughed*.

"That's a miserable business," I said to the rough-faced man.

He squared off his shoulders as though I'd asked him to step outside for a punch-up. "It's business, love. You don't like it, you don't have to play that way. But don't be crying to me like the other have-nots. Us haves are the ones who are smart enough to do what it takes."

I turned to Josh. "Do you believe this rubbish?"

Josh shrugged, clearly uncomfortable. "It is a valid business strategy, Em. You don't know much about it. But I think he has a point. We all do what we have to do to get ahead. You did when you were dancing. Lord knows you ignored my feelings all the time when you were preparing for a show."

The conversation moved on. I sat there among it all, and I knew with sudden certainty that I wasn't meant to be here. These people were not my people. This future was not my future, and I had made a terrible, terrible mistake. I had stepped out of this life, then stepped back in expecting everything to be the same—and it was, but *I* was different.

"Josh," I said quietly.

He didn't hear me, was still talking to the real-estate mogul.

"Josh," I said more forcefully.

He turned, looked at me. In his eyes, I saw it. He knew, too. He wasn't stupid: I had changed, it couldn't last.

"I need to go home," I said.

"Okay," he said, scooping up his glass urgently. "Let me just finish this glass of wine and we'll head straight back."

"No," I said. "Not home to your apartment. Home. I don't belong here."

For the second time that evening, the conversation stopped. Josh laughed nervously. "Emma, can this wait?"

I shook my head. "Take me to the airport," I said. "I belong at Wildflower Hill."

THIRTY-TWO

I climbed into a taxi at Hobart airport at seven in the morning Australian time, but my body had no idea what time it was. I was completely topsy-turvy, but one thing I was certain of was that I had made the right decision.

"Where to?" the driver asked.

"Do you have any objections to taking me all the way up to Lewinford? I'll tip you really well."

He switched on his meter. "I aim to please."

"Battery Point first," I said.

I couldn't remember Mina's address, so I directed the driver there. Monica had been right: I owed the girl an apology. I'd resisted phoning her because I wasn't sure if she'd understand how far away London was, what it meant that I'd gone there when I should have been helping her through the last few dress rehearsals.

Outside her house, I instructed the driver to wait. I went up to knock on the door and wait, with the warm yellow sun on my back.

Mina's father answered it.

"Hello, Mr. Carter," I said. "Is Mina here?"

He frowned at me, looked at the taxi waiting down on the street. "Are you intending to take her somewhere?"

"No, no. I just wanted to talk to her briefly."

He didn't take his eyes off me. "Mina!" he called. "Visitor for you." He nodded. "Do you want to come in?"

"I should be quick. The meter's running."

Mina came to the door. When she saw me, she broke into a grin and raced up to hug me. I squeezed her tight.

"You came back!" she said.

"I did."

"Marlon and Patrick said you had gone forever."

"I changed my mind. I didn't want to miss your concert." I stood back to look at her. "I'm so sorry I ran off like that."

She looked back at me blankly, I realized she hadn't much understanding of what I'd done; nor would she think it a sin. I touched her cheek. "You're a good girl. I can't wait to see you dance."

Her father touched Mina's shoulder. "You go inside now, Mina. I need to have a word with Emma alone."

She beamed at me, then did exactly what her father had said. I looked at him curiously.

"Let me walk you down to your taxi," he said.

"Sure."

I walked with him down the path, and he seemed embarrassed about something, so I said, "What did you want to speak with me about?"

"I'm sorry," he said. "I had thought you . . . I didn't realize who you were. When Mina said you were a famous ballerina . . . well, that means nothing to me. Mina doesn't understand the world all that well at times. But you are, and I'm sorry that I thought you were just . . ." He must had realized he couldn't go on without insulting Patrick and Marlon, so he trailed off. "I'm sorry if I was rude."

We had come to a stop on the footpath next to the taxi. As tired as I was, as dicombobulated from jet lag as I felt, I knew that this was my moment. "Mr. Carter," I said. "I don't care what you think about me. But I want to urge you, really strongly, to come and see Mina's performance."

He wouldn't look at me. "You are very persistent," he said.

"Answer me this, then: why don't you want to come?"

A long silence drew out between us. The taxi driver was peering up at us through the window. The sun glinted off the water, and a warm breeze moved in the tips of the plane trees. Finally, he said, "Because I will feel embarrassed."

This was the last thing I had expected him to say, so it took me a while to understand what he meant. And when I did, it was so profoundly sad that I couldn't hate him for saying it.

"I promise you," I said, "she won't embarrass you. She will make you so proud."

He shook his head. "You aren't me. You can't know that. I love my daughter, Emma, but she is not a normal teenager. I can't pretend she is. I know her, I see her every day. I know that she can't dance properly, and to see her try will simply make me uncomfortable. She doesn't mind. She gets great joy from rehearsing and performing. She is better off without me there, squirming in my seat." He tried a smile. "She'll be happier without me."

The taxi driver wound down the window. "Are we still going to Lewinford?"

"You're taking a taxi all that way?" Mina's father asked.

"My knee's still no good for driving," I replied.

"I could have taken you."

"It's fine." A breeze off the water caught my hair, and I brushed it away from my face. "I promise you," I said again. "The girl has talent."

He shrugged, and my taxi fare was creeping up, so I said goodbye and climbed back in the car. Mina's father was still standing, thoughtful in the sunshine, as we sped off down the street.

I had no idea what kind of groceries I had left in the fridge at Wildflower Hill. It felt like a lifetime had passed rather than one hectic week. I instructed the taxi driver to stop in town and quickly dashed into the grocery store for bread, milk, and a premade lasagna. As I was heading back out into the sunny street, I literally ran into Penelope Sykes coming the other way.

"Penelope!" I said, taking a step back.

"Emma? We thought you'd gone to England."

"I went. I came back." I smiled weakly. "Changed my mind."

She raised her drawn-on eyebrows at me. "Are you staying on at Wildflower Hill, then?"

"I haven't made any firm plans either way. I wanted to be here for the Hollyhocks concert that I've been helping Patrick Taylor with." I dropped my voice. "If he forgives me."

"I'm sure Patrick will," Penelope said. "I'm not so sure about Monica."

"Yes. She's very protective."

"We all know how protective she is." Penelope shifted her empty shopping basket onto her other hip. "You know that Patrick was engaged a few years ago?"

A barb of completely unjustified jealousy hit me out of nowhere. "Really?"

"It ended badly. The young woman was seeing someone else at the same time. Monica found her out; she was the one who had to tell him."

I thought I had reached my high tide of guilt over Patrick, but I was wrong. No wonder Monica hated me.

I glanced at the taxi. The fare was already astronomical; it didn't matter if I took another five minutes with Penelope. "I have to tell you something," I said. "I found a memorial—a cross with a name on it—at Wildflower Hill. Under the big cabbage gum near the house. It said CHARLIE."

She tilted her head to one side. "Is that right?"

"You know something?"

She nodded slowly. "Maybe. I've been tracing some of the local stories, as you know. There was a stockman—far more than a stockman, really—who worked in Bligh for some years. Charlie Harris. He was well known for his affinity with the work, and in great demand. He left there in 1935, and I often wondered where he went. I wonder if he did go up to Wildflower Hill."

I grew excited. "Yes! He must have. Grandma would have come to rely on him; I can just imagine it. Penelope, I think he was the person she wrote the letter to. You know . . . the sexy letter."

She was already shaking her head. "I don't think so, love. It was the thirties, after all, and a mixed-race relationship would have been frowned on."

"Mixed-race?"

"Charlie Harris was Aboriginal."

"Oh."

"I doubt he was her lover."

But the memorial just outside her window. I didn't say anything to Penelope Sykes, but I was almost certain she was wrong.

I was surprised—almost frightened—by how good it was to open the front door of Wildflower Hill and drop my bags. The familiar scents of the soap powder I used, the wood paneling, the years. I put my groceries in the fridge and put the kettle on. My answering machine blinked at me.

It was Mum. "Emma? Where on earth are you?"

She sounded worried. No, worried wasn't the right word. She sounded frightened, and my sudden realization of her vulnerability gave me a sense of vertigo. The folly of my trip to London was becoming more and more apparent. How many people's feelings had I trod on? My poor mother. I picked up the phone and called her.

I told Mum everything: Josh, London, the realization that I wasn't what I had been. But most of all, I told her that I loved her, because I hadn't said it nearly enough in my lifetime. I cried, felt embarrassed for crying. But Mum was wonderful, knowing just what to say and when. I don't know why I'd locked her out of my life so firmly. I kept talking long after the kettle had whistled and exhausted itself, and I eventually found the courage to admit to Grandma's secrets—the photos and the poker game, Charlie—and ask her what she made of it all.

The silence was brief, prefaced with a sigh. "I don't know, Emma," she said. "None of it sounds like Mum, but then . . . she sometimes did unpredictable things."

"Like giving away her money to charity?"

"Exactly."

"But why would she keep it a secret? I don't understand."

"Think about all the things you just told me, Emma, then imagine it's the fifties and you're married to a senior politician and have two little children . . ." She trailed off sadly.

"I'm sorry, Mum, I wasn't going to tell you any of this. I didn't want to upset you with stories about secret children and so on."

She went quiet again, then said, "Beattie once said something to me in an unguarded moment. And it always made me wonder."

"Go on."

"It was when I first got pregnant with you, and I was asking her about her first pregnancy and the birth. I was worried, I supposed. I needed some reassurance. And she told me her first birth was fast and at home, easy and natural. Then a few years later, I heard her tell Michael that his birth was awful, too many doctors, strapped on a table. A completely different story."

"So either she was lying to make you feel good . . ."

"Or Michael wasn't her first baby." Her voice broke.

"Are you okay, Mum?"

"It's all right, love. It just makes me sad to think . . . that she felt she couldn't tell me." She sniffed. "I miss her so much. I wish she were still around to ask."

"So do I."

I was dead tired at midday and went upstairs to have a nap. I set my alarm for one o'clock but must have turned it off in my sleep, because I slept for much longer than an hour. I was having a dream about Grandma. I couldn't see her, as she was off in the distance on a horse, but I knew it was Grandma. Beside her, on another horse, was a man with dark skin. They were out on the ridge that I could see from my bathroom window, and they were laughing . . .

I woke to a knock on the door downstairs. Quite a loud knock. As though somebody had been trying to rouse me for a while. I sat up, disoriented. Looked at the clock: four in the afternoon.

"Coming!" I called.

I descended the stairs, hoping whoever it was would give me a chance to get there.

I opened the door, saw Patrick's car reversing out of my driveway.

I ran down, waving madly: a crazy, bleary-eyed woman with sweaty hair. He stopped, turned off the engine, and climbed out of the car.

"Hello," he said.

"Hello," I said.

"I heard you were back."

"No secrets in this town."

"Indeed."

We looked at each other for a minute. Then I said, "Do you want to come in for a coffee?"

He shrugged. "All right."

We went inside, and he sat at the kitchen table while I filled the kettle and put it on.

"I really just wanted to talk to you about the concert," he said. "Ask if you were still coming. It's this Saturday night."

"I know," I said. "It's why I came back." I glanced at him, but he wasn't looking at me. "One of the reasons I came back."

He looked up; his eyes were sad. "I don't know why you went."

"Because I'm a fool."

He didn't say anything. I made two cups of coffee and sat with him at the table.

I took a deep breath. "I had unfinished business there," I said.

"With Josh?"

"How did you know his name?"

"Monica told me."

I put my head on the table. "Monica. She's never going to speak to me again."

He laughed softly. "She's got a fierce side, especially where I'm concerned."

I sat up again. "I'm so sorry, Patrick, I didn't mean to send you such confusing signals. But I didn't know what I wanted myself. I had to go back."

"And do you know now?" he asked. "Do you know what you want?"

"I don't want Josh," I said. "For certain."

A long silence stretched out between us. Neither of us touched our coffee. I suspected he was trying to decide whether he should trust me.

"I should go," he said. "Give you a chance to settle in."

"I didn't sleep with him," I blurted.

"That's really none of my business," he said in a cool voice, and I felt embarrassed for saying it.

I saw him to the door, then asked him to pick me up for the dress rehearsal on Wednesday night.

"I can't," he said. "I have to pick up the rest of the lights, so there won't be room in the car. But you can come with Monica and me to the concert on Saturday."

In the car with Monica for an hour. I shuddered. "Great, thanks."

"I'll pick you up at five," he said.

"Looking forward to it."

I watched him drive away, hoping I hadn't blown it.

I spent most of the week thinking. Oh sure, I also did laundry and shopped and reset my body clock. But most of the work was going on inside my head. I knew for a fact that my life in London, the life I had thought of as my dream life, was over. I didn't want Josh—I didn't know why I'd *ever* wanted Josh—and London wasn't as much fun without a glittering and highly paid career to keep me busy. But I wasn't ready to give up the dancing. My knee would never let me move like that again, but that didn't mean I couldn't enjoy moving, or teaching, or even seeing ballet. My future didn't seem so bleak anymore. In fact, I wondered that it had ever seemed bleak, since I was alive and healthy and young.

My only anxieties about the future were related to Patrick. I kept replaying his kiss over and over in my imagination. I was wary of getting too caught up in a fantasy, but it seemed to me that I'd never met a better man. And that I never would.

THIRTY-THREE

I was ready half an hour early on Saturday afternoon, pacing my sitting room. I was nervous for so many reasons: having to face Monica, desperate to make a good impression on Patrick, wondering how Mina would do. I wished I'd been able to see the last dress rehearsal to tell her how great she was, how proud I was . . .

Mina. I had an idea, and it staggered me that I hadn't thought of it before. I went upstairs to my bedroom and opened my dresser. Inside was my *Swan Lake* tiara: she would look divine in it. I realized sadly that the reason I hadn't thought of it before was that it was too precious to me, a symbol of my old life. I would have been too selfish to let it go.

I put the tiara in my handbag and went downstairs to wait. The summer afternoons went on forever, mild and balmy. Long shadows and lazy breezes. Patrick turned up the driveway right on five. Monica was in the front seat.

"Hello," I said, climbing into the back.

"Hi, Emma," Patrick said, putting the car in gear and

turning it back toward the road. He looked sharply at Monica, who said hello grudgingly.

I sat back and looked out the window. She was cold toward me—if not hostile—for the whole journey, much to my discomfort and Patrick's obvious embarrassment. I was relieved when we pulled in to the car park outside the school hall; I could get out of the car and have some space from her.

Patrick handed us our tickets. "I have to go over the sound system again," he said. "If you'll excuse me."

"I need to see Mina, if I can," I said to Patrick. "Is it okay if I go backstage?"

"Of course."

I found my way backstage, where Marlon was parading about, singing happily to everyone. There were nervous children and their nervous parents everywhere.

"I'm looking for Mina," I said to one of the mothers.

"Over in the wings on the other side of the stage," she said.

I walked around the back. Stages smelled the same anywhere in the world: hair spray, greasepaint, hot electricity, the rubbery scent of duct tape. It was dark in the wings, with only the pinprick torchlight of the technical assistants to light my way. I found Mina sitting on a stool, gazing into middle distance.

"Hi," I said.

She looked up and smiled. "Hi."

"Are you excited?"

She nodded. "A little scared."

"That's normal. That's good. The best ballerinas are always a little scared."

"Really?"

"Absolutely. It means they care. Hey, I have something for you."

"What is it?"

I pulled the tiara out of my bag. "Remember this?"

She reached for it, set it on her head. I arranged it properly, pinning it securely while I talked to her. "I can't dance anymore, Mina. Not the way I used to. So I don't have any use for this tiara anymore. Would you like to keep it?"

Her eyes went wide. "Yes, yes, yes!"

"You must be gentle. It's delicate. It was . . ." It meant nothing to her that it had been hand-crafted for me in the Czech Republic. "It was special to me once," I finished.

"It's not special anymore?"

"I've redefined special," I said, and I laughed. "You have it. It looks beautiful on you."

She nodded. "You know something? My dad is coming."

I was shocked; maybe I had finally gotten through to him. "That's wonderful. He'll be so proud."

"He's taking me out for pizza afterward. I really like pizza."

I gave her a hug. "I'd better go find my seat. Good luck, sweetie." I left her there, sitting in the dark, entranced by the whirl of excitement around her.

The auditorium was starting to fill up. I checked my seat number and noticed that it was right next to Monica's. Of course. Patrick had been given the tickets, and they were together. I braced myself and sat next to her.

She glanced up but didn't say anything.

"I'm sorry," I said. "Do you want me to sit somewhere else?"

She shrugged. "I don't mind. I've got a friend meeting me here soon." She patted the empty seat next to her. "We won't have to try to make awkward small talk. I can just pretend I don't know you."

I had to laugh. "Wow, Monica, I had no idea you were this ferocious."

The corners of her lips twitched, but she didn't let herself smile.

"Can I explain something to you?" I said.

"You can try."

"Up until recently, I didn't know what was important. I think I had to lose it for a little while to realize how much I missed it."

She turned to look at me. "Are you talking about Patrick?"

"Among other things."

She considered me silently for a few moments, as the chatter and movement of the auditorium increased. "He's smitten with you, Emma. If you break his heart, I will kill you." Now she smiled.

A light, bubbling sensation ran over my ribs. "Really? Smitten?"

"I don't want to have to kill you."

"You won't have to. I'll be good."

Her friend arrived soon after, and I sat back to wait. Gradually, the seats were all filled. There was a hubbub of voices, a sense of expectation in the waiting gloom. I closed my eyes for a second and remembered—so many performances, all over Europe—then opened them. The sadness was fleeting.

That was when I saw Mina's father. He had arrived just before they closed the doors and was finding his way to his seat, tripping on people's feet, eyes scanning for his seat number. Finally, he found it, four seats away from me. He sat stiffly, hands resting on his thighs. I watched him for a few moments, but he didn't see me. Then the lights dimmed and the spotlight came on, the audience roared, and the concert began.

The first piece was a disaster. The youngest children got themselves completely spooked and didn't start dancing until the eighth bar of the music, and then they were out of sync for the rest of the piece. But they were spirited and happy, and the audience cheered them as though they'd hit every beat. By the second piece, things were running more smoothly. It was an old show tune, and a couple of the kids were so determined to get it right that the floor shook with their stomping feet.

I relaxed in my seat, enjoying the show, the warm feeling of community. I felt blessed.

Mina's piece was the last. The music started, and six children in white filed out and formed a semicircle. Then Mina, queenly in her tiara, walked gracefully out to the center of the stage and beamed. She was so beautiful, made of starlight. She raised her arms . . . and off she went. Every beat precise, every movement of her arms full of energy and care. I got so swept up in her performance that I almost forgot to see what her father was doing. During the closing bars of the song, I looked across at him. He was palming tears off his face.

* * *

Monica left straight after the concert with her friend. She was going to spend the rest of the weekend in Hobart. I was left waiting for Patrick as he and Marlon saw off excited families and watched over the packing up of the sound and lights.

"I'm sorry," said Patrick as the last piece of equipment was loaded onto the truck. "You're going to be home late."

"I don't mind," I said. "Nobody waiting for me."

He smiled at me. "You talked Mina's dad into coming."

"I know."

"I would have just let it go. But you didn't. You were right about that one."

"Right about something. At last."

"All right, let's head home."

The night was soft and cool, with starlight on the river. In the car, it was dark except for the colored dashboard lights that reflected on Patrick's skin. The radio mumbled too softly to hear. We talked in short bursts about parts of the concert, then fell into long silences. The wide fields, the noble silhouettes of dead trees, the clear starry sky, the magical dark, and us speeding through it to my home.

He pulled up in the driveway but didn't turn off the car. He was going to make me ask.

"Will you come in?" I said.

"Are you sure you want me to?"

I was glad it was dark so he couldn't see me blush. "Oh, yes."

He cut the engine, and we got out and walked to the front door. Closed it behind us. I was in his arms before I'd taken breath. His lips on mine were firm and warm. I wrapped my arms around his neck, and we kissed like teenagers. His hand crept up to stroke my breast, and my skin seemed to turn to liquid.

"Upstairs," I said.

"Upstairs," he answered.

I woke, and the birds were there. Calling and singing and chirping, as rowdy as ever. I opened my eyes and saw Patrick, still asleep. His pale, bare shoulder above the sheets. Patrick, naked in my bed. I could have swooned all over again.

I watched him for a while, and eventually, his eyelids flickered. I snuggled against him and kissed his shoulder.

"Good morning," he said softly, his fingers in my hair.

"Yesterday's surprise," I said.

We lay like that for a while, twined around each other, listening to the noisy birds.

Then he said, "What are you going to do now?"

"What do you mean?"

He extricated himself and sat up, looking down at me. "Now the concert's over. Are you selling the house? Going back to Sydney?"

"Of course I'm not selling the house," I said.

"Then you're staying?"

"I guess I must be."

He smiled.

"If you want me to."

"Oh, I want you to."

Over breakfast, I listed all the things I had been putting

off because I hadn't wanted to commit to staying. "Buy a new fridge," I said. "One with a freezer that works."

"Get the piano tuned. Please," he said.

"Yes. And I'll get a television. And a proper washing machine."

"It'll be like a home."

"It *is* home," I said. I snapped my fingers. "The master bedroom. I'll move in finally, like Monica's been telling me all this time. I'll move in today."

We finished eating and went upstairs to the master bedroom. He made love to me there, on the dusty covers, sweet and fierce. I opened the curtain afterward and looked out at the cabbage gum and thought about Grandma and Charlie.

"Are you going to buy a new mattress for this bed?" Patrick said as I dressed. "The springs are gone in this one."

I turned. He was lying, still shirtless, on the bed.

"Probably. I'll just turn it over for now."

"Want some help?"

"Sure."

We pulled the linen off the bed, sneezing from dust, and lifted up the mattress to turn it over.

"Emma."

"I saw it." The cardboard folder, squashed flat from years between the mattress and the bed base. While he held the mattress up, I reached for it. He let the mattress go with a thud, and we sat on the bed and opened the folder.

Photos. Dozens of photos. The little girl, whoever she was, in a dozen different dresses and poses. On a horse, playing with dogs, bent over in the garden, posing by a Christmas tree.

"Oh, my," I said, leafing through them. Here was Grandma, a young woman, with the little girl, waving to somebody behind the camera. And here was a tall, dark-skinned man, his face obscured by his hat, sitting comfortably on the back of a horse. I flipped it over: *Charlie*, Grandma had written on the back. I showed it to Patrick.

"Mystery solved," he said.

"There was more than one mystery," I replied. I started looking on the backs of the other photos. One name appeared over and over again. *Lucy*. "Lucy," I said. "Her name was Lucy." I don't know why this affected me so; I was close to tears.

"I wonder what happened to her."

Right at the bottom of the folder, I found a letter. I read the address. "She went to Scotland," I said.

Patrick read the address over my sholder. "Why didn't Beattie send this?"

"The same reason she never told us about Lucy. An illegitimate child meant something different back then." The envelope was sealed.

"Are you going to open it?"

"It doesn't feel right."

"Open it," he said.

I handed it to him. "I can't. You do it."

He picked open the envelope and pulled out a letter. "You want me to read it to you?"

I nodded, not trusting myself not to cry.

My darling Lucy,

It has been many years now since I saw you and held you. You were only a girl then, and light as a bird when I hugged you goodbye. I know that your father and Molly have done what they thought was right for you, but if I had known that last time I would never see you again, I would have held you much tighter. I would never have let you go.

You are a grown woman now with children of your own, and now that you know how intense the bond is between mother and child, perhaps you judge me for letting you go. I did try to stay in your life, as you know. When you told me to keep out of it, I took you at your word. Of course I should not have. I should have persisted, because you were barely an adult and didn't know what you wanted. But I had grown ashamed— not of you, never of you—of myself, my past. I married a man with a very public life, and so common sense dictated that it was better to let you go, especially as you were insisting to be free of me.

But we will never be free of each other, you and I. You grew inside me and came from my body, your heartbeat depended on my heartbeat. And when you were born, I needed you as much as you needed me. No matter what happens, that bond cannot be undone. Molly, though she liked to think she was all the mother you ever needed, could never know that primal love. We belong to each other, Lucy, even though we have been far, far apart for many years now.

I do not know that this letter will ever be welcome in your life, so I suppose I will not send it, but it has made me feel better to swear my love for you again, and tell you how devastating the loss of you has been. A piece of me, always missing. My Lucy, my darling soft-skinned child. Do not ever doubt that I loved you, that I continue to love you, and will do so until the stars go out and the silence comes.

Your loving mother, Beattie.

My heart squeezed tight. My beloved Gran had hidden this pain from all of us, for years and years. Patrick rubbed my back gently. I hadn't even realized I was crying. Finally, wiping away tears, I was able to look again at the photographs. Beattie and Lucy. Grandma looked so beautiful and so happy.

"She looks like you," Patrick said.

"Everyone says that. Mum looks more like Granddad. Tall and striking. I look like Grandma."

"No, I mean the little girl. Lucy. She looks like you."

I picked one of the photographs up and examined it. Lucy, smiling. She *did* look like me. The smile, Grandma's smile. My smile.

"What are you going to do?" Patrick asked me.

I turned to him. His face was soft, his eyes connecting warmly with my own. "I'm going to do the right thing," I said.

EPILOGUE

Spring had officially come to Glasgow, but it looked to me like the snow was going nowhere. I wasn't conditioned for the extreme cold anymore, and Patrick teased me as I pulled on extra layers before we left our hotel.

"I don't know how you're going to manage a Tasmanian winter," he said.

"There is actual snow out there," I said. "Very cold snow."

We walked through the heated foyer and out onto the street. Patrick had the map, and we followed it carefully. It had been surprisingly easy to find Lucy MacConnell's address—or Lucy Sutherland, as she was now known—but surprisingly hard to work out the right thing to do. If I posted the letter, she could reject it. If I phoned her without the letter to give her, she might reject me. I figured the only way to approach her was in person, with the letter in my hand. The rest was up to her.

I'd asked Mum to come with me, but she'd canceled her flight at the last moment. Not out of jealousy or ill will toward Lucy; just in the spirit of not overwhelming her with too much at first. If Lucy was willing, there would be time for Mum and Uncle Mike and big noisy gatherings. I saw my role as only to deliver the letter.

"This is it," Patrick said, coming to stop outside a run-down cottage with a beautifully kept garden.

I looked up at the front door, my breath fogging in front of me. "I'm so nervous," I said to Patrick.

"You want me to come up with you?"

I nodded.

"All right, then. Here we go."

We walked up to the front door, and I let Patrick knock because I knew he could do it much more confidently.

"You have to talk, though," he said.

"Agreed," I said, checking in my pocket for the letter again.

Footsteps inside. Somebody was coming. *Please let it be her.*

The door opened. An elderly woman stood there. Her hair was mostly gray, but there was still a touch of ginger through it.

"Can I help you?" she said kindly.

When she smiled, I almost lost my nerve: echoes of my grandmother. The world held its breath for a moment.

Then I bravely pulled out the letter and offered it to her. "This is for you," I said. "It's been on its way for a long, long time."

ACKNOWLEDGMENTS

I'd like to thank a range of people who helped me research and develop this story.

Tim and Jane Parsons at Curringa Farm were marvelous, generous with their time and knowledge, and welcomed my family warmly into their wonderful farm-stay cabin. The family at Fonthill Farm provided me with wonderful pictures and footage of their beautiful homestead. Charlotte Nash-Stewart and Kevin Stewart operated as my left brain, wrangling the numbers for me. Sue Williams generously allowed me to read an early draft of her book about the Merry Makers.

Other bits and pieces of research and encouragement came from Julie Hinchliffe, Ian Wilkins, Meg Vann, Robyn Haig, Keely Double, Mary-Rose MacColl, Ron Serduik, and my Facebook cheer squad. Kate Morton, as always, kept reminding me to trust myself. My family put up with all my nonsense with good grace and minimal tantrums. Selwa Anthony continues to provide an endless supply of love and support to me and my career.

Most of all, I want to express my gratitude for my cousin Janine Haig. Not just for helping me understand horses (and for laughing so hard when I asked how to steer one that I could hear her all the way from Chinchilla) but also for her unfailing support, pride, and love. Bless you, cuz.

TOUCHSTONE
Reading Group Guide

Wildflower Hill

INTRODUCTION

Wildflower Hill is told as a dual narrative, one story following Beattie Blaxland as a young woman in the 1920s, the other following her granddaughter Emma Blaxland-Hunter in modern day. The two women's stories become intertwined across the decades when Emma gradually uncovers her grandmother's history after inheriting her sheep farm in isolated Tasmania.

In 1920s Scotland, Beattie Blaxland became pregnant by her married lover Henry just before her nineteenth birthday. Abandoned by her family, Beattie and Henry set sail for a new life in Australia. After a tumultuous and trying course of events, Beattie manages to secure a Tasmanian estate, run a successful sheep farm, and later establish a highly successful woman's wear business.

In modern day, after an injury ends her dancing career and her boyfriend breaks her heart, Emma leaves London and returns home to Australia to recuperate. There, she discovers she has inherited her beloved grandmother's Tasmanian sheep farm, *Wildflower Hill*. While cleaning out her grandmother's house and sorting through her belongings, Emma discovers secrets about her grandmother's past and begins to reevaluate her own life and priorities.

Discussion Questions

1. Which story did you enjoy reading more, Emma's or Beattie's? How did you relate to both of them?

2. Early in the novel, Beattie's friend Cora tells her: "There are two types of women in the world, Beattie, those who do things and those who have things done to them." How does Beattie adopt this motto throughout her life? Does Emma live by the same credo? Do you agree with Cora's theory about women?

3. How did you feel when Margaret went behind Beattie's back to let Henry see Lucy? How do you feel about Mary, Henry, and Molly's determination to "keep Lucy away from sin"? Is this just a selfish excuse to keep Lucy away from Beattie?

4. Discuss how religion is treated in the novel. Being a good Christian is emphasized by characters such as Mary, Henry, and Molly, but Lucy feels closer to God when she prays privately, and Beattie seems to feel more in tune with the land. Talk about each character's concept of God and "good vs. evil."

5. Beattie remarks that it doesn't matter how she earns money, as long as she can feed her child: "Children can't eat morals." Do you agree? Do you think Beattie did the

right thing working for Raphael and serving drinks illegally?

6. Discuss the poker game that leads to Beattie's ownership of Wildflower Hill. Why does Beattie come up with such a risky proposal? Why does Raphael agree to it?

7. Beattie often blames herself for letting Lucy be taken away. Did she do the right thing by relinquishing more and more control to Henry? Should she have filed for sole custody? Which is more important, for a child to have contact with both of her parents or to be raised in the most stable, "proper" way possible?

8. Compare and contrast Beattie's relationships with Henry, Charlie, and Ray. Do you think Beattie should have told Ray about her former relationships? How do you think he would have reacted?

9. How do you think Beattie would have reacted if she knew Charlie's death was actually a murder? Do you think Leo was right to keep the truth from her?

10. Why do you think Beattie kept every record from her past at Wildflower Hill? Was it, as Emma muses, that she was clinging to every scrap, or do you have a different theory?

11. The setting of the book is described beautifully through the vivid description of Wildflower Hill and its contrast to the city of London. What was your favorite scene?

12. How does Emma's sense of identity, priorities, and relationships change throughout the novel? What event has had the most impact on her? Compare and contrast her transformation with Beattie's.

13. Discuss Mina's father's reluctance to see Mina perform. Do you understand his embarrassment? Why does Patrick refuse to get involved?

14. Emma decides finally to visit Lucy and deliver her grandmother's letter even though her grandmother never intended to send it. How do you think Lucy will receive her? What do you envision happening after the close of the novel?

ENHANCE YOUR BOOK CLUB

1. Do a little research on Tasmania to help envision the setting of Wildflower Hill. Visit http://www.discover tasmania.com/about_tasmania for information, maps, and photographs. To take a virtual tour, visit http://tourtasmania.com/.

2. Visit Kim Wilkins's blog at http://fantasticthoughts .wordpress.com/ and read her thoughts on the writing process, her many novels, daily life, and more!

3. Before her injury, Emma was a prima ballerina. Go to the ballet with your book club and see the dance that Emma dedicated her life to.

4. Emma is greatly impacted by her involvement with Mina and the rest of the Hollyhock dancers. Watch a video about the Adaptive Dance Program, a dance class for children with Down syndrome founded by Children's Hospital Boston and the Boston Ballet in 2002 at http://www.childrenshospital.org/patientsfamilies/videos/Adaptive_Dance_Final.mov.

A Conversation With Kim Wilkins

You've written many acclaimed books in the fantasy and horror genres. What made you decide to branch into women's fiction? How does writing in these genres differ? Do you have a preference?

I had written a lot of books very close together, basing them on mythology and history, and I was a little burned out. Also, I felt I had said all I had to say in that genre for the time being. So I sat with my agent on her couch, and we were talking about the books we used to love in the '80s, like Lace *and* A Woman of Substance, *and she said, "Why don't you write something like that for a change?" I loved the idea of doing something fresh and different.*

What made you decide to use the pen name of Kimberley Freeman on some of your books and your real name, Kim Wilkins, on others?

I used the pen name because I didn't think there was much cross-over between the readerships. Freeman is my grandmother's maiden name, but "Kim Freeman" sounded it like it could be a man. So I made it Kimberley. It's very strange to walk into a bookshop and have the staff call me Kimberley though.

Tell us about the research that went into writing *Wildflower Hill*. What inspired you to set it in Tasmania? Do you have any experience with ballet?

I did ballet as a small child and I was just terrible at it. I was a blue fairy at the end-of-year concert, and somehow ended up on the side of the stage with the pink fairies and never really recovered from the shame. But I read a lot of ballet books and I still enjoy watching ballet. I decided to set the book in Tasmania because it's such a wild, breathtaking place. And it's right down there at the bottom of the world, tucked away, out of sight, and so underappreciated! Apart from that, I had to do a lot of historical research, but I always enjoy that aspect of my work immensely.

We never hear from Cora again after Beattie leaves Scotland. What do you think happened to her? What kind of life did she end up living?

I imagine she would have had a privileged life with few worries, financially anyway. I think it says in the book that she has a baby, and Beattie is jealous at the idea of the life of ease she might have. But of course, money doesn't guarantee happiness.

The original title of the novel was *Field of Clouds*. What was the origin of that title, and why did it change to *Wildflower Hill*?

I called it Field of Clouds *because when I was down in Tasmania researching (in the middle of winter) there was one day on the farm that the fog simply didn't lift, and it felt like the fields were full of clouds rather than crops. But the name of the farm was always* Wildflower Hill, *and we thought it was a much more vibrant, inviting title.*

You mention on your blog that you struggled at times through the writing process of *Wildflower Hill*. Was this book more difficult than your others? How do you overcome obstacles such as writer's block?

I struggle with every single book. Sometimes I wonder why I continue to write them! Every book is difficult, every book has unique challenges that I have to find unique solutions to. But I am just psychologically better equipped to deal with them because I've written so many now (twenty-one including children's books). So writer's block doesn't present as a big problem for me. I know that there's only one way around it, and that's to think a bit more, then write a bit more, and chip away at it slowly. Then I'm back in the swing and off again. But yes, I do sometimes moan about how hard it all is on my blog.

Gambling plays quite an important role in Beattie's life. Did you have to do any kind of research or are you familiar with cards yourself?

No, but my dad was a gambler so I was well aware of how much one can win or lose. As for the card game that plays an important part in the plot, I had to get a couple of friends who are mathematicians to work out how much should be bet at each stage to achieve the right result. I am pretty bad at math.

You have created two very different protagonists with Emma and Beattie. What made you decide to tell the story through their alternating viewpoints? Did you enjoy writing for one woman more than the other? Whom do you identify with more?

I loved them both so much. I loved how prickly and self-absorbed Emma was and how she slowly softened and found out what was really important. I do identify with her (being a sometimes prickly and self-absorbed person!). But Beattie had my heart. No matter how much life beat her down, she just kept getting up. She had a strong moral compass and an unbreakable spirit.

Wildflower Hill has been enthusiastically received in Australia. How do you think it will translate to an American audience?

I am so pleased and proud to be sharing the book with the US. I really hope that my characters connect with your readers and that the parts set in Australia will be interesting to them. At its heart Wildflower Hill *is a simple story about a woman who didn't know a big secret about her grandmother, and I think that's a story that any audience can relate to.*

The ending of the novel leaves the reader wondering what happens next. Any plans for a sequel? What do you think happens after Lucy opens the door to Emma?

I have no doubt Lucy would welcome her with open arms. Age makes people wise, and Lucy would definitely want to know her family. So, no plans for a sequel. I had one reader over here who was so distressed that I didn't say exactly what happened that I opened her book and handwrote the last line, "And Lucy took Emma inside and loved her to pieces." So, yes, that's what I think happened next.

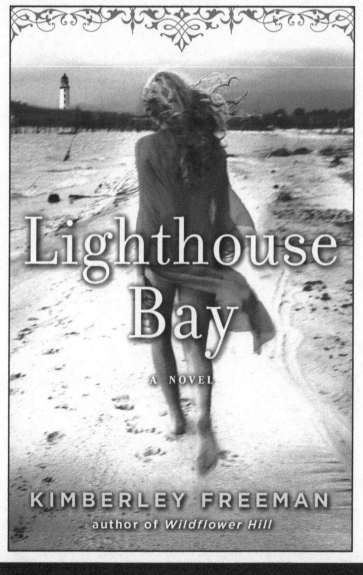